COMING HOME

BY MIKE DOWD

To Isabella and Nicoletta,

"Life, like golf, is a journey that is best played boldly. Never lay-up, play it safe, or leave an eagle putt short. Don't judge each day by the number you put on the scorecard, but by how you shared that time with others. Each round must eventually end, so make sure you've loved the playing of it and those with whom you've played to the fullest. For it's not that the end comes too soon, it's that too often we wait too long before we really start to play."

-Daddy

TABLE OF CONTENTS

COMING HOME

"It's a funny thing coming home. Nothing changes. Everything looks the same, feels the same, even smells the same. Then you realize what's changed is you."
- F. Scott Fitzgerald

A week after suffering the biggest setback of his life in his first attempt at PGA Tour Qualifying School, Tyler decided to crawl back home in search of his coach Mack. In truth, he had nowhere else to go. In his most despairing moments, he had half entertained the idea of quitting the stupid game altogether and going to work in his old man's garage. But, when Tyler stopped by to give him the obligatory explanation for what had gone wrong, that first smell of grease had unleashed a flood of memories that only reinforced why he had gone to college in the first place and what golf was for him: his ticket out of Poplar Bluff.

It's not that Poplar Bluff was a bad place, but in Tyler's mind, it was more one stoplight than bright lights; a small Midwest town just a bit too bereft of any real opportunities besides marrying his high school sweetheart and settling down to a life of comfortable mediocrity. A simple life whose highlights would have likely included coaching Little League, starring in the Thursday night softball league, and turning enough wrenches during the week that he'd have some extra spending money to play poker with his high school buddies on the weekend. Besides, that ship had sailed when Katherine, the girl who would have happily played Bonnie to his Clyde in just about anything if he'd just asked, and the only part of that vision he regretted leaving behind, had gone. He couldn't blame her. She'd run off to chase her own dreams after he'd broken her heart by telling her he needed to chase his, none of which she had pointedly told him apparently included her.

His old man was another part of the problem. Jack Foster was larger than life in Poplar Bluff. A legendary high school quarterback who had gone on to star at Mizzou for three years; an All-American and Heisman Trophy runner-up. That was all before an ugly knee injury ended his NFL dreams and sent him back home along with his own high school sweetheart to start a business with his other true love: cars. Jack Foster was still a legend in Poplar Bluff, though. And, to get out from under that big shadow was what had led to Tyler disappointing his folks, and just about everyone else in town, by accepting a scholarship from rival Vanderbilt. He argued that it was one of the top golf programs in the country, and played a better schedule than Mizzou. But in truth, he was tired of being 'Jack's boy' and wanted to strike his own course. Jack had been supportive of his son's decision to play golf, partly because his own larger-than-life father, Jack Sr., had introduced Tyler to the game, and partly because Jack came to the realization that his 'boy' didn't have the requisite size to likely make football or basketball something he could excel at.

"Hey, Pop," Tyler said as he walked into the all-too-familiar sight of his old man with his head under the hood of someone else's classic car.

"Son," Jack Foster said in way of response without looking up from what he was doing. "Can you hand me a 3/16?"

Tyler did as he was asked, grabbing the wrench from the opened giant Snap-On tool chest that seemed to follow his old man around wherever he went.

Jack finished tightening up a couple more bolts and then finally broke the silence by grabbing a grease rag to wipe his hands and looking up from under the hood.

"So what are you gonna do now?" he asked.

"You heard?" Tyler asked.

"Of course I heard," his old man said flatly. "You think we live in a vacuum here? I know this town's a bit backwater for your big city tastes, son, but we have managed to get the Internet."

"Well, I'm gonna call Mack." Tyler said as if that statement alone was sufficient.

"Aren't you a little worried you might have burned that bridge, son?" his old man said only half condescendingly. "The man only spent a decade teaching you how to play, and treating you like one of his own, and then you snub him when you likely could have used him most. Besides, I think your problems might run a bit deeper than just how you swing the club."

Tyler listened to the rest of his old man's I-told-you-so speech, partly out of respect and partly because he knew he had earned it.

"I'll make it right, Pop," Tyler finally said once his old man had said his piece. "I screwed up. I should have taken Mack. I know that now. But I had my reasons, and it just didn't work out. Mack will understand, and he'll help me get back on track."

"So you're not giving up on this thing?... I spent a good portion of what I had set aside to re-do the kitchen for your mother to finance your little meltdown. How are you going to pay for the next go-round? Where are you planning on living? The way I see it, you need a job, son."

This was the part of the conversation Tyler had dreaded most. It was half statement, half offer. It was bad enough having to come back and explain to his old man what had happened, but having to ask for his help in the same breath was the worst part. He hadn't finished his degree at Vanderbilt, falling 12 units short of a liberal arts degree that in the back of his mind would have allowed him to get a job as a P.E. teacher someday as a worst-case scenario. His eligibility had run out, and when he chose to go to Q-School that fall, instead of returning to Vandy to finish his degree, neither of his folks had been too happy. But they begrudgingly supported him, at least partly because they knew it was his dream and because everyone knew he was that good. The other part, Tyler suspected, was because his old man was getting to the age when he wanted to start taking a step back, and he needed help to do that. Tyler knew he half hoped that if the golf thing didn't work out he could ultimately talk his son into coming back home to work in the garage, and they could put a plan in place for him to take it over someday.

The problem with that plan, and why Tyler had always resisted spending too much time around the garage, was that it meant giving up and giving in. Golf was his ticket out of Poplar Bluff, and he knew his old man would want a full-time commitment, which meant giving up on his dream. And he wasn't ready to give up on a goal he'd been working toward for the past decade. Tyler also secretly felt that his old man resented the fact that his son might make it in a way that he never had. As good of a life as his old man had built for himself, and as much as he was still a legend around town, Tyler knew there was a part of his old man that still dreamed about what might have been. And when Tyler talked about getting out of Poplar Bluff, he would always disgustedly say something like, "This life isn't good enough for you, son?" or "What do you think you're gonna find out there you can't have here?" He didn't understand.

"I think Mack might take me on as an assistant," Tyler finally replied. "That way I could work in the mornings and practice every afternoon until dark."

Tyler knew that wasn't the answer his old man wanted to hear, but he bit his tongue for the moment and simply said, "Well, even if he does take you on, son, that's not enough money to live on. You plan on moving home or have you got other ideas?"

Tyler didn't have other ideas, unfortunately. Moving back home after living large in Nashville as the 'Big Man on Campus', at least as large as a college golf star can, seemed like such a huge step backwards from what he'd gotten accustomed to, but he didn't have a lot of other options at the moment.

"Would that be a problem?" Tyler finally said. "Between work and practice, and playing in all the local events I can get in, I really wouldn't be there all that often."

"I'll talk to your mother," his old man said after a long pause.

Tyler knew his mother wouldn't object – in fact, she'd be ecstatic. He'd called on his way home to break the bad news to her ahead of going to see his old man and she'd already assured him he was more than welcome to move home for the time being until he decided what his next move was. Sure, she'd work on him every day, try to get him to settle down, listen to his father, and finish his degree so he'd have the backup plan that his own father never had. But in that brief call he'd understood that she relished the idea of having her only child home again.

"Thanks, Pop," Tyler said. "I'm going to call Mack and see if I can go by and see him today."

Mike Dowd

A SHORT WALK

Tyler left his car at the garage and decided to call Mack while he walked home, which was only about 10 blocks away. His coach would take his call, Tyler thought, if for no other reason than to make sure he didn't miss out on his opportunity to tell him I told you so, too. Tyler supposed he deserved having to listen to it, and he knew he needed to man up and apologize for how he had left things. It was the price he needed to pay for refusing his advice, his offer to help, and for hurling a particularly disrespectful parting shot at his coach once he'd become frustrated.

"You know, I think I might know just a bit more about what I need to do to play well than someone who can hardly break 80 anymore," Tyler had said after Mack had put him on the defensive.

The crux of their falling-out was over Tyler's decision to take his college roommate Gabe as a caddy instead of his longtime coach. Mack had finally conceded that Tyler didn't want him on the bag, but said, "Well if ya' don't want me, at least take someone who knows which end of the club to hold. Ya' might as well flush the whole thing right now if ya' think taking that airhead wannabe frat boy trust-fund baby as a caddy is a smart decision."

That's when Tyler had unloaded on him. Gabe was a decent golfer, he'd been the best on his high school team actually, and his ever-present sense of humor, Tyler felt, kept him loose. The rest of Mack's description, though, wasn't too terribly far off the mark. Gabe was a bit of a free spirit whose dad had invented some type of machine that cleaned laundry and linens for hotels and resorts without using soap, and it was used all over the world, so he was financially set. And he did like a good party. They had gotten into a bit of trouble in town when he brought Gabe home for Christmas break their junior year, and he took him bar-hopping around town to celebrate Tyler's 21st birthday. It was mostly innocent college boy antics. Being from St. Louis, Gabe had never been cow-tipping, and somewhere around two o'clock in the morning, after they had closed down the last of all four bars they had in Poplar Bluff, he talked Tyler and a couple of his high school buddies into taking him to the dairy out on Route 142 to give it a try.

Well, they hadn't even gotten that far, because once they noticed that someone had left the keys in an old tractor, that seemed like a lot more fun. Two fenceposts, a mailbox, and ten minutes later, the foreman had come out of his trailer in a t-shirt, boxers, and holding a shotgun while threatening to call the police. Tyler recognized him as an old friend of his dad's, and when he dropped his name, the foreman instead called Tyler's father out of respect for Jack Foster. None too happy about being awoken at that hour, and embarrassed by what would certainly get around town by breakfast time, Tyler's father had rounded them up and, to sober them up, made them ride home in the back of his pickup on an uncharacteristically cold and snowy winter night. Then he marched them right back early the next morning, hung-over, and made them fix the fence and mailbox.

Mack had coached Tyler since he was 12. Tyler's grandfather, Jack Foster Sr., was the retired head of the nail plant in town, and he had taken him to Mack one summer with instructions to get him course-ready in a month so he could tag along with him and some of his golfing buddies without getting in the way. Tyler instantly fell in love with the game, recognizing it as something he wouldn't have to be as big as his father to be good at, and jumped in with both feet, hoping to be able to join his grandfather and at the same time impress his father for once. He was good enough to play along with his grandfather and his cronies in just a few weeks, and within a few years, Mack had coached Tyler into one of the best young players in the state. They were close, especially in those early years when Tyler would tag along darn near everywhere Mack went when he would let him, soaking up his pearls of wisdom and everything he was willing to share about the game. As Tyler got older and better, won more events and began to attract the attention of colleges around the country, their relationship had grown a bit stale, though. Mack had become almost like family, a close uncle or the even the big brother Tyler never had, but as his confidence had grown, Tyler had begun to suspect his success had more to do with his own hard work and talent than it was any specific guidance from Mack. And he began to think more and more that he could just as easily figure things out himself if his game ever really went south.

Tyler had chosen to play for Vanderbilt at least partially, he argued, because it was just a few hours away in Nashville, and close enough that he could drive home on weekends and see Mack if and when he needed to. The influence of his larger-than-life college coach, a former Vandy All-American who had played the Tour briefly in the early '80s, however, had made those almost weekly trips as a freshman become something he was doing less than once a month by his senior year

Tyler hit Mack's name on his phone and waited enough rings before he got an answer that he momentarily feared that his coach actually wouldn't speak to him.

"Hey, Coach," Tyler opened once he finally got an answer, "I guess you probably heard what happened…" He braced himself for the lecture that he knew was due.

"…Yes, of course," Mack replied after a bit of a long silence.

"I know what you're thinking, so go ahead. You can tell me I told you so if you want. I deserve it," Tyler responded.

"Don't think there's much need for that," Mack said. "Sounds like you've been doing it enough yourself already, or at least been hearing it from your old man."

"Well, I guess I needed to learn things the hard way. And I did. I'm sorry, Coach…" Tyler said, pausing long enough to realize Mack wasn't going to immediately respond, so he continued, "It's just that when I decided to quit school, I started to feel a lot more pressure than I ever have before, and I thought I needed to do something to stay loose so I could play my own game. Gabe may not be a swing coach, but he's actually a pretty good caddy and usually keeps me relaxed, and besides, he damn near grew up on that course."

"Yes, I'm sure," Mack finally broke in, "Just as I'm sure he was pretty familiar with all the bars and nightspots in the greater St. Louis area too."

Tyler hadn't told either of them the specifics of what happened, but he knew that both his father and Mack suspected the biggest problem with Gabe caddying for him was the fact that Q-School was being held just 20 minutes outside of St. Louis, and Gabe's reputation, combined with the fact that they would be a stone's throw from where *he* grew up, would present a host of distractions during the week. And while that hadn't been a problem for most of the week, it had predictably reared its head the night before the final round.

Tyler had been fighting his swing all week, but grinding things out just the same. If it hadn't been for a double on the last hole the day before the last round, he would have gone in to it right on the number needed to advance. He was wound up tight, frustrated, and headed to the range to go do battle with his driver for a couple of hours to try and figure something out. That's when Gabe, who had been largely a good soldier and helpful during the week, said, "You're trying too hard, Ty."

"What?" Tyler looked up from his self-imposed trance as they walked back toward the range.

"You're trying too hard, buddy. You need to relax, man. I told you three times on 18 you needed at least an extra club into that green, and I don't think you even heard me you were so in your own head," Gabe continued. "You need a drink, man. Your driver's fine if you'd just slow down, relax, and let everything else catch up."

"What?" Tyler said again, apparently still in the trance that not only had caused him to ignore his buddy's advice on 18, but to either not hear him now or at least not comprehend what he was saying.

"Let me take you out for a beer and some barbecue," Gabe said. "I know this great place walking distance from our hotel. Once we've eaten and you've relaxed and stepped away for about an hour, we can come back and hit balls until dark if you want. You'll be in a better frame of mind. You haven't even been laughing at my jokes today, Ty."

Maybe Gabe was right, Tyler thought. He was wound up way too tight. More than half the reason he brought him along was he thought Gabe would help keep him loose, and he wasn't even allowing him to do that.

"All right," Tyler said, "but just one beer, and I *am* hungry."

"Great!" Gabe said. "You're gonna love this place."

To make a long story short, it didn't end up being one beer. They ran into some girls Gabe had known from high school, and while the barbecue was really good, the beers tasted even better. Six or eight later (Tyler couldn't remember), they stumbled back to the hotel and passed out. Tyler woke in time for his tee time the next morning, but only barely, and after arriving on the first tee with barely a warm-up, he started off with back-to-back doubles. He never recovered, shooting a final round 76, and even though the field came back considerably that day, he missed advancing by two shots.

He had hung out with Gabe in and around St. Louis for the next few days, mostly drowning his sorrows and trying to figure out what his next move was. Eventually, he realized that he would need to head back home to Poplar Bluff. While Gabe had felt really bad about keeping him out so late, and spent most of that time apologizing, Tyler knew ultimately it had been his decision. And he alone had to go home and own up to it.

"I should have taken you up on your offer, Coach," Tyler finally admitted. "I was fighting my swing all week, and I could have used your help. I thought by now I could pretty much fix everything myself, but I guess not. It got pretty ugly in spots."

"Ya' can, Tyler," Mack surprised him by saying. "Ya' just need to learn what to pay attention to … and what not to."

"What do you mean?" Tyler asked.

"Ya' always think it's about your swing, Tyler," Mack said. "Ya' think it's the one thing you have control over… Your emotions, how ya' think, what ya' think about, how you choose to frame everything, and where you choose to place your focus – these are things you have control over. Ya' can hit balls until your hands bleed trying to get control over your swing, but that'll never really happen."

"I don't understand," Tyler said.

"Meet me out at McLane Park tomorrow morning at 6:00," Mack said.

"What for?" Tyler said. "Why not at the range?"

"I think you and I have spent far too much time out on that range already. I think that might have been my biggest mistake," Mack replied.

"What can we do at McLane Park? Isn't it just some ball fields and walking trails?" Tyler asked.

"Yep," said Mack. "You're gonna join me for my morning walk."

"I need a job, Mack," Tyler said, changing the subject and as way of an inquiry.

"We can talk about that, too," Mack said. "If you're going to stay at this, swinging wrenches in your father's garage isn't likely going to get ya' any closer than ya' are already."

Mike Dowd

COMING FULL CIRCLE

Tyler hung up the phone feeling that things had gone better than expected. Mack had obviously forgiven him. He wasn't quite so sure what taking a walk with Mack out at McLane Park was going to do for him, but if Mack wanted him along, then humoring his coach was the least he could do, all things considered.

As he pondered why it was that Mack wanted him to take a walk, Tyler rounded the corner and headed up the slight hill toward his childhood home. He could see his mother's car in the driveway of the big old mid-century two-story at the edge of the old part of town. It was dated, but Tyler's neighborhood had once been the nicest in all of Poplar Bluff. That was before some new developments came along in the late '80s, right after the Briggs & Stratton plant opened up.

As he walked up the street, Tyler thought about the conversation on the phone he'd had with his mother earlier. He'd always been able to talk to his mother in a way that he just couldn't open up to his old man. He had known he would need to tell his father in person, but he wanted his mother's sympathetic ear in advance of that meeting. He'd expressed his frustration, his sorrow for letting them down, his embarrassment at having to crawl home with his tail between his legs, his determination to press on, and a host of other thoughts and emotions that all told her how much he'd been humbled.

And she'd listened as only a mother can, mostly without interrupting. Interjecting only support and encouragement in just the right doses, during those moments when she knew he needed it most.

As he bounded up the steps of the old front porch, Tyler smiled for what seemed like the first time in a week. At least Mack was back in his corner, and the difficult conversation with his father, a confrontation he'd dreaded from the moment he'd signed his scorecard, was behind him. His mother, wearing an apron and looking every bit the Stepford wife Tyler had always teased her of being, beat him to the door and met him with a warm embrace that said she was more than glad to see him, felt his pain, and loved him unconditionally all in one.

Mary Jane Foster was a throwback to a bygone era. She looked every bit the part of Marion Cunningham from that old TV show *Happy Days*. She was a petite woman, standing only an inch or two over five feet, and the obvious reason for Tyler ending up almost eight inches short of the massive 6-foot-4 frame of his father. Unless she was headed to town, to the grocery store, to meet her Tuesday bridge group, to church choir practice on Thursdays, or out to dinner or a fundraiser with his father on the weekends, she almost lived in the kitchen in her apron. Tyler believed that she loved cooking and being domestic in the way that he loved playing golf. She was always baking something for someone, for a fundraiser, for church, or just for him and his father to take in their lunches back in the days when Tyler lived at home. Mary Jane Foster – it was Williams back then – had been the head cheerleader at Poplar Bluff High back in the day, the sweetheart of the star quarterback, and had followed her future husband to Mizzou, majoring in hospitality management until Jack's injury had sent them both packing and back home to Poplar Bluff. Tyler had often teased her growing up, saying if his old man had been some gypsy following the Grateful Dead around the country, she'd have been right there with him, wearing dreadlocks and a peace-sign T-shirt while cooking his cage-free eggs and whole grain toast for breakfast. She was as devoted to his father as any wife could be, and Tyler thought that was why she had been so close to Katherine, his own high school sweetheart, recognizing a kindred spirit. She had taken it almost as hard as Katherine had

21

when they broke up after Tyler had chosen to go to Vanderbilt, and for a while she'd kept in touch with her, giving him periodic updates on how she was doing, hoping he would contact her and they would reconcile. He never did, though, and after a couple of years she seemed finally convinced he never really would and gave up.

"Hey, Mom," Tyler said, smiling as he broke off their embrace.

"Well you're in a much better mood than when we talked earlier," Tyler's mother said with a sly smile of her own as she turned to walk in the house. "I didn't quite expect that after the conversation with your father... I guess you must have seen her?"

"Seen who?" Tyler said suddenly confused, as he had been just about to tell his mother about the conversation with Mack.

"Katherine," she said matter-of-factly as she walked back into the kitchen. She picked up a wooden spoon and a bowl of something she'd obviously been stirring and then turned her full attention back to him.

"She was just here. Came by to say hello and invite me and your father to a fundraiser. Didn't I tell you? I guess she moved back home a few months ago after she got her degree and is working for The American Cancer Society. I don't know how you could have missed her."

Tyler just stood there a moment, stunned, and feeling like his entire life was suddenly coming full circle.

"…No," Tyler finally said, realizing his mouth had fallen open. "No, you didn't. I guess I must have just missed her."

Mike Dowd

KATHERINE

It had been almost four months since Katherine had moved home after getting her degree in Business Administration from Mizzou. She had entertained a few offers to work in Columbia after graduation, but in the end decided to move home for a few months to weigh her options, rather than commit to something right out of the gate that she wasn't sure her heart was in.

The pragmatic side of her had ultimately settled on business as her major, that and the fact that she knew her father would be just a bit more approving of his only daughter's sensibility. After initially intending to get a teaching degree, she had almost switched to majoring in Social Work, but Edward Anderson, her no-nonsense financial planner father, had thrown more than a bit of cold water on that idea over Easter brunch the spring semester of her freshman year.

"Be sensible, Katherine," he had said. "Getting by on a teacher's salary is one thing, but do you really want to clip coupons and shop at Wal-Mart for groceries the rest of your life? I know you want to do some good in this world, but you can do a hell of a lot more good with money in your pocket than without. Show me one social worker that isn't ultimately dependent on someone else in this world to have a decent life and a family and I'll show you a hundred others that are. Do you want to work for a cause, or found one? You don't want to be dependent on someone else. Now I know your mother would've been proud of that notion, and I know your heart lies with helping people just like she did, but if you really want to make a contribution, make an impact. It's a lot easier from the top of the totem pole than it is from the bottom."

Katherine's mother. She felt like she hardly knew her anymore, other than from a handful of pictures they still kept up around the house and memories that had seemed to have faded over the years in ways she had promised herself they never would. She had been Katherine's world and her biggest role model until the cancer had taken her from both of them way too soon. Twelve years is too short a time for a young girl to have with her mother, and while her father did his best after she was gone, she instinctively knew that he had needed her almost as much as she did. Daddy had buried himself in work after her passing, never trying to replace Katherine's mother, but she wasn't sure how much of that was out of respect for Katherine or if his own heart was just too broken to risk being vulnerable again. What she did know was when he talked about being dependent on someone else, his concerns for her ran deeper than just the financial.

Katherine had pretty much taken her mother's place around the house after she had gone. Her mother had set quite an example up to that point, both at home and in the community. At home she kept things running with a cool efficiency that seemed to seamlessly complement all she did outside of it. In Poplar Bluff, she had made an impact and a name for herself with her selflessness, alternating between being the PTA President, a school board member, and chairing the Butler County Community Resources Council, all while volunteering more than her fair share of time for their church. When cancer had reared its head the first time, she didn't even let it slow her down, adding The American Cancer Society to that list and working right through her chemo to help found their Annual Gala. After that, she became their local standard-bearer, first as a survivor, and later as a victim when the cancer returned with a vengeance just a few short years later.

And Katherine had always been happily in tow, helping her mother with the small details of organizing this fundraiser or that, championing everything from bake sales to car washes, and she looked up to her mother and all the gratitude and wonder she seemed to inspire from nearly everyone in town for all she did. And that is why when her mother's long-time friend Karen Gibson came calling for help with the Society's Annual Gala, shortly after hearing Katherine was home from college, it was a no-brainer for her to agree to work in the office while she was weighing her options.

"Katherine," Karen said in that all-too-familiar bubbly voice over the phone that unleashed a flood of memories of her mother and her busying themselves with the business of helping others, "I'm so glad to hear you've come home. And just in the nick of time, really. I'm in desperate need of an extra hand around here with the Annual Gala coming up and, all things considered, just knew you'd be the perfect person to help insure I keep this thing honoring your mother's memory in a way that is fitting."

"Oh," Katherine had said with a knowing smile and only a hint of sarcasm, "I'm happy you called, Karen. I'm not doing a thing at the moment and, as Mother always said, we wouldn't want to drop the ball."

In truth, Katherine really hadn't had anything else concrete in mind when she had come home after graduation. If she was going to get involved in some way before charting her post-graduation course and heading off somewhere to meet her future, she couldn't think of a much better cause to occupy her time with. Daddy had predictably let the house fall into what her mother would have called a *"shocking state of disarray"*, but that would only take a handful of days to put in order, something she had gotten used to having do for him every time she came home on break. In truth, there were days she wished he would finally meet someone that'd be able to take care of him in the way his mother had at first, and she had later. It'd had been a decade now since her mother had passed and she no longer thought of the idea of her father seeing someone as replacing her, but rather finally getting on with life, and trying to find his own way to be happy. He had been there for her during those tough years, and she him in a great many ways. But going off to college had only made it more obvious to her how there was still something missing in his life that would keep him from ever being truly happy– a void that Katherine could never fill no matter how much she loved him and she had a life of her own to live.

A life of her own, just what that life was supposed to look like was the thing that still had her puzzled, and why she had returned to Poplar Bluff after graduation. Four years of college hadn't gotten her as close to figuring that out as she thought it would. Part of her said she should have thrown caution to the wind and taken one of the job offers she'd had in Columbia and just get on with life, but something else kept pulling her back home. She felt she had unfinished business there, and she wanted to weigh her options before making a commitment because she knew she was the type that once she had her mind made up, she would see it through. She'd told herself at first it was to check on Daddy, and to let him know that he could get on with life while making sure he understood that she not only was okay with that. But it's what she really wanted for him. Something unexpected had happened this morning, though, something that had suddenly made things all too clear to her about why she had really come home. And she was livid with herself once the truth had finally become clear. It was Tyler.

She had been walking the neighborhood dropping off tickets to a handful of her mother's old friends that were annual supporters on her lunch break when she suddenly realized she was staring up at the nice old two-story where Tyler's folks still lived. In the three years she and Tyler had dated, Mary Jane Foster had become almost like the mother she no longer had. She was funny, kind, and unfailingly devoted to her family, and Katherine found she could talk to her in ways and about things she just couldn't talk to her father about. And when she had a problem, or her and Tyler had an argument, she more and more realized that Mary Jane was the one she instinctively turned to. And after Tyler had left her to head off and chase his dreams, there were days when she wasn't so sure if she missed her more than she did him. They had kept in touch for a while, Mary Jane saying she would always be there for her. She was convinced her son would come to his senses after being away at school for a few months, but as months turned into years, Katherine became more and more angry with herself for what she began to think of as how she had emotionally just sat around pining for him while the rest of life had moved on. And as the realization that he likely never would sunk in, she realized also that her relationship with his mother no longer really made sense. In her bitterness, Katherine had ended it.

Looking up at that house brought back so many truly *good* memories, and Katherine suddenly regretted that she had abruptly cut off the woman that had been so kind to her for so many years. She had a few tickets still in her envelope, and after all, money was money, so she hesitantly walked up the steps to that big old front porch. Mary Jane and Jack almost certainly would be invited by someone, if they hadn't been already, and so ultimately she would bump into them at the Gala anyway, she thought, and so the right thing to do would be to invite them herself. She hesitated at the last second and almost turned around as she reached for the bell, but then hit it quick before she changed her mind.

Mary Jane came to the door in what seemed like seconds, almost as if she had been waiting for her, wearing that familiar blue apron that Tyler had always teased her about and a smile that was as warm and inviting as it had ever been.

"Katherine dear," she said, reaching out to greet her with a hug as if no time at all had passed since they had last spoken. "What a nice surprise. Please come in, I was just, well you know, doing what I do and I've got to get something out of the oven," she said with a somewhat self-deprecating smile and gesture towards her faded apron.

The kitchen was mere steps from the entry hall with a view of the street, and why, Katherine remembered now, Mary Jane had gotten to the door so quickly. She had seen her coming.

31

"How've you been, Mary Jane?" Katherine asked a bit awkwardly as they walked towards the kitchen. She felt more than a bit guilty about not staying in touch, that and the fact that she had been home for more than four months now and hadn't reached out to at least say hello to the woman that had just about adopted her as the daughter she never had.

"Well, I've been fine, dear, but how about you? I heard you graduated from your father when I ran into him a few months ago. He's extremely proud of you, you know, convinced you'll be off to be the next CEO of something before long," she said with a knowing smile as she pulled some fresh baked bread from the oven and set it out on the counter to cool.

"Well, I'm good, and you obviously remember Daddy all too well," Katherine said smiling. "I actually decided to move home a few months ago after graduation and take some time to weigh my options, so to speak. I didn't want to make a mistake by just taking the first thing that came along."

"Very sensible," Mary Jane said, wiping her hands on the apron and taking it off. "I'm sure your father is happy to have you back home too, even if it is just for a bit, and I'm sure you've got plenty of opportunities and time."

"Yes," Katherine said smiling. "He needs me to check in on him now and again. Lives like a bear with furniture when I'm not around. I do wish he'd finally meet someone, you know. I can't take care of him forever."

Mary Jane laughed that sweet warm laugh that always filled every room she was in and Katherine knew immediately that even if she had ever been upset with her for not keeping in touch, it was just the disappointment she felt at losing a friend. But she obviously understood and all was forgiven.

"Well," Katherine continued as if finally getting to a long belabored point, "the reason for my rudeness in springing this unannounced visit upon you this afternoon is that I've taken a short-term position with The American Cancer Society to help them out with the Annual Gala. Karen Gibson roped me into it as soon as she smelled my blood in the water. Truthfully, I'm happy to be helping and I just wanted to bring by a couple of tickets and ask if you and Jack would like to come. It's the third weekend in November, on the 22nd at the new Heartland Community Center."

"We'd love to, dear," Mary Jane said, smiling and reaching out to accept the two tickets Katherine had produced from the envelope, but then she paused as if considering whether or not to ask a question and continued a bit hesitantly. "Of course we'll pay for them, it is a fundraiser after all, and I so appreciate the invitation, but do you by chance have a third?"

Katherine felt a lump in her throat suddenly, as if she was being briefed of some potentially troubling news she wasn't so sure she wanted to hear.

"All things considered, I'm not exactly sure how to bring this up, but you'll find out sooner or later anyway, Katherine, so I guess

I'd rather it be from me," Mary Jane continued. "The timing of your visit this morning is truly ironic… Tyler's coming home. Today actually, and not just for a visit. He failed to qualify for the Tour and his eligibility at Vanderbilt has run out. He's apparently not going to return to school. He called on his way home from St. Louis earlier to tell me and was planning to stop by the garage to break the news to Jack before coming here."

Katherine just looked at her blankly as she reached back into the envelope for the remaining ticket. As she handed it to Mary Jane, she realized suddenly her hand was trembling slightly and tried to cover it up by quickly blurting out, "W-why, yes, ironically I do have one ticket left."

"I don't have any money on me, Katherine," Mary Jane began again matter-of-factly as if she was discussing the weather, "I can just drop it by the office in the morning when I'm running my errands, if that's okay?"

"Sure," Katherine said, forcing a smile through the whirlwind of emotions and thoughts that suddenly flooded her brain. "Speaking of the office, I actually really must be going. I'm covering for Karen this afternoon so she can make her hair appointment and I need to hustle or she'll be late."

"It's really been so good to see you, dear," Mary Jane said, walking her to the door and reaching out to embrace her in a way that told her all-at-once that she knew exactly what had to be going through Katherine's mind. This meeting and the timing of it all seemed more than just a bit serendipitous, and even Mary Jane seemed almost flustered with an odd mix of anxiety and excitement.

"You too, Mary Jane," Katherine said, and then before heading out the door, she turned adding, "I'm really sorry I stopped keeping in touch so suddenly, Mary Jane. It's just..."

"Please, Katherine, don't," Mary Jane said almost embarrassed. "You know I love you, dear. And you know that I know how difficult everything was for you. I know, dear. Now hurry along before that son of mine comes home and you have another meeting I'm not so sure you're ready for at the moment."

Mike Dowd

A LONGER WALK

Tyler didn't sleep much that night. He'd eaten dinner with his folks the previous evening and watched some obligatory highlights of that weekend's Mizzou game with his old man before begging off to bed early, explaining he was tired and needed to get up early to go meet Mack. He'd tried to act just as matter-of-factly as his mother had when she'd given him the news of Katherine being back in town, but she knew him all too well, he thought, and knew good and well that news would have an effect on him. In truth, and despite the fact that he really was tired, thoughts of Katherine and the confusing mix of emotions that came along with them had kept him up most of the night.

When 5:00a.m. rolled around, he finally gave up in frustration, turned off his alarm, climbed out of bed, and put on some old sweats and a pair of sneakers. It was useless, he thought, and he realized he needed to get going anyway since he had to first walk to the garage to get his car before he could go meet Mack. When he finally arrived about an hour later, he saw Mack's car parked right next to the sign that read Jerry F. McLane Park.

"I like this place," Mack said as Tyler walked up. "Like to think they named it after me."

It was the first time Tyler had made the connection. Mack's full name was Angus McLean. He was a Scottish immigrant, a bit unusual for Poplar Bluff, and had always just gone by Mack, a fairly plain Americanized nickname which for some reason seemed to fit his understated persona. Mack had apparently, as far as Tyler had always been told, been a close friend of the son of one of the club's original founders. When the longtime local pro suddenly departed some 30 years ago, Mack had been asked to come over and assume the head professional's position. His Scottish burr, apparently once very pronounced, had softened over the years to the point where you only noticed it on certain words or when he was excited. His teaching style had always been a bit minimalist too, saying little and listening much, which Tyler appreciated when he was playing well, but which slightly annoyed him if he wasn't. Mack seemed to measure everything he said, hoping to pick just the right word or couple of words with an economy of prose that made Tyler fill in the blanks. He had apparently been quite a player before coming over, but hadn't been blessed with many very talented students on this side of the pond until Tyler came along.

Mack had known Tyler was different from the first time they were together on the range. He obviously had inherited a bit of the legendary athletic ability of Jack Foster, even if it was in a somewhat smaller package. But it was the dogged determination that Tyler displayed on that first visit that left an impression. He initially hit the ball off the tee high and straight, but as soon as they had dropped it on the turf, Tyler struggled to get it airborne even once. An hour later, when Tyler's grandfather had come to corral him for lunch, he was still at it and told his grandfather he couldn't take a break until he figured it out. And he didn't. So when his grandfather came back from lunch with his cronies 45 minutes later, he found Tyler beaming and saying, "Watch this, Poppa," before dropping a ball on the turf and hitting a 7-iron high and soft, landing it next to the target pin almost 125 yards away. That was the start of it all.

Mack had worked with Tyler all that summer, teaching him at first just the basics of what would get him around the course without embarrassing his stoic grandfather or slowing their game. In a little over a month, though, they had progressed from the basics of how to swing the club and hit the requisite short-game shots, to things like hitting off uphill, downhill, and side-hill lies, as well as how to shape shots to the left and the right intentionally. Tyler was like a sponge that summer, a young prodigy soaking up everything

Mack told him with the unbridled enthusiasm of a kid who has found something he has fallen in love with. By the time he had to go back to school, he was breaking 100 consistently, a pretty fair feat considering he'd been at it just a bit over two months and hadn't yet cracked the five-foot mark. And he'd talked his father into putting a net up in the backyard so he could hit balls once school started because he wouldn't be able to get to the course except on weekends. He would still go see Mack on those weekends, all throughout his sixth-grade year, and typically play nine holes with his grandfather on Saturdays after his regular morning game. By the time the next summer rolled around, he was shooting in the mid to low 80s occasionally and beating his grandfather on a pretty regular basis.

And all the while, Mack was there with a small suggestion here, a subtle comment there, an occasional demonstration when Tyler didn't quite understand something (which was rare), and enough patience to allow him to develop his natural talents without trying to over-coach him into some perfect little model of the ideal golfer. Mack had kept it fun by continually challenging him, having contests with him, and slipping in just enough instruction to keep him on the right track. He was like a master sculptor, knowing just what pieces to chip away to allow the natural masterpiece that lay beneath in his young pupil to shine through. And while Tyler wasn't aware of it at the time, he realized now that was why he had clicked so well with Mack. He liked figuring things out on his own, and Mack gave him the space to do that, stepping in just enough when he could see his pupil was either struggling or headed down a road that wouldn't ultimately get him where he wanted to go.

"Let's go this way," Mack said, suddenly interrupting Tyler's thoughts about what had eventually led him to this point in his life – in a public park at the crack of dawn walking with a curmudgeonly old Scot nearly three times his age.

"You do this a lot?" Tyler asked as he took in the crisp morning air and the smell of the freshly cut grass.

"Every morning," Mack replied in his typically economical style. "Doc's orders."

Mack had taken off at a pretty brisk pace, one that had initially surprised Tyler, and it took him a few minutes to adjust his stride to match that of the much older man.

"So, first of all," Mack broke the silence after Tyler had caught up to him, "ya' need to get back to what made ya' so good all those years ago."

"I work as hard on my game as anyone, Coach, probably harder. I always have. It just doesn't seem to be paying the dividends it used to," Tyler interjected.

"Yes, you've always been a hard worker, Tyler, but that's not the biggest part of what made ya' so good," Mack said. "When ya' were younger, it definitely helped ya' get better faster than most kids who pick up the game, but it wasn't the real difference maker."

"I don't understand," Tyler said. "You always praised me for what a hard worker I was."

41

"That's right," Mack said, "because if ya' want to be successful at anything, ya' have to work hard at it. And the game came easy enough for ya' at first that I didn't want ya' to believe ya' could just get by on all that God-given athletic ability that seems to run in your family. Hard work is important, but it's not what ultimately made ya' so good."

"Well, what are you talking about then?" Tyler asked, confused that Mack had just basically ruled out talent and hard work; the two things Tyler had always felt had set him apart.

"Curiosity, joy, a love of learning, and playing the game for your own reasons," Mack said.

"Huh?" Tyler said, really confused now.

"Think about it a moment, Ty," Mack continued. "When ya' were younger and improving so much, ya' loved to learn new things and always wanted to find new ways to get better. At the time, you were the most curious student I'd ever had, always asking questions, wanting to know how to hit this shot or that, what to do in this situation or that, and when I wasn't around, ya' didn't stop asking those questions. Ya' just asked them to yourself and figured out a way, and ya' couldn't wait to get back to show me what you'd come up with. As you got older, ya' began to think you had the game all figured out, and ya' stopped asking those questions, and when I tried to give ya' the answers anyway, ya' stopped listening. Just when I could have taught ya' the most about what ya' needed to be really successful at this game, ya' stopped believing there was more to learn and became convinced that it was your own talent and hard work that ultimately made the difference."

"I'm not sure that's fair," Tyler said. "I still came to see you when I could since I went away to school, but it's more than three hours' drive. It wasn't as easy as it used to be, and besides, I had Coach Pohl there, and it's not as if he doesn't know which end of the club to hold."

Tyler's last comment was a bit of a shot at Mack's statement about Gabe, and a testament that he had begun to think Mack was at least still partially lecturing him for not taking him along to Q-School.

"Yes, Coach Pohl knows a thing or two, but his path to the Tour was never going to be your path, and his hit-balls-until-your-hands-bleed approach didn't exactly feed into your best instincts. Sure, ya' came to see me now and then, but ya' were there in body, not in spirit, and that's the way you've been playing the game the past few years. Golf is supposed to be enjoyed, and ya' began to treat it like a job, something ya' had to do to keep your scholarship, best your old man, and ultimately put this town in your rear-view mirror. When ya' stopped loving the process, playing for yourself, and playing with curiosity, ya' stopped really enjoying the game, and that's when ya' stopped learning and getting better."

Tyler was quiet for a moment. He wanted to object, particularly to the part about playing to best his old man, but too much of what Mack was saying was hitting home all of a sudden.

"Think about it, Tyler," Mack continued. "You've basically been shooting the same scores since your freshman year. I know ya' thought back then, and so did a lot of other people, that you could have skipped school altogether and tried for the Tour, but ya' weren't ready. I think ya' knew that. I knew that. But in truth, four years later you aren't much better than ya' were then. I know going to school and playing golf can be a grind, but when ya' stopped playing for the right reasons and ya' turned golf into an extension of school and what ya' were going to do in this world to prove yourself, ya' began to feel pressure for the first time and stopped getting better."

"Well, it's a different type of pressure," Tyler said. "You aren't just playing for yourself, you're playing for the team, and everyone is relying on you to help get them somewhere. They've all got dreams too, whether it's getting Coach a conference championship or getting the team nationally ranked so we collectively get noticed. They don't articulate it, but when you're the star recruit they all expect you to take them somewhere. I was actually looking forward to the idea of just getting back to playing for myself again."

"It sounds like ya' thought that was going to be easier," Mack replied, "…Q-School isn't exactly the venue to turn to if you're tired of the pressure, though."

"Well, that's not exactly what I meant," Tyler objected. "It's just that it was kind of a relief once my eligibility ran out because I thought I could get back to focusing on my own goals. I kind of felt like I put my goals on hold for four years in a way to help everyone else get theirs. I know I got some individual accolades along the way, but it didn't always seem to be getting me any closer to where I ultimately wanted to go-in some ways, but instead further away because I knew I could end up being right back here."

"The last place ya' wanted to be," Mack finished for him, letting it hang there.

As they rounded a bend, they came upon a picnic bench just off the trail. Mack walked over to it and took a seat on the table with his feet on the seat. Tyler realized all at once he was actually a bit winded and was glad for the break. The older man kept a brisk pace, and Tyler realized he had let his conditioning slip a bit. After they had both caught their breath a minute later, Mack finally broke the silence.

"Ultimately, Tyler, when golf stopped being something ya' did because ya' loved it, and started being your ticket out of here, is when ya' started feeling all that extra pressure and stopped enjoying it. I understand that... Did I ever tell ya' why I left Scotland?"

"No, I don't really think you did," Tyler said. "I know you said you played competitively and wanted to try some tournaments over here."

"Well, my own father was the pro at our club back home. He was a big, loud, fiery, larger-than-life, redheaded Scotsman who had a pretty fair playing career and was the best player our small town had ever produced. He actually qualified and played in The Open

Championship seven times as a club professional, even made the cut once and finished in the top five three times in the Scottish Open. Pretty big footsteps for a quiet, soft-spoken young lad to follow in. Now he wasn't too hard on me, and he taught me everything he knew, expecting and more than half-hoping I would be even better than he was someday. But he couldn't help who he was, and I always felt the weight of his expectations, and when he realized I wasn't likely to live up to those expectations, I felt the weight of his disappointment.

"I played well, especially in regular rounds. I could shoot 65 any day of the week when it didn't mean much, but as soon as I was in some kind of an event where I felt the eyes and hopes of my own old man on me, I would wilt under the shadow of those expectations and shoot a 75. When it was clear to me, him, and everyone else that I wasn't going to be the competitive successor to Colin McLean, he started teaching me to be his successor as the club professional. However, living in that shadow was something I just couldn't ultimately handle. I had a student from America who often came to see me when he was in the area on business, and when he told me they had a sudden need for a club pro back at his home club, I jumped at the opportunity."

"Wow," Tyler said. "Old Garret Williams was a student of yours? I had always heard he was the one responsible for bringing you over."

"I had no idea where Poplar Bluff even was at the time, Tyler. Hell, I didn't even exactly know where Missouri was, but I knew it was about a million miles away from my own old man and that little Scottish seacoast town where it seemed like the only opportunity I was ever going to have was to take over for him someday when he was good and ready, and all the while I would continue to be known as Colin McLean's boy. At first, I told myself that once I was here I could work on my game and start playing competitively again without all the weight of the expectations of my dad and the whole town. And I did a bit, just enough to satisfy myself that I could still do it. But in the end, I liked this town. It was small, like where I was from, the people were generous, kindhearted, and looked out for each other. I traveled enough to know that's not always the case, and so I ultimately decided I would stay."

"Was your dad upset with you for leaving?" Tyler asked.

"Mad as hell," Mack said. "He ranted and raved and swore in a colorful display of language that only a Scot could, which told me more about the fact that he truly loved me than just about anything else he had ever said. It hurt to disappoint him, but in the end he relented and understood that it was something I had to do and, I think, partially because deep down he understood just how hard it really was to be his son. Especially in that town."

"I never knew all this," Tyler said.

"Ya' never asked," Mack replied. "Ya' were a kid, self-absorbed and interested mostly in your own hopes and dreams, but that's okay. That's the way most kids are, at least for a while."

"Let's go," Mack said, suddenly getting up from the picnic bench. "We've got to finish our walk, and I've got a lesson at 9:00 o'clock with just about the most talented 12-year-old kid I've ever had the pleasure of working with." He winked at Tyler.

"Really?" Tyler said, instantly curious, but believing Mack was just giving him a hard time. "Who is it?"

"Your cousin Jackie."

"What?!" Tyler said. "Little Jackie's playing now? I thought my uncle had him playing basketball 24/7."

"Well, I guess big cousin Tyler going off and being such a big shot has had quite an impression on him. After your grandfather brought him to me this past summer, he went home and told his folks he wanted to quit basketball and be like big cousin Ty."

"Wow," Tyler said, "I bet my uncle was pissed about that."

"A little disappointed at first," Mack said, "but once he saw how good Jackie was, he got over it pretty quick. And he's got a pretty good mentor to look up to, I think. You want to come by and impart any words of wisdom on him as he gets started on this journey? I know he'd love to see ya' now that you've come home."

Home. In four years at Vanderbilt, Tyler had adopted Nashville as his hometown and had quietly told himself that going back to Poplar Bluff would never be for more than a visit. But for some reason, the thought didn't bother him quite as much at the moment.

"Yeah, I'd love to see him and see his swing," Tyler said. Jackie was the son of Tyler's dad's younger sister, Candace. He was named after Tyler's dad and was the closest thing he ever had to a little brother.

"I guess I should tell him to never stop learning and make sure he's playing for his own reasons," Tyler continued with a wry smile at Mack. "Oh, and don't' forget, we still need to talk about that job. I've got to do something to start saving up for the next go-round."

Mike Dowd

A LONG AWAITED MEETING

They got back to the cars and Tyler agreed he would head home, get cleaned up, and then meet Mack back at the range a little after nine o'clock to surprise his cousin.

"Let me get at least fifteen minutes in with him," Mack had said in mock exasperation. "Once his legendary cousin shows up, I've a feeling we won't accomplish much."

Tyler felt a lot better on the ride back than he had in a long time. He was digesting the weight of everything Mack had said and coming to the realization of how true a lot of it was. For some reason, while it technically didn't change anything, just recognizing where all that pressure– not just at Q-School, but for the past four years– had really come from seemed to take some of the weight off his shoulders.

He pulled up in front of the house and opened the garage to see his father had already left. Jack Foster was an early riser who loved to open the garage just before the sun topped the tree-line of the Black River that wound through town. The thought of spending his days under the hood of a car in a hot garage like his father did just didn't appeal to Tyler. And with any luck it wouldn't need to. That was his dad's thing, and that was all right. Golf was his thing. As he got out of the car and headed back out to the driveway to pick up the newspaper, he thought about the irony of his "little brother", as Jackie liked to call himself, wanting to follow in his footsteps. It made him smile as he mounted the front steps and opened the door to the smell of his mother's cooking.

"Mornin', Mom," Tyler called from the entry hall.

"Good morning, dear," Mary Jane replied, echoing tones of June Cleaver.

"Did you hear Jackie's taken up golf?" Tyler asked as he walked into the kitchen.

"Yes, I heard," Tyler's mother replied. "Poppa Jack was over here for dinner a few weeks ago boasting to your father about how little Jackie is going to give you a run for your money someday soon, and how he ought to be a talent scout for the PGA Tour since he claims he saw the raw ability in both of you before anyone else did."

"That sounds like Poppa Jack," Tyler said, chuckling as he rifled through the cupboards for the cereal. "I've got to eat something, I'm meeting Mack to watch Jackie hit some balls at the range at nine… and talk about a job."

"Let me fix you a proper breakfast," Tyler's mother said. "You're getting too skinny."

"That's okay, Mom," Tyler replied. "I just need something quick. I've still got to shower and change."

"Well, since you're headed that way anyway, you can do me a quick favor then," his mother continued as if suddenly remembering something. "I owe Katherine for the tickets. Stop by the garage and get some money from your father for me and take it over to the ACS office. It's just around the corner."

"What?!" Tyler said with more emphasis than he had intended. For some reason he still didn't want his mother to think that Katherine being back in town was a big deal to him, but he suddenly realized that it was, and he wasn't at all mentally ready to actually see her. "I-I'll be late. You know how Mack is about punctuality. Can't Dad do it?"

"Your father's really behind, Tyler," his mother continued. "He could really use some help around that place you know, and I've got to finish nine more loaves of bread I promised this morning for the VFW Ladies' Auxiliary fundraiser."

Tyler quit protesting, again not wanting his mother to see how the prospect of seeing Katherine had thrown him for a loop.

He ate his cereal in silence as his mother buzzed around the kitchen doing what she loved to do and humming like a domestic little bee in the process. She and Katherine had been close, and once his mother had stopped updating him on how things were with her a couple of years ago, Tyler had half feared Katherine had met someone and started a new life in Columbia. Apparently not, he thought as he finished his quick breakfast and headed off to shower and change.

Initially, he was just going to wear some comfortable golf clothes, but after the shower Tyler realized about thirty seconds into staring into his closet that his clothes seemed old and tired, and that he had been wearing mostly the same things for years. He settled on a pair of jeans and a bit of a nicer button-up shirt that he realized had been shuffled towards the back of his closet without ever having been worn since he hadn't taken it to school with him. Not very golf-like, he thought suddenly, and so he grabbed a golf shirt too and threw it over his shoulder.

He tried to shuffle out the door without his mother seeing him, shouting a cursory, "See you this afternoon, Mom," in her direction as he headed out the back door to the kitchen and down the side steps that led to the driveway and his waiting car below.

"Tyler," she called from the landing as he hit the bottom step. "The tickets are $50 each, I took three of them," she said smiling down at him almost mischievously. "You aren't much dressed for golf are you?"

***

Twenty minutes later, Tyler was walking down the sidewalk towards the ACS office after having procured the necessary $150 from his old man at the garage. Jack hadn't asked many questions once Tyler told him what it was for, but Tyler detected just the faintest hint of amusement in him as he was leaving when he called out, "Tell Katherine hello for me," as he slid back under a car on his creeper.

The American Cancer Society Office had taken up residence in one of the many abandoned storefronts on old Broadway, one of the two main streets in Historic Downtown Poplar Bluff, a couple of blocks from the old Rodger's Theater. The scene was not unlike a lot of Midwest towns that had been originally settled at the turn of the 20th Century. The once bustling Main Street and Broadway area of town had been largely abandoned by modern businesses, in favor of bigger traffic arteries with space for expansion to big box stores and fast food chains easily accessed by the casual passer through. In some instances, space in these historic old buildings could be had for almost nothing as the handful of landlords just wanted tenants of some sort. Therefore, charitable organizations often found them the cheapest place to set up shop.

Like a window-shopper from a bygone era, Tyler stopped to stare into the big empty display window of one such abandoned storefront before he got to the ACS space, and almost turned around as he considered what he was about to do. While hardly a week had gone by without him thinking about it, it had been more than four years since he had spoken to Katherine, not since the day he had broken her heart. It was the biggest regret he had about leaving Poplar Bluff in the first place, but some combination of pride, regret, embarrassment, and just not knowing how to express it all, or even really understanding it all, had kept him from ever reaching out to tell her so. What would he say to her? Katherine, in a way, had come to represent a past that he had left behind, and contacting her would be a sign of weakness; a kid who couldn't abandon the old security blankets of his youth and stretch his wings to chart his own course in life. He had dreams that were much bigger than Poplar Bluff and Katherine, despite his feelings for her, had almost come to represent a step back– back to a life that was just too small, simple, and unsophisticated. But had that really been fair?

Katherine was a smart girl. Somedays he even felt she was just a bit too smart. Smarter than him for sure. And between his mother and her, he sometimes felt like they were conspiring to map out a course of life for him that they weren't quite letting him in on. She was a girl so much like the girl his mother had been, instinctively seeming to know when to look out for him, and at times almost picking up, it seemed, just where Mary Jane had left off. But she was more than that, and she wasn't just a girl anymore, he suddenly realized. She had left and tasted life beyond their small town in her own right, heading off to Columbia and Mizzou for, what did his mother tell him it ended up being, a business degree of some sort? That almost didn't sound like the Katherine he'd known. Unfairly, he now realized, he had always pictured her majoring in something like home economics, seemingly so cut from the same cloth his mother was, but there was a bit of her own old man in her, too. A shrewd, no-nonsense sensibility and pragmatism combined with her own mother's almost legendary philanthropic heart that was both attractive and intimidating all at once. She was bigger than Poplar Bluff too and she surely would figure out just how much once she got away from it. He had told her that at that fateful final meeting, but he now realized that was at least in part to assuage his own conscience, and he hadn't completely believed it.

They had long talked about going away to college together and she had just assumed he would go to Mizzou like everyone else, the only school they had really talked about and the one she could follow him to because the in-state tuition break allowed her father to afford it. She knew he had other scholarship offers and had made a handful of visits out-of-state with Jack. Tyler had told her they were mostly obligatory. Jack was a Mizzou alum and everyone knew he was steering Tyler hard in that direction too, so Katherine hadn't even applied anywhere else. Something changed, though, when he saw Nashville for the first time and met with Coach Pohl. And when Tyler finally indicated he was going to take their offer, it was too late. In the end, he had a lot of reasons for choosing Vandy, and while he never articulated it, one of them was that the Mizzou route had sounded just way too much like a replay of his parent's lives. He knew it would be impossible for Katherine to follow him to school in Nashville, and when he had finally tried to explain what he was thinking she was not only shocked, but at first in confused disbelief that he had been considering going somewhere he knew she couldn't follow. Once the ramifications of his decision had finally sunk in, however, she had been justifiably upset.

"I guess we obviously just didn't mean as much to you as we did to me, Tyler," she said as the tears began to stream down her face. "You really think we can still see each other when we'll be living almost seven hours apart? Are you serious? What has this been to you? Just a little fun and a way to pass the time until you got your shot at the big time? Even if your dream had been to stay right here and take over that stupid garage of your father's you know I'd have supported you, and even set my own goals aside to help you make that happen. You're not just chasing your dreams, though, you're doing it in a way and a place where you know I can't even be a part of them. I'm obviously not a part of them. How could I have been so stupid... *We* not only didn't mean as much to you, Tyler, *I* obviously don't mean that much to you. Well, just leave then, and don't look back, Tyler, because you're not going to find me waiting around in the rear view mirror if things don't work out!"

That had been just across the street in old Vern's Diner, he suddenly realized, as he caught the reflection of the vintage 1950's neon sign that hung above Vern's in the display window he was absently staring into. It was more than four years ago, but it suddenly seemed like yesterday, and the regret and awful way he had felt about how he had gone about it all came rushing back. He could see her getting up without even drying her eyes and leaving abruptly without a goodbye or even a glance back. He had watched her stop outside and collect herself, putting her hair back and walking off in the opposite direction he knew she needed to just so she wouldn't have to walk by the window where he sat in the booth they had shared side by side for the previous three years.

Now, for whatever reason, they were both right back here, and she apparently had more to show for those years than he did. He suddenly realized how unprepared he was for this meeting, or what he should even say. Had she changed? Was her hair different? Was she seeing someone? Engaged even? The image of an engagement ring on her finger suddenly flashed in Tyler's mind and he almost became sick to his stomach, but no, his mother would have said something or at least not sent him down here. How twisted she had been to send him on this errand all of a sudden, he thought, but then his mother didn't do anything without having first thought about it. All at once, he took a deep breath and decided to just do it. If he waited around and thought about it much longer he knew he really would just turn around and suddenly he realized he wanted, more than anything, for good or bad, just to see her again.

Tyler looked at himself in the reflection of the display window one last time, ran a hand through his hair, straightened his shirt a bit, put his hands in his pockets, stood up straight, and began to walk around the corner to the next old storefront where he knew the ACS office was. As he rounded the corner and walked past the double display windows that had been decorated with all sorts of images of various past fundraisers the Society held, he realized he couldn't see past the reflection inside to the space beyond. He put his hand on the door a bit hesitantly and then opened it to the agonizingly loud sound of the jingling bells that had obviously been put there to alert someone of the presence of a visitor. As he looked around, he saw a fairly large room with a handful of unoccupied work-stations on the left-hand side and some tables that looked as if they were preparing centerpieces for an event to the right. He walked over to these to look at the pictures that had been fanned out on the table when a voice from the back room suddenly called out, "I'll be right there." It was Katherine, and seconds later there she was, walking hurriedly with two armfuls of fake flowers and other decorations.

"Sorry, I was just getting some…" She stopped suddenly as she finally looked up from the load of things she was carrying to see Tyler. And then she dropped all of it.

She was wearing jeans and a red fleece pull-over with The American Cancer Society logo on it, but above that casual outfit was a woman he almost didn't recognize. Her hair had been pulled back away from her face and was tight up on her head in some sort of bun, but it had an obvious curl to it, evidenced by the two tendrils that tumbled down from each temple almost to her shoulders. She wore smart, somewhat thick-rimmed glasses and a serious expression that made her look more like thirty-two than twenty-two. She definitely wasn't the same girl who had walked out on him at Vern's Diner more than four years ago.

"Hello, Tyler," she said, very business-like as she reached down to retrieve the load of flowers she seemed more than a bit embarrassed to have dropped now.

"Hi," Tyler replied a bit hesitantly, suddenly dumbfounded he hadn't scripted at least something to say in advance, but then remembering his manners he quickly stooped to help her retrieve everything.

"I've got it," she said, again coolly, as if she was dealing with something mildly irritating.

"I wanted to…"

She cut him off, "I know, come by and pay for the tickets I gave your mother yesterday. I should have known Mary Jane would put you up to this."

"I-I didn't realize you moved back home," Tyler said.

"It isn't permanent, just helping out around here temporarily," Katherine replied with a dismissive wave of her hand as she deposited her load on the table where she had been building centerpieces.

"I guess I'm kind of in the same boat. I'm actually on my way to talk to Mack about going to work for him for the time being... Don't you have any help around here?" Tyler asked, gesturing to the empty work-stations and obvious lack of other people around.

"Oh, sure, Karen Gibson just about lives here. She went to get us some coffee, and a couple other volunteers will come by in the afternoons." She busied herself with what she had been doing, seemingly determined not to give Tyler another glance and treating him about as significantly as a UPS driver who'd stopped in to deliver a package.

"Look," Tyler said, "I want to start by saying I'm sorry, really sorry, for a lot of things. I was wr..."

"Honestly, Tyler," Katherine cut him off again with a wave of her hand and note of slight exasperation as she barely looked up from what she was doing, "That was a long time ago, and I'm not the same girl you left across the street. And Karen ought to be back any moment, so even if I was inclined to get into it, which I'm not, it's not the time or place. If you've got the money to pay for those tickets, just leave it on the desk there and thank your mother for me profusely. I'm just way behind here and I've only got a few weeks left before the Gala to get caught up."

"Oh, okay," Tyler said as he began to pull the money his father had given him out of his pocket. "I understand. I'll get out of your hair... My father said to tell you hello."

"Tell Jack I said hi," she replied with a note of finality.

He put the money on the desk closest to him and turned to walk out. At the last second he turned back to her and said, "Maybe I'll see you around?"

"I'm sure, Tyler," she said, again without looking up. "This isn't exactly Nashville. Pretty tough to avoid someone altogether in this town even if you want to."

And with that Tyler turned and walked out, the loud jingling of the bells letting him know he'd let the door slam just a bit harder than he'd intended. After all this time it certainly wasn't the type of meeting he had expected. Despite the fact that he had never contacted her, hardly a week had gone by in the last four years when he hadn't thought about what had happened with Katherine, wished he'd done things differently, and envisioned what this meeting would be like if and when it ever happened. But in his mind it had never gone like this. A confused mix of emotions washed over him as he walked back to the garage that ultimately left him feeling that his first impression had been correct. Katherine was not only not the same girl he had known; he wasn't so sure now he'd ever really known her. And that left him suddenly feeling like the biggest idiot in all of Butler County.

Mike Dowd

GOING TO WORK

Twenty minutes later, Tyler pulled into the familiar parking lot at Butler Bluff Country Club. It was only twenty minutes after 9:00, so at least his all-too brief encounter with Katherine hadn't made him too late to meet Mack and surprise his young cousin. He parked around in the side lot where only the staff usually parked so Jackie wouldn't be immediately alerted of his presence when he saw the classic Mizzou Tiger Orange '68 Camaro he and his father had restored the summer before his sophomore year in high school pulling up. That car, and that summer he spent with his old man fixing it up in anticipation of his sixteenth birthday, was one the best memories he had of spending time in the garage. He was excited to not only have his own ride, right out of the gate when he got his license, but a sweet ride on top of it. Jack had taken his enthusiasm as a sign that his son was cut from the same cloth when it came to his love of cars, and agreeing to paint it Tiger Orange just about sealed that conviction. But once the car was done, his interest in hanging around the garage waned as the lure of the links called him back.

As he got out of the car, he decided to walk around the back side of the clubhouse past the kitchen loading dock and cart barn so he could sneak up behind Jackie on the range and surprise him. He loved his little cousin like the little brother he never had, and that affection was definitely reciprocated as Jackie had always begged him to play with him at every family occasion, from throwing a baseball in the backyard, to a football in the street, to shooting baskets in the driveway. And, not having any siblings, Tyler had never minded. In fact, he enjoyed it and Jackie was a great kid, always laughing and playing little practical jokes on him that he had dreamed up whenever he knew big cousin Tyler was coming over to the house.

As Tyler rounded the corner and passed the cart barn, his thoughts of his cousin were interrupted suddenly by a girl's voice calling out to him from just inside.

"Hey Tyyy," came a familiar drawl that he couldn't immediately place. Then he heard the sound of the old beverage cart start up as it emerged from the shadows, and with it came a stunning head of blond hair he hadn't seen since high school. It was Whitney Robertson, ex Homecoming Queen and head cheerleader from his Poplar Bluff High days. She stopped short, playfully pretending she was going to run him over, and then jumped out and wrapped him up in an almost overly friendly embrace.

"W-Whitney," Tyler fumbled. What a day this had been already. "Sorry, I-I didn't see you in there. It's been a long time, how've you been?"

Whitney held on to him a bit longer than was probably customary of old friends, which they hadn't even exactly been, but after the chilly reception he'd gotten from Katherine, Tyler didn't exactly mind. Whitney had sat behind him in Economics class their senior year, and they had become somewhat friendly, somewhat more friendly than Katherine had been happy with, but Tyler had explained to her that attention was an obvious ploy to glean some free Econ help. And if it made her arrogant captain of the football team boyfriend Garett Daniels a little jealous at the same time, well, Whitney probably didn't mind that either, Tyler reasoned.

Whitney was beautiful, the kind of beautiful that seemed effortless on her part and that he knew made most of the other girls in school resent her. And while she didn't flaunt that, she seemed not to be able to help the fact that she attracted men and always acted as if that attraction was almost surprising to her. Tyler had come to learn in that semester that she was actually a pretty nice girl, and smarter than most gave her credit for, but despite that she seemed eternally saddled with a never-ending line of unfortunate jealous comments and commentary heaped upon her by other girls. The kind who wanted to make her out to be someone less than she was just because it made them feel better about themselves and who felt it was wrong that any one girl could be so effortlessly attractive.

"I'm fine, Ty, just fine. Well, aren't you all grown up," Whitney said looking him up and down after she finally let him go. "Big city must've agreed with you, I see."

Tyler smiled, a bit embarrassed and suddenly at a loss for words. For some reason he felt a bit like a kid who was being assessed by an older relative he hadn't seen in years, but then he regained his composure. "Well, you look as great as ever. Are you working here at the club now?"

"Yeah, was waitressing for a few years and then started tending bar for a while to pay my way through school, but I find these golfers are a bit better at keeping their hands to themselves than the fellas down at the Liar's Bench."

Tyler chuckled. "Yeah, I can imagine. I've only been there once, but if I remember it definitely doesn't seem like your type of crowd. Actually, I'm moving home for a bit and was talking to Mack about coming to work here myself in the time being, so maybe I'll be seeing more of you."

"Well, it'd be good to see more of you, Tyyy," Whitney said with a wink and drawing it out again. "But I better get back to what I'm supposed to be doing. For a game that's so dang slow, these golfers aren't a real patient lot if you're not there with a drink when they want it."

"Yeah, I'm late to meet with Mack myself. I'm sure I'll see you around," Tyler said, suddenly wondering what had ever become of old Garett Daniels. Whitney sure could have an effect on a guy.

With that Tyler headed up the steps that lead to the back side of the practice tee and walked through the opening in the tall box hedge. Over in the familiar, somewhat isolated corner of the practice tee Mack used for teaching, he could see his cousin hitting balls and Mack standing nearby, leaning on a club and watching intently. Tyler tried to walk casually along the back side of the tee as if he was headed to the practice bunker, hoping to go unnoticed until the last minute. The first thing he noticed was that little Jackie wasn't exactly all that little anymore. He had sprouted up a bit since he'd seen him last Christmas and even though he was just shy of 13, he was now only a few inches shorter than Tyler. The next thing that caught Tyler's eye was how effortlessly he swung the club and how far he was hitting what appeared to be a 7 or 8 iron; easily 130 yards in the air as each shot was flying right over the old 125 bulls-eye. Jackie had always been a good little athlete, better at most sports than most of the kids his age, but he looked like he'd been doing this for years, not months. And, Tyler was suddenly filled not only with a sense of pride, but a touch of awe at the same time.

"You're gonna' have to hit it a lot better than that if you think you're gettin' in my pocket," Tyler said loudly as he stepped up on the tee behind Jackie and Mack.

"Ty!" Jackie exclaimed as he looked up, dropping his club and running over and nearly knocking Tyler over as he jumped up to wrap him up in a huge bear hug. Jackie obviously didn't realize himself yet that he was a lot bigger than last time he had seen Tyler and didn't yet know his own strength. "I didn't know you were home. Mom didn't say a thing."

"Well, she didn't know either," Tyler replied. "I just got back yesterday afternoon. Q-School didn't exactly go as I'd have liked so I'm going to be spending a bit more time around here for a while if that's okay?

"Okay? That's awesome," Jackie said. "I mean, I'm sorry about the tournament. I made Mom look up your scores every day, so I knew, but you'll get 'em next time."

"That's my plan. I just need to spend a little more time with Mack here to get things back on track," Tyler said as he turned to finally acknowledge his coach. "Sorry I'm a little late, had something... I guess you could say unexpected come up this morning after we talked."

Mack noticed the slightly curious expression on Tyler's face and decided to wait to ask questions. "So, what did ya really think of my young protégé here, Tyler? Remind ya of anyone?"

Jackie had gone back to hitting balls, wanting to show off his ability to his big brother Ty, and no sooner had Mack finished his sentence when there came a loud *whack* as Jackie's iron shot hit the bulls-eye.

"Whatt'ya think o' that, Ty?" Jackie looked up beaming. "Last week I hit that thing four times in a row at the end of our lesson."

"That's awesome, Jackie." Tyler replied. "Really, I don't remember hitting that thing once all summer when Mack first taught me to play. And trust me, I tried a lot. I guess I really am going to have to get to work on my game, or before you know it you'll be giving me strokes."

Jackie smiled and went back to hitting balls after switching to a driver. He obviously wanted to show his big brother how far he could hit it too and Tyler was only too happy to cheer him on. After about another 20 minutes of Jackie hitting balls, interspersed with occasional words of wisdom from Mack, and plenty of encouragement from Tyler, Mack eventually said they should go sit down while Jackie headed off to the practice bunker. They walked over to the back of the range where Mack always kept a couple of chairs under a big old Sycamore tree so he could sit and talk with students either before or after their lessons.

"So ya need a job?" Mack finally said, as much a statement as a question. "What for? Ya need to actually support yourself, or ya got that part worked out for now?"

"Well," Tyler said after a bit of a pause, "I know I'm going to at least need to save up enough money for the next go-around, that and for a handful of mini-tour events within a few hour's drive I can get into just to make sure I stay sharp. My folks fronted me last time and I won't ask them for it again, even if my father hadn't already indicated that well has run a bit dry for now. I mean, I don't need to make a ton of money, and I'll do whatever you need."

"So then, I take it you'll be staying with your folks for now?" Mack asked.

"Yeah, I mean, I need to be able to work on my game too and if I was to get my own place I'd need to work full-time to afford it and if I'm going to do that then I might as well just give the whole thing up."

"So, your old man's okay with all this?

"Well…," Tyler said, "You know he'd prefer me to come help him at the garage, but if I did that he'd work on me every day to do a little more, help him an extra day here and there, or he'd come up with reasons to take a long lunch or something else that would keep me from getting out here where I need to be. He keeps hoping I'll come around, and I understand he needs some help and sure, it's security, but I know how that story ends and I just don't think it's me. At least here I can practice before or after work and people respect me here. At the garage, I'm just Jack's boy, and most people who come in there don't really take me all that seriously."

"Hmmm," Mack said, thinking as he looked off in the direction of the practice bunker, apparently scrutinizing what Jackie was doing even at over 100 yards from where they now sat. "And you don't think that would change with time? Maybe the reason they don't take you seriously has a little bit to do with the fact that you've never taken it all that seriously."

"It's just not me, Mack. I love playing golf. I like being around golf, the game, the people, hell, I just like talking about golf. It's like football was for my old man. I mean, if I couldn't play any more like him then maybe I'd have to find something else, but I don't want to. And even if that were the case, I'd rather do what you do and help people play. If I've got to spend a hot summer afternoon working, I'd sure as hell rather do it out here than spend it under somebody else's car in that stuffy old garage."

"Okay then," Mack said, suddenly getting up as if he'd made a decision. "I see you've thought about this enough. We're not exactly headed into the busy season right now, but I suppose if you're willing to not just watch the counter in the afternoons while I teach, but wash carts, pick up the range, and help out with a handful of my younger students like Jackie when I'm booked up, then I could find 20 hours a week or so through the winter, and then likely a bit more once springtime rolls around. If you work out, that is."

"Thanks, Mack, I really appreciate it. In truth, I'd love to learn the ropes around here, and you can send Jackie or any of the other kids my way as often as you want. I can't wait to get him out there. If the rest of his game is anything like how he hits that 7-iron you've done an amazing job."

"A man in my line of work only has a kid like that come along maybe once in a career, Tyler. You'll learn that if you stick with it long enough," Mack said with a suddenly far-away look. And then turning back to look at Tyler, he smiled and continued, "Now I've had two… I might just be living on borrowed time."

Tyler chuckled at that, and then, as they both headed off towards the practice bunker where Jackie had hit about 100 balls up onto the green already, he said, "So when do I start?"

"Right now," Mack replied. "Go shag all the balls on that green and put 'em in five equal piles on the other side. I've got a chipping clinic in about 30 minutes. And then ya' can straighten the range tee back up and take Jackie home after you've watched him putt for 30 minutes. I told his mother you were coming by and wouldn't mind doing that. Make sure he keeps his left wrist flat and his shoulders moving, especially on the short ones. He tends to get a little flippy on those just like another member of his family I know. After that ya' can have the rest of the day off, but be back here by 10:30 tomorrow and I'll show ya' the rest."

With that, Mack headed off in the direction of the Pro Shop, leaving Tyler with Jackie and the balls to clean up. At least this part of his plan was working out like he'd hoped. As he picked up the old shag bags Mack left by the green, he turned to look at Jackie, still whaling away in the practice bunker and smiled. Yes, this could work out just fine.

AN OLIVE BRANCH

When the slamming door and jingling of the bells told Katherine that Tyler was gone, she finally looked up and exhaled. It was only now she realized she had been almost holding her breath during the entire exchange. He had caught her by surprise, but she had rehearsed that first meeting in her head so many times in the past four years that, once she had collected herself, she knew exactly what she wanted to do. There was no way she was giving Tyler the self-satisfaction of thinking she wasn't over him. Aside from dropping the flowers, she was proud of how cool and collected she had been, maybe almost too dismissive she suddenly thought, but no, she wanted him to suffer. At least a bit. He deserved it after all this time and there was no way she was letting him off the hook easy, if at all.

The bells jingled again and Karen walked in carrying coffee and a bagful of bagels, almost as if in a hurry, and suddenly blurted out, "Katherine, you're never gonna' believe who I just saw walking down the street..."

"Let me guess…" Katherine said, pausing for effect, but not looking up. "Tyler Foster?"

Katherine not only didn't want Tyler to think seeing him again suddenly was a big deal, she realized she didn't want anyone else to think that either. The whole town practically knew what had happened between them and it had embarrassed Katherine to an extent to be jilted in such a public way. Four years later, she was determined the tables were going to be turned, if anything. Leaving Poplar Bluff, living in Columbia, getting her degree, and experiencing life had given her a sense of self-confidence that inwardly she might have lacked before even if it hadn't showed. She always had been a catch, but she knew that now, and the soft-spoken pretty little girl next door had come back home with a sense of self that allowed her to feel like she could own any room she was in if she wanted to. At least in this town.

"He was just here, Karen, dropped off some money for Gala tickets I had given his mother. It's on the desk over there." Katherine continued working and said the whole thing so matter-of-factly that Karen seemed speechless for a moment. And that never happened.

"Well, you sure seem to have handled it pretty well," Karen finally said. "After all this time I'd have thought you might have had a few choice words for him at least. Is he just visiting or has he moved back home?"

"Apparently he's more than visiting," Katherine said as if that fact was mildly irritating to her more than anything. "He's looking for work."

"Looking for work?" Karen replied, a bit confused. "Why doesn't he just work for Jack at the garage? Everyone knows he wanted Tyler to take that place over."

"It never was his thing," Katherine said in the most disinterested way she could muster. "Still chasing his dreams, I guess."

"Hey, that gives me a grand idea, Katherine," Karen said in that irritating way of hers that meant she wanted Katherine to do something. "We still need more items for the silent auction. Maybe you could talk to Tyler about getting Jack to donate some memorabilia. He's got to have some old pictures we could frame and have him sign from his Mizzou days or an old football or something? Just about anything with Jack's name on it would still sell in this town, Katherine. Whatt'ya say?"

"I don't know, Karen," Katherine said. "Jack's given away so much over the years I can't imagine he has much left. And I wasn't exactly friendly when Tyler was here. I'm not so sure he'd welcome a visit from me right now, let alone want to help me."

"Hogwash, Katherine," Karen said as excited with her new plan suddenly as if she'd discovered gold. "Look at you, dear. You could have that boy eating out of your hand if you wanted to. If there's one thing I know it's that playing a little hard to get at first just makes a man even that much more interested. He probably hasn't stopped thinking about you since he left. It's for a good cause, Katherine. At least go ask Jack if you won't ask Tyler. He's only around the corner and you know he'd do anything for you."

"I'll think about it, Karen," Katherine said, still acting disinterested and not wanting her to know how much this whole morning had thrown her for a loop as it was.

***

By the end of the day, Katherine had agreed she would visit Tyler sometime in the next few days to see if he would help by procuring some things from Jack for the Gala. She made Karen beat her down, and in the end put up a pretty fair fight. Enough she thought to not only convince Karen that she really didn't want to do it, but that she just did it to get her to shut up about it.

"Enough already, Karen. I'll go, I'll go," Katherine finally gave in. "I'm not promising anything, though, and I'm definitely not begging."

Despite all her outward protestations, Katherine had to admit to herself in the end that she wanted the opportunity to see Tyler again. As much as she had handled herself exactly the way she had always wanted to in that first meeting, there was still a small frustrating little part of her that felt guilty about it. She was truly such a nice person by nature, and acting arrogant, stand-offish, and cold just really wasn't her. And as much as she hated to admit it, even though she had told herself for years now she was over him and would never again be interested, there was a part of her that didn't want Tyler to think he didn't stand a chance with her. He was a guy, after all, and if he thought she was completely disinterested he might just move on to the next likely candidate. She wanted to make sure she was still on his mind, but at the same time didn't want him thinking that she would just take him back either. He wouldn't suffer if he didn't think he at least had a shot, though, so she was going to have to find a subtle way to make him think just that.

On the other hand, she thought, just as she wasn't the same girl as she was four years ago, maybe Tyler wasn't the same guy. Four years away from home could change a person, and not always for the better. She realized she had held onto this image in her mind, even after what he had done to her, of the Tyler she always wanted him to be and that, if anything, the reality hadn't lived up to the fantasy. He'd let her down, in a big way, a life-changing way, and she wasn't so sure she could ever trust him or wanted to even. He had at least attempted an apology, though, before she had cut him off. At least there was that, but more than four years later? Common sense told her that was way too little too late, and were his regrets even genuine? And what did he really regret? Not making it? Having to crawl back to Poplar Bluff with his tail between his legs? No, she wasn't going to fool herself into thinking that Tyler would have come back here, back to her, or to any of this if he'd had bigger and better options. She was the one with options now, and she chose to be right where she was. He apparently didn't, and that fact alone meant she couldn't exactly trust that apology because it wouldn't likely be coming if he hadn't been forced to come back here and make it. In truth, considering the circumstances, she wasn't sure she could imagine how he could ever earn her trust again. She wouldn't be that stupid twice, and no, she wasn't going to take it easy on him.

So Katherine decided to wait a few days before contacting Tyler. The next day would look too eager, she reasoned, even the day after that and contradict the disinterested way in which she had handled that first meeting. Three days would be long enough to make her reaching out to him look incidental enough, but not so long as to make him start to forget about her.

Tyler had inherited Jack's good looks, if not his height and build, and there'd be no shortage of girls around town who'd die for his attention were he left alone too long. She knew he wasn't the carousing type, or at least hadn't been, and could lock himself away on that golf course for hours on end given an option, but she didn't want to take a chance, and she decided to track him down there since Tyler had mentioned he was going to work for Mack.

"Butler Bluff Pro Shop, this is Jeremy," came a voice she didn't recognize on the other end once she had hit the number on her mobile.

"Uh, yes, I was looking for Tyler Foster. I, I heard he might be working there now?" Katherine said, a bit unsure of herself all of a sudden for some reason

"Tyler?" Jeremy said as if a bit confused why someone would be calling the golf shop to talk to him. Katherine knew enough about golf and the club after following Tyler around for most of high school to know that everyone at the club knew who Tyler was. He was pretty much royalty around that place, so, she sensed immediately that this Jeremy wasn't exactly excited that the local 'Golden Boy' had come home. "Oh, he's out picking the range. He's not really one of the shop staff, ma'am. I can take a message if you want. He'll be in here a little later around 1:30 when Mack's teaching."

"Oh, that's okay, I'll try back later," Katherine said, and then hung up the phone. She didn't want to alert Tyler to the fact that she had called and she didn't really want to just talk to him on the phone she suddenly realized. He had caught her unaware the other day, and she'd be prepared for the next meeting. Tyler was picking the range? The Golden Boy out shagging balls? It seemed Mack was making him grovel a bit too which brought a brief smile to her lips. She could just drive over there this afternoon, right after lunch she thought, and the thought of that meeting suddenly brought just the hint of butterflies to her stomach for some reason. This was stupid, she chastised herself, it was just to get some memorabilia, nothing more. But she knew if she really just wanted some of Jack's memorabilia the reality was she could just walk around the corner and ask him, or Mary Jane for that matter. Mary Jane would certainly tell Jack to donate just about anything he could part with for her. No, right or wrong, she wanted to see Tyler so she made up her mind to go see him.

Katherine went home for lunch before heading over to the club. She hadn't been exactly dressed for the Country Club, she reasoned, but the fact that Tyler had seen her at what she hadn't felt was her best the other day was also something she wanted to remedy. If she was going to make him suffer she needed to make sure he knew exactly what he had given up back at Vern's Diner all those years ago, and she was going to make sure she looked good enough to not just make him jealous, but every other guy in that place for them not being the one she had come to see.

When she left the house, after changing a half dozen times, she'd let her hair down and settled on a business length skirt and sleeveless button-up blouse that was a bit summery for early November and more than a bit form-fitting. She threw a sweater in the car to be sensible since she would be going back to the office afterwards, but she knew she wouldn't be wearing it. At the last minute, she even decided to throw on a pair of heels. She had never worn heels back in high school when her and Tyler had been dating. In fact, she thought, she hadn't even worn them to prom since she was only a couple of inches shorter than Tyler to begin with, and she knew wearing heels would have made him feel short. She didn't mind that thought at the moment, though. In truth, it's what she wanted. She wanted him looking up to her in more ways than one.

When she rolled up the drive to the old club, she decided to use the valet just to heighten the effect. She didn't really expect Tyler to be anywhere around the front of the club, but she wanted to make an entrance, and getting out of the sports car Daddy had bought her for college graduation and tossing the keys to an admiring young man was something she'd never done, and almost felt like something out of a movie. As she entered the club and walked the long hall past the lounge and then the restaurant, she felt the eyes on her. She knew it was mostly retired guys and a handful of businessmen entertaining clients for lunch, but she didn't care. She hadn't grown up having that kind of an effect on men and, as superficial as she knew it was, she couldn't deny that she liked it. She had come into her own in those four years away at school, blossoming in a way that left her confident that the only real reason she hadn't had that kind of effect before was because she hadn't really ever tried.

She rounded the corner and headed out the door that headed towards the Pro Shop. It was a separate building, about 30 yards away from the main clubhouse and restaurant, bridged by a walkway with a covered canopy. She had rehearsed what she would say to him all morning. She would be sweet, but business-like, ask him for the favor and leave it at that. She knew he would do it, and it would possibly open up the door for another meeting once he had acquired whatever it was that Jack could part with. That was enough for now.

Katherine opened the door to the Pro Shop and immediately saw Tyler running a vacuum around the counter while another guy, not much older than Tyler, sat disinterestedly behind the counter staring out the window in the direction of the first tee. They both looked up when she came in and Tyler shut off the vacuum.

"Can I help you, ma'am?" came the voice that had greeted her on the phone this morning. It was Jeremy, and he was asserting himself over Tyler by being the first to address the attractive young woman who had obviously just mistaken the golf shop for the restaurant and was lost.

"Uh, actually, I'm here to see Tyler," Katherine said, glancing in his direction, but holding Jeremy's gaze just long enough to see the disappointed look on his face.

"Oh," Jeremy said. "You're the gal that called earlier. I'm gonna go see what the hold up on the tee is, Tyler. I'll leave you two alone. Old Man Johnson's been just standing there for at least ten minutes." And then he excused himself.

"Katherine," Tyler said, standing up tall and dusting himself off as he put aside the vacuum cleaner.

Katherine looked him up and down appraisingly with a slightly amused grin. He was wearing an old golf cap, a pair of khaki's, and a Butler Bluff Staff golf polo that was positively dirty; a likely by-product of working on the range. My how things had changed, she reflected, fighting back a wise-crack about his disheveled appearance.

"I didn't think you much wanted to see me after the other day," he continued.

"Oh, I don't," Katherine said, but instantly regretting how blunt that sounded. "I mean, I'm not here for that… I need to ask you for a favor."

"Go on," Tyler said, obviously surprised to see her and confused by her comment. It was he who had been caught unprepared this time.

"Well, I guess Karen Gibson spotted you walking down the street after you left the office the other morning," Katherine explained. "And she was suddenly struck with the revelation that if we could procure something from your father, maybe some signed memorabilia of some sort, it would be great for the silent auction at the Gala coming up."

"I see," Tyler said, coming closer now so that there were only a few feet between them. "And you thought *I* could talk him into it?" he asked, looking into her eyes for the first time.

"Well, it was Karen's idea," Katherine said, becoming a bit flustered for some reason now with Tyler suddenly so close and averting his gaze by absently picking up a women's shoe on the table next to her and pretending to look at it. She had kept her distance at the office the other day, intentionally, and she had been fine when he was across the room, but with Tyler so close now she was suddenly finding it a little harder to breathe.

"I'm not sure you're barking up the right tree, Katherine," Tyler said. "You know my mother has a lot more influence over my old man than I do. Why didn't you go ask her?"

She didn't have an answer to that question and suddenly felt stupid for not anticipating him asking it, so she thought up a quick lie for cover and looked down at the floor as she put the shoe down to try and avoid looking at him directly.

"Oh, well, a-as I said, it was Karen's idea, and since I had to meet a potential donor here for lunch today anyway I just figured I'd pop in and see if you were here. I can ask your mother if it's too much trouble." She had been so confident the other day, so confident all the way over and walking in here. What was going on now?

"Well, no, it's not any real trouble I suppose," Tyler said. "I just meant, well, I'm not exactly on Dad's good list at the moment since I chose to come out here over helping him in the garage, but if it's for you I'm sure he'll come up with something. Obviously, since they're going anyway, I suppose it's only appropriate."

"Aren't you going?" Katherine asked, looking up at Tyler instinctively and with a note of disappointment she hadn't been able to hide.

"Well,..." Tyler said, and then he paused as if he was considering what to say. "I didn't get the impression you much wanted to see me there after the other day, so I told Mom to give that other ticket away, or to take my aunt." He paused again and looked around as if he expected Jeremy to come back in any moment, or a member, and didn't want to be caught in the middle of saying something he really wanted her to hear. "Look Katherine, I really wanted to..."

The door opened suddenly and Jeremy burst back in as if in the middle of a conversation they had just left off.

"You know that Johnson thinks he owns the place," Jeremy complained as he brushed by Tyler and Katherine on his way back to the counter, obviously irritated by something that had gone on outside. "Next on the tee: Jackson, Williams, Jarrett, and Reed. Second up Johnson," he almost shouted over the P.A., and then looking back at the two of them as if he thought they should have concluded whatever business they had added. "That vacuum cleaner don't run itself, Foster," he said with a smirk that spoke volumes about the fact that he enjoyed being a bit higher on the totem pole right now than the legendary Tyler Foster.

"I've got to get back to work," Tyler said with a bit an irritated glance back at Jeremy. "I'll talk to Pop, and if that doesn't work I'll talk to Mom, but I'm sure he'll do something."

"Thank you, Tyler," she said, her tone suddenly softening with him, and then added "You know, if your Mom already got rid of that ticket I could always use some help the night of the Gala…"

"I'd like that," Tyler said.

"We're short of bus boys," she said then, getting business-like again, and looking Tyler up and down with an amused little smile as if she was imagining him bussing tables as she said it, and then shooting a glance back at Jeremy as if she too were now bringing Tyler down a notch.

"I'd be happy to," Tyler said, though, without a hint of the annoyance he had when Jeremy had done the same thing. "There's still some things I'd like to talk to you about, but this obviously isn't the best time. Just let me know where I need to be and when."

"Here's my cell number," Katherine said suddenly a bit caustically, handing Tyler a business card she had procured from her pocketbook. "In case you lost it, it hasn't changed. Call me once you've talked to your father about the auction items because I'll need those in advance if he's willing to do anything. The Gala's in two weeks, Saturday November 22nd. We can discuss time, place, and anything else necessary over the phone."

With that Katherine turned on her heel and almost strutted back out the door of the Pro Shop and into the restaurant, leaving Tyler more confused than ever.

Mike Dowd

TRUST YOUR GUT

When Katherine walked out of the Pro Shop, Tyler just stood there and stared for a moment before turning the vacuum cleaner back on and finishing what he had started. She had just thrown his head into a tailspin for the second time in a week.

"That's some woman," Jeremy said interrupting his thoughts. She'd obviously drawn his attention as well. "That the one I hear you left at the altar when you ran off to play for Vandy?"

Tyler ignored him for the moment, pretending not to hear. In just a few days Jeremy had already managed to get under his skin. He was only a couple of years older and knew he couldn't hold his own with Tyler on the golf course, so he decided he'd use the slight seniority of his position to try to bring him down a few notches.

Tyler was lost in thought about Katherine, though, and really wasn't processing much else at the moment.

"Well, if she ain't good enough for you, Golden Boy, I'll keep her warm this winter," Jeremy said, pushing Tyler jokingly as he walked by and headed back toward the door of the shop just as Mack was coming in from a lesson.

Tyler let it go. He hadn't been back in town a week and he decided he needed to pick his battles.

"What was that all about?" Mack asked. He had caught the tail-end of the exchange and saw the barely disguised look of contempt on Tyler's face.

"Oh, nothing," Tyler replied as he turned off the vacuum cleaner. He knew Mack wouldn't likely let Jeremy get away with too much, but at the same time Tyler knew that with their relationship Mack was likely going to be looked at as playing favorites with him around here to begin with and he didn't want to perpetuate the 'Golden Boy' line of talk any more than it already was for both their sakes. He would earn his way around here. Mack had given him the job, but he would prove that he deserved whatever he got, for however long he was around, and wouldn't give anyone a reason to complain about him for anything.

"Didn't exactly look like nothing," Mack said, "so ya' let me know if it becomes something."

"… What? Oh… I will," Tyler answered after a moment, having returned his attention to the vacuum to feign disinterest. "It was really no big deal."

As he bit his tongue, though, Tyler realized suddenly how much it bothered him that another guy had made comments about Katherine like that. He felt protective, was pissed off at how it objectified her, and suddenly realized he still thought of her as his girlfriend despite the fact that it'd been four years since they'd been together. What had he really expected? That she would just hang around waiting for him to come back and collect her once he got his ducks in a row some day? He understood now that part of the reason he hadn't called, or even wanted to hear about her from his mother in all that time, was the fear that he would hear she had moved on and found someone else. And this little exchange, if nothing else, had served to make him realize how much that was a thought he couldn't really handle.

***

A few hours later, after picking the last of the balls on the driving range, Tyler cornered Mack as he hit a few shots from the old practice bunker to wind down at the end of the day. Mack was hitting one after another, alternating between the three flags on the practice green and tossing them up about as softly as if he was actually lobbing them each up there underhanded. Tyler just stood there, mesmerized at first by the mindless ease with which Mack executed the shot. Bunker shots, Tyler silently lamented, were likely the biggest hole in his game, and so after Mack had holed his third ball in a couple of dozen, Tyler finally decided he had to ask him a question.

"What are you thinking about on that shot, Mack?" Tyler interrupted him suddenly.

Mack hit one more that just lipped out of the closest hole, paused a few seconds, and then looked up at his protégé in what Tyler could only interpret as a look of confusion.

"…What am I thinking about?" he finally replied. "I don't know, Tyler… I'd hate to think how I'd be hittin' 'em if I actually started thinking."

Tyler gave Mack a slightly exasperated look and put his hands on his hips as he shook his head. "You know what I mean. Your technique. I guess I should have said what exactly are you doing there from a mechanics standpoint? How do you get it to just land so softly and roll out without checking?"

Mack seemed to be genuinely considering Tyler's more elaborately articulated question, and after a moment began, more slowly this time, as if he was simplifying his response for the benefit of a slightly thick-headed young student who wasn't getting his point.

"You can't think about technique, Tyler… at least not while you're playing," Mack replied. "There's no quicker path back to your father's garage than to start thinking while you're swinging, especially thinking about technique. That's my job."

"Mack," Tyler insisted, "How am I supposed to learn to hit that shot without understanding the technique? I've got to do something different than what I'm doing now. I'm putting too much spin on my shots and I can't always tell when it's going to check and when it's going to release a little. How do I fix that?"

"Well, not by thinking, certainly," Mack fired right back as if it was the most ridiculous line of inquiry he'd ever heard. "A good bunker shot can be heard, Tyler, and felt, but ya' can't do either of those if you're focused on your technique. Ya' feel it inside of you before you even think about actually hitting it. Watch, and listen."

With that Mack swung down at the sand and made a thump sound as his club went through the soft upper layer of sand and bounced on the firmer sand below.

"Ya' hear that?" Mack asked. "That's what a good bunker shot sounds like. If ya' can hear it, then ya' can feel it. If ya' can feel it, then ya' can make it, but ya' can't make that sound until ya' hear it first. Your body takes care o' the rest. Ya' don't have to actually tell it what to do."

Tyler still looked puzzled, but, knowing Mack as he did, this was the kind of explanation he knew he should have expected. Coach Pohl would have gone into an eight-part dissertation on grip, stance, club path, release points, weight transfer, and so forth, and Tyler suddenly realized how much he'd come to adopt his college coach's way of thinking in the past four years. Mack though? He just said you've got to hear it.

"Get in here," Mack said suddenly, gesturing to the bunker and offering the wedge to Tyler. "Now close your eyes."

"What?!" Tyler almost protested.

"Just do it will ya'," Mack insisted.

"Okay, okay," Tyler replied, humoring his coach.

"Can ya' hear it?" Mack asked.

"Hear what?" Tyler answered. "All I hear is you."

"Hear that sound, that thump." It was Mack's turn to be exasperated now. "It was only moments ago when I made it for ya'. Can't ya' still hear it?"

"Oh, remember it you mean," Tyler said. "Okay, I know what you mean now. I remember it."

"No, ya' obviously *don't* know what I mean," Mack replied. "I wanted to know if ya' can hear it, in your mind, hear the actual sound. Not remember that I'd made it. There's a big difference."

Tyler suddenly did feel kind of dumb. He wasn't picking up what Mack was getting at, at least not exactly how he wanted him to get it, and so he sat there with his eyes closed and gripped the club like he was going to hit a shot, waggled it a bit as if he was getting ready, and then opened his eyes again.

"Okay," he said suddenly. "I think I can hear it now."

"Don't open your eyes," Mack almost hissed. "Now make it, make that sound. Make that thump."

Tyler swung down sharply and buried the head of the wedge into the sand where it almost stopped before exiting.

"That's not a thump," Mack said shaking his head. "That's a thud. You can't even get the ball out with that pitiful effort. Give me that!"

He took the wedge back from Tyler and said, "Now watch and listen."

Mack made a handful of swings at the sand, each one resulting in a soft thump as the club bottomed out and then deposited a handful of sand out of the bunker. Tyler watched each time as the head of the club came up sharply, went down again, hit the sand, and came back up abruptly in a slightly abbreviated elliptical arc. Each time Tyler listened to the sound, embedding it as he studied how the club entered and exited the sand. Mack stopped suddenly and handed the club back to Tyler.

"Now *you* make that sound," he said, "and as ya' do remember how it feels in your hands, your forearms, your chest, and most importantly in your head."

"What?" Tyler asked, looking back up at Mack, confused at his last comment.

"Just do it," Mack said. "Hear it, feel it, then do it, but don't do it before ya' can hear it and feel it. Now close your eyes."

Tyler did as he was told, closing his eyes and then settling his feet in as he tried to picture in his mind what Mack had been doing. At first he just stood there waggling the club until he could see the image in his mind of Mack hitting the sand repeatedly, and then he could hear the soft thump as the club hit the sand. He started to swing, but was interrupted by Mack's voice.

"Can a' feel it?" Mack said. "Don't go until ya' can feel it."

"Well, at first I could see the image in my mind of you hitting that shot over and over again," Tyler said, opening his eyes and looking at Mack, "and then I could hear it. It sort of followed right in behind it."

"Ah, the image is a good starting point, but ya' can't just see it and hear it, but ya' need to feel it," Mack replied, pointing to his head. "Feel it in here, and then ya' can feel it here," he continued, putting his hands together like he was gripping a club. "Now close your eyes again."

"Okay," Tyler said, not sure he was getting it, but finally bought in. He settled in again and began waggling the club until he could see Mack swinging and hear the subtle thump of the sand. He let it just loop in his mind, over and over again, until suddenly he could feel it like he was the one doing it, and then he swung.

Thump came the sound as the flange of his wedge hit the sand. It was *his* swing, but it was different, maybe not to the naked eye, but in the speed, the level of tension, and the release. He opened his eyes again, almost tentatively, and looked at Mack with a combination of curiosity and amazement.

"I felt it that time," Tyler said in voice that seemed to resonate within him from somewhere in the past. It almost sounded like Jackie's in its exuberance.

"Yes…good," Mack replied patiently. "Now close your eyes and do it again, but make sure you can feel it before you pull the trigger."

Tyler settled in again, waited until, like the last time, he could see it, hear it, and then finally feel it… *Thump*… Something was slightly different this time, though, and Tyler opened his eyes to notice Mack kneeling down next to him. He had quietly deposited a ball into the place where Tyler had swung. Tyler looked up in the direction of the green and the target flag he had been aiming towards just in time to see a ball slow to a gentle stop about four inches from the flag.

"… How'd you do that?" Tyler said, almost in wonder now.

"I didn't," Mack replied. "You did. Ya' just had to stop thinking. See it, hear it, and feel it. Once you feel it, you can believe it. Anything more is more than we need. Any questions?"

As Mack turned to walk up out of the bunker, Tyler just stood there shaking his head a moment, looking at the spot in the sand, and then back up at the green as if to confirm the ball he'd seen roll to a stop was still there. "I guess I've still got a lot to learn."

"Well… yes and no," Mack said cryptically as he turned back to look at him. "Ya' pretty much know how to hit all the shots, Tyler. You've hit every one of them at one time or another. You've just got to learn how to empty your head of all those instructions so you can focus on finding the shot ya' need when ya' need it. It's in there somewhere."

"It's hard to explain," Tyler said, "but a lot of times I walk up and think I somehow just instinctively know what shot to hit without even thinking about it. I just kind of see it and feel it. It's when I start to analyze things a bit more closely, factoring in all the things I know are important to consider like the wind, keeping away from the short side, where I want to putt from, and the best trajectory or shot shape for the situation, that I often start to second guess that feeling."

"Ever heard the saying paralysis from analysis?" Mack asked. "It pretty much describes those moments."

"Yeah, I get it," Tyler replied, "but all that information is important. You have to consider everything and not just make a rush decision."

"Sure, information is important, but ya' can't get lost in it," Mack countered. "Whether it's golf, or just about anything else in life, Tyler, ya' need to learn to trust your gut. You've hit hundreds of thousands of shots in your life, Tyler. All those shots leave a mark. They leave an indelible little mark that gets filed away in your brain subconsciously, getting stacked one on top of the other. And after years of playing the game those stacks and stacks of shots create an instinctive reaction to each situation. It's like gravity. It pulls ya' in a certain direction so much that most of the time ya' almost know what club ya' should hit before ya' even know the yardage. Trust that, Tyler. Go with it, and know that first instinct comes from experience. There's more wisdom in those gut reactions than just about anything else."

"…Thank you," Tyler said after considering it a moment. "I think that'll really help."

"You're welcome," Mack replied. "Now rake that bunker for me and clean the balls off the green. I want to get things closed up before dark."

Mike Dowd

SUNDAY MORNING RITUAL

On the way home that night, Tyler decided he would talk to his father about the donation for Katherine at breakfast the next morning. Their Sunday morning ritual had always been to go to church early, and then to Vern's Diner for breakfast afterwards. He hadn't been back to Vern's since the day he and Katherine had split, avoiding the place and the memory of what had happened there every time he had come back to town for a visit. He knew his father would likely be in a better mood after church, and while he didn't really think he'd have that much of a problem procuring a little something for Katherine, his mother would see to that, just having a conversation with and being around his father for any reason since he'd been home and chosen to start work at the club had been a bit tense. Mack had given him the morning off, saying he wouldn't need him until that afternoon to pick the driving range and help put away carts, so he had some free time anyway.

Vern's was pretty much the only diner in the old part of town. It was fixture for locals, primarily a breakfast and lunch spot, but it doubled as an after school hang-out for local high school kids, a place where they could get a burger, fries, and a shake in an environment where they wouldn't be chased out just as soon as they were done eating. Old Vern had been around for as long as anyone could remember and he claimed the kids kept him young. He would let them hang around until about dinner-time before closing during the week, and stayed open until 9:00 or 10:00 on Fridays and Saturdays, with young people often occupying the booths right up until closing.

At the last minute, Tyler had decided he would even go to mass with his folks. He hadn't done that in years, other than Christmas and Easter, and he knew it might even further soften his father's mood. Despite still feeling that his coming back to Poplar Bluff was more pit-stop than homecoming, there was something comforting about getting back in touch with some of the rituals of his childhood, and church had been one of them. His father was a devout Catholic and his mother had followed him down the street to Sacred Heart Catholic Church from the Faith Episcopal Church she had grown up in. It was only about four blocks from Vern's and they typically parked at the garage and walked to breakfast after mass when he was younger. Occasionally, when he was much younger, he and Jack would hang around the garage afterwards with his old man teaching everything Tyler ever wanted to know about cars while his mother would go shopping or back home to start readying for the week and making dinner. Except during football season when they would all go back and spend the afternoon in front of the television while Tyler's mother made them snacks, sandwiches, and whatever else they wanted the rest of the day. It was football season, so they likely wouldn't hang around at Vern's too long and Tyler would excuse himself after breakfast to go to the club and get a little practice in before work.

They had met at church, Tyler driving himself down to Vern's and walking the four blocks to church on his own so he'd have his car and the ability to make a get-away as soon as he had finished breakfast. There had been relatively little conversation that morning between he and his father until mass had let out and they had begun the familiar walk down Vine Street to Vern's.

"What've you got going on this afternoon, son?" Tyler's father eventually asked after a bit of an awkward silence that had lasted nearly a block.

"Well, Mack wanted me to come in a little after lunch time to help out with the range and carts," Tyler replied.

"No time to catch the game?" he asked in a way that that sounded like part question and part accusation.

"I kind of promised Jackie I'd practice with him for a while before work and help him out a bit with his short game," Tyler replied. He was glad he had seen Jackie the day before and his cousin had asked him if he had time to help him because he knew his father wouldn't' complain about him begging off early for that. In the past, it hadn't been uncommon for Jackie, his father, and his mother Candace, Jack's younger sister, to join them after church for breakfast, but Candace had become increasingly involved with the church's foundation and it seemed she was forever attending meetings or working a fundraiser of some sort after mass the past few years which usually meant Jackie and his father were commandeered by Candace to help out in some way.

"How's he doing?" Tyler's mother chimed in, obviously wanting to steer the conversation in a somewhat neutral direction.

"He's really doing well," Tyler replied. "Amazing really, for only just picking it up this summer. I don't think I was that good that quickly, and boy he's really sprouted up. He's obviously taking after his father in that respect."

Jackie's father, James, had been a basketball player, a center, and was as big as a house. He'd grown up in Dexter, about thirty minutes away, and moved to Poplar Bluff to attend the Community College and played there for a couple of years. That's where he met Candace, and being a fellow athlete, Jack had immediately given his stamp of approval. Jack and James could talk and watch sports for hours, which they often did, while Candace and Mary Jane made an excuse to slip off to the kitchen and talk while making drinks or snacks for the boys, leaving Tyler and Jackie to entertain themselves.

That's how they had bonded. Tyler and Jackie had spent many a Sunday going to church, then breakfast, then all afternoon in the yard playing catch or shooting a basketball when Jackie was just a little kid.

"The kid's a natural athlete," Jack said, allowing the conversation to go in that direction for the moment. "He'd be good at anything he wanted to play. I guess like a lot of kids, though, he seems to prefer to take after someone other than his old man."

Tyler let that last comment go. He knew it was directed at him in more ways than one, and that it went way beyond sports. His father had long ago come to terms with the fact that Tyler didn't have the size to follow in his footsteps on the gridiron. What he hadn't exactly accepted yet was the fact that Tyler didn't seem to want to follow in his footsteps in just about anything else either.

They had reached their destination and Jack opened the door for Mary Jane, allowing her to enter in front of him, and then Tyler. Jack preferred a table, the booths being a bit snug for him, and they had a regular one near the back that Vern always held for them as long as Jack called ahead to let them know they were coming.

"Mornin' Fosters," came a familiar voice from the kitchen door as they were seated. "And, well, Tyler, haven't seen you in quite a spell. How's life in the big city treatin' ya'?"

"Just fine, Vern." Tyler got up and shook Vern's hand. "At least it did. I've moved back home for a bit. How've you been?"

"Oh, same as ever," Vern said as he turned to set the next table. "Mary Jane, how've ya' been, darlin'? Keepin' Jack well fed when I'm not?" he said with a chuckle, stopping what he was doing just long enough to give Tyler's mother a big warm smile while nodding to Jack.

"Yes, yes, Vern," Tyler's mother said, "and glad to have Tyler home for now."

"Well it's good to see ya', Tyler, glad yer' back," Vern called over his shoulder as he moved to clear another table."

Some things never changed, and Vern's, and Vern in particular, was thankfully one of them. He would make his way around the dining room, carrying on running conversations with just about everyone while he took orders, cleared a table here and there, and generally just made people feel welcome. He seemed to live for it and knew everyone, and just about everything about his regular customers at the same time as he was always asking questions, checking in on people, and making sure they didn't need anything. If you wanted to know anything that was going on in Poplar Bluff, chances are you could find it out from Vern, and if he didn't know, he pretty much knew who did.

They looked over the menus in silence for a moment, but all knew what they wanted for the most part, setting them aside pretty quickly and waiting for the young gal who had seated them to bring back some waters and coffee and take their orders. She did fairly shortly, and once she had, it was Tyler's mother who ultimately opened the conversation.

"So, Tyler," she said, "I know you finally talked to Katherine a few days ago after more than four years. You've been pretty tight-lipped about it, other than to say you wanted me to give away that ticket. What exactly happened, if you don't mind me asking?"

"No, I guess not," Tyler said while looking off out the window in the direction of the ACS office where the meeting had taken place. "There really wasn't much to tell, Mom. She just didn't seem too thrilled exactly to see me. Almost indifferent, really. After everything I guess I can't blame her. I tried to apologize, but she didn't even want to hear it."

"Little bit late for that don't you think, son?" Jack chimed in. "Don't think she's going to be quite as quick to forgive as Mack was. You weren't exactly a fine upstanding young man when it came to the way you handled that one."

Tyler had heard this from his father before. He liked Katherine almost as much as his mother had, but also didn't seem to ever want to miss an opportunity to let Tyler know when he screwed up. At the moment, though, Tyler didn't really protest.

"I know, Dad," Tyler finally said after realizing his mother wasn't exactly rushing to his defense. "I'd definitely do things differently if I could go back, but I can't. I've learned that at least. Actually, Katherine is something I wanted to ask you about. She came by the club yesterday when I was working."

Tyler's mother noticeably stirred in her chair at that and began stirring the coffee the girl had brought with a little cream as she waited for Tyler to expand on what he had said.

"She's helping run that big Gala now that her mother started years ago. She says they could raise some pretty good money potentially if you would be willing to sign some old memorabilia and donate it."

"That was a hundred years ago, son. Nobody cares about anything I did back then, let alone wants to actually pay money for it," Jack said with a bit of false modesty. Tyler knew his old man still loved hearing that at least someone thought people remembered what he'd done back in the day.

"Well, apparently Katherine thinks they do," Tyler said. "I know you donated a lot of stuff years and years ago and it's been a long time, but you have to have something left in that old steamer trunk down in the basement or some of those bins?"

"I don't know," Jack said. "There really isn't much left, and most of it's pretty important to me."

"Oh, come on, dear," Tyler's mother intervened. "It's for a good cause, and we're going to the event. And it's for Katherine. You can't just keep all that old stuff forever. You haven't even looked at most of it in years."

"Why didn't she just come ask me?" Jack finally asked after a lengthy pause as if he was really considering saying no. "If she really isn't too keen on seeing you anymore, why'd she drive all the way out to the club? She could have walked a block and asked me herself."

"I asked her the same thing," Tyler said. "I was pretty surprised to see her, but she said she had a meeting there with a donor or something."

"Is that all she wanted?" Tyler's mother asked with a curious tilt of her head.

"Well, pretty much, I think... She did ask me if I wanted to help out, after I told her I wasn't going."

"Hmm," Tyler's mother considered. "And you said?"

"I told her I'd be happy to," Tyler replied. "But I'm not so sure she isn't taking advantage of me and the fact that she thinks I feel guilty now about everything. She says they're short of bus boys. I'm sure they could use all sorts of help, but she'll probably stick me with the most menial job she can just to get back at me."

"That's not Katherine. She's not petty like that," Tyler's mother said, coming to her defense. "But is that what you feel, do you feel guilty about everything? You've never even wanted to talk about it."

"Well, I'm not sure the Katherine you knew and the one who came back from college are exactly the same person, Mom," Tyler said. "I don't know how much you talked when she came by, but she's definitely changed. I mean, she was always smart and I knew she'd be successful in whatever she did, but she's... well."

"Grown," Tyler's mother finished for him. "I think being on her own has been a good thing for her, Tyler. She's a very confident young woman now, and from what I hear she's pretty much taken that office over and has been running it since she got back. She may not have wanted it, and still may not know it, but I think you two going your separate ways has been good for her. She seems to have found herself after she left home and I don't know if that would have happened if you'd been around. You haven't answered my question, though... Do you just feel guilty, or do you have other reasons you regret the choice you made?"

Tyler looked up from his coffee and his gaze fell on the old booth that had been his and Katherine's. He had resisted talking about it and his feelings whenever his mother had brought it up in the past, and for some reason he was particularly uncomfortable doing it with his father around. After a handful of seconds passed he finally answered.

"I wouldn't say guilty, exactly. I regret how I did it, and especially how it hurt Katherine at the time. I know I never told you guys, or Katherine either, but I honestly really struggled with that decision and she was a big part of the reason why. I know she didn't believe it, but I didn't intentionally wait to decide until after it was too late for her to try and apply too, but in the end that's what happened. I can't exactly explain it, and it's not consciously why I made that decision, but looking back now I think I somehow instinctively knew that I needed to be on my own, too."

"Alright, I tell you what," Jack suddenly interrupted as the young gal brought their food and set it down in front of them. "I'll go down in the basement once we get home and take a look around. I'm not promising anything, but I might be able to come up with a handful of things that still have some value."

"Thanks, Dad," Tyler said as he cut his steak and eggs and poured a generous helping of tabasco sauce on both. "Katherine will really appreciate it, I'm sure. And if it's good enough maybe she won't have me washing dishes all night after the Gala."

"Don't count on it, son," Jack said. "Hell hath no fury like a woman scorned and I'm sure she's not done making you pay. Anyway, you can repay me with a little help this week if you can fit it in to your busy schedule. We aren't exactly the Red Roof Inn and room and board does come with a price. I let Denny take the week off to go fishing with his cousin and I just got three new jobs Friday."

Tyler's expression noticeably soured as his father brought up the garage. "What do you need? Mack's got me working almost every day this week too, and I haven't gotten hardly any practice time in since I've been back."

"Too busy to help your old man, huh," Jack said with a disgusted note as he shoveled a forkful of food into his mouth."

"I didn't say that," Tyler replied defensively. "I'll help you. The club is closed Mondays, so I've got tomorrow off and I could come in then, and maybe another morning or two because I'm working mostly afternoons at the moment."

"Oh, don't go out of your way," Jack continued. "What are you planning on doing over there anyway, Tyler? The man can't pay you half what I pay you and you're not even working full-time. How are you going to support yourself? You can't live at home forever and you've got two full-time assistants in front of you over there that don't look like they're going anywhere soon."

"Part-time is all I can really handle right now, Dad," Tyler said. "I've got to try to get in 4 to 5 hours a day of practice and once spring rolls around there'll be at least one or two tournaments a month I'll be eligible for."

"Tournaments cost money, son, a lot of money. And so does Q-School. Even if you work enough for Mack in the next 11 months to save up the money for another shot, I don't see where you're going to have enough to travel around playing in mini tour events to get prepared and they certainly don't pay anything to speak of. Have you thought about that, or were you thinking of asking me for money again?"

Tyler shifted uneasily in his seat and stopped eating. "I might be able to get some sponsors. Maybe Poppa Jack could organize a syndicate and they'd be paid back when I make it. A lot of guys do that. I was so close, Dad. I know I learned from it and I'm still learning. A lot of guys take four, five, even six times before they pass."

"A syndicate?" Jack almost laughed. "You mean instead of asking me for money now you're going to ask your grandfather to go begging his cronies for cash to keep you out there chasing this dream? The way I see it you had your shot, son. It's time to grow up now. Your girlfriend seems to have figured that part out. What's holding you back?"

Tyler was getting upset now. This wasn't exactly fair. His father didn't really know golf and he didn't understand. He was making it sound like Tyler was going to go asking for charity. That wasn't the case. All sorts of guys had syndicates backing them for their first few years when they were trying to get out on Tour.

"Look, Dad, it's done all the time. It's like an investment and investors get a return on that investment. I'm not looking for charity. This is my thing. I know you had your chance taken away from you, and I'm really sorry about that, but I've still got a shot. I've got to see it through. If I give up now, I'll just end up…"

"Being like your old man," Jack finished for him.

"That's not what I was going to say," Tyler protested. "I'll end up feeling like I just gave up when things got tough. I *can* make it and I'll always regret not trying again if I don't."

"Sounds like your definition of making it still doesn't involve anything around here. Well, you better be careful, son, or before you know it this life might be too good for you. At least Katherine's got a degree to show for the past four years. Ever think that might be why she didn't give you the time of day? Maybe she doesn't want someone who's working part time for minimum wage holding her back."

"Look, I said I'd help you, and I can always finish my degree later if things don't work out," Tyler almost shouted now. "What do you want from me?"

"Settle down boys," Tyler's mother said firmly but quietly as she grabbed both of their wrists. "Remember where we are."

"Nothin'," Jack said as he got up, wiping his mouth and dropping his napkin on his plate while not even looking at Tyler. "Nothin' at all. I've lost my appetite, Mary Jane, and I've just realized how much work I have to do. I'm going to the garage."

As Jack walked out, Tyler resisted the urge to get in the final word. It seldom worked with his father anyway and he didn't want to embarrass his mother any more than they already had. His father had hit below the belt when it came to Katherine, almost goading him into a reaction, but he wasn't going to take the bait.

"It's okay," Tyler's mother said after a long moment. "He'll settle down after he's been under the hood of a car for a while."

"Look, I know he didn't get to realize his dream, but why does he have to take that out on me?" Tyler replied. "It's like he doesn't want to see me get any farther than he did. Is he that afraid someone in this town might end up taking his place as the big man on campus around here?"

"That's not it and you know it," Tyler's mother said. "I understand your father casts a pretty big shadow around this town and it's only natural to want to get out from under it, but your father has also spent far more than you probably realize so that you could have the opportunities you've had. It's just, he's had plans for his life, too. And one of them was to provide for his family. He's built up a pretty nice little business from nothing, a successful one, and you know he doesn't want to see all that hard work go away some day and he can't do it forever. He's starting to feel his age. Believe it or not, he'd like to relax someday, maybe even take up golf, or start fishing again, something. He can't do that the way things are right now, though, and he doesn't trust anyone enough to hand them the reins even part-time. Except you."

"I know," Tyler said. "I get it. I truly wish it was my thing, but it's just not, Mom. I've got to at least know I gave it my best shot or I'll always wonder what might have been and who I could have been. I'm not trying to knock being a mechanic, or anything else that someone around here might be, but I just know I can do more."

"I understand, honey," his mother said. "I really do, and believe it or not your father deep down understands, too. You can't get as close to your dream as he did and not understand the frustration of not realizing it. Wondering what might have been, he gets that. But what he also knows now is that maybe that wasn't what was ultimately most important."

"Do you think he's right?" Tyler said, suddenly looking distractedly off in the direction of the booth he and Katherine used to share.

"Right about what, honey?"

117

"About Katherine?" Tyler replied. "Do you think she thinks she's better than me now? I never really thought of it that way, but I'm picking up balls on the driving range. I was vacuuming the Pro Shop when she came in the other day. Do you think she looks at me now as someone who'll just hold her back?"

"Tyler, now I'm your mother, and I know I'm biased, but I think I know Katherine about as well as anyone and while I can't speak for her, I don't think she's that kind of person. She had more than a few opportunities in Columbia after she graduated from what I understand and for some reason she chose to come back here. Does that sound like a girl who's worried about being held back? If you think you still have feelings for her, though, I wouldn't wait around forever to tell her. She's waited around for more than four years already, but sooner or later she's going to get on with life and if you're not ready to she'll ultimately find someone who is."

"I understand," Tyler replied. "I really need to talk to her. I don't think she ever really understood why I had to do what I did, but maybe now that she's had opportunities of her own she'll see why I've got to see it through. I don't want to hold her back, and I don't want her ever thinking she'd settled for less than what she could have had either."

Tyler's mother considered what he said for a moment as she drank the last of her coffee.

"Sounds like you two do need to talk, but I'd consider this before you do, Tyler. I know you need to see this through, at least once more or you'll always wonder what might have been. I don't know if Katherine will understand that or not, or even if she would take you back on any terms. I do know, though, that there's a difference between chasing your dreams and running away. Just make sure you know which one you're actually doing before you talk to her because she's a smart girl, and no matter what you tell her, she'll likely see it for what it really is."

Mike Dowd

A PEACE OFFERING

Tyler stayed late after work that night, putting under the floodlights on the practice green for almost three hours, and when he finally got home his folks were in bed. But he found a signed Mizzou game-worn jersey of his father's, a signed NCAA official college game-ball from a win over Vanderbilt when his father had played with the score and the date written on it, and a signed Mizzou pennant from the last year his father had played for them lying on his bed. It was a surprise, to say the least, and probably as close to an apology as he was going to get from his father. But the fact that the ball was from a win over Tyler's Alma Mater wasn't lost on him either. His mother, he was sure, must have had at least something to do with it. She was forever playing the mediator between them when

121

he had been growing up and he knew she had a way of making his father see things in just a bit of a different light once the emotions of the moment had passed.

He decided to get up early the next morning and go help his father in the garage. If he was going to be living at home for now, he needed to make peace, and the best way he could do that was to try and help his father out when he could. At the same time he figured it would give him an excuse to walk the things his father had given him over to Katherine. He didn't say anything to either of his folks about his intentions and decided just to show up ahead of his father and have the garage opened and ready with all of his things set up and ready for the day. When Jack rolled in around 7:45, he reached for his phone to call the police when he saw the front garage door rolled up and then hung up once he saw Tyler's car parked in the yard out back.

"What are you doing here?" he asked Tyler through the open car window as he paused before parking his own car out back.

"Earning my room and board," Tyler quipped with just enough of a smirk that he knew wouldn't leave his father feeling the comment was meant to be disrespectful. "Thanks for the stuff, by the way."

Tyler had donned an extra pair of coveralls and they got started working on a carburetor rebuild for a '74 Challenger Rallye that someone had restored to near mint condition. As well as a more extensive project that left him a little more appreciative of what his father was facing at the moment. Someone had bought a junked '57 Chevy, one that was more rust than actual sheet metal, and told Jack that he wanted to make a funny car out of it and race it. It was so bad it was almost actually funny, but apparently the client didn't think so and expected Jack to work his magic. Plus, money was apparently no object. Tyler spent most of the morning working on the carburetor, and he was surprised at how much came back to him from his years of following Jack around and soaking up everything there was to know about cars. His dad stayed busy, not only because he did great work, but because there were increasingly fewer and fewer shops where guys had the expertise to do things of the past like carburetor rebuilds.

When they broke for lunch just before noon, Tyler told his dad he'd finished the project but he was going to skip lunch and go drop off the stuff his father had agreed to donate at the ACS office with Katherine. Tyler got out of the coveralls and went into wash up before heading out back to grab the stuff out of his car his father was donating. At the last second, he put the stuff back and decided to walk over empty-handed. He really wanted to see Katherine, and if Karen was the only one there she would gladly accept the donation and Tyler would lose his excuse to see her. If she was there, he'd come back and get it he reasoned. And if she wasn't he'd have a good excuse to come back again when she was.

As he walked around the corner, the irony of the situation he found himself in began to set in. More than four years earlier he had left this town, this life, and the girl that had loved him to strike his own path because he was convinced it was what he needed to do to succeed, and for people to think him a success. But just who was he trying to impress? For the most part he didn't care what people in Poplar Bluff thought of him, unless you counted Mack, his family, and that very same girl he'd left behind. And now here he was. No better than when he'd left, and the girl he left behind had become a respected young woman. And this left him feeling humbled, and increasingly focused as if he now needed that success just to be worthy of her again.

Tyler opened the door to the ACS office, and unlike last time, it was abuzz with activity. He scanned the room and saw Karen at the table showing another woman pictures they were assembling into a photo collage of local survivors and the work the Society was doing. A delivery driver was at the front desk where a younger gal who couldn't have been much more than 18 or 19 was signing for packages. She looked up as Tyler entered and turned to him with a smile.

"Can I help you?"

"Is Katherine in?" Tyler asked.

At the sound of his voice, Karen turned around, along with the other woman, and she started to speak when there came a sudden voice from the back hall.

"I've got this Annie," said Katherine and then, as she walked up close, "Hello, Tyler. I didn't expect to see you again so soon. Have you got anything for me?"

She wasn't dressed quite as stunningly as she had been at the Country Club the other day, but then again, with heels, a business length skirt, a close-fitting sweater, and her hair pulled neatly back up away from her face, she wasn't dressed anywhere near as casual as she had been the first time he had walked in on her unexpected. Tyler suddenly had the thought that she wasn't likely to let him catch her unprepared again, physically or otherwise.

"Y-yes," Tyler stammered at first. "Well, I've got something over at the garage for you. I didn't know if you would be here, but I can go grab it if you like. It's a jersey, a football, and a pennant. Pretty cool stuff really. You might be able to make a shadow-box with the jersey and pennant and sell the football as a separate item. Or you could package all three."

"That's great!" Karen butted in suddenly as she walked up, putting her hands on her hips and sizing him up. "And hello, Tyler. It's good to see you back in town."

Tyler suddenly wished it was just the two of them. He didn't want the audience and didn't feel comfortable talking to Katherine in front of everyone at this point for some reason.

"Thank you, Karen. Good to see you, too," Tyler said, but then turning back to Katherine he added, "I can just run back over and grab the stuff if you want it now?"

"I'll go with you," Katherine said, surprising him and maybe feeling a little the same way, he sensed. "I need to get out of here for a little bit anyways and stretch my legs. I've been sitting on the phone with potential donors and attendees all morning."

Without a glance back, she headed out the front door calling back to no one in particular, "I'll be back in about an hour, I've got an errand to run after this." She certainly did act as if she ran the place, Tyler thought as he stood there a moment just watching her walk out, but then he hurried to catch up as she looked back holding the door and waiting for him.

They walked side by side, not talking for a moment, rounding the corner to where the shop's side door entrance was. The front roll-up was closed, which meant Jack had headed to lunch and the two of them would be alone. Realizing this, Tyler's stomach suddenly turned a somersault, and for a moment he almost wished they were back at the office. As he fished the key from his pocket, Katherine walked up close and interrupted his thoughts with an unexpected question.

"You smell like grease. Have you actually been working for your father?"

He opened the door, and turned sideways to allow her to enter in front of him.

"Well, Dad needs some extra help this week," Tyler said. "Denny's on vacation and he's suddenly got a few more jobs than he can keep up with."

"It seems miracles never cease," she said as she entered the narrow side door to the old brick building. She brushed so close to him he could smell the subtle fragrance of her hair as she stepped into the garage, saying, "I thought you'd sworn off auto repair years ago. Didn't like getting those precious golfing hands dirty."

"That wasn't it," Tyler said, suddenly a bit defensive. "It just wasn't my thing. You know I did plenty of it, but it wasn't exactly helping me get where I wanted to go at the time. Things change, though."

"I always kind of liked the smell of grease," she said, running her finger along the engine block of the Challenger, which still had the hood up. "Did I ever tell you that?" she asked playfully as she brought it in front of her lips, and turned back to Tyler with a sidelong glance that, as confused as he now was, he found he couldn't interpret as anything other than seductive.

"N-n-no," Tyler said, completely shaken. Who was this woman?

She laughed suddenly as if she knew exactly what was going through his mind, and turned away to walk towards the back roll-up door that lead to where she knew the yard was. She was toying with him.

"Let's get that stuff, Tyler," she called back over her shoulder indifferently, getting business-like again. "I've got things to do and I haven't got all day."

"They're in my car, out back," he said. "Let me just roll up the door."

Tyler walked up to the chain and pulley where Katherine stood expectantly with her hands on her hips now, wearing the irritated expression of someone who's had to wait in too long a line at the DMV. Tyler rolled up the door and went out back to fetch the things from his car. Katherine walked up right behind him as he grabbed the stuff out of the back seat, and as he stood up and turned around she was right in his face.

"Thank you," she almost breathed on him, holding his gaze in a way that felt like an invitation.

Tyler instinctively reached for her and the football he held bumped the edge of the door, fell to the ground, and began rolling in the direction of a waiting puddle of muddy water.

"Son of a -," Tyler exclaimed, scrambling to grab it before part of his father's donation was ruined.

Katherine laughed again, obviously enjoying the effect she was having on him.

"Here," Tyler said as he scooped up the ball and turned to hand it to her like a hot potato along with the other things his father had donated. "You're responsible for 'em now. That way he can't kill me if something else happens.

"What else do you think could possibly happen, Tyler?" she said with a mischievous grin, but then before he could even answer, she got all business-like, took the things, and then turned to walk out, saying, "Thank your father for me, Tyler… You still willing to give up your busy Saturday night to help a good cause?"

"Absolutely," Tyler said as he closed his car door. "Like I said, just tell me where and when and I'll be there."

"Well I told you the 22nd already," she replied, "and service staff needs to be there by 3:30 for a crash-course in training for the evening. It's at the new Heartland Community Center."

"What should I wear?" Tyler asked as they walked back into the garage.

"Black slacks, black shoes, white dress shirt, and a black tie," she said and then turning back to him, "I can provide the tie if you don't have one. Any of that a problem?"

"No," Tyler said. "Not a problem."

"Now, Tyler," she said with the almost disapproving tone of a mother, "no taking the spikes out of your golf shoes. That doesn't count. Get yourself a decent pair of shoes if you don't have one."

"Really, Katherine," he said, "I'm not a child. I haven't done that in years."

She looked him up and down appraisingly as if she was deciding whether or not he was really up to doing this.

"Alright, but I'm counting on you, Tyler," she almost sighed. "This event's important to me and I want it to come off well. It'll be my first and I want it to be the best one they've ever had."

"I understand," Tyler said. "I'm sure it'll be great, and I'll do everything I can to help make sure that happens.

"I appreciate that," Katherine said, a bit more softly as she turned to walk out of the garage and apparently to head off and run whatever errand she had.

"Katherine," Tyler called after her. "I'd still really like to talk. Can we do that?"

She turned to face him again and paused as if considering whether or not that was even a possibility. "Sure," she said finally. "I suppose, but I'm busy at the moment and truthfully I'm going to be busy non-stop between now and the Gala. Let me get through that night and then if you've still got something you need to get off your chest, I might be ready to listen."

Katherine turned and walked out the door then, not looking back but calling over her shoulder once again in that same almost irritating motherly tone of voice, "Don't forget to thank your father for me, Tyler."

LIKE OLD TIMES?

The next eleven days passed in a way that felt like two for Katherine. She really was busy, non-stop, and surprisingly didn't spend as much time thinking about her encounter with Tyler as she expected. At the same time, her woman's instinct told her Tyler wasn't having nearly so easy a time keeping her off of his mind. She had laid it on pretty thick at the garage. She'd weakened momentarily when they met in the Pro Shop and come off a bit too vulnerable, so she had decided that she'd make sure she still had the upper hand at their next encounter. She also wanted to give him a little taste of what he'd given up so many years ago when he left her behind and she knew she'd had an effect on him. She was the same girl, she reasoned, but she wasn't, and she didn't mind the thought of him wondering; wondering what she might do, or say, and after all she'd been through on his behalf she didn't exactly feel bad about keeping him guessing. Especially now that she felt certain he wanted her back.

The day of the Gala dawned and Katherine found she was a bit nervous. She went through her checklists, her itinerary, the volunteer lists and assignments, the instruction for the valets, the catering company, the clean-up crew, and all the details about the guest list, the donors, the silent auction, live auction, raffle items, and everything else she could think of one last time. She had originally agreed to help Karen with the Gala, but once she had come aboard, everyone involved quickly realized it was her show. Without even being asked, she had taken over just about all the details of the event and when her cool efficiency became apparent to just about everyone involved, they sort of just got out of the way and let her do it. Even Karen Gibson, the event's chair, recognized to everyone involved that she was really in charge in name only, and she ran all the big decisions by Katherine before doing anything. Everything was ready to go, she finally declared at noon that day of the event organizers luncheon she had put together to run down last minute details. So why was she nervous?

Three o'clock rolled around and she began to understand why. The service staff had been asked to show up by three-thirty for training and when a certain orange classic Camaro rolled into the back lot thirty minutes early while she was unloading table centerpieces, the source of her nervousness became clear... Tyler. As he got out of the car in a full black suit and tie, she stopped short. She didn't remember ever seeing him in a suit and tie in all the years they'd dated, even when they attended the funeral of one of his relatives once, and she'd almost forgotten how painfully handsome he could be when he made an effort. He was getting her back, she thought, or at least trying to for the Pro Shop the other day, and how she'd teased him at the garage. She wasn't going to let him know he'd gotten to her though.

"A bit over-dressed to bus tables," Katherine said off-handedly as he walked up. "And you're early."

"Just in case you needed some extra help," Tyler replied. "And I can always ditch the jacket if you can't find anything better for me to do than bus tables."

She looked at Tyler appraisingly and thought a moment. In truth, she had plenty of busboys, and then a last minute thought hit her. Her plan was to greet everyone at the door personally and thank them for their support. She then would show them on the diagram she had on an easel where their table was, what number it was, and let them head to the bar for a drink. She could give Tyler an alphabetical table assignment list and have him show each guest to their table personally and ditch the easel. It was the only first impression guests were getting after they walked in that she hadn't been happy with and this could add a bit more of a personal touch.

The overall room size wasn't that big and Tyler could easily show people to their tables and be back in time to take the next guests.

"Alright," Katherine said, "Grab two more of those centerpieces for me, and *don't* drop them, and then follow me."

They went inside and she directed Tyler where to deposit the centerpieces, how exactly to place them, and then asked him to retrieve all the remaining ones from outside and do the same thing at the rest of the tables. It would keep him out of her hair for a little while and let her think about what to do next. She was suddenly acutely aware of why seeing Tyler tonight made her nervous. They were really going to talk after the Gala. She knew he wanted to apologize, for real this time, and likely talk about the past, and maybe even the future. The problem was she really hadn't had time to think about how she felt exactly. She'd been busy, but at the same time she realized that had also been a convenient excuse not to confront her own feelings. As much as she hated to admit it, she still had feelings for him, but she wasn't even quite sure what those feelings were. A part of her had sworn she would never forgive him, but somehow her bitterness over what he had done had softened a bit over the years with perspective. Some days she looked back on it and reasoned they were both kids, neither really ready to continue down the road they had seemed headed. And as much as it had hurt her, she knew deep down too that he done her a favor. She was proud of the strong independent young woman she had become and if she'd been with Tyler all that time, she doubted she'd be the same.

She'd eventually dated in college, once she became convinced that it was really over, and at the urging of her friends there who kept telling her how she was wasting the best years of her life crying over someone who obviously wasn't worth it. And she'd had fun, even though she'd never met anyone she could really see getting serious about. So was that why she was back here? Had she never really quite moved on? Was there still some kind of closure she needed? Did she just need the chance to finally give him the piece of her mind he so deserved, or was it more than that? Part of her wanted to forgive him, at least once, if she thought he was sincere. Tyler wasn't just handsome, he was thoughtful, kind, and had an endearing, almost incidental way of making her smile. At least he used to. And everyone deserved a second chance, didn't they? And if he truly regretted his decision, shouldn't she at least give him the opportunity to prove that to her? So many questions, she suddenly thought. Why hadn't she really thought about all this before tonight? The only way to ultimately get answers to those questions, she finally determined, was to have that long-awaited talk.

An hour or so later, once Tyler had placed all the centerpieces, she went up to him with the list and began to explain what it was she wanted him to do.

"Take the woman's arm," she said, "and lead them to the pre-assigned table, pointing out the number so that they don't forget where they will sit once they've come back from the bar. There are thirty-six tables out there, and it's easy to get mixed up if you're not paying attention. Tables with sponsors, however, will have the company or individual name on the table, so make sure you point that out as well when you've got one of those."

"Alright, I can handle that," Tyler said. "What do you want me to do once everyone has been seated and dinner starts to be served?"

"Well," Katherine said, "most of the service staff will be back in the annex behind the kitchen during dinner and when they're not needed. You can hang out there and I'll come get you if I need you. I have to give a brief presentation during dessert and I'll be busy until the dancing starts. It'll be all hands on deck to clear the tables after dessert and you can help with that, too. I'll find you after that."

Katherine busied herself by ordering different volunteers to finish doing this and that for the next fifteen or twenty minutes, and then excused herself to get ready. When she emerged from the ladies' room thirty minutes later, she looked every bit the hostess of a high ticket fundraiser. Smart, professional, and elegant. Her mother would have been proud, she thought, and she was suddenly so sad she wasn't here to see this. Her father would be sitting at her table, by her side, beaming at the sight of his daughter moving among the guests and talking to everyone in the easy way her mother always had. She so wished he'd brought a guest. Maybe she could introduce him to someone tonight, she thought. There had to be at least a few eligible ladies in Poplar Bluff.

She corralled Tyler just before the guests were to arrive and they went over what she wanted one more time just to make sure he got it. She was suddenly glad he was here. She would be at his side while everyone that was just about anyone in town came in, and they would talk for sure. But she was the star of the show now, and he would be taking a back seat.

The next ninety minutes or so were a bit of blur as guests showed up in an almost non-stop procession, and despite the fact that Tyler was by her side for much of it, they had barely talked. She welcomed people, thanked them for coming, for their generosity, and handed them off to Tyler. When Mary Jane and Jack had shown up, they had gotten an obvious kick out of the irony of Tyler playing second fiddle to Katherine in such a public way, a fact that Jack obviously wasn't going to let him forget too soon by the sound of how he was ribbing him while he led his mother to the table. And Katherine couldn't help but smile at how well her little last minute idea had worked.

Katherine's own father had shown up at very nearly dinner time, and when he got there he hung in the back until all the other guests had been shown their seats so he could escort his daughter to the table. He looked good, she thought, and he even smiled politely and shook Tyler's hand before he took her arm, something that wasn't lost on either of them. While they had never been close, Katherine's father had liked Tyler, but they hadn't spoken in almost five years either. Katherine had always expected that he wasn't too heartbroken himself when they had split, as he had always felt they were moving just a bit too fast for his taste and that they were too young to be talking as serious as they were.

They ate dinner with Katherine's father asking her all about the details of the evening, amazed at what he had now come to realize was largely an evening that she had pulled together. When dessert was served, Kathrine excused herself, and the lights dimmed as a projector screen lowered from the center of the curtain behind the dais. When the video began to roll, an image of The American Cancer Society logo came up on the screen along with pictures of bald patients in the hospital who had obviously been through chemo and a sudden woman's voice-over.

"Cancer isn't somebody else's problem anymore. It's all of our problem. Whether it's your mother, father, sister, brother, or even, God-forbid, your son or daughter, someone in your family will be faced with this disease in their lifetime. Having a branch of The American Cancer Society in our own town now means we will be raising money that not only goes towards finding a cure, but that goes towards helping the families of cancer victims right here in Poplar Bluff. I know, all things considered, some may think this plea a bit self-serving, but the founding of this chapter will bring help and healing to so many families here in our town long after I'm around."

The screen faded and an image of a pretty woman of about forty came up on the screen, along with a name, Caroline Anderson, and a date, 1965-2004. A single spotlight lit the dais as Katherine walked up on the stage, adjusting the mic ever so slightly.

"Thank you all for coming. I'm Katherine Anderson, and the voice you just heard was my mother's." She paused for just a moment, seeing her father through the bright spotlight at the front table, tears unashamedly streaming down his face. And then she stood tall and continued in a clear and commanding voice, "For those of you who don't know it, Caroline Anderson founded the Poplar Bluff Chapter of The American Cancer Society in 2000, after her first bout with the disease. She was also the woman whose vison made this evening a reality. Many of you knew her as a woman whose tireless efforts made an impact on people in this room and all around our town. Whether it was organizing events like tonight, serving as President of the PTA, on the School Board, or the Butler County Community Resources Council, Caroline Anderson was known as a role model for community involvement. I knew her as Mom. And I knew her for far too short a time. Cancer took my mother from me at the age of twelve, just when a young girl most needs a mother around for oh so many reasons. But, I am not alone. Cancer takes people of every age, every year in this community, and they are all important. They are our parents, our grandparents, our siblings, and our children, and if they suffer from this disease, whether they're seven or seventy, they all suffer, and they all leave us too soon.

"I want to see an end to that, and while I may sound naive in making that statement, we can put an end to it. At least for someone, and that's something. And, it starts here tonight. We can't bring my mother back, but we can honor her and all those like her by remembering her spirit of giving and by doing what we can to help insure that as many of our community's members as possible are given the physical, emotional, and financial support they need when they're facing this same fight, while helping contribute to the fight to finally find a cure once and for all, for all cancers... Now we still have our live auction to come, and then please stay for dancing afterwards, but for those of you who don't win an auction tonight, on each of your tables there are a handful of envelopes. Inside each is a donor card, along with potential donation amounts and a place to put down your bidder number. You can just drop these at the table on your way out the door tonight and be guaranteed that more than 75% of your donation will stay right here in Poplar Bluff. And whether it's a family member, the kid that was on your son's little league team, in your daughter's Girls' Scout Troop, or the young person who waited on you at dinner tonight, you can guarantee that donation will mean more to them in ways you might not even be able to comprehend... Now, I'd like to leave you with this thought, Terry Tempest Williams once said, *an individual doesn't get cancer, a family does.* Well, when it comes right down to it, we're all family here, so let's make sure we're there for each other. Thank you all again for coming."

Katherine turned and walked off the stage to a rousing ovation, and when she finally got out of the bright spotlight and could see the room, she realized not only was everyone standing, but more than just her father had been crying, and she too finally let go. Mary Jane and Jack had been at the table closest to where she had stepped off the stage and, seeing what it had taken out of her, Mary Jane instinctively caught her in an embrace that was as close to what she could have wanted if her own mother had actually been there. And for the first time in a long time, she felt like she actually was.

"Thank you, Mary Jane," she said, pulling away just slightly to look into her face. "Thank you. I need to go be with my father."

"Of course you do, dear," she said. "That was an absolutely beautiful speech. Your mother is so proud."

Katherine only hesitated slightly at the comment, smiled back at Mary Jane, and walked over to the table where her father stood. He wrapped her up in a hug and held her so long that most everyone other than those at their table had actually begun to sit down as the auctioneer had taken the stage. When they finally separated, he looked her up and down as if he didn't quite know what to say.

"That was, well… you should have warned me," he finally said almost laughing. "You are certainly something, Katherine. I didn't come here expecting to cry my eyes out in front of everyone in town tonight."

"Sorry, Daddy," Katherine replied. "I know hearing Mom probably wasn't easy. I guess I should have said something. But why are you laughing?"

"Well, these tears aren't for your mother, honey. I hope you don't think this is wrong, but I've finally gotten to a place where I just don't think I have many tears left in that department. I was just so proud to see you up there, so strong, and it just hit me all at once that you're not my little girl anymore. Your mother would have been brought to tears too just because we would have been so proud of what a confident and capable young woman you've become. I'll just have to be proud enough for the both of us."

Katherine and her father finished out the auction period speaking about the evening and all she had done to make it so successful. Katherine begged him to stay around for the dancing and so she could introduce him to a few people, but he begged out early.

"I said I'm out of tears, Katherine," her father said, "but I don't think I'm quite ready for my daughter to start playing matchmaker with me. Baby steps, honey."

The evening progressed as planned, with various people coming up as they were leaving and either telling her what a wonderful evening it had been, what a moving speech she had given, or a combination of both. When the band had inevitably announced it was time for their last song, she realized she was finally alone. And as if on cue, that is when she noticed Tyler walking up from the vicinity of the kitchen.

She hadn't really had a lot of time to wonder what exactly he was doing most of the evening, but she realized now how much she hoped he had caught her speech and wondered what he thought.

"You are full of surprises," he said as way of an acknowledgment not just of her speech, but of the entire evening. "I'm not sure I'm equal to asking you this anymore, but would you like to dance, Katherine?"

Katherine looked around, almost as if she thought there might be someone else he was speaking to. "You're asking me to dance, Tyler Foster? I don't know that you've ever done that. Seems you've got a few surprises up your sleeve as well... I'd be happy to," she said as she held out her hand to him and he walked her over to the dance floor where a small handful of couples ended the night with a slow song. He kept his hands, and the space between them incredibly respectful, but by half way through the song she surrendered to the moment and laid her head on his shoulder as if the night, the situation, and maybe a whole host of things unspoken had finally worn her down. When it ended, they stayed like that for a moment, and when the lights came on she pulled back and said, "Come on."

Katherine took his hand and lead him back past her table where she grabbed an unopened bottle of champagne, and then out the back door of the Community Center to the office building. She produced a key from her pocketbook, opened it, and pulled him inside. There was a small waiting room inside with a couch, some end-chairs, and a coffee table. Katherine kicked off her heels, plopped down on the couch, and handed Tyler the bottle.

"Would you do the honors, Mr. Foster," she said, indicating for him to open the bottle.

"Have you got any glasses in here?" he asked.

"Nope," Katherine said. "They're all rented and the clean-up crew needs to get them washed and accounted for. I'm fine drinking from the bottle. And I don't mind sharing, unless whatever it was you wanted to talk to me about includes the fact that you picked up something communicable during your time in the big city."

She laughed and smiled at him as she said it, but it wasn't the same mocking laughter she had used with him up to this point. Something about the evening had softened her to him even more, and maybe she was just plain worn out from the planning of it all and was ready to relax and enjoy the fact that it was over.

Tyler popped the cork and it bubbled over just a bit. He handed it to her and she took a long pull off of it before handing it back.

"That's better," she said. "So what is it, Tyler, that it's taken you going on five years to get the courage up to finally talk to me about?"

"Well... I don't exactly know where even to begin. I've started this conversation in my head so many times, in so many ways, but ultimately the first and most important part of it always seems to start with I'm sorry..."

"Go on," Katherine said. She was studying him, looking into his face for the answers to the questions she had as much as listening to his words. He took a small drink of the champagne himself, handed it back to her, and continued.

"Can I sit?" he asked, gesturing not to one of the chairs, but to the couch next to her.

"Not so fast, Mr. Foster," she teased, "I don't know your intentions yet. I agreed to the dance, but let's start with the chair for now considering we're alone."

Tyler took the seat closest to her as she took another draw off the champagne and handed it back to him as she pulled her feet up under her and got comfortable.

"I honestly never wanted to hurt you. Leaving Poplar Bluff was easy, but leaving you behind was the hardest thing I've ever done in my life. And when I saw and realized how much I'd hurt you, it got so much worse than I'd even imagined because I didn't know how and what I could do to ever make it right. I didn't let you in on it, or anyone else for that matter, but I struggled so much with what to do that I put off making the decision until it was too late. I knew how much it would upset my father, Poppa Jack, and just about everyone else in town, but most of all I knew how much it would impact you and all of that was why I felt for some reason I needed to grow up and make that decision on my own. You were my best friend and much more than that, and I didn't let you in on the biggest decision of my life because I was afraid you'd talk me out of it if I did. I was ashamed for doing that. In my mind, making my own way was what I thought I had to do to grow up, but I realize now that doing it the way I did was probably the most cowardly thing I could have done."

Katherine realized suddenly that she'd been almost holding her breath, and when tears began to well up suddenly, she stopped him by getting up, moving over, and motioning for him to join her on the couch. As brave a face as she had put on these past weeks in front of him, she couldn't help it now. Like it or not, and as much as she had tried to bury it, almost five years later this wound was somehow still fresh. This was one hell of an apology, though, she suddenly thought. If he wasn't sincere, he was a damn good actor. She had found herself almost feeling sorry for him now. She laughed lightly at her emotions suddenly, waving a hand in front of her face and exhaling heavily.

"Sorry," she said. "I guess I didn't quite expect this…" She wiped the tears that had formed at the bottom of her eyes away and collected herself. "I-I still just don't understand why you shut me out, Tyler. You should have known I ultimately would have supported your decision, even if I didn't like it. I know you had a lot of good reasons for it, despite how you did it, but if I was truly your best friend, and you really loved me. Why didn't you fight for me? Why did you just let me walk out, without a word, and never ever try to make things right?"

"I didn't know how to undo it. I didn't know how to make you believe me. I felt that I'd betrayed your faith and trust in me, and didn't know what words I could say that wouldn't have rung hollow after my actions. At the same time, I was really conflicted. There was a part of me, I think, that thought if we'd stayed together somehow I'd end up right back here. I know that's totally unfair to you because, well, look at you. Look at tonight. You're so much bigger than this town, Katherine, yet for some stupid reason, at that moment you represented all things Poplar Bluff and the small town life I wanted to leave behind."

"When I visited Nashville, I got caught up. Coach Pohl, his enthusiasm, the city, and the seemingly endless possibilities that were out there. Common sense told me there really wasn't anything out there that I didn't have here, but somehow I couldn't put that genie back in the bottle. Ever since I picked up a club I wanted to play the tour, travel the world, and make something of myself, for myself. Something that not only you and my folks would've been proud of, but that I would have respected.

"I somehow came to believe that casting aside all the security blankets of my youth was what I needed to do to grow up. I didn't forget your number, Katherine. I must have dialed nine out of ten of those numbers a hundred times sitting in my dorm room in Nashville, or on the road, but I think part of me thought that if I talked to you, even once, I'd be giving all those dreams up."

Katherine stopped fighting the tears now, but still, there was something that held her back from completely surrendering.

"I still don't know, Tyler…" she said. "Maybe it's a fluke or maybe it's fate that we both ended up back here, at exactly the same time. I had a number of opportunities for work after school. Some really good offers in Columbia. In the end, though, I chose to come back here. I told myself it was just to check in on Daddy, weigh my options, blah blah blah, but it was my choice. You apparently didn't choose to be here. If you had qualified for the tour a month ago and earned your card, would I even be talking to you right now? I chose to be where we are right now, and I'm happy with that. You seem to have just ended up here, despite all your best efforts not to be and if fate hadn't intervened I don't know that we'd be having this conversation, and I guess I'm struggling a little bit with that."

They both took another pull off the champagne bottle and he looked deeply into her eyes as if he was trying to get her to see in him what he couldn't exactly find the words to articulate.

"I'm afraid you might be right," Tyler said after a long moment, "but I can tell you this at least. Whatever brought us back here, together, at this time, I went to church for the first time in a long time last weekend and prayed to God, thanking him for the fact that He did. You see, another reason I never called was in the back of my mind I was always afraid that you might have found someone else, moved on, and I knew I couldn't take hearing that you had. When you left the Pro Shop a couple of weeks ago, that idiot Jeremy made a somewhat ungentlemanly comment about you. I almost decked him. But I need that job right now and I thought better of if it for the moment. I can't stand the idea of you being with someone else, Katherine, and that's never changed."

"It was selfish of me to leave, and I don't know if in some backwards fantasy I always figured you'd still be here waiting when I finally did what I needed to do, but I know now that was selfish too. You're the best thing that ever happened to me, and I screwed that up, royally. I don't know if you can ever forgive that, I don't know if I even deserve for you to forgive that, but I do know this. If you do, I won't make the same mistake twice."

Katherine instinctively put her arms around Tyler and he held her close, but she still held something back, just a bit. They were awfully pretty words, but she'd been hurt enough to know now that it was the actions that backed up those words that ultimately made the difference. She pulled back after a few moments and reached for the champagne bottle again to drain the last couple of sips.

"What a day," she said with a bit of a light-hearted note in her voice again. "And so what do we do now? Did you expect you'd just give me that nice little speech and we'd go back to being Jack and Diane like old times? That was a pretty good start, Mr. Foster, nice words. And thank you. I do think you've given me some things to think about. But it's just a start, and it's going to take more than pretty words for me to just fall back into your arms and start trusting you again. What are your plans?"

Katherine had drunk more than half the bottle of champagne herself and she was starting to feel a little bit of that self-confident young woman that had just given one of the best speeches anyone in Poplar Bluff could remember re-emerge.

Tyler looked a little confused at the question suddenly.

"For the future," Katherine said, reading his expression and filling in the blanks.

"Well, you know I'm working at the golf course, for now," he said almost as if he was a bit embarrassed.

"For now?" she inquired with the raise of an eyebrow. "That isn't a career move?"

"No, well, I'm working so I can save up enough money for Q-School again next fall while still getting in enough practice time to keep my game sharp and play in a few mini-tour events. I'm making it on my own from now on. I'm not asking my parents for money again. I was so close, Katherine. I should have made it."

"And your degree?" she asked next.

"Well, I guess I can always go back and finish it if I have to. I'm about 14 units short. Playing and going to school full-time wasn't the easiest thing. There was a lot of travel. Made it hard to do everything I needed to do and take all the classes I needed to get my degree in four years."

"So you're not giving up on…" she seemed to be choosing her words carefully, "playing for a living?" She'd suddenly gotten a bit cold with him again. She didn't really expect him to give it up so quickly, but something in how he talked about it suddenly filled her with doubts about whether he ever would.

"Giving up?" He sounded almost incredulous. "Geez, you're starting to sound like my old man now. Are you going to ask me if I'd reconsider taking over the garage next?" he said, trying to pass it off in a somewhat humorous tone.

"No, I just want to know where your priorities are, Tyler," she said. "I apparently didn't quite fit into your plans last time. Has anything really changed?"

"Well, everything's changed," Tyler said, suddenly a little flustered. "You've changed, I've changed, we're older, wiser, and even though we're right back where we started, I know now it wouldn't mean anything if you weren't here with me. Hell, the only thing that hasn't changed is the fact that I still need to make something of myself. Look at you, Katherine, you're so smart, you've got your degree, and you just pulled off one of the most successful fundraisers anyone's probably seen around here in at least a decade. You've got such a bright future. Do you really want to settle for a school teacher or a mechanic? Would that make you happy? You could be with anyone you want. I think you know that, and don't you think that I know that? And do you think I could handle always thinking that deep down you were the one who settled for me?"

"I don't know, Tyler," she said coolly, getting up off the couch and slipping back on her heels "but thanks for at least asking me this time. We are older, I'll give you that, but I'm not so sure a whole lot of wisdom has come with that. You've definitely given me something to think about. I'm just not so sure I can trust someone a second time who it's starting to sound like felt as if he would have been settling for *me* the first time." She turned and started to walk out the door, and then turned back and looked at him very soberly as she opened it.

"I appreciate your apology tonight, Tyler, I really do. I believe it was sincere, and I really appreciated your help. You were very good tonight. I've still got work to finish up here, though, and so I think it's time for you to leave. And if memory serves me, you're pretty good at that, too." And with that she walked out.

SIZING UP THE COMPETITION

The day after the fundraiser, Tyler decided to call Katherine. Was she testing him again? He originally wasn't even going to just leave that night, like she had asked. It was late and he didn't want her leaving the community center and driving herself home, but when he finally walked out of the office a few minutes later, Karen Gibson had caught him on the way back the ballroom and she had told him to just let it go for now.

"I'll give her a ride home, Tyler. Give her a call tomorrow. She's had a big day, a big night, and has been under a lot of stress with this whole thing. She'll be in a better frame of mind to listen to whatever else it is you have to say after a good night's sleep."

He had poured out his heart to her that night, finally, and for the most part thought he had told her what he needed to say. For the briefest of moments, he had almost felt relieved. He had gotten through to her, and she understood. And their lives, lives that had so obviously been on hold for the past four and a half years, could maybe begin again. But no sooner had he broken through all those layers of protection had he said something to cause her to put those walls right back up. He was foolish, he thought, to have believed she would just take him back that easily. Like she said, she was going to need more than just pretty words, and he was going to have to prove himself to her this time.

Tyler called Katherine's cell first thing the next morning. It was Sunday and he didn't call too early, so he was still a little surprised and a whole lot disappointed when it went to voice mail. He left a message, asked her to call, and left for church with his parents. He skipped breakfast with them that morning, pretending something had come up at the club that Mack had needed him for, and decided to try and get caught up on his short game practice. But his pre-occupation with the whole situation resulted in him being there more in body than in mind.

She didn't call back that day, or the next, even after Tyler had called and left her a second message, and he started to get a little depressed. She could be stubborn, he knew, but with that came a determination he had always admired. He just wished for once she would set that aside. They were so close, and he couldn't prove anything to her if she wouldn't even return his calls. By the time Wednesday rolled around, however, after having left her messages on each of the past three days with no response, he decided the ball was in her court, and was even starting to get a little irritated with the fact that she wouldn't even call him back to say, "Stop bothering me." or something so he could at least stop wondering.

Mack had asked him to come in early that day and help set up for a clinic he had after lunch and then watch the shop before picking the range that night. The second assistant, Tom, had called in sick the previous evening, forcing Jeremy to open, and leaving Mack short-handed. When the clinic ended, Mack relieved Tyler behind the desk and told him to go hit some balls for a little while if he wanted to.

"Have I been keeping ya' too busy?" Mack asked with a bit of a playful smile. "I've noticed ya' haven't played much of late. Ya' better take advantage of it while the weather's still decent. It'll turn Scottish ugly here pretty quick and then I'll just make ya' go play!"

It had been men's guest day, and there were a lot of members and guests out that morning, but it was finally starting to die down with just a handful of guys coming in here and there to post their scores. Tyler had about 45 minutes to kill so he decided to grab his driver from his bag, which he kept on Mack's cart in the cart barn, and go work on some cut shots. As he was just about to walk out of the barn, the beverage cart came flying around the corner and nearly knocked him down.

"Whoa," came a familiar voice, "We've gotta' stop meetin' like this, Tyyy. You were right, you can't see a thing inside there when you're out here."

It was Whitney, as pretty and gregarious as ever, at the end of her shift and putting away the beverage cart for the afternoon.

"You're right, Whitney," Tyler said. "And it seems I'm the one who's going to get the short end of the stick of one of those meetings."

"Whatt'ya off to whack some more balls? Workin' on your form, Tyyy?" she said with a wink and in that almost caricature drawl she liked to use when she was teasing someone.

"Yeah," Tyler replied. "Gotta a few minutes to kill and I've got to get it in when I can."

"Why'nt ya' show me how sometime?" Whitney asked. "I used to be a pretty fair softball player, you know. I bet I could hit those things just as far as you do."

"Well," Tyler chuckled as he started to turn and walk towards the range, "when you can pry yourself away from that beverage cart some afternoon, you know where to find me."

"Why not right now?" Whitney asked. "I'm done for the day and I've got a little time to kill myself before I go home and get ready for my night class."

"Are you serious?..." Tyler asked.

"Why wouldn't I be serious, Ty?" Whitney challenged him. "I figure it'll help me to know a bit more about this game, and they say you're the best so if I'm gonna' take up this sport I might as well start at the top."

Tyler looked around almost incredulously. Here was arguably one of the most attractive women in Butler County asking him to give her a golf lesson and he was more than half balking at the proposition. A little nagging part of him said there was something not quite right about it, but then, Katherine wasn't even taking his phone calls right now and it was just a golf lesson. Or was it? Whitney had been awfully flirty with him on their handful of encounters since he'd been back. Up until now, he'd just written that off as Whitney being Whitney, but was there more to it than that. Tyler knew enough to know that once you got past her little act she could be quite genuine, and maybe this was one of those instances. He could score some brownie points by passing her off on Jeremy, who he knew had a thing for Whitney anyway, but he didn't in any way deserve that with how he'd been treating Tyler to this point since he'd been back. In fact, Tyler knew it would get under Jeremy's skin to see him working with Whitney, and that suddenly felt like a bit of poetic justice.

"Okay," Tyler said after obviously hesitating. "Get changed and meet me out on the range in ten minutes."

"Changed?" she said confused. "What's wrong with what I'm wearing?"

"Well, I know this doesn't make sense exactly," Tyler said. "But while they allow you to dress like you're working at Hooters on the beverage cart, hell, they almost encourage it, it's against the rules to go play golf or practice looking like that. If there are any ladies sitting up there in the clubhouse, they'll be sending Mack down here in less than five minutes if I let you go out there looking like that."

"More silly rules in this game than you can count," Whitney said throwing up her hands and rolling her eyes. "Alright, alright, I've got something else in my locker. I'll get changed and meet you out there. You got a club for me, too?"

"Sure," Tyler said. "I'll get one."

As she walked away, Tyler shook his head. Whitney sure was an attractive woman, but Tyler still wasn't so sure this was a smart thing to do. Someone could get the wrong idea, someone who knew Katherine, but in the end the allure of a very pretty woman and the chance get back at Jeremy won the debate and he decided it was really no big deal. Besides, Whitney was being nice to him, a step up from how Katherine was treating him at the moment, and what if she never really would forgive him?

When Whitney walked on to the range ten minutes later, she had not only changed into a fairly conservative pair of shorts that stopped just above the knee, but amazingly, a close-fitting ladies golf polo and tennis shoes too. She actually almost looked the part, and shocked him even further when he noticed the golf glove tucked into her back pocket with the fingers hanging out. Something about a woman who played golf, especially an attractive woman, had always done something for Tyler that he couldn't quite explain. Katherine had always supported him, even went to tournaments with him during the summer in high school and followed him around, but she'd never really seemed interested in actually taking up the game herself.

"Don't you look just about like an LPGA Tour star," Tyler cracked as she walked up to where he had been hitting balls.

Whitney stopped, did a half curtsy, smiled that big smile of hers and pulled out her glove to put it on as if she was ready to get down to business.

"Well, before we get started, you need to have a glove that fits," Tyler said laughing. "Where'd you get this stuff?"

"I got the shirt the first day I worked here," she said. "Mack let me pick one off the rack when he explained that my tank top wasn't likely to go over too well. I found the glove on the course one day and I've been carrying it on the cart ever since, but nobody wants to claim it."

"Well, as they say, you've got to look good to play good," Tyler smiled as he handed her the club he brought, "so I think you've more than got that aspect covered."

Whitney smiled warmly at the compliment, and Tyler. He knew she probably was pretty used to being complimented on her looks, though, and hoped suddenly that he didn't sound like just another guy flirting with what they assumed was an empty-headed beverage cart girl.

"So do you know anything?" Tyler asked. "Grip, stance, set-up, which end of the club to hold?"

Whitney cocked her head to one side and gave him a look that said, "What do you think I am, an idiot?"

Tyler kicked himself inwardly for doing what he had just vowed to himself not to do. "Sorry," he said quickly, trying to recover. "It's just another way of saying have you ever had a lesson before?"

"No," she said, "My dad took me to the driving range at Club of the Ozarks once when I was about 14, but I haven't picked up a club since then."

"Alright," Tyler said, coming right up next to her and putting her hands on the club in the correct grip. "This is a 7-iron. It's a good club to start with. It doesn't hit as far as my club would, but it's easier to hit and get up in the air at first."

As he stood there, manually adjusting Whitney's grip and putting her into the correct posture, Jeremy drove up in a cart shaking his head at the sight of him teaching her. Jeremy himself had been trying to get somewhere with her, but up to this point had been striking out and the fact alone that it so obviously irritated Jeremy made Tyler suddenly glad he had decided to do this.

"Hey, Golden Boy. Mack says he's gonna' need you back in the shop in a few minutes. Somethin's come up out on the course, so he needs to go Marshall and I'm already on o.t."

As he looked back towards the Pro Shop, suddenly irritated that his little impromptu lesson with Whitney was being interrupted, he saw Katherine standing in the middle of the path leading from the range to the Pro Shop, arms folded, and looking in their direction in a none too friendly pose.

"Oh, and you've got a visitor," Jeremy said, suddenly amused. "Same gal who was here a couple of weeks ago. Seems you're leading a charmed life, my friend. Need me to take over for you?"

Tyler was suddenly dumbstruck, and he quickly shoved his hands in his pockets like a kid who got his hands caught in the cookie jar. Katherine was a good sixty or seventy yards away, but what had she seen? What had she thought she'd seen?

He started to walk towards her and she immediately turned around and headed briskly back up the path. He remembered Whitney then, and turned back to her feeling suddenly horrible about more than one situation.

"I'm sorry, Whitney, I've… I've got to go," he said. "I'll explain later. I'm really sorry."

He quickly jogged back up the path to try and catch Katherine before she got around to the front parking lot where they'd make a scene. When he rounded the corner, he found her already at her car. She'd used the side lot where the employees park, and so he called out to her to stop as he ran to catch up. As she opened the door and got in, he reached the car.

"Katherine, wait," Tyler said breathing heavily. "It's not at all what you think."

"Well if that isn't the cliché to beat all clichés," Katherine said as she put on her seatbelt without even glancing in Tyler's direction. "Not what I think, huh, Tyler. I think it's pretty obvious to me at this point that you're not incredibly concerned with what I think, or what anyone else thinks for that matter. Half the people in the clubhouse up there saw us together at the Gala the other night. Regardless of what it was to you, don't you think they're up there right now talking about how you're out there flirting with that Prom Queen? Did you even stop to think about how embarrassing that might be for me, or how it'd make me feel once I heard about it from someone else?"

"I was just being nice, Katherine," Tyler said. "She works here now and wants to learn how to play. It meant nothing, and I don't know what I was thinking, you're right, I wasn't thinking, that was totally stupid of me. I almost told her to ask Jeremy because I honestly didn't totally feel comfortable with it. Hell, I would have if I didn't know how much it was going to get under his skin."

"Oh, that's exactly what I want to hear, Tyler. You were just harmlessly flirting with probably the one woman in all of Poplar Bluff that you knew would hurt me to hear about you with more than any other just to get back at some idiot you have to put up with for a few hours a day at work? Didn't totally feel comfortable? You looked pretty comfortable to me with your hands all over her a few minutes ago. No, now I've seen enough and heard enough. What an idiot I am, *still*. And to think I was coming here to apologize for how I ended the other night and to invite you to dinner at the house. Goodbye, Tyler," she said finally, turning and looking at him sadly as she started the car, closed the door, and drove away.

Mike Dowd

HOME FOR THE HOLIDAYS

A week, then two went by after Katherine had said goodbye to Tyler at the club after walking in on him giving a golf lesson to Whitney. She had kept herself busy with the aftermath of the Gala to try and keep from thinking about it, but before she almost realized it Christmas was just around the corner. She had felt that goodbye was for good when she said it, but after she'd had time to cool down and think, she had to admit to herself that she almost couldn't stand the idea of losing Tyler to Whitney as much as she was disappointed in him. He had called her, repeatedly, and each message was so pleadingly apologetic it had almost gotten pathetic. But to this point those calls had gone unanswered, just as they had after the Gala. And was that at least part of what had driven him to succumb to the allure of those sickeningly natural blond tresses?

Whitney... Katherine was self-aware enough to know that her feelings towards her were more jealousy than anything Whitney had ever actually done to her. Sure, Whitney had been a little too friendly towards Tyler back in high school, but Katherine had made it abundantly clear to him at the time that she wouldn't put up with him being too chummy with her no matter how innocuous he claimed her intentions were. Katherine was smart enough to know that not only was Tyler still a catch, but he was also a man after all, and the attention of a woman like Whitney was the kind of thing that kept most guys up at night. And Whitney wasn't stupid. She got a lot of the stereotypical bimbo comments dumped on her by other girls who were jealous, and she knew how to play that hand when it benefited her. There was a shrewdness to her, though, one that lay just beneath that acrylic veneer that a lot of people chose to ignore, or were too blinded to because of her appearance. Tyler was naive. Disguised in innocence, Katherine knew that Whitney's attention those many years ago had been a bit more than just a ploy to get some help with her homework. And now here she was again, moving in on him just like she had all those years ago. Did anything ever change around here? Well, she was every bit the woman Whitney was, and more... No, she definitely wouldn't be giving him up to her that easy, she finally decided. And so she picked up the phone.

She needed to get a Christmas tree, as decorating the house had fallen on her each year since she had been in high school, and her father had left for a few days on business. She could get the guys at the lot to load it up for her, but her little sports car was too small to do anything but strap it on top and even then it would have to be small. She wanted to surprise Daddy with a big old natural tree when he got home, like they used to get, because he had invited a handful of relatives over for Christmas Eve dinner this year. Tyler's father had a truck, and so she had her in.

"Katherine," came Tyler's voice on the other end. "Thank you for calling. I trust you got my messages? I'd almost given up hope you'd call me back."

"I need a favor, Tyler," she said a bit matter-of-factly as if nothing at all had even taken place. "Can you get your father's pickup either tonight or tomorrow and give me a hand?"

"Sure," he said. "How about tonight? I'm supposed to close the shop tomorrow."

"That'll work," she said. "Pick me up at 6:00 and wear something you can get dirty."

"May I ask what we're doing?" Tyler asked.

"We're getting a Christmas tree. Daddy's out of town and I'm going to surprise him. I just can't stand that old fake tree he keeps having me put up each year anymore."

A few hours later, she saw Tyler's father's classic old Chevy pickup pulled up in front of her house. It was truly a beauty with a wood laminate bed and a Kelly green paint job that made it look like it belonged on the front of a John Deere Tractor brochure. She locked the front door and walked down the front walk as Tyler made his way around to open the door for her.

"You sure Jack isn't going to kill you if you get a little dirt on it?" she asked as she got in. Jack kept all his cars immaculate. They were like business cards, each bearing the All-American Auto magnetized stickers on the doors. He always kept two or three parked out in front of his shop, kind of like a standing car show, and it drew people in to admire his work and showed them what was possible when it came to their old clunkers. The old Chevy had always been one of his favorites, Katherine knew, and she figured Tyler must have had to do a pretty good sales job or promise some extra time around the garage for Jack to agree.

"Well, I'll clean it first," Tyler said. "I brought a bunch of towels from the garage to lay down so we don't get any scratches on the bed. He might actually kill me if I did that."

She smiled politely in his direction at that, without really looking at him and decided to continue with safe small-talk for now. She had something she wanted to say, and she knew he did too, but it could wait until later.

"There's a big lot on South 5th across from the Black River Coliseum. I went by there on lunch today and they're holding a tree for me," Katherine said. "We need some rope, though. They didn't have any they would sell."

"I brought some," Tyler said. "It's behind the seat."

It was only a five minutes or so from Katherine's house to the lot, depending on how many lights you hit, but even in that short time they were both suddenly aware of the awkwardness that lay between them at the moment. She wasn't completely done being angry with him, but she figured that was a step up from just being done with him period. They had ridden in silence for a couple more blocks when Tyler suddenly hit the steering wheel with the palm of his hand and swore.

"Dammit!" he said. "That was Dad that just drove by us. He must have forgotten something at the garage. I didn't actually tell him we were borrowing the pickup."

Katherine burst out laughing as Tyler's cell phone went off. It was pretty much dark now, but there was no mistaking Tyler's father's old Chevy driving down the street in any light.

"Yeah Pop," Tyler said as he picked it up to a loud voice he didn't need to put up to his ear to hear. "I know, I know, I'm sorry, I should have said something. Katherine needed help picking up a Christmas tree and I've got plenty of towels to lay down across the bed."

Katherine was trying to suppress her laughter, but she was obviously enjoying Tyler getting an earful from someone other than herself. When he finally hung up with his father, after assuring him they wouldn't get a scratch on his precious old Chevy, they were pulling into the lot. They got out of the truck and Katherine walked up to the guy running the place, produced a receipt, and pointed to the tree that had been netted and leaned up against the temporary cyclone fence they had erected around the entire lot. The guy went and grabbed it while Tyler began laying down the towels he had brought to protect the truck. When he was done, he grabbed the trunk end with one hand and the middle of it with the other while Katherine held the top and they laid it in the bed of the pickup as carefully as if it were a large carton of eggs.

"There," Tyler said. "Now as long as we don't drive too fast I might even be able to get out of this with my life."

They drove back to the house and Tyler carried the tree up the front walk and into the house as Katherine held the door. She had cleared a spot in front of the big window facing the road where her father and everyone else would be able to see the tree from the street, just the way she remembered her mother always had.

"Thank you," she said to Tyler, assessing the tree after he had placed it in the stand, cut off the netting, and adjusted it until they got it straight.

"You're welcome…" he said, and then as if finally addressing an unanswered question that lay between them he continued, "What now?"

"Have you had anything to eat?" she asked with a note of such casual curiosity as though he could have been anyone who'd just popped in to say hello.

"No," he said. "I was sort of hoping we might have the opportunity to do that."

"Good," she said. "I'm not too fond of eating alone and I threw something in the oven before we left. And besides, I could use your help getting the star up on top. It's just about an inch or two out of my reach."

Katherine turned and headed towards the kitchen with Tyler in tow. She knew he could smell the baked lemon chicken now, a favorite of Tyler's, and a recipe she'd gotten from his mother many years ago.

"Is that…" he started, smelling the air as if he was trying to place something.

"Oh, it's just a little something I threw together," Katherine said, turning slightly and smiling a sly smile that she knew would make him think.

She busied herself with finishing things up and asked Tyler to pour them each a glass of wine from the bottle she'd left out on the counter next to two glasses.

"You know, I can't figure you out," he said incredulously and chuckling slightly.

"Well, I don't think that's necessarily a bad thing," Katherine quipped.

"One minute I'm practically picking out engagement rings, and the next minute you won't even return my phone calls," he said.

Katherine dropped the salad dressing bottle she had been pouring from and it landed with a loud crash on the tile floor which sent ranch dressing flying all over the cabinets and the floor. Engagement rings? Did she hear him right? She looked up at Tyler who had stopped pouring the wine suddenly at the sound of the crash. He looked startled, but his look didn't betray whether or not he had understood the gravity of what he had just said, how it had affected her, or whether or not he was even serious. She moved quickly to grab some paper towels and Tyler began picking up the broken bottle fragments and pieces of glass from around the kitchen.

"I hope you were in the mood for Italian," she said as way of covering up the accident and diverting the conversation from his previous comment while she wiped up the mess.

"Sure, whatever you've got," he said.

She got the Italian dressing from the fridge and put it on the small round kitchen table with the small bowl of salad she had prepared. Tyler grabbed the two full glasses and put the bottle on the table in between them. She dished up two plates with plenty of rice and chicken, and as she brought it over motioned for him to sit.

As they sat, Tyler picked up his wine glass as if in preparation for a toast.

"I don't know much about wine," Tyler said raising his glass, "but I do know you can use it to do this… to the smartest, classiest, prettiest, most forgiving, and by far and away most intriguing woman I've ever been fortunate enough to know… Merry Christmas."

"Thank you, Tyler," Katherine said beaming back at him genuinely as they toasted and she took a sip. "I'll trust you're not talking about Whitney Robertson," she couldn't help but add with a smirk and an arch of her brow.

"Oh, you're bad," Tyler said, laughing carefully and smiling back at her in that roguish way that, despite his betrayal and all her protections, still had a way of stopping her heart like a traffic light.

"And no," he continued, "I'm definitely not talking about anyone other than you. And I'm betting on the come with the forgiving part."

Katherine felt at ease suddenly. A part of her was still thinking she was letting him off the hook way too easy, and quickly, but enough of her wanted to believe him and believe in his genuine feelings for her that she decided to let go. Her sensible side said that they had been apart now longer than they'd actually been together, and she still had a lot more questions. But she couldn't answer those questions alone, and it was the holidays. And now that Tyler was back in her life, for good or bad, she couldn't bear the thought of spending one more of them by herself, or the thought of him spending them with someone else.

"We've got to get something straight, though," Katherine said, getting business-like with Tyler again suddenly. "If you really expect me to believe in your sincerity, and to start trusting you again, I better not hear about any more golf lessons, or anything else for that matter, with Whitney or any other girls younger than your mother from now on."

He laughed genuinely this time, noticeably relaxing as he sensed that she was finally softening to him and was ready to at least give him the benefit of the doubt. She'd made him suffer for weeks, and arguably should have made it more considering how long he'd made her suffer. But now that she understood he too had suffered in his own way during that time, something felt different. She was tired of playing this game. It just wasn't her. And so she decided she was ready, and willing to at least try and get on with life.

THAT'S MY LITTLE BROTHER

The holidays came and went with Tyler and Katherine hardly spending a day apart. They were making up for lost time, Tyler thought, and for all the holidays they had spent apart during college. Katherine's father was a little cold towards Tyler at first, but by the time New Year's rolled around, even he had come around when he realized how happy his daughter was. Tyler's mother and Katherine had picked up their relationship like no time had passed, and it was immediately obvious to Tyler how much they had genuinely missed each other when he saw the two them together at Christmas. Things seemed right again, right in a way that made him realize just how wrong they had been all the years they were apart. And when Tyler finished second by only one shot in the first mini-tour event he played in after the first of the year, he began to wonder how much just being in a great place mentally had a spill-over effect on his game.

At the same time, there were still some issues between them they had both chosen to ignore for the moment. Almost winning had bolstered Tyler's confidence, and when he finished fourth six weeks later in an event where he'd gotten a handful of bad breaks and hadn't even struck the ball that well, he became even more steadfast in his belief that he was on the right track. At the same time, Katherine seemed to be getting more entrenched back in Poplar Bluff by the day. With the success of the Gala, and the understanding in the community that she was the driving force behind that, she had more than a couple opportunities come her way, and she was thoughtfully considering her next move. They both wanted things to work, though, and while neither of them were exactly sure what that was going to ultimately look like, and how it was supposed to happen, neither of them seemed to want to immediately concern themselves with that for the time being either. They were enjoying each other for now, and the more serious issues could wait. At least a while.

When spring rolled around, and the weather got better, Tyler's propositions at the club changed slightly as well. Jack had invariably kept working on him about the garage, and he truly tried to help him as much as he could, but when Jeremy got the opportunity to take a position as the first assistant at a bigger, more prestigious club just outside of Branson, he took it. Mack said that

Tyler had proven himself all winter, and if he wanted the spot it was his. So, Tyler officially became a part of the Professional Staff at Butler Bluff. It was more hours and meant he wouldn't be able to help his father as much, but it was better pay and also meant he wouldn't be picking the range anymore and washing carts until well after dark. Mack had agreed to give him mostly morning shifts so he could practice in the afternoons, and the time off he needed to play in a handful of events. And since the other assistant, Tom, was much easier to work with than Jeremy had been, even that element of it was an improvement.

Up until that point, the only person Tyler had worked with on any kind of a regular basis was Jackie. Mack had kept a regular appointment with Jackie, every other week, to make sure he kept him on track, but he and Tyler had spent at least a couple of hours together, usually on the course, two or three days a week all winter. And it showed.

"I just want ya' teaching him what ya' know about playing the game, Tyler," Mack had told him one morning after his session with Jackie, "Don't concern yourself with his mechanics or technique. I'll deal with that part. The less he even thinks about that stuff the better. Ya' just report back to me if you notice he's struggling with a particular element of his game, or ya' see too many misses of one type or another and I'll find a way to address it."

Jackie was so much like Tyler at that age, Mack had said, it was scary. The biggest difference, though, was Jackie was a lot bigger… and he had Tyler. Not many kids learn to play the game by spending a few days a week with someone who was about as close to a Tour Player as you could come across, but that's just what Jackie was doing in all that time with his big brother. And when the local Junior Tournament season began in late spring, Tyler declared that he thought Jackie was ready. He hadn't broken 80 yet, but he was getting close, and playing in the boys 12 & 13 division of the Southeast Missouri Jr. Golf Association Tyler thought he would be competitive. The first event that came up was just a one-day event, and, unlike many of the events, you could have a caddy.

"You want me to carry for you?" Tyler asked Jackie after practice one afternoon just a few days before the event.

"Would you really?" Jackie asked. "That'd be awesome!"

"I already asked Mack about it," Tyler said. "He said he'd give me the morning off and we're only going to Club of the Ozarks. We can be back here by 1:30 or 2:00 so I can close."

Jackie was beside himself and declared he was going to win the thing now.

"Hold your horses," Tyler said. "There's some really good kids from all around the state playing. It's the first event of the year and some of them might be knockin' the rust off after the winter, but let's keep things in perspective."

"Yeah, but they don't have you caddying for them," Jackie said, still really excited about the fact that his big brother would be carrying his bag.

When the day of the tournament rolled around, Tyler found he was almost as nervous for Jackie as he would have been if he was playing in a big event himself. He and Mack had conferred over dinner the night before about what his game plan should be and in the end they decided to just let him have fun and see what happens.

"Ya' can over-coach, Tyler," Mack said, "and over-control. It's his first time playin' in a tournament. Just see how he reacts to it. Let him ask ya' for advice, don't force it on him. It's your chance to see how much he's been payin' attention to all that advice ya' been giv'n 'im. The first question you should always ask is, what'cha thinkin', Jackie? Let him tell ya' what he plans to do. If you're gonna be a good caddy someday, and a good coach for that matter, you've got to learn to listen more than you talk."

"Alright," Tyler said, "I'll try to resist. He does some awful boneheaded things sometimes and he wants to hit that lob wedge for darn near every shot inside of 70 yards, even when he's three feet off the green!"

"Leave 'im be, Tyler," Mack said. "He's havin' fun with it more than anythin' right now, so don't take that away from him. Remember, what'cha thinkin', Jackie? That's it, and don't give any unsolicited advice. He'll learn eventually."

They got to the event and Tyler watched Jackie look around wide-eyed at all the other kids there. At Butler Bluff, he was one of only a couple dozen kids that were ever out there on any kind of a regular basis, and most of them were older than him and in high school.

"I can't believe all these kids," Jackie said when they started walking to the tent set up for check-in. "Where they all come from?"

"Like I said, Jackie," Tyler reminded him as they gave his name and picked up his scorecard, "All over the state. These are the best of the best, so to speak, the best handful of kids from each club all over Missouri. And some from Tennessee and Arkansas, too. Let's go putt first. You want to spend the most time gettin' used to the speed of the greens. That's the biggest difference from course to course and has the biggest impact on your score day to day."

They did that for a while and then headed to the range. Jackie was still pretty wide-eyed and Tyler was really enjoying watching him experience it all for the first time. He remembered back to his first tournament and how pumped he was. And how he thought that he was going to win the thing too. He'd finished almost in last that day, and it made him realize how much better he needed to get and upset him enough he just wanted to work even harder. He didn't want Jackie to fail that badly, he thought, but inside he wondered if being humbled a bit right out of the gate like he had been wouldn't be too bad a thing either.

When Jackie started warming up and Tyler began looking around to size up the competition, he wasn't so sure if that would happen. They were early, and since they blocked the tee-times by age, and Jackie had the first one in his flight, Tyler figured most of the kids on the range were about his age or even a bit older. Jackie was a head taller than all of them, and when he began cracking drives out there a good 230 to 240 yards, a bunch of the other kids started looking around to see who the big kid was that none of them obviously recognized. How many more tournaments could he have won when he was a kid if he'd been blessed with Jackie's size, Tyler thought shaking his head.

Thirty minutes later, when they were walking to the first tee after rolling a few last minute putts, Jackie turned to Tyler and smiled a smile as big as Texas.

"This is sure fun, Ty. Just in case I forget to tell you later, thanks for bringing me."

"Oh, don't thank me now," Tyler said smiling back at him. "If you're still telling me how much fun it was when we're done, I'll say your welcome."

They got to the first hole and Tyler was about to start telling him about the way to play it, since he'd played it a hundred times, when he remembered what Mack had said. "What'cha thinkin', Jackie?" he asked, imitating Mack's Scottish accent.

"Driver," Jackie said, reaching out his hand just like the guys he'd seen do on TV. And that was it. Tyler laughed and handed him the big dog with nothing more than a, "Let her rip."

For his first tournament, Jackie played surprisingly well the first nine holes, shooting a 41 and only really asking for Tyler's advice on one hole when he lost his ball in long rough and didn't remember for sure what the rule was. As they walked off the 9th green, Tyler was like a proud father watching his kid hit a triple in his first little league game, and he found himself thinking about how really scary good Jackie could be. The other kids were visibly discouraged by how far he hit it too, and even though his game was still pretty raw in spots, the talent was there. And looking at his father, he'd only likely continue to just get bigger. The modern game favored distance and Jackie had a built-in advantage he'd likely not lose in the years to come.

Jackie kept it going for the first few holes on the back, making pars, but when he drove it through the fairway on the thirteenth and out of bounds, making triple, he was visibly disheartened.

"Man, Ty," he said as they were walking to the next tee, "I was doing so good, I could've broke 80."

"You still can," Tyler said. "A lot of golf still to play. Don't let one bad hole turn into three."

But he did, bogeying the next, a short easy par three, and doubling the hole after that when he hit it into a fairway bunker and tried to hit a hero shot out and caught the lip, leaving it to roll right back at his feet. He was smart enough to ask Tyler for a different club the second time, and he got out, but Tyler could see that mentally he was more than rattled.

"What'cha thinkin', Jackie?" Tyler asked as they walked to the 16th.

"I don't know," Jackie said a bit down. "We're not there yet. I don't even know what the par is."

"I'm not talking about the next shot," Tyler said softly. "What's going on in your head right now?"

"Well," Jackie said, "I was hoping you weren't disappointed in me. I wanted to play well for you. You took the day off to come out and caddy for me and I feel like I'm letting you down."

Tyler stopped him right there in the path, let the other kids and parents walk by, and then turned to Jackie to look him in the eye.

"Look, Jackie, you play this game for you and no one else. You're never going to disappoint me with what you shoot. You'll only disappoint me if you stop enjoying it and let that stop you from trying your best. We all have bad holes now and then, and bad rounds too, no matter how good we ultimately get, but I want you to remember this... this is the best game in the world, Jackie, and you can play. You're just at the beginning of this journey and you've still got so much to learn, so don't you dare go being hard on yourself or worrying about what anyone else thinks. This is the most fun I've had on the golf course since I was in high school, and if you really want to know why I didn't make the Tour last year, just about the biggest part of that was because I stopped having fun. I started treating this game like a job, and when I did that I not only stopped having fun, but I started feeling pressure. Now go have fun and stop giving a damn about what I or anybody else thinks about what you shoot!"

Jackie looked at him and smiled as a wave of relief seemed to pass over him, and then he exhaled loudly. "Got it. Let's go have fun."

Jackie parred the last three holes for an 83. When he signed the scorecard and turned it in to the scorer's tent, he was the leader in the clubhouse. But with more than a half a dozen groups left to finish in his age flight, that was likely to change. In the end, he came in fourth, a pretty fair showing he thought for his first tournament, but Tyler could tell he was really disappointed when he found out they only gave trophies for the top three.

"Just two more strokes!" he said, recounting all the places he could have easily saved those shots all the way home.

Tyler just smiled and said, "You'll get 'em next time, Jackie. You see what happened once you stopped worrying and started having fun with it again? The important thing is just to make sure you learn something from that." He had, and he was hooked.

A RETURN TO VERN'S

Things between Tyler and Katherine had been good all that winter and spring, really good. So good in fact, she'd light heartedly brought up a couple of times the fact that he'd mentioned he'd almost been shopping for engagement rings at that first dinner she'd made during the holidays, and she wondered why he was waiting so long to actually give it to her. The first time she could see it made Tyler visibly uncomfortable, but as things had been going so well she passed it off as either embarrassment that she'd beaten him to the punch, or possibly even that he didn't have enough money to buy one. When she tested those waters again a couple of months later and got a similar response, though, she began to worry about why that was.

She had continued to work for The American Cancer Society, feeling committed to it now, even though she'd had some better offers. She had impressed a number of the right people in Poplar Bluff, and she had options. But she hadn't quite made up her mind which one, if any of them, was the right move for her. And a big part of the reason for that, she realized, was she wasn't one hundred percent sure where she and Tyler were headed and where they stood on some very big issues. Tyler was committed to trying for the Tour again, and if he actually made it through the first stage, where did that leave her? Did she want to go with him? The first year, at least, wasn't even the full PGA Tour anymore, and she didn't exactly cherish the idea of living like a vagabond in cheap motels while he struggled just to make cuts. And even if she did, that'd mean she was pretty much giving up on her own goals. She might have done that four or five years ago, but she couldn't hardly fathom it now. Or did he expect her to just stay home while he travelled the country, playing golf, eating out every night, and finishing his evenings with a nightcap in some hotel bar with the boys or, worse yet, one of those groupies she'd always heard followed the tour around?

Just the thought of these things made her uneasy. She'd only half-jokingly brought up the idea of an engagement and let it drop when it hadn't exactly gone well. Why was that? Was Tyler saving every extra penny just to try and qualify? And what if he didn't make the Tour? Would that just begin all over again? Would he ever give up on this dream? At some point could he come to terms with the idea of settling down and decide that something less than making it could make him happy? That she could make him happy? She knew she wanted a family, not right away, but eventually, and what was he going to do to help make that a reality if his tour dreams didn't pan out? She was happy he started working full-time as an assistant at the club, but even with the lessons he'd been starting to give, and the couple of checks he'd made playing in mini-tour events that spring, the pay was still horrible. Unless he actually worked himself all the way up into something like Mack's position somewhere eventually, it would barely be enough to raise a family on. And she didn't exactly relish the idea of someone else raising their kids someday while they both worked full-time just to make ends meet. They were having fun for now, and she knew now that she loved him every bit as much as she ever had, but they weren't in high school anymore, and they couldn't just keep living at home and dating indefinitely like they were. Yes, they'd been avoiding it, but it was time for an overdue talk... a talk about the future.

"Butler Bluff Pro Shop, this is Tyler," he answered when she called the club.

"Tyler," she said, "What time are you getting off later?"

"Oh, I close the shop about 6:00," Tyler said. "What's up? You want to go get some dinner? I already practiced this morning so I'm free."

"Yeah, I do," Katherine said. "Why don't you pick me up at the office? I'm going to be working a little late."

When Tyler showed up at the office about 6:30 that evening, he'd obviously stopped by the house first to clean up and change.

"Where we headed?" he asked as he walked up behind her at her desk and began to rub her shoulders. It felt good, really good, and so she just closed her eyes and let him do it for a few moments before finally looking up.

"Let's just go to Vern's…" she said, pausing to see his reaction. They had avoided the spot of their break-up ever since they'd been back together in an unspoken way that both of them just understood. Vern's was still a painful memory for her, and she knew that even though his parents loved going there for breakfast, he wasn't all that comfortable there either.

"Vern's?" he said confused. "What's up?"

"It's a Tuesday, it'll be quiet," she said, "and I think we need to talk."

"Ooookay," Tyler said, drawing it out. "We'll go to Vern's."

She locked up the office and they walked across the street. Most of the after school crowd had dissipated and there were only a couple of tables occupied in the back.

"Well hellooo there Tyler, and my goodness, Katherine," Vern called out as they walked in. "Haven't seen the two of you in here together in pertineer a whole year of Sundays. Where'd you like to sit?"

"How about that booth right down there," Katherine pointed to their booth. "I think we're past all that now, aren't we, hon'?"

Tyler almost winced when she said it. "Uuuh, sure. Absolutely."

She knew he didn't exactly know what she wanted to talk about, but he was visibly uncomfortable now and was likely about to become even more so she figured.

Vern left them with menus and waters and, sensing something was up, did it without his usual small talk and banter. "Just holler when you're ready."

Tyler picked up the menu and started to look it over, maybe hoping to stave off the inevitable. But this moment had been building for a while and so Katherine decided the best thing to do was dive right in.

"Tyler," she began, "I'm considering leaving ACS because I've got a couple of pretty intriguing offers."

"Really," he said. "I know you said that construction company talked to you about running their business office, but I didn't think you were serious about that. Has something else come up?"

"Yes," she continued. "I was approached by someone at The Gates Corporation. They have an opening in finance that has the potential to advance to the executive level, and there's a relatively new start-up out of St. Louis that has some local ties. They're expanding rapidly and want to open up an office here."

"Well that's great," Tyler said. "They both sound promising and they're right here."

"Well, no," Katherine said calmly and slowly. "It's not exactly great, Tyler."

He looked first confused, then concerned and waited for her to clarify.

They were sitting across from each other in the same place they had been so many years ago. Right back in the very same place, only this time Katherine was starting to feel like their roles had been reversed. Katherine took Tyler's hands in hers. It almost hurt to look at him knowing what she felt she had to say, and not knowing how he would take it.

"You know I love you, Tyler. I think I even loved you when I hated you. I've come to realize that's something I just can't help anymore."

He smiled broadly, momentarily relieved as if whatever it was she was about to say wasn't nearly as bad as he had started to fear. "I love you too... So what's the problem?"

"Well... I need to know where we're headed, Tyler. You're not the only one with goals here, and I can't move forward with mine if we're standing still, or at least until I know what you want, and what you expect. I know what your goals are, but how do I fit in with them, that plan, and what do you really expect of me if and when you accomplish them? And how long do you plan to keep trying for them if things don't work out again this time? I can't commit to this job, or that job, or anything else if you expect me to up and quit a few months from now if and when you accomplish what you want."

Tyler held her hands and her gaze in a way that she knew immediately how much he loved her too, every bit as much as she did. But in that gaze she could also see he didn't have a clue.

"You haven't really thought about these things, Tyler, have you?" she said after a moment. "You're so focused on your goal that you haven't really even thought about what would happen if you accomplished it. If you make it to the Tour this fall, a couple months later you'll be packing up to head out on the road, and while I know it's a huge accomplishment, that's essentially just the minor leagues for at least another year. At that point what exactly do you expect me to do? Just quit my job and follow you around, stay here, something in between, or what? I can't make a commitment to someone and just up and say sorry, thanks for the opportunity but my boyfriend made the Tour, gotta' go now. That's not me, and besides, I don't even know if that's what you want."

Tyler obviously wanted to say something by now, but was apparently trying to choose his words carefully. "I'm sorry, Katherine," he started. "You're right, I guess I've been selfish. In my mind, I guess I sort of figured that when two people love each other things just work out, like it did for our folks, but I can see now that thinking that way hasn't been considerate of you. I always thought I'd already have my ducks in a row at this point, and I guess part of me is embarrassed that I don't so I suppose I've been avoiding the hard questions. We've been so happy I think I've avoided these things because I don't exactly know if I have all the answers right now. I do know that I love you, with all my heart, and I want us to be together. Isn't that what's ultimately most important?"

"Yes," she said, smiling at what he said. "But I need to know that you have a plan, that we have a plan, and what that is. I know better than anyone how long and hard you've worked towards your goal and I'm not asking you to give up on your dreams, but I need to know what you expect and what you want. I'm a patient woman, Tyler. To an extent, I can wait for you, if I have an idea what I'm waiting for. But then again, I've been waiting for you for five years now, and I'm still waiting to start that next chapter. It's not just your dreams anymore, Tyler. I've been out of school for a year now. I'm pretty good at what I do, and I like doing it. I'm seeing opportunities come and go and I can't keep watching them pass me by because I'm not sure exactly where we're headed. We may need one of these opportunities, for our future, to help get us on the right track."

"I understand," Tyler said. "I really do, but how are we supposed to start that next chapter the way things are? You said it yourself, you've got opportunities. This is my opportunity, my best opportunity to really provide for us, and give us a better life, something much bigger than just Poplar Bluff."

"Well, what does that life look like to you, Tyler? And how long do you expect me to wait? Am I supposed to just commit to something while you struggle to play the mini tours for a few years until you make the big time and then, what, just quit whatever it is I'm doing to follow you around the country, or the world? I don't know if that's me, and it's no way to raise a family someday. And if you think I'm sitting at home by myself all the time while you traipse around the globe playing golf, coming home on holidays or whenever you don't make the cut then, well, I'm afraid you might have the wrong girl."

"No, no, no," Tyler said, "I would never expect that, or want that for you, for us, but we could still have a normal life, and we could live anywhere we wanted. Wherever it would be most convenient and that I could have the most time at home. I could arrange my schedule, especially once I've established myself, so that I didn't need to play every week. A lot of guys do that once they're established, and they're home fifteen to twenty weeks a year."

He was getting a little desperate now and grasping at straws, and she could see he was struggling because the life and lifestyle he'd dreamed about for half his life had begun to unravel before his eyes with her questions. He really hadn't thought this through at all.

"Fifteen to twenty weeks a year, Tyler?" she said incredulously, "and that's if and when you establish yourself? Do you really think kids only need their father fifteen to twenty weeks a year? Do you think that's all *I* want to be with you? I grew up in a one parent household for a good portion of my life and that's not what I want for our kids. And what happens if you *don't* make it? As good as you are, I know the odds. What did you say once? 25 or 30 guys a year out of ten thousand ultimately make it. That's less than one percent. What then? Are you gonna' keep working as an assistant and living with your parents so you can save up enough money for the next go-round and the next? Am I supposed wait around for you until that finally happens? An assistant golf pro doesn't make enough money to support a family, Tyler. Do you expect me to be the bread winner, helping you to keep trying, year after year? And if so, when does it all end?"

"What are you saying, Katherine? Do you want me to just give up? Do you really want me to just quit, take over Dad's garage someday, finish my teaching credential, or settle for working my way up into Mack's or a similar position at some other club someday so that you can stay home clipping coupons while we struggle to raise our kids? I can do better than that, we can do better than that. I want you to be proud to be with me, Katherine, like I'm proud to be with you. Not wake up someday and feel like you settled for the local washout who never really lived up to his potential."

"You're underestimating me, Tyler, if you think how much money you make determines whether or not I'm proud to be with you. Who you are as a man, how you treat your family, and how you handle your responsibilities determines that. I'm 23-years-old now, though, and whether we like it or not, life is moving on, and if we don't start making a plan for it, we're gonna' wake up one morning and it will have happened anyway."

"Just giving up will suck the life out of me, Katherine, especially when we both know I can do so much better. Can't you see that?"

"I'm not saying you should."

"I know that's not what you said, but it sure sounds like it. Don't you want to set your sights higher than all this? Will you really be happy with just staying in Poplar Bluff the rest of your life?" Tyler was gesturing wildly with his hands now and getting visibly frustrated.

"I could be. That just depends on who I'm with," Katherine said with a soft smile, still very calm and holding his hands. "And really, Tyler, what have you got against this town anyway? This is home. We grew up here and we both have family and friends here. Where else can you say that about? Do you really think we'd be happier somewhere else just because it has bigger buildings, or fancier restaurants? Do you want your kids to even know their grandparents, their aunts, their uncles, their cousins, and everyone else who's really important to us?"

"But don't you at least want to see what else is out there, Katherine?" Tyler said, obviously restless now, like he almost wanted to get up and pace the floor. He was visibly agitated and looking around almost like he wanted a little help in the discussion, from somewhere, anywhere.

"I'm not giving up, Katherine." He stood up all of a sudden. "I've worked too hard for too long to just give up. You can't ask that of me."

"I didn't, and I'm not, Tyler. I was just asking what the plan is because I have decisions I need to make, but it sounds a lot like you've already made a decision and you just haven't let me in on it."

"What decision, I didn't make any decision," Tyler said. "What did I decide? I don't know what you're talking about."

"Can't you see this is happening all over again?" she said exasperated and finally letting go of his hands. "Look, Tyler, I just laid out the only two scenarios for our life if you make the Tour that I can envision, and on the surface at least, neither of them look all that appealing. And you say you're not giving up. Is there a third scenario you're not letting me in on? And while I believe in you, we both know even getting there is still a pretty big long shot. I told you I love you and I can wait, but when I ask what happens if you don't make it, then what? You say you're not giving up. I can't wait forever, so that sure sounds to me like you've made a decision. And unless I'm missing something, you've not only made that decision without me, your choice doesn't seem to include me."

Tyler sat back down again, obviously trying to calm down and trying to be thoughtful about what he said next. He was actually breathing heavy and Katherine couldn't exactly tell if he was angry or possibly even scared.

"I spent more than four years apart from you, Katherine," he said finally, and she realized he was trembling. "And when God finally, amazingly, somehow brought you back into my life, I was so thankful that I vowed I'd never let you go again. But when you came back to me you knew this is who I was. You say you love me and you know how important this is to me and how hard I've worked for it, but in the next breath you say all that doesn't really work for you..."

"I just want you to be realistic, Tyler, and to know exactly what," she began, but he cut her off as a solitary tear rolled down his cheek and landed on the table.

"Realistic?" Tyler replied, almost dumbfounded. "Don't console yourself by thinking that I'm the one who's made a decision here, Katherine. You were right about one thing, I've been so happy and so blindly optimistic about things I guess that maybe I hadn't thought everything all the way through, but you apparently have. You say you believe in me, but in the next breath say that who I am and who I want to be isn't realistic, or doesn't exactly work for you? You're the one who's made the decision here, and you're asking me to make a choice you know I can't make. I love you, Katherine, with all my heart, and I'd put a ring on your finger tonight if that would make you believe it... But you ask too much."

Tyler got up from the booth, wiped the tears that were now running down both his cheeks with the palms of his hands. And then he turned and walked out.

Katherine sat there for a moment, not sure exactly what to do. She felt sick to her stomach, but she didn't cry. She had spent nights up crying already over this moment, almost knowing the outcome before it happened. She had needed to know what was more important to him, being with her or being somebody. And despite the fact that she had so hoped it would be otherwise, her worst fears had been confirmed. She suddenly realized she was now the only one in the place and as old Vern walked out of the kitchen in her direction, she took a drink of her water and started to get up. It was getting late and they obviously weren't ordering so he probably wanted to close.

"You know, Katherine," he said as he walked up, almost as if they had been in the middle of a conversation that had been interrupted. "Tyler and his folks have been coming in here since he was a boy. Almost every Sunday. I've seen a lot of things in that time and watched him do his best to grow up in that awfully big shadow Jack Foster casts 'round here. Handled himself pretty well over the years all things considered, but sometimes a man's just got to make his own way."

Katherine looked at Vern disapprovingly. "Do you listen to everyone's conversations around here, Vern?"

"Look, I probably see and hear more than is good for me around here, or is really my business for that matter, but before you go running off thinking the wrong things I think you might ought to consider this… it might never have been about you. It just might have been about Jack."

Mike Dowd

AN ALL-AMERICAN BOY?

When Tyler left Vern's that night, he couldn't help but think of the irony of it all. Part of him said it was karma finally rolling around for what he'd done five years earlier. In a sense, he'd gone through almost exactly what Katherine had, just from the other side of the booth. This time she held all the cards, though, and despite her statements to the contrary, she was still pretty much telling him he needed to choose between her and everything he'd worked for and dreamed of. God, life just wasn't fair sometimes, he thought. They had really been so happy that a big part of him wanted to walk right back in and tell her fine, he'd give it all up. Anything so they could be together. But as he walked back across the brick cobbled street to pick up his car, he looked up and stopped. There, flanked by two old spotlights that illuminated it from below, was the big old wooden sign that seemed to bring all the reasons why he just couldn't back into focus. All-American Auto. The words that arched along the top of the oblong sign that mimicked the shape of a football were separated from the silhouette of two classic cars facing each other by the laces. No, he just couldn't go back.

The next few days passed with Tyler doing what he had always done when he wasn't sure what else to do. He focused even harder on his game. He worked his morning shifts, helped Jackie a bit afterwards, and then practiced or played until dark. Even well past dark on a couple of nights when he putted under the floodlights on the clubhouse until the timer went off at 10:00 pm.

He and Katherine had survived a few fights when they were younger, usually nothing terribly consequential, and their pattern in the past had been always to wait a few days until they had calmed down and then they would both apologize and make up. This was uncharted territory, though. Things had gone so well since they'd been back together that they really hadn't even had a disagreement, and somehow this felt to Tyler like it wasn't just a fight. It almost felt like they were engaged in a twisted game of chicken, with each of their lives' ambitions headed straight for each other and if one of them didn't blink the collision would tear them apart. Why did it have to be so damn black and white, he thought. Was there no compromise that wouldn't allow for them to be together, and at the same time not force one or the other to give up what was important to them? He had heard somewhere once that love meant sacrifice, and more and more he was starting to understand what that meant.

Four days after their fight, Tyler's father surprised him by calling the Pro Shop. "Son," he said once Tyler had picked up the phone. "I'd like you to have dinner with your mother and I tonight if you're free. Will that work for you?"

"Uh, sure, I guess," Tyler said, hesitating. He had been about to break down and call Katherine to ask her to meet him after work so he could apologize for getting so emotional and just leaving her there like that. There had to be a way they could come to a compromise. She wanted to know what his plan was, well he would come up with one. One that would allow them to make things work for the both of them. His father calling him was unusual, though, and something in his tone told him this was more directive than request.

"Where?" Tyler asked.

"Just at the house," Jack said, "but we hardly seem to see you before ten o'clock at night these days and I'm not staying up that late to get an appointment with you."

"Okay," Tyler said. "I'll be there. Five-thirty work?"

"That'll be fine, son."

Despite the unusual nature of his father's call, and how busy they were at the course that day, Tyler still couldn't get his mind off Katherine. He spent the rest of his shift running over potential scenarios in his head that he thought would allow them to make things work. At 2:30 when he got off, he went to the range to practice, but he was there in body only. And after an hour of beating balls he decided he wasn't really doing himself any good and just drove home.

When Tyler walked in he was surprised to find his mother wasn't there, but she'd put something in the oven. Maybe she'd run a quick errand, he thought, before he and his father had gotten home from work. Tyler felt a need to talk to his mother all of a sudden. He hadn't shared what had happened with her yet, but her mother's intuition, he knew, sensed that something wasn't quite right. She knew Katherine as well as anyone, and since she and Tyler had gotten back together he knew a week hadn't gone by where they hadn't gone to lunch or at least talked on the phone. It really wouldn't have surprised Tyler if Katherine had actually talked to her first, he suddenly thought. They truly loved each other, and, if anything, had become even closer than they were before, with Katherine often seeking his mother's advice. Tyler was saddened by the thought of what another break-up would do to them both.

When Tyler heard his mother's car roll in the driveway at just before five o'clock, he was surprised to hear his father's pull in immediately behind her. Had they been somewhere together? His father typically would have been at work until closing at 5:00 and his mother never went to the garage for any reason other than the Annual Car Show and Spaghetti Feed his father held for his customers because she would cook. Something was definitely up.

A few minutes later they both came in the house, their moods obviously a bit reserved, and Tyler's father headed straight to their bedroom while his mother went to the kitchen.

"You're early," Tyler's mother said looking a bit tired. "I won't have dinner ready for about thirty minutes or so."

"Oh, that's fine," Tyler said, but he was concerned now. Had something happened to Poppa Jack or any of his other grandparents, he thought. They obviously weren't going to talk about whatever it was until his father was ready. When they finally sat down to dinner almost an hour later, it was Jack, predictably, who finally broke the silence.

"Son, something has come up and your mother and I need to make a decision, but we didn't think it'd be right without at least talking to you about it first."

"What's going on?" Tyler asked. "I was afraid someone was sick or dying."

"No," he said flatly. He shoveled another forkful of food into his mouth while looking down into his plate and then after a moment looked up at Tyler. "Now, I know we've been down this road often enough that I think I pretty much already know your answer, but seeing as how you and Katherine look to be getting pretty serious, your mother felt it was only fair to go down it one last time... You know I bought the building the garage is in a few years back, right?"

"Yeah, sure, I remember." Tyler said, "right after I went away to school."

"Well, your mother and I thought it would be a good investment because of the rent we'd get from the space next door and because if you didn't decide you wanted to take it over I could ultimately close it and rent that space as well so we'd have at least have some income once I couldn't do it anymore."

"Yeah, I remember that whole conversation," Tyler said. "Are you really getting to that point already, Dad? Have you saved up enough money to retire? I thought that was at least another five years away, or more."

"Well, not exactly," he said, thinking on another forkful of food and then turning to Mary Jane. "This is really good, hon."'

"Thank you, dear," Tyler's mother said, speaking for the first time and then turning to Tyler. "Listen, Tyler, sometimes things happen in life that can change your perspective. I know being back here, living at home, and working at the country club isn't exactly where you thought you'd be right now when you went away to school five years ago. I also know that you weren't exactly expecting Katherine to be back here either, and the two of you to be heading down the road it appears you might be heading. It's no small secret that her and I spend time together, Tyler. I love her like she's my own daughter, dear, and I think I know what's important to her by now. A big part of why your father has hounded you all these years about taking over the garage some day is because we want you to be able to have some stability in your life and the ability to start your own family at some point. We wanted to be able to pass something on to you for your future and that's the best we can do. I know you've heard me say your father can't do this forever and you think it's just my way of saying he's getting older, but there's a bit more to it than that. He hides it pretty well, but a lot of those old football injuries are catching up to him, and arthritis is starting to make a lot of what he does every day pretty challenging."

"It's not that bad, Mary Jane," Tyler's father interjected. Tyler knew in his mind part of his father still clung to the idea that a few months of working out and he could damn near be back out on the football field, but a handful of occasions down at the garage now flashed into Tyler's mind when he'd seen his father struggling and showing his age. He'd helped out enough down there since he'd been back home to realize there was something to what his mother was saying. He definitely wasn't getting around like he used to, but Tyler hadn't really thought much about it until now.

"Is it that bad, Dad?" Tyler asked, suddenly concerned. The legendary Jack Foster had always been such a strapping imposing figure, even to his own son, that the thought of him struggling physically just to get around and do what he loved to do was suddenly both sad and shocking to Tyler.

"I'm fine," Tyler's father said suddenly and obviously uncomfortable with the direction the conversation had taken. "A few aches and pains is all, and besides, this would still be coming up regardless of whether or not I had 'em."

"What's coming up?" Tyler asked.

"A developer wants to buy the building, son," Tyler's father said, obviously tired of all the beating around the bush. "They want to buy the whole block, level it, and build some fancy new office complex. We're just down from the County Courthouse and there's a need for more office space apparently now and there's only two spaces suitable for three blocks in either direction that have been modernized or are available. They've already got the landlord for the next two buildings to agree and all they need is me."

"What will you do?" Tyler asked, having a hard time really fathoming his father without the garage and all his beloved cars. The garage was all Tyler had ever known. He'd grown up there and it was part of his family identity. And it *was* his father's identity. As much as Jack Foster was still remembered around town for his glory days on the grid-iron, he knew he was just as known anymore for the classic car shop he owned and it was something he was really proud of.

"Me?" Tyler's father questioned. "I'll be fine. It's a good offer, son, and I've been thinking of getting back into a little coaching on the side. Coach Calhoun over at the high school has a need for an assistant. It doesn't pay a heck of a lot, but I won't need all that much. Besides, nobody's got a gun to my head. I don't have to sell."

Mary Jane rolled her eyes at his last comment. "Tyler, your father's going to sell the garage and the whole building with it. That is unless you want to put a plan into place to take it over yourself. We know your goals, and we get all that and are proud of you for how hard you've worked since you've come home, but we didn't think it'd be right to just do this without at least telling you first and giving you one last chance to think about it. With Katherine back in your life now, we thought maybe your thinking might have changed. You need to really think about the future, what you want, and where you want to be. We know you're planning on going to Q-School again in a few months and that's what you've been working towards all year. But if that doesn't work out again you'll be right back where you were a year ago and really no closer to supporting yourself or anyone else."

Tyler was still having trouble digesting it all. His folks had wanted him to think about taking over the garage as far back as he could remember. Even when he was a kid his dad used to say, "Now, son, pay attention. One day this'll be all yours, so you better focus so you'll know what to do when the time comes." But golf had changed all that and even though he had made up his mind years ago that it just wasn't for him, in the back of his mind, he suddenly realized he always thought it would be there. "How long do you have?"

"A week, maybe two," his father said. "They've got options on another spot, but ours is their first choice. If I bail, though, they'll move on. They're anxious to get the project rolling."

"Look," Tyler started, "I appreciate this, I really do. It's a lot to digest, and I know you think I'll immediately say no, Dad, but..."

"We understand, honey," his mother interrupted, "but before you say anything I think it's only fair to really tell you what you'd be getting into, or giving up. We've never really talked money with you when it's come to this before and so I think you need to know the details."

She was right, Tyler thought. He knew his dad did okay, and his mother had never worked other than a stint with a catering company apparently before he was born, but they didn't really share their finances. They lived modestly, but his old man was a saver too, and not one to spend money frivolously.

"Over the past ten years, on its own, the garage hasn't netted less than $125,000 at the end of the year. That's after paying all the overhead and Denny's salary. There've been a few years where it's been close to $190,000 and its' averaged about $160,000 over that time," his mother started. "Since we bought the building, the business pays a little over $1,000 a month on the mortgage, but the space next door rents for $1,500, so it actually nets us about an extra $5,000 a year."

Tyler's eyes noticeably rounded as his mother spoke. He understood now why they felt it was important to tell him all this first. This was quite a bit more than Tyler had thought. His father clearing more than $150k per year? In Poplar Bluff that'd make him better off than most of the guys Tyler worked for at the Country Club. Working on cars and wearing cover-alls pretty much every day except Sundays, Tyler had never thought of his old man as among the better off men in town, but he realized now why his father was saying he'd be okay.

"Now that you understand what it is Tyler, here is what we're proposing," his mother continued. "Your father could maybe continue doing what he does now, with help, for another five years. Up until that point he's willing to pay you $5,000 per month if you work full-time Monday through Friday. It's a thousand a month more than what he pays Denny now, and it'll cut into our income a little, but we're willing to do that for you. After five years, your father can retire and he'll turn it over to you. At that point, if business stays as it is, that means your income will just about triple. We'd keep the building and still collect the rent off the other space for another 7 years when it will be paid off and we can start collecting social security. And ultimately, if we need the money for some reason, we'll give you the option to buy the building off us down the road. And if we don't, it'll be yours when we pass on."

Tyler swallowed hard at the thought of his parents ultimately passing on. He didn't like to think of those types of things and it had always seemed so far away, but this talk of plans and money seemed to bring it so into focus. His instinct was just to say no, like he always had, but he realized now why his parents had laid all this out for him. It was certainly true that they figured Katherine in his life again might have changed his thinking, but it was just as true that they had realized that by keeping him in the dark financially all these years they had never given him an accurate indication of what he'd be inheriting. This was a lot of money, almost twice as much as what Tyler had sort of figured in his head that his father actually made. And it could be his. All he had to do was say okay.

And then he thought of Katherine suddenly. She would be ecstatic if he settled down. They could get engaged, maybe rent a little apartment for a couple of years, but with his father paying him as much as he was saying, it wouldn't be long before he could save up enough for them to buy their own house and Katherine would certainly be working too. Everything he had railed against for as long as he could remember suddenly didn't sound so bad. He looked up at his mother who had her hands folded in front of her on the table and had pushed her plate to the center almost untouched. She was looking at him with a soft expression, almost as if she was waiting for questions. And then he turned to his father. Jack still looked uncomfortable, or irritated, as if he just wanted to get all this over with.

"I suppose a part of me just," Tyler began slowly, "just didn't really didn't think you'd ever give up the garage, Dad. You love that place."

"Well, life goes on, son," he said, suddenly looking thoughtful. "At some point we all have to say goodbye to things we love and move on to that next chapter no matter how important they are to us."

"I hope you're not offended by this," Tyler began hesitantly, "I really appreciate all this, but..."

"I told you, Mary Jane," his father burst out. "This has been a complete waste of time."

"For once will you let me just finish, Dad," Tyler said, raising his voice with his father in a way he almost never did. Jack settled ever so slightly back in his seat, allowing Tyler to continue. "I was going to say that I just have to think this through if that's okay? You have to understand how much I appreciate this offer. It's honestly more than I expected and probably more than I deserve considering the off-hand way I've dismissed the whole idea in the past. I'm really grateful you believe in me enough to make this offer. You also have to understand that everything I've done and everything I've been for the past decade has been leading towards one goal, and this wasn't it. It's a lot to digest, and I think I need to talk to Katherine."

"I think that'd be a good idea, honey," his mother said, putting a hand on his father's arm as an indication for him to calm down.

"Well, I'll just say this then," his father said, leaning over the table and looking him squarely in the eyes. "You only get so many chances in life to figure out what's most important, son. And this might be your last one. It's definitely your last chance when it comes to the garage. I'll give you a few days, a week at the most."

A BIRD IN EACH HAND

When Katherine left Vern's after Tyler had walked out on her, she resolved that it was time to take the reins of her life. She hurt, and she hurt for Tyler at the same time. She realized she had blind-sided him to a degree, and that he hadn't been ready to answer the questions she'd asked him. At the same time, she felt that if she hadn't forced the issue Tyler would have just allowed things to continue on the way they were, hoping things would ultimately work out. She needed to make some decisions. She felt like they were in limbo and they'd very likely stay there unless she took things into her own hands.

She thought about what Vern said. Maybe it had always been about Jack. Tyler's leaving in the first place, the fact that he never reached out to her, his working at the golf course, his disdain for Poplar Bluff, and the fact that he seemed so hell-bent on doing whatever it took to get them out of there, even if he had no real idea where that was. It made sense, to an extent. Tyler had always keenly felt his father's disappointment in the fact that he hadn't been cut out for football. He looked at his accomplishments on the golf course as nice, but not on the same level as he would have had he been carrying or throwing a ball instead of hitting one. Tyler had wanted to make his own way, prove to his father he could, and Jack's domineering personality had obviously played a role in that.

Despite all that, it still didn't make Katherine feel a whole lot better. Whatever his reasons for chasing his dream, he had them, and he seemed prepared to ultimately let her walk out of his life in order to continue to pursue them. She tried playing devil's advocate with herself, wondering if she was more in love with her own goals, and the idea of ultimately setting them aside on her own terms when she was ready to raise a family, then she was with Tyler? If she really loved him wouldn't she follow him to the end of the earth, as the old saying went? Or at least around on the Tour for a few years until he either made it, or made the decision in his own time that it wasn't going to work? The thought of just following any man around, even Tyler, suddenly felt so weak and old-fashioned, though, and she was a strong independent young woman now. But by pushing him to make a decision before he was ready, wasn't she setting them up for failure? Would he live the rest of his life thinking *what if* every time they got in a fight or money was tight? Had she over-played her hand?

Four agonizing days later she decided she couldn't put it off any longer. She needed to make a decision. She couldn't pass on the opportunities in front of her, they were just too good. But she was really undecided about which position to take. They both had their plusses and minuses and, despite her frustration with him, she knew she really wanted to talk to Tyler. She wanted his advice and knew she should include him in any decision that would affect their future. It was the right thing to do. They were a couple, and possibly more, and couples made their decisions together. That was at least part of the point she'd been trying to make the other night, that and the fact that he obviously didn't have a plan. And just then the phone rang...

"Katherine," Tyler said on the other end of the line. "I'm really sorry about the other night, but something's come up and I need to see you. Can you meet me somewhere?"

She paused. She suddenly realized that as much as she wanted to see him, she was still upset with him. What was so important that he had to see her right now?

"I don't know, Tyler," she began. "I've got a big day tomorrow and I'm not sure I'm ready to talk to you just yet the way you walked out on me the other night."

"Look, I'm really, really sorry about that," he said, almost hurriedly, "but I really need to talk to you right now. You were right about everything, I didn't handle it well, and you can punish me later all you want. Can you please just meet me somewhere now."

Something was definitely up, Katherine realized, something out of the ordinary. She expected Tyler would cave in and apologize at some point once he'd calmed down and thought about things, but this really didn't seem like just a ploy to avoid having to go through all that.

"Can't you just tell me what it is?" she said.

"I'd really rather not," he said. "Just meet me somewhere, anywhere. Anywhere other than Vern's that is. I think it's cursed."

She smiled at his attempt at quick humor. "Oh, alright," she said. "I've got to get dressed. Why don't you just pick me up in twenty minutes and we'll go wherever you want to go."

"Fine, and thank you," he said before hanging up the phone.

Twenty minutes later, Tyler pulled up in front of her father's house. She'd put on a pair of jeans, an old sweatshirt of Tyler's she was fond of, and just pulled her hair back in a pony-tail and so she was sitting on the porch step waiting for him when he pulled up. He had started to get out to let her in, but she waved him off and jogged around the passenger side on her own. She could take care of herself, she thought momentarily, and whatever this was about, it certainly wasn't a date.

They rode along in silence for a minute once she'd pulled the door closed. Tyler seemed far away and deep in thought.

"Where we going?" Katherine asked, finally breaking the silence.

"Huh?" Tyler said, looking over at her like he had just realized she was in the car with him. "Oh, sorry. That Mexican place over off Westwood. They've got some quiet booths in the back where we hopefully won't be interrupted by half the town."

He got quiet again, and she let him. For being so adamant about needing to talk to her, he sure didn't seem to be in much of a talkative mood. It wasn't really all that far from her father's house and less than five minutes later they pulled into the parking lot. They got out, walked in, and Tyler requested one of the booths in the back when the hostess walked up. Once they were seated, Tyler still didn't speak for a minute, ordering a couple of waters and waiting for the girl to bring them back while eating some chips and salsa she'd placed on the table as she sat them.

"Okay," Katherine finally broke the silence, "you got me out of the house, and you said you needed to talk. But it doesn't seem like kissing and making up is exactly what's on your mind, Tyler. It doesn't exactly seem like talking is even on your mind at the moment. What's up?"

He looked up at her finally, as if her question had brought him back from somewhere else.

"I'm sorry," he began, "It's just. I got some news and you're the only one I can talk to about it. Hell, you're not only the only one I want to talk to about it, it affects you too."

"What's wrong," Katherine said, suddenly concerned and getting a sick feeling at the pit of stomach. "Are you sick? My God, is your mother sick?"

"Well, no, it's not exactly like that," Tyler said.

"What is it then?" Katherine asked a bit relieved. "For a second there I thought you were going to tell me someone was dying."

"My father, … I guess his years of playing football are finally catching up to him," Tyler continued. "He can't keep doing what he does much longer and a developer wants to buy the whole building and the whole damn block for an office complex."

"Are they going to evict him? Are your parents going to be okay?" Katherine asked concerned, but still a little confused.

"No, and yes," Tyler said, "…I never told you because I'd actually kind of forgotten about it, but my dad owns the whole building. They bought it about the time we went away to college. The developer wants to buy it *from* him."

"Do your parents intend to sell?" Katherine asked, suddenly a little hurt by the fact that Mary Jane hadn't mentioned anything to her about it and that she didn't even know they owned the whole building. They were close, she thought, they talked about everything, and this was a big deal.

"That depends," Tyler said.

"Depends on what?" she asked.

"On whether or not I'm willing to give up trying for the Tour once and for all and take it over," he said in one breath like it was the most obvious thing in the world.

"Really," Katherine said. "They'd turn down developer money and give it to you? I'm sure that's a pretty big number. Wouldn't they be set?"

"I think it is, and they would," Tyler said, "but they want me to have the opportunity to be set. They want us to be set."

Katherine looked at him almost in disbelief. Was he saying what it sounded like he was saying? Was he considering it?"

"It's an unbelievably generous offer, Katherine," Tyler continued. "They laid it all out for me for the first time tonight, in financial terms. I never realized my father did as well as he does. He makes more than $150,000 a year on the average, but he just can't do it anymore like he used to. His arthritis, his injuries, they're all catching up to him. He wants to pay me $5,000 a month for five years while he takes a progressively smaller role. At that point he'd retire and give the entire business to me. They'd keep the building, until they pass, and then it would go to us, too."

"To us?" Katherine said, tears welling up in her eyes. Was she really hearing what she thought she was hearing? "W-w-what did you tell them?" she asked hopefully.

"I told them I had to think about it, and that I had to talk to you," he said.

"You had to think about it?" she almost blurted out, but then calming a bit she continued, "Tyler, I know it's not what you'd envisioned, but doesn't this change your thinking at all? That's an unbelievably generous offer. It's a future. We could settle down, buy a house, and I could afford to quit work eventually when we decide the time was right to start a family. What was there to think about?"

"Well, first of all," he said a bit shortly, "I wasn't so sure you were even speaking to me an hour ago, and despite the generosity of the offer, there isn't any part of it that sounds all that appealing to me if you aren't a part of it."

Katherine softened. "Come on, honey, did you really think I wouldn't get over you being upset the other night? I pretty much knew you weren't going to be happy when I made you think about the future, but I was beginning to think that if I or someone else didn't you likely wouldn't have, at least not for a long time. You're an optimist, and I love that about you, but that sometimes comes with a sense that everything will just work itself out whether you plan for it or not."

"I have plans," Tyler said a bit defensively. "I think about the future, and I wanted to include you in this decision. Katherine, it's just… this isn't what *I'd* been planning on. You know I love golf, and I've been working towards playing professionally for as long as my dad spent playing football. If he had never been hurt and Poppa Jack had come to him on the eve of the NFL Draft and said, come on home, son, I've got a nice position waiting for you at the nail plant, good pay, pension, real security. Come on, you might get hurt, or you could wash out in a year or two with this football thing. You and Mary Jane can settle down and raise a family... Do you really think he would have done it? Do you honestly think he would have given up on his dream for a little security?... I don't think so."

Katherine looked at him. A minute ago it seemed like everything she wanted was right there in front of them. All Tyler had to do was to reach out and take it and everything she'd dreamed about would be theirs. But she could see the turmoil in him, and that hurt her.

"Dad's given me a few days," Tyler said finally after a few moments. "Says the developer has other options down the block if he won't sell."

Katherine decided to try a different angle. "Look Tyler, I know you love golf, I get that, but with the money you'd be making you could join the Country Club yourself, not just be working for everyone up there. What do you think that playing the Tour is ultimately going to provide you, provide us? At some point everything becomes a job, and if it's financial security how is this really any different?"

"You don't understand, Katherine." Tyler looked at her dejectedly. "Do you really think I want to ride Jack Foster's coattails the rest of my life? All I've ever been around here is Jack's boy. I'm 23-years-old, Katherine, and people still introduce me that way. Hey, let me introduce to Jack Foster's boy, this is... What's your name again, son? My own father doesn't even call me by name. What are you tryin' to prove, son? What are you gonna' do with your life, son? When you gonna' help me at the garage, son? The garage is Dad's thing, golf is mine, it's the thing I can do that has always made me most proud of who I am. It's my identity, and now everyone wants me to just give it up.

"Don't get me wrong, I'm not ungrateful, I know just about every guy in this town would kill for an opportunity like this and tell me how stupid I am for even thinking about passing it up. I should have immediately got down on my knees and said yes while thanking them profusely. It makes me feel like I don't even deserve it, and the fact that I know it's what you want, what it would mean for us, for our future, don't you see how that makes this hardest of all? It feels like I've got a bird in both hands and yet I'm still intent on chasing the one in the bush."

Tyler put his head on the table and hands over his head. Katherine looked at him with a mix of love, understanding, sympathy, and disappointment, and at first she couldn't decide which emotion she felt deepest. She put her hands on his and tried to think of what to say. He'd come to her to talk about what he obviously felt was the biggest decision of his life. He said he wanted her advice, and that he wanted to include her on the decision, but it suddenly hit her that what he really wanted was her support, no matter what he decided. She so wanted to give it to him. She understood his reasoning, his ambition, his desire to stand on his own two feet, and the pain he felt at the idea of abandoning his long sought goals… But as selfish as it felt, she knew that if she told him what he wanted to hear from her, she'd be lying.

"I I don't know what to say, Tyler," she began slowly. "I think I know what you want me to say, but honestly… I can't. You've never needed to prove yourself to me, Tyler, but it sounds like you need to prove yourself to yourself… You say you wanted to include me in this decision, but in truth this decision is yours to make, and it sounds like you've already made up your mind. You know how I feel, and I know how difficult this is for you, but I guess ultimately I just can't support the idea of giving away everything your parents have worked so long and hard to provide for you. If one-upping your father is really what's most important to you, if that's ultimately what this is about, and what it's going to take to make you happy then I think you need to take me home."

He looked up at her, devastated and speechless. She knew the look. He felt abandoned, deserted by the most important person in his life. She knew it well because she'd seen it herself five years ago. Every time she looked in the mirror.

Tyler left a tip and they got up without even ordering. They walked to the car, got in, and rode the short distance back to her house without either of them saying a word. They pulled up in front of her house and he turned to her, searching for what she felt were words he didn't possess. Something he could say to change her mind.

"Look, Katherine, you're obviously what's most important to me. This isn't about my dad, that wasn't fair... Can't you see this is about who *I* am?"

"Tyler, you know I love you," she said pausing, and then turning to him, her eyes moist with tears. "But I'm not your mother, Tyler. I'm not always just gonna be here once you run out of other options. This is a chance for us to have a great life... but if that life isn't good enough for you now, I don't know if it'll ever be. Maybe I'm just not good enough for you."

"That's not true, Katherine," he said emphatically, trying desperately to grab her arm to keep her from getting out of the car.

"Don't, Tyler," she said, pulling away without looking at him. "Don't! If you need to keep chasing your father's legacy I wish you luck, but I can't stand by and watch it anymore." And then she turned back to look at him as she got out of the car. "Have you ever even stopped to consider the fact that maybe, just maybe, you actually are that legacy, Tyler?"

THE WEIGHT OF REGRET

When Katherine shut the door and walked up the path to the front porch, Tyler felt as alone as he'd ever felt. No one supported the decision he felt he needed to make. No one understood it. No one, he suddenly thought, except maybe for Mack. Mack had grown up trying to live up to his own father's accomplishments, and ultimately chose to make his own way. Not just by leaving his town, but his whole country. And ultimately he ended up alone. Sure, he had the members at the club and a few close friends he'd made over the years, but he'd never married, had no children of his own, and no family. At least not anywhere near Poplar Bluff.

The next morning, Tyler pulled Mack aside shortly after he came into the office.

"Have you got some time for me this afternoon?" Tyler asked.

"Was beginning to think ya' thought you had it all figured out again," Mack chided him.

"Well, no, definitely not, but I'm not exactly talking about working on my game," Tyler said. "I need some advice, and I think you're just about the only one in this town who can relate to where I'm coming from."

"Ah, well, sure," Mack said. "I've got a 1:30 with Mr. Jensen, but I'm free after that. I'll meet ya' on the range. I can watch ya' hit a few while ya' tell me what's on your mind. Q-School's creepin' up again and if I'm going to give ya' the week off I want to at least know you're in a good place."

"Thanks, Mack," Tyler said.

When 2:00 rolled around, Tyler grabbed his 7-iron out of his bag and headed out to the range. Even with working full-time and seeing Katherine the past ten months, he'd still managed to put in a pretty decent amount of work on his game. And with the success he experienced in the handful of mini-tour events and pro-ams he'd played, he actually felt a little better about it in some ways than he had heading into Q-School off his final year of eligibility at Vanderbilt. His senior season had been a bit of a disappointment to him, and in retrospect he thought the impending reality of all that lay in front of him after school had maybe already started to creep into his psyche. He felt different now, at least he had. With Katherine in his life, he'd felt a weight lifted, and like he had told her, that ultimately everything would just work out one way or another. When he felt he had her support, he'd been in a great place mentally. Now that she'd made it painfully clear that she couldn't stand by and watch him throw away everything his parents wanted to give him, he didn't know if he felt quite so confident. He began to fear that if he decided to put all his eggs in this basket, choosing golf over the life his parents had built for him, that even if Katherine came around and decided to support him, the weight that he felt had been lifted would return to hang around his neck like an albatross.

He took a space next to where Mack was finishing up with his lesson and began to loosen up while listening to Mack at the same time in hopes of picking up a few pointers for his own lessons.

Teaching. He was in some ways surprised to find how much he enjoyed it. He'd spent the early part of the year cutting his teeth by mostly working with Jackie, but as more and more members had begun to ask Mack about working with Tyler, he'd finally relented and let him start teaching a bit in the spring. Mack had spent some time with him prior to that, explaining things like ball flight laws and some of his philosophies on the fundamentals before turning him loose, but he'd spent enough time with Tyler over the years to understand that he had a fairly decent grasp of the nuts 'n' bolts. The members, predictably, respected how good of a player Tyler was, and they all seemed to want to see if he could pass along a little of that to them in some way.

When Mack finally finished and walked over to where Tyler was, he'd already hit about thirty balls and was good and loose.

"So what do you think?" Tyler asked, knowing that Mack, as always, had been keeping an eye on him from the next space over, even while he worked with someone else. Mack had a way of doing that. He could be working with one student and then break away for a second here or there and help someone who was struggling next to him on this side or the other, and sometimes both. He couldn't stand to see people struggle, and he wanted to help them whether they were paying him or not. Tyler liked that, and he noticed he'd adopted the same habit when he was teaching, always keeping an eye on everyone around him and quick to offer a tip or a pointer if he thought it was welcomed and would be helpful.

"It' rubbish," Mack said with just the slightest hint of a grin. "We'll need to tear it down and start over if ya' expect to even break 80 in a few weeks. Save yer' money, Tyler, so ya' can buy Katherine a nice shiny Christmas present this year. The good Lord knows she's waited long enough."

"You too," Tyler said smiling and shaking his head. "I get enough of that at home you know."

"Wayll, therr' moot be a reason fa' tha', laddie," Mack said, mocking his own accent by exaggerating it. "So what's got ya' all worked up?"

"Developer made my father an offer he shouldn't refuse to buy his garage and the whole building along with it," Tyler said.

"I see," Mack said. "And how's this going to affect *you*?"

"They don't want to sell," Tyler said. "They want me to take it over so my father can ease into retirement and then give it to me in a few years once he does."

"I sort of figured ya' wouldn't be out here with me if cars were really your thing," Mack said. "Something change?"

"No, but it's a really generous offer," Tyler said. "He makes a fair amount more than I ever figured, and, well, Katherine really wants me to settle down and, you know, buy her that shiny present so-to-speak."

"Will ya' be happy swinging wrenches all day? Can ya' be happy?" Mack asked. "I know it's all well and good for people to tell ya' what a great opportunity it is, and what you'll be giving up if ya' don't take it, but, unless ya' feel some responsibility to take it, at the end of the day ya' just have to ask yourself whether or not ya' will be happy doing that. All the money in the world won't be enough if you're miserable, and not that I speak from the voice of experience here, but I doubt you'll be much of a husband or a father if you are. Can ya' be happy working at the garage every day?"

"It's not that simple, Mack," Tyler said, continuing to hit balls all the while he was talking, as if it helped him think. "For one, my dad can't do it much longer. His body's giving out on him and my mother doesn't think he can make it much more than another five years the way he's going."

"Will they be okay if you don't take it over?" Mack asked.

"Well, they say it's a good offer, and my father says he can coach football at the high school, but I sense things will be a bit tighter financially. They're making me a great offer, but I don't doubt part of that is because it's really what they want. I know they want the best for me, but my dad built that business from nothing and he's proud of it. It's part of who he is. It can't be easy for him to admit to my mother or anyone else that he can't do it anymore and I know he doesn't want to just see it go away."

"You're getting a bit shallow," Mack said, changing the subject suddenly and putting a second ball about a foot behind the one he was hitting and an inch inside the line. He looked up at Tyler, "Now don't hit that."

Tyler hit the shot and the ball came off a bit lower and the lazy three to five yard draw he'd been hitting straightened out.

"I like that," Tyler said. "I'm gonna' use that one. With your permission of course."

"Of course," Mack said matter-of-factly. "Don't have a son of my own ya' know, and I can't do this forever either. If I'm gonna' pass my bag of tricks on to someone it might as well be you."

"There's another problem," Tyler said as he stopped hitting for a moment and looked back at Mack. "Katherine isn't exactly supportive of this either," he said while holding up his club and making a wide gesture towards the golf course, the club, and everything else around them.

Mack's eyes rounded from the half squint he typically wore to ward off the bright afternoon sun, but he didn't say anything.

"She's got opportunities of her own now," Tyler said defending her. "Good opportunities that she's let pass her by because she's been waiting on me. In a sense, she's been waiting on me for five years and wants to get on with living life. She wants a plan, a time-table, and ultimately that whole white picket fence with two kids and a dog. She's losing patience with my dream. Hell, even if I make the Tour, she's made it pretty clear that the idea of the whole lifestyle isn't something she's exactly thrilled about. All the travelling and me being away from home half the time or more. She doesn't ultimately want a part-time husband, no matter how much money I make."

"She's got a point there," Mack said. "I did the whole traveling thing myself enough to know it's not something everyone's cut out for. Did I ever introduce ya' to my friend Ray Alder?"

"I think so," Tyler said. "Isn't he a that old club pro from Cape Girardeau, the guy who can really play?"

"Yep," Mack said, that's the one. "Did I ever really tell you his story?"

"I don't think so," Tyler replied. "At least not that I remember."

"As ya' recalled, Ray could really play," Mack said. "He actually made the Tour back in the late 70's. He wasn't out there four months when he came home, homesick as an 8-year-old kid on his first sleepover. He couldn't do it, he had a wife, a young kid, and he just couldn't take being apart from them, tucking his kid into bed at night over the telephone, all that kind of stuff. He gave it up and just came home."

"Really?" Tyler replied. "I don't believe it."

"Honest to goodness," Mack continued. "I mean, ya' understand the money out there wasn't near as good back then, and he kept playing over the years while he worked as a club pro, playing in all the local stuff around the state, stuff where he could travel to in a day and be home at the end of the night. Made a nice little side income while doing it, too. Twenty some years passed and when he was about to turn 50, his members came to him and said they wanted to sponsor him on the Senior Tour just as it was really starting to blossom. The guy could still flat play, and they all figured his kids were grown, things were different, and they wanted to give him another shot at playing for a living. Well, he agreed, and he qualified right after he turned 50. Ya' know what happened?"

"What?" Tyler said, enthralled now and amazed Mack had never told him this story.

"Six weeks into the season he came back home and paid back all the members with money from the handful of royalty checks he'd cashed. He was good enough, but he hated it. Said he couldn't stand living in a hotel room, eating out every night half of the time by himself, and playing golf every day with people he didn't know and didn't really care about."

"Really?" Tyler said. "He just came home, just like that? Are you making this up, Mack? Did Katherine get to you?"

"By Saint Andrew I'm not," Mack said, holding up a palm like he was on his honor. "I'll give ya' his number if you want to talk to him. I've played with him in lots of club pro events over the years and we became good friends. The guy's almost 70 now and he can still play. Could probably teach ya' a thing or two."

Tyler went back to hitting balls, thinking on everything Mack said and everything he'd had to digest in past 24 hours. It was all so overwhelming. He felt like he'd come to an almost unexpected fork in the road in his life, and he wasn't remotely prepared to make a choice. But he was being forced to anyway and there was no going back.

"The thing about any choice in life, Tyler," Mack said, suddenly interrupting his thoughts, "is no matter what anyone says, no one can tell ya' exactly how it's going to work out in advance. But we still have to make that choice. Lewis Carrol once said, *In the end, we only regret the chances we didn't take, the relationships we were afraid to have, and the decisions we waited too long to make.* You've got a decision to make my friend, and from where I'm sittin' it seems you're going to have regrets no matter what you decide. What ya' need to figure out is which regrets ya' can live with. And then make that decision quick because if ya' wait around too long sometimes ya' find it's already been made for ya'."

"Thanks, Mack," Tyler said. "I appreciate you listening."

"My pleasure, Tyler," Mack said. "Now I've got a question for *you*. Depending upon what ya' decide, of course, have ya' settled on a caddy yet?"

"Well, not exactly," Tyler said. "I hadn't even truly decided whether or not I'm even going. Dad gave me a few days to make up my mind about the garage because the developer is going to pull his offer sometime next week if they don't give him an answer." Then he looked up at Mack with a bit of a wry smile. "Gabe called and said he's available, though, if I'm willing to give him the chance to redeem himself."

"You're not really thinking of going with the frat boy again are ya'?" Mack said, a bit incredulous.

"Well," Tyler said, "I was waiting to see if I'd get a better offer."

"…I'd be honored to," Mack said after a bit of a hesitation, "if, that is, you decide you're more a professional golfer than ya' are a mechanic."

"How's your blood pressure?" Tyler said, with a note of true concern. "First stage is four rounds, four days in a row. You sure?"

"Ah," he said, waving his hand in the air like he was shooing away a mosquito, "my little walks in the park this past year have done me good. I'm up to 7 miles a day now if ya' can believe that. Truthfully, it's a good thing ya' took Gabe last year. I might not have made it, but now, not a problem."

"Well it's settled then," Tyler said. "Now all I've got to do is figure out what to do."

***

Tyler stayed late into the evening that day, hitting balls on the range, out of the practice bunker, chipping, pitching, and even putting on the putting green until the timer on the floodlights finally clicked off at ten o'clock. He was practicing, but he was thinking more than anything. He needed to make a decision and he couldn't help but think in a way how cruel it was that all this hadn't come up a month from now, after he'd already at least given Q-School another shot. He could put his father off until evening, but tomorrow was the day he'd promised to give his parents an answer. Tomorrow's decision would change the course of his life for good. He was at that proverbial fork in the road and it was time to decide. And by the time he put his clubs in and slammed the trunk, he was pretty sure he knew the one regret he just couldn't live with.

Mike Dowd

GOODBYE MARY JANE

When Tyler dropped Katherine off that night, she was truly conflicted. It hurt that she just hadn't stood by his side. It hurt her because her heart told her she needed to stand by her man. And she could plainly see how much it devastated Tyler. But her head had won the day. The pragmatic side of her said she was looking out for the both of them, and that she just couldn't stand by and watch him throw his future, their future, away like that. She understood his desire to make his own way in the world, but she couldn't help but feel he was proving once again that his dreams were ultimately more important to him than anything else, even than she was. She'd given him a second chance, and in doing so had hoped that it was just youth and immaturity that had caused him to give her up before.

239

She'd prayed that this time he understood what was ultimately most important. And those prayers seemed to be going unanswered.

The next morning, Katherine decided she needed to go by and talk to Mary Jane about her dilemma. She had little hope that she could talk her son into changing his mind. Tyler was stubborn once he'd made up his mind. It's just that she knew there was a chance that if she held firm, and Tyler wouldn't come around to her way of thinking on his own, she wouldn't be just giving up on Tyler, but giving up the mother she had so desperately wanted for so many years. She loved Mary Jane and had talked to her on so many occasions these past nine months about life, her plans, and even about raising their family someday. She had finally admitted to herself that she had wanted Mary Jane in her life almost as much as Tyler, and if she lost them both for a second time it was going to be even more painful than the first. They had become instantly close again, and in truth Mary Jane had become like her best friend. Her strong, steady, but gentle way was so reassuring to Katherine that she found herself instantly wanting her advice in almost every situation. And she needed it now, even if that ended up being for the last time.

"Hi, Mary Jane," Katherine said when she'd picked the phone on the other end. "Have you got a few minutes if I come by?"

"Certainly, honey," came Mary Jane's concerned reply. "I've just put on a pot of coffee if you haven't already had some."

"That'd be great." Katherine said. "I'll be over in about ten minutes."

Katherine got into her car for the short drive over to the Fosters and rehearsed what she was going to tell Mary Jane. She wanted to thank her and Jack for the offer they'd made to Tyler. She knew it was more than half an offer to her, and that, considering how many times Tyler had already shut his father down on the subject, it was most likely Mary Jane looking out for their future that had talked him into giving him one last chance. Katherine so appreciated what she knew Mary Jane was trying to do for them, and she needed to tell her so, even if her son didn't. And she needed to tell her personally why she felt she would need to move on if Tyler made the decision she was afraid he was going to make.

As she pulled up in front of the house, images of all the future times she had imagined pulling up to that house flashed in her mind. She saw Sundays with the boys watching football while she and Mary Jane spent hours talking in the kitchen, making snacks or dinner while planning the details of their wedding. She saw them pulling into the driveway with Mary Jane and Jack standing at the top of the landing, Jack ribbing Tyler for the mini-van they'd traded in his precious Camaro for as he proudly produced their new grandchild from the sliding door of the second row. And she saw summer barbecues in the back yard with Jack manning the grill, Tyler running around the yard playing with their kids like just another big kid, as she and Mary Jane looked on, all the while smiling at how blessed they were. As she walked up the steps to the front porch, though, all those images seemed to fade, becoming blurry through the tears that had begun to well up in her eyes over the life she began to feel like she was walking away from.

"Come in, dear," Mary Jane said, pulling her in and wrapping her up in a long heart-felt embrace once she could see Katherine was obviously upset. She pulled back and took her in after a few moments. "Goodness, Katherine, please come in and sit. Let me get you some coffee and you tell me what's wrong."

"Oh, Mary Jane," Katherine said, wiping her eyes and walking into the kitchen with her. "I'm so sorry. I didn't want to do this." She gestured to her face and how emotional she'd suddenly gotten.

"It's fine, dear," Mary Jane said, waving her hand dismissively and handing her a cup of coffee as they both sat at the kitchen table. "Please, don't think twice about it. Just tell me what's wrong."

"Well…" Katherine said, pausing and sipping on the coffee to steady herself, "Tyler told me last night what you and Jack offered him… I know where that came from, Mary Jane, and I can't begin to tell you how grateful I am for you two being willing to give him another chance."

Mary Jane looked almost a bit embarrassed, and then she put her hand over the one Katherine had been resting on the table and looked at her. "I want what's best for my children, dear. Other than our love, it's all we really have to give, and we want you to have it. We want you to have at least as good a life as we've had."

"I know, Mary Jane," Katherine said crying unashamedly now. "That's why this hurts so much."

Mary Jane looked confused momentarily, and then Katherine's phone buzzed on the table. It was Tyler.

"Not now," Katherine said, muting it and continuing. "Has he given you his answer then?"

"No," Mary Jane said. "Jack said when he got in late last night that he wanted to talk about it tonight. Do *you* know what he's decided?"

Katherine's phone buzzed again. She looked down with irritation and saw it was Tyler again and muted it for a second time.

"Well," Katherine began, "it's probably wrong for me to say anything then, but I think…"

Katherine's phone buzzed annoyingly on the table for a third time and she reacted by just picking it up angrily and blurting out, "God, what is it, I'm trying to talk to your mother?"

She listened on the phone in stunned silence for a moment, and then said, "Okay, okay, of course. I understand." And then she hung up and looked up at Mary Jane in shock as she put a hand to her mouth.

"Mack's had a heart attack," she explained as she began trembling. "A jogger found him lying on the path at McLane Park about 45 minutes ago. He's at Poplar Bluff Regional and he's unconscious. Tyler's on his way over there now. He wants us to meet him there."

Mike Dowd

IT JUST CAN'T BE

The morning after his talk with Mack, Tyler opened the shop as usual. It was ladies' day at the club, which meant that once Mack came in at 7:30, Tyler would patrol the parking lot picking up bags and welcoming the ladies as they arrived. As soon as he arrived, Mack would take over the counter and check the ladies in. At 7:35, Tyler looked at his phone to see if there was a text from Mack saying he'd be late. It was unlike him. Mack was a stickler for being on time and it was rare he didn't actually show up early. The ladies were starting to show up and began coming in complaining about the fact that that no one was out in the parking lot to help them with their bags. Tyler was just about to call Mack when the Pro Shop phone rang. Tyler put down his own phone and picked up the golf shop line.

"Butler Bluff Country Club, this is Tyler," he answered. A woman's voice came on the line that sounded like it was coming through some kind of an intercom.

"Hello, this is the operator at Poplar Bluff Regional Medical Center. Is this the place of employment for Angus McLean?"

"Uh-yes," Tyler answered, struck almost dumb with instant concern.

"I'm sorry," came the voice on the other end, "we were trying to locate any family members and one of the EMT's that brought him in recognized him and said he thought he worked there. A jogger saw him go down on the path out at McLane Park this morning. He appears to have suffered a heart attack. Is there someone there who knows how to get in touch with his family?"

"Is he okay?" Tyler almost yelled at the woman on the other end, alerting a few of the ladies in the golf shop to the fact that something was obviously wrong.

"I'm sorry," came the woman's voice. "We need to contact the family. Do you know how we can do that?"

"He doesn't have any family," Tyler said, calming just a bit, "at least not in this country. He's my boss, my coach. I'm about as close to family as he has. He's my friend. Can you tell me if he's okay?"

"He's unconscious, sir," the woman's voice came after pausing a moment. "That's all I can say. If you know how to get in touch with whatever family he has, you should do that. He's at the new facility on Oak Grove out by the freeway."

"Okay, thank you," Tyler said, hanging up the phone. "I've got to go," he said suddenly to no one in particular.

One of the ladies who'd been standing nearby and waiting to check in looked at him concerned and asked, "What's the matter, Tyler?"

"It's Mack," Tyler said. "He's had a heart attack. He's at the hospital unconscious. I've got to go."

Tyler explained what had happened to the cart attendant who had just brought in keys for the carts and asked him to watch the counter for him. On his way to the parking lot, he alerted the clubhouse staff and the GM as to what had happened and then called the other assistant, Tom, who wasn't due in for another couple of hours and told him to come in immediately to cover the shop. Everyone was in shock, and Tyler was numb. He needed Katherine there.

As he got in the car, he hit Katherine's number on his phone. It rang twice and went to voicemail. He hit it again, knowing full well her phone didn't go to voicemail in two rings unless she'd done it manually. It went immediately to voicemail again.

"Damn it!" he exclaimed, hitting his steering wheel as he pulled out of the parking lot, "Would you pick up?!"

Tyler hit her number a third time and after a single ring Katherine picked it up and almost barked at him, "God, what is it, I'm trying to talk to your mother?"

"Mack's had a heart attack," Tyler barked back at her. "He's at Poplar Bluff Regional, the new one. I'm on my way over there now. I need you right now. Grab my mother and come down here please."

"Okay, okay, of course. I understand," Katherine said, and Tyler hung up.

The new hospital had been built in an area of new development out by the freeway interchange and was less than ten minutes away from the Country Club because of both their proximity to route 67. Tyler knew, even if they had left immediately, it would take his mother and Katherine almost twice as long to get there going through town with all the lights they would likely hit and traffic. He felt a sense of urgency, and everything Mack meant to him flooded his mind on the way over. He'd told the woman on the phone that Mack was his boss, his coach, and ultimately his friend and Tyler was suddenly and painfully aware that Mack had been all those things and more. He had taught him the game of golf for sure, but Tyler now realized that he had learned a whole lot more than golf from Mack.

While Tyler hadn't actually become aware of it until just this past year, Mack had lived a life as a young man that in so many ways paralleled his own. He understood Tyler and where he was coming from. And that was in no small part because of where he'd come from. He'd been almost like the older brother Tyler never had. Someone who he could talk to when he couldn't talk to anyone else. And aside from their fall-out over Q-School the previous year, he'd always seemed to know what Tyler needed to hear and said it in an understated way that was rarely preachy.

Tyler suddenly regretted that he'd not been even closer to Mack and that he'd not asked him more questions. Not just about his own life, but about life in general. He thought about the story Mack had told him about his life in Scotland, his own father, and how the pressures of living up to the accomplishments of his father had ultimately brought him to Poplar Bluff. And there was obviously so much more he could have learned from Mack if he'd just asked. If he'd just stopped being so self-absorbed for long enough to really pay attention. So many stories Mack could have likely still told, and so many lessons Tyler still needed to learn. Had he just asked…

Tyler pulled off the freeway and almost instantly into the hospital parking lot. He parked his car and jumped out of it awhile it was practically still moving. He ran into the emergency room entrance and walked up to the receptionist's desk

"Excuse me," Tyler asked the woman behind the glass. "I'm looking for Angus MacLean. I got a call from the operator here saying he had a heart attack."

"Let me check, sir," the woman said, "and you are?"

"I'm his," Tyler paused, considering his response momentarily after the experience he had with the woman on the phone. "I'm his son."

The woman pecked away at her keyboard for a moment and then looked up at Tyler, "I'm sorry, Mr. McLean, he's in intensive care right now. We can't allow anyone in there. I can get word to them that you're out here and have one of the nurses come out and discuss his condition with you."

"Okay," Tyler said, "I would appreciate that."

Tyler paced back and forth in front of the receptionist's desk looking mindlessly at everything from the décor to other people in the waiting room. It was a new hospital and he hadn't been here before. Everyone seemed to be either waiting to be seen, or nervously waiting for their own friends and family who were being treated for one reason or another. The mood was an odd mixture of irritation and trepidation, and the quiet concern that registered on most everyone's face seemed to say the same thing. No one had planned on being here today.

The automatic door slid open behind him and Tyler turned around to see his mother and Katherine. They had made better time than he expected, and as they walked up he realized immediately that they were both as concerned for him as they were Mack.

"What's going on, honey?" Tyler's mother spoke first, clasping his hand in hers.

"I don't know," Tyler replied looking at his mother. "They're supposed to have a nurse or a doctor come out and tell me what's happening. They said he's in intensive care."

He turned to Katherine and she wrapped him in a long firm embrace, and it was only then he realized he was shaking.

"I know what he means to you," she whispered in his ear.

"Mr. McLean," came a woman's voice, almost yelling into the waiting room.

Tyler whirled around and raised his hand. "Here," he replied, and then turning back to Katherine and his mother, he whispered, "I told them I was his son because I didn't think they'd let me see him otherwise."

Tyler turned and walked over to where the nurse stood waiting at the door, motioning for his mother and Katherine to follow. There was a small room with some chairs just inside the door.

"They're with me," Tyler said to the nurse as she held the door and indicated for him to take a seat. They sat down as the nurse closed the door. She looked down at her clipboard, and then up at him solemnly.

"Mr. McLean, your father's suffered a severe heart attack. Luckily our facility is very close to the park and paramedics were there almost instantly once we got the call from the man who saw him go down. He's in intensive care and he isn't conscious. He's on a ventilator. The next 24 to 48 hours will tell us a lot more about what his chances are."

"Will he stay in intensive care until he's conscious?" Tyler asked. "Will they move him? When can I see him?"

"As long as he isn't able to breathe on his own he'll remain in ICU," the nurse replied, "and I'm sorry, but we can't allow anyone in there. If his condition stabilizes and we can move him to a regular room, then you'll be able to see him. Are there any other family to contact?" she asked.

"No," Tyler replied, looking down. "Well, I don't really know how to get in touch with his family. He lives alone and the only family he has that I know of are somewhere in Scotland."

"You're his son?" she asked puzzled, "and you don't know how to get in touch with his family?"

"Well," Tyler said, looking up at the nurse with tears welling up in his eyes, "I'm as close as he has to a son, and I'm all he has here aside from a little dog. He never even told me what town in Scotland his family is from. I might be able to find that out if I had the keys to his house, but I don't have much to go on other than his father's name."

"I understand," the nurse said, "I'll see what I can do. Wait in the waiting room and I'll talk to the charge nurse and come find you."

As they walked back to the waiting room, Katherine put her arm in his, holding his hand as they sat quietly.

"It doesn't make sense," Tyler said to both of them at the same time, still not exactly able to process where they were, why they were there, and what had really happened. "He's been walking every day for way over a year. He was in good shape. I couldn't hardly keep up with him. He'd even offered to caddy for me at Q-School. Said his doctor gave him clearance, that his blood pressure was down and everything was fine. How does this happen?"

"It just does sometimes, honey," his mother said after a moment. "He's at an age where those kinds of things just happen sometimes, even when you're in good shape. We just need to pray for him right now and hope that they revived him in time."

Ten minutes later the door to the emergency room slid open again and Tyler's father walked in. He spotted the three of them and walked over to where they were sitting.

"How is he?" he asked, taking a seat next to Mary Jane.

"He's unconscious," Tyler said without looking up, "on a ventilator. They said the next 24 to 48 hours will be critical for him."

"I'm sorry, son," Jack said. "He's a good man, and I know how important he is to you." He looked back at Mary Jane and continued, "I called Candace. Jackie's in school and I don't know if she'd really want him here right now, but I figured they'd want to know."

"I need to call the club," Tyler said suddenly. "Everyone's waiting to know what's going on."

Tyler got up and walked away from the three of them to an area where he could make a call without disturbing anyone. When he hung up the phone, he returned and sat down in silence next to Katherine without saying a word. She put her arm around him, just pulling him in close as they sat together in silence for what seemed like hours, but might have been minutes. Just as Tyler began to wonder how long it might have been, and was about to get up and inquire about what was going on, the door to triage opened and a young nurse began walking in their direction.

"Are you Tyler Foster?" she asked.

"Yes, I am," Tyler answered, his eyes suddenly brightening with the hope that maybe Mack had awoken.

"One of our EMT's apparently knows you," she said. "He's the one who identified Mr. McLean because he apparently golfs at the club where the two of you work."

The brief hope Tyler had momentarily had faded and he just looked at her blankly and replied, "Oh?"

"This is a little unorthodox," she said, "but the only thing on him when he was found was a set of keys. If it weren't for the EMT, we wouldn't have even have known who he was. Normally this is something the police would be handling, but since we had someone here who can vouch for the fact that you are as close to a family member as he has, they've given us permission to give you his keys if you like. We don't know where he lives, but we assume he likely has a car parked at the park. If you want to retrieve that and take it to his home, you can see if you are able to locate something that will make it possible for you to get in touch with his family. We can't say for sure, but it could be quite a while before he wakes, if he does, and there's really nothing you can do here until that time. We can take your information and call you as soon as that happens."

"Thank you," Tyler said. "I think we should try to do that. I don't know if his folks are even still alive, or if he even has any siblings, but they should know if I can figure out somehow to make that happen."

"Okay," the nurse said. "If you'd come with me I'll get the keys and take down your information. We'll need to see your i.d."

When Tyler walked back to where they were sitting twenty minutes later, they all got up at once, waiting for his cue.

"Are you going straight over there, son?" Jack asked. "I called Poppa Jack and he's going to ask around the club to see if anyone knows anything about Mack's family. If any of them have ever visited him, or if he's ever told anyone anything about them that would help get in touch with them. He said Mack took some time off years ago to go home, but he doesn't remember now what that was for."

"Thanks, Dad," Tyler said. "I'm going to go to the park first. I know where he parks his car and if we don't pick it up it'll be towed by tomorrow. I'll drive it to his house from there and see what I can find."

"Can I come with you?" Katherine asked. "I can follow you in your car so you don't have to leave it at the park."

"I'd appreciate that," Tyler said, reaching out for her hand. "I'd really appreciate that." Despite all that had happened, and the uncertain situation that lay in front of them, it was her and her alone he wanted with him right now.

LETTERS FROM THE PAST

They all walked out of the emergency room and Tyler's folks headed off together, asking him to call as soon as he found something out. He agreed and he and Katherine walked to where he'd parked the car in silence.

Tyler let Katherine in, and then walked around to the driver's side, opening the door slowly and deliberately, almost as if he was in a trance. It just didn't seem real to him.

"I can't believe this," he said holding the wheel, but not even putting the keys in or starting the car. He turned to Katherine, "Why's all this happening?" He pounded the wheel with his fists all of a sudden and cried out, "God, I'm an idiot!"

Katherine put one hand on his and another around his shoulder while resting her forehead against his. "It' gonna' be okay. He'll wake up... I know it. I'm so sorry... You need to be strong right now, though. Let's go get his car and see what we can find out about his family."

Tyler started the car and they drove to the park. It was so close to the hospital Tyler wondered momentarily if Mack had originally chosen McLane Park for that very reason. Whatever the reason, he was grateful that he had because if he had been more than a quarter of a mile from the hospital help might not have gotten to him in time.

They pulled into the park and found Mack's car in the same spot it had been when Tyler had met him there almost a year previously. Tyler opened the door but left his car running, and Katherine slid over from the passenger side.

"Just follow me," he said to Katherine as he got out. "He lives in a little old house right across from the club on Westwood. If you lose me, just call."

With that, Tyler got out and went over and got in Mack's late model Acura and drove off. Ten minutes later they pulled into the long driveway to Mack's home and Tyler parked his car in its usual spot in front of the little detached garage. Tyler had been over to Mack's house a number of times, but only inside a few. He kept a plethora of old golf clubs, training aids, memorabilia, and a hitting net in the garage, which he had converted into sort of a makeshift teaching studio that he could use during the winter months if there was snow on the ground. When he was in high school, Tyler would come by and work with Mack in the garage in the winter sometimes when the weather kept them off the range, but Mack was a bit of a private person, and that invitation usually extended just to the garage. Tyler felt a little weird being here without him and told Katherine so when they got out.

"As many times as I've been here," he said, "I can count on one hand the times I've been inside and that was just to use the bathroom. He lived pretty Spartan, being a bachelor and all, and I think he was a bit self-conscious of that. He had a little teaching studio in the garage, mostly golf stuff in there if I remember, so let's check the house first."

They walked up the old front porch and Tyler fumbled with the keys until he found the right one. When he opened the door, they were met with a bit of musty smell, and Mack's little Scottish Terrier running up to meet them.

"Hey, Bogey," Tyler said, bending down to pet the excited little dog, and then turning to Katherine, "Mack comes over on his lunch to let Bogey out back to go to the bathroom. He loves this little guy. Even brings him to work sometimes when the weather is bad and it's slow."

Immediately to the left of the entry hall was the kitchen with one big picture window that looked out over the yard and across the road to the course beyond. It was plain, but neat, with little in the way of any kind of décor. To the right were a handful of hooks on the wall for coats, and then a small hallway that had a door on each side and an open door at the end. Immediately in front of them the entry opened into the living room where there was a small sofa, a recliner, and a credenza with a fairly large flat screen TV.

"I think the only time he spent here was to eat lunch, dinner, watch golf that he'd taped in the evenings, and sleep," Tyler said. "He was usually at the club six days a week, and probably would have been seven if they weren't closed Mondays."

"It's quaint," Katherine said as she scanned the walls and living room, "but kind of sad at the same time. It needs a woman's touch. It feels lonely. There aren't even any pictures on the walls."

"Like I said," Tyler said, a little defensively, "he spent all his time at the club. He had a few friends, but the members were his real family. I know a couple of the old timers he was close with would come over here sometimes and watch and talk golf with him, but that was about it."

There was a small end table by the sofa with some drawers and Tyler opened those just to find some golf magazines and the TV remote. Katherine looked in the kitchen for any sign of something personal.

"Most of the drawers in here are empty," she called back to Tyler. "There's one with silverware, another with utensils, and a cabinet with some plates and bowls, but that's it outside of the small pantry. He doesn't even have a junk drawer."

She came back into the living room where Tyler was looking through the cabinet under the TV in the credenza. He looked up to report basically the same thing.

"He definitely wasn't a hoarder," Tyler said. "He's got a lot of stuff in the garage, but it's all golf stuff pretty much if I remember. Let's check the closet and the bedroom."

They walked down the dark paneled hall and Tyler opened the first door on the right which revealed a small coat closet. Coats, a handful of boots and shoes on the floor, and a what looked like a faded old shoebox up on the shelf. Tyler pulled it down and opened it, hoping it would reveal something other than more shoes. The box was full of letters, all addressed to Mack here in Poplar Bluff by someone with a graceful spidery hand, and a few of them appeared unopened.

"This is strange," Tyler said, turning the box so that Katherine could see it. "It's a bunch of letters someone wrote to Mack from Scotland. There's only what appears to be a first initial and a last name on the return address, M. MacIntyre, and it's obviously a woman's writing. Some of them aren't even opened."

"Look at the date," Katherine said, pulling the first envelope from the box. "It's postmarked June 1985. That's more than thirty years ago."

"They all are," Tyler said, flipping through them. "They're in order by date. They go back more than a year to 1984. I think that's the year Mack started at the club."

"Only the first few look like they've been opened," Katherine said. "This is really odd. They're all addressed by the same person, obviously. Do you think we should read one, at least one that is already opened to see if we can get a first name? We've got the address, but who is it?"

"I don't know," said Tyler. "It seems kind of private. Let's set it in the living room and see what else we can find first. Let's check the bedroom."

The rest of the house revealed very little. The bedroom was furnished just as minimally and, aside from a plethora of golf clothes and more shoes, they found little in the way of anything you would call very personal with two small exceptions. There was a large framed map of Scotland with dots and names next to all the golf courses apparently in the country. It was unbelievable, Tyler thought. It appeared that every village in the small country had a course, and some more than one. What a place to be raised, Tyler thought. No wonder it seemed that everything in his life was about the game. On the map, a small red dot had been placed next to the Craigewan Golf Links.

"What was the name of the town on the return address of those letters?" Tyler called out to Katherine who was in the bedroom.

"Aberdeen something or other," she said. "I think there was something else on it too and a bunch of odd letters and numbers. Let me look again," she called as she walked back into the living room where the box was. She came back with the box, reading one of the envelopes as she did, "M. MacIntyre, 37 Blackhouse Terrace, Peterhead, Aberdeenshire Scotland, and then a bunch of letters and numbers."

"Look at this," Tyler said. "There's a small red dot next to the Craigewan Golf Links. It's right next to this town called Peterhead. I'll bet that's where Mack is from. Who do you suppose M. MacIntyre is?"

"Her," Katherine said, holding up a small handful of photos. "I found these in the nightstand. There's only a few and they're all old. Looks like they were taken in Scotland. She's very pretty, and this one sitting on the hood of a car has to be her with Mack. He was a pretty handsome young man thirty plus years ago. The back of the small portrait has Mairi printed on it."

Tyler looked through the handful of photos of the pretty young red-headed woman that had somewhat yellowed with age, and then the final one with Mack in it. What exactly did this all mean, he thought. Who exactly was this young woman?

"I guess the only way to find out for sure is to open one of those letters," Tyler said, "but I don't know if that's exactly right. We could look up that club, get a number, and call and see if anyone knows or knew Mack's father, mother, or his family. His parents would likely be dead by now, but someone might know if there's family about."

"Maybe," Katherine said, "it's worth a shot. And then if you don't get anywhere I suppose you could open one of the letters."

Tyler pulled out his phone and began searching the internet for the club and any information about it. After a few minutes, Tyler looked up and said, "Apparently the Craigewan Course is part of the Peterhead Golf Club, but I just realized it's like six or seven hours ahead of us. It's evening there so they'd likely be closed by now."

He hit something on his phone, waited a few moments, and then looked back up at her.

"Nothing, just a funny buzzing," he said. "Now what?"

"I don't know," Katherine said. "If he wakes up and we went through his things to try to find some way to get in touch with his family do you think he'll be upset? I mean, this seems pretty personal," she said holding up the box. "But what else do we have to go on? Do you want to look through the garage first? Maybe he keeps some things out there."

"Alright," Tyler said after getting briefly choked up at Katherine's statement about if he wakes up. "Let's check there first. I don't remember a lot of things in there outside of golf stuff, but there could be. It's been a while."

They went out to the garage. "It wouldn't be like Mack to be really upset with me, considering we were trying to get a hold of his family. I mean, he's a private person so he might be more embarrassed than anything, but I don't think too upset."

Tyler opened the side door of the garage with one of the keys and flicked on the light. There was a single uncovered bulb hanging from a fixture in the ceiling that illuminated the garage rather poorly, keeping the perimeters almost in shadow.

"It this all the light he has in here?" Katherine asked.

"Well," Tyler said, "when it was just raining, and not too cold, he'd just roll up the door and let the daylight in. There used to be shop light too, though, for those times when it was too cold to open up the door. Let me open it and we'll get some more light in here."

The old hitting net was still in the same place Tyler remembered. There was a desk and chair adjacent to the net where Mack liked to sit and take notes while watching his students, and there was a line of clubs along the wall opposite the small door that had been arranged by sets. He rolled up the door and the flood of light revealed little more than that, but allowed for at least a little better inspection.

"You're right," Katherine said. "He definitely wasn't a hoarder, unless you count golf clubs. There must be a dozen sets here at least."

"Mack kept every set he ever played," Tyler said. "Too many memories to ever part with he once told me. They're like old friends, he said, and you never know when you want a visit with an old friend. He'd hit them sometimes too, at least in here, and tell a little story about a shot he'd hit one time with this club or that, where he was, what the situation was. He remembered them like they were yesterday. He'd say, *when you're really present, Tyler, you can remember every shot from every round,* and he'd quiz me sometimes about a club I hit on a certain hole in a tournament weeks earlier just to see if I could remember, and if I couldn't, he'd shake his head and say, *remember, Tyler, if you can't remember you won't learn from your successes or your mistakes.* He was funny like that. A lot of his coaching was similar. I mean he'd tell me things about my swing now and again, but less and less as the years went on. In retrospect, I think I mistook the fact that Mack wasn't telling me much about my swing once I went away to college for him not having much left to say he hadn't already said. Now I think it was more because he knew the things I most needed to learn at that point didn't have much to do with my swing."

Katherine picked up a few of the clubs leaning against the wall, looking at them and putting them back in their exact spot. "Are these really all the clubs he ever played?" she asked.

"As far as I know," Tyler said. "At least that's what he told me. I mean there aren't any junior clubs here so I don't think he kept those, but he showed me the first set he played in competition when he was in his early teens and they're all the way to the right. He kept them in order. Occasionally he'd bring out one of the old putters and put it into play for a while, but once he retired a set it stayed retired in his own little personal museum here."

"Let's take a look in the desk," Katherine said. "There aren't even any boxes or file cabinets out here. No old trophies or awards?

You'd think if he was such a great golfer when he was younger he'd have had a bunch of that stuff."

"Left it all behind," Tyler said. "I asked him the same question once when I was first starting to compete. I think I wanted some sort of proof that he really knew what he was talking about and he said something like, *all that rubbish is just for show, Tyler. I don't have anything to prove to anyone, I play for me and me alone.* I found out last year his father was a champion golfer and the pro of their club. He apparently kept a huge display case in the house with all their golf trophies and awards. He let his parents keep all that stuff there along with all his father's when he left for the U.S. I think it just made him keenly aware of the fact that he'd never measured up to his father's accomplishments and he didn't want the daily reminder."

Katherine opened the desk drawers and began rummaging through them. Most of what she found were old golf magazines, note-pads with Mack's blocky printing on them and diagrams about things related to the golf swing, pens and pencils, and a flashlight. In the bottom-most drawer she came upon a huge dark brown leather-bound journal that was tied closed with a heavy integrated gold ribbon. She brought it up on the desk and turned to Tyler who had become distracted with some of Mack's old clubs.

"Here's something interesting," she said.

Tyler turned to her and his eyes grew wide at what she had.

"That's Mack's bible," he said. "I saw it once when I walked in on him reading something from it and he didn't realize I was there.

He said it came from his father, but it was his to finish. It's thoughts on the game, playing the game, teaching, and little bit of their lives as well if I remember. I only saw it once, sometime last winter, and he didn't really let me look at it so much as just showed me a few pages… I'd forgotten about it, and I'd never seen it before or since."

Katherine untied the ribbon carefully and began turning the pages. It was hand-written, with hand-drawn diagrams, mostly, and the occasional old article from one golf publication or another folded and neatly tucked into the page. The initial pages were in a bold, formal looking script.

"That has to be Mack's father's writing," Tyler said, and when they had turned a page that apparently ended a section it was signed, Colin McLane.

She turned a few more pages and there was a yellowed black and white photograph tucked in the between the pages.

"That's Tony Jacklin," Tyler exclaimed, pointing to the individual on the right in the picture. It was a picture of two men laughing, the larger of whom, on the left, had one arm around the shoulder of the smaller, while pointing with his club to a small boy of maybe seven hitting a ball ferociously on a driving range somewhere. "He's a famous British golfer. I wonder if that's Mack's father on the left. He said he was a big man."

"You think Mack is the kid?" Katherine asked.

The photograph had a date stamped on the white border. 1962.

"That'd be about the right time," Tyler said, doing the math in his head. "I think Mack is 63 this year."

They thumbed through many more pages and didn't find anything anymore revealing. At one point, about a quarter of the way through the almost four-inch thick tome, they came to an almost entirely blank page that just said 'Part II', and then the following pages changed to what was obviously Mack's writing. Mack had obviously invested more time in putting down his thoughts on the game than his father had because it filled about eighty percent of the pages that had something written on them, but then Tyler thought about the fact that Mack had likely possessed the journal quite a bit longer than his father had. Still, there was little more than golf swing thoughts, thoughts about the mental game, famous quotes and ancient wisdom. Tyler couldn't help being fascinated with it, though, and found himself wanting to really sit down and delve into it, but he remembered that Katherine likely didn't understand much of it and the fact that it wasn't the real reason why they were here. He put the journal down on the desk and looked up at her.

"I could read this stuff all day," he said a bit sheepishly, "but I don't think it's really getting us anywhere."

It was now almost three o'clock in the afternoon and Tyler had not only begun to realize he was getting a little hungry, but he felt bad about not checking in with Katherine about it. She was here for him, had been amazingly understanding, and he didn't want to take that for granted.

"I'm sorry, Katherine," he said "with everything that's happened today I've completely lost touch with the time and I don't even know if you needed to be somewhere or if you want to eat. I'm so sorry, I…"

"Tyler," she said, cutting him off, "I'm a big girl. I can take care of myself. This is important. I'll let you know if I need something. I know it's personal, but I think we need to take a look at those letters. Unless there's a basement or attic I'm not aware of, I don't think we're going to find anything else out here other than golf tips."

Tyler just stared at her, emotion welling up in his eyes, and then reached out and hugged her so tightly he was almost embarrassed when he finally let go.

"Sorry," he said pulling away slightly to look her in the eyes, "but thank you. You're right. Let's go have a look."

Tyler closed up the garage and rolled down the door and they went back into the house. Katherine grabbed the shoebox with the envelopes off the small end table where she'd left it and they sat down on the small sofa. She pulled the first one that had been opened, the oldest dated letter, from the box and opened the flap carefully to reveal the hand-written letter and slid it out gently. She looked up at Tyler, took a deep breath, and then began to read aloud.

Angus,

It has been almost three hours since you left and I can't begin to tell you how much I miss you already. Selfishly, I still wish you were willing to just wait for the day your father retires, but please know how much I support you despite my last minute display of weakness. I know it's a great opportunity, one you might not have gotten here for years. I just wish you didn't have to go all the way to America for it. I am looking at the beautiful ring you gave me as I write this and I know, as you say, it will be the little piece of you that I carry with me each day that keeps me going until we can be together again. My father was terribly upset when he found out about this whole idea and thinks you should have told him yourself that you were leaving and what our plan was. If you don't at least come back so we can have the wedding here in Peterhead, I'm not sure he'll ever speak to me again, but you know Daddy. He'll come round. I don't know how long I can stand this, so I'll be saving every schilling of my tips and praying you win a tournament or two in your off time so I can come be with you just as soon as possible. Please tell me that won't actually take a year like you said it could. In truth, I am excited for you, and excited to hear everything about Missouri. Such a funny name. I think I will miss the sea, but as long as you're there I'm sure it will feel like home. Please write back as soon as you get there and tell me all about it. Love you,

M.

"Wow…" Tyler said, digesting it all as Katherine looked up from the letter, "Mack had intended to bring his fiancé over here with him eventually. I wonder what happened. I never heard anything about Mack being married, or even having a fiancé for that matter, but this was before we were even born. I don't even remember him dating as far as I can recall. I remember some of the ladies at the club tried to set him up last year and he just politely declined. I teased him a little at the time, but he was kind of sensitive about it so I just let it drop. He said something odd like, *I'm sure she's a nice lady, Tyler, but that ship has long since sailed for me."*

"She signed it M," Katherine said, holding up the small handful of photos, "just like on the return address, so we can't say for sure, but I'd bet a million dollars these are her."

"Makes sense," Tyler said. "Let me look something up."

Tyler did a Google search on his phone for the name Mairi MacIntyre in Peterhead Scotland. After a handful of moments, he looked up at Katherine a little frustrated.

"Appears that MacIntyre is about as common in Scotland as Smith is here," Tyler said. "And the same goes for the first name Mairi."

"What do you want to do, Tyler?" Katherine asked. "There are plenty more letters here, and we can read them all in hopes of a few clues. But if she signed them all 'M', it won't give us much to go on."

Tyler considered for a moment, and then said, "Let's just look at the other opened letters and if we don't find anything more we'll wait until morning and I'll try and call the club over there to see if anyone knows anything that could help us get in touch with his family. I feel a sense of urgency I can't explain. But then you may be right. This may not get us anywhere."

Katherine opened up the next letter and began to read.

Angus,

I really wish it wasn't so expensive to call, but since we're supposed to be saving up every last bit for the wedding and our reunion, I guess I'll have to settle for writing more letters. It's hard not to be able to talk to you every day and you can't know how reassuring it was to hear your voice last week. I'm so happy to know you're settled and that things seem to be going well at your new club and that the people have been so welcoming. Mr. Williams was very generous to give you this opportunity and I hope that you are planning on giving him free lessons for life or something similar. Poplar Bluff sounds like a very pretty old town, and at least they've an Episcopal Church to help to make it feel a bit more like home. Aside from golf, though, things sound so foreign there. The football you say they play seems very strange, and baseball? What's wrong with cricket? Mum and Daddy really want to know when we're going to set a date for the wedding now that we've announced it. Do you think we can plan for the fall? I know coming home will cost you some of the money you've saved for me to come over and may put that off a bit longer than we both want. Mum says we need a proper wedding, though, one with all our friends and family about, and I have to say that I'm starting to agree. I can't wait to be your bride, Angus, but I want to share that special day with everyone we know and love, not a gaggle of strangers. I'll have plenty of time to get to know all your new American friends once we've been married. Speaking of friends, Thomas says hello. He started working at the pub a couple of weeks ago and misses having a pint with his best mate. He'll be your best man, right? Alright, I've got to get ready for my shift, dearest. Bye for now, and love you,

M.

Katherine looked up at Tyler when she finished the second letter. "This one was dated only about three weeks after the first one. They obviously had talked on the phone at some point and it sounds like there may have been other letters, too."

"Sounds like Mack wanted to bring her over as soon as possible and get married here," Tyler said. "But her family obviously was pressuring them to do otherwise. I can't imagine they were too excited about her moving so far away."

"Sounds a little like she was having doubts to me," Katherine said as if she was contemplating something and then continued, "she mentions how foreign things sound and while she says she can't wait to be his bride, she also says she wants to be surrounded by the people they know and love… I think I can relate to that."

Katherine looked up at Tyler as she said this, as if she wanted to see understanding in his eyes. He knew what she was referring to and didn't want to make a mistake so he chose his reply carefully.

"I think you're right, Katherine," Tyler said. "And that goes for a lot more than just these letters."

She smiled at him in a way that lit up her entire face and then leaned into him as she pulled out the next letter.

"This one is dated about six weeks after the last. It must be multiple pages, it's much thicker than the last two," Katherine said as she pulled it out, and then gasped. "There's a ring folded up in it!"

Katherine pulled out a small thin silver band that looked as if it was woven into knots and had a single round cut diamond in it. She held it out for Tyler to hold and look at as she unfolded the letter and began to read.

Angus,

So much has happened in the past six weeks that I find it hard to explain it all. I tried to on the phone when you called a couple of weeks ago, I really did, but you were so upset that I didn't want you to just come over as soon as possible and I didn't have the heart to disappoint you even further at the time. I honestly am not as strong in my resolve when I'm actually talking to you because hearing your voice makes me weak. Where do I begin… I truly believed in my heart of hearts when I told you I loved you and said that I would marry you, that no distance between us could ever change that, and that it wouldn't matter where we were ultimately because home would be wherever you were. What I didn't understand, Angus, is how hard it would be to be apart from you and how important everyone else here was to me until the thought of leaving them all behind became more and more of a reality. It sounded very exciting to come to America, at first, but I realize now it was the kind of excitement that one has when they're anticipating going on holiday. I'd like to visit, I really would, but I know now I don't want to live there. This is my home, Angus. The Old Blue Toon, with its weathered stone streets, it's fish markets, the boats, the pub, the people, the sea. I belong in Peterhead, Angus, I know that now, and I'd be a fish out of bleedin' water were I anywhere else.

I feel dreadful doing this, and for agreeing to marry you and follow you to America because a part of me says that had I not maybe you wouldn't be there. Maybe I should have tried harder to talk you into staying and working for your father, and we could have had a proper wedding and been happy together right here. That is my heart speaking, though, and my head tells me that your mind was made up, and you were going with or without me. It might have made that decision a little easier in the end to believe I was going to follow you and that you wouldn't ultimately be alone, but you're a strong man, Angus, and once you've made up your mind you've made up your mind. You'd have ultimately made that decision anyway and I'd still be right where I am now. And I won't fool myself into believing that I can talk you into coming back. I know that ship has sailed, Angus. You've charted a course for your life that is your own. You needed to make your own way, I understand that, and you're doing it. No one can take that away from you and I know that just as you've moved on from your life here, you'll ultimately move on from us too. I need to believe that because it makes it easier to do what I have to do, and what I know is the right thing.

I will always love you, but I am giving you up and giving your ring back, Angus. It is a beautiful ring, but I don't deserve it. So before I go, and before you call or come rushing back to try and talk me out of this decision, I need to tell you something else I've figured out so you don't. I know this is selfish, but I realize now that I need someone who is so devoted to me that that is enough to make their life complete, and that includes being here. You've seen the world beyond now, Angus, and Peterhead will never be good enough for you again. I will never be good enough for you.

Your family and I are not the only ones you left behind. Angus. Almost since the day you were gone I've watched, at first from afar, how much it hurt your truest friend, Thomas. You two were thick as thieves from the time you was lads and he looked like an absolutely lost puppy round here once you'd gone. At first, I thought I understood it because I missed you just as much and took it as natural because of what a good friend you'd been to him. Once he started working at the pub, though, and I came to know him much better. I began to realize what it said about him, and the type of devoted person he was and the true friend he'd been to you. He sat round here many nights, long after closing, like he had nowhere else to go, and waited to walk me home because he said it was the least he could do for his best mate since you couldn't do it yourself. He looked after me because you couldn't.

Now before you go thinking what I know you're thinking, he's been totally honorable, and never once made any kind of a move on me, and if you really know how good of a friend Thomas was to you, you'd likely know that. At first, it made me wish I could find someone to set Thomas up with because he is such a good man and deserves to be with someone special. I kept trying, but he resisted, and the more I got to know him the more I realized that I didn't know anyone that I believed was good enough for him. And the more I began to understand that, the more I began to realize something else... I wanted to be with him. As honorable and devoted a friend to you as he is, though, I know he will never consider being with me because of his loyalty to you. Now that I've seen it, I know that type of devotion is what I need, Angus, and while I feel wretched telling you all this, I know now that I could never be that to you or you'd still be here.

So, that is where I am, Angus. I can't be with one man I love because he doesn't want to be here with me and I can't be with the other because he loves the first one too much to even consider loving me in return. It's a fine mess, and one I guess I'll have to sort out on my own, but please please please know this. I wish you all the very very best of everything in this life, Angus, and I truly hope with all my heart that you'll have an easier time dealing with all of this on your end than I have on mine. This has been by far the hardest thing I've ever done in my life and I know now I'll never be the same because of it. Hoping that you can,

M.

Katherine stopped reading and realized only then that tears had begun to roll down her face. "My God this is so sad," she said looking up at Tyler, who wiped the tears from her cheeks with his thumbs. "Despite what she says, it doesn't appear that he ever moved on."

"I had absolutely no idea," Tyler said looking at her, then the ring and the letters. "I wonder whatever happened to her. As far as I know he's never had any visitors from Scotland, and he didn't make practice of going back to visit."

"She wrote at least four more letters after this, Tyler," Katherine said, "over the period of almost another year. And he never even opened them. I don't understand it. Did she change her mind, regret giving him up, want to come over after all? You'd think he would want to know, but it's like he just kept filing them away in this box until she finally gave up."

"Maybe it was too painful," Tyler said. "Maybe he was afraid to hear she'd moved on when he couldn't. Maybe he was afraid his best friend broke down ultimately and she was going to marry him. I think I understand… they both wanted someone that loved them enough to give up everything to be with them. Seems they both figured out at some point that the other one wasn't the person they had hoped they were."

Katherine sat there a moment as if she was processing what he said, and then looked at him like she wasn't completely buying it. "I don't know. I get what she was saying in that last letter, but it doesn't add up. Why would she keep writing if…" she said, letting it trail off. "Oh well, unless you've changed your mind about opening the rest of the envelopes, though, I think we should go for now and you should try calling that club in the morning. We've learned something about Mack's past, but I don't think we're any closer to finding out how to contact his family, and seeing as how they haven't exactly kept in touch on either side maybe that's how he wanted it. I think you're pretty much his family now, Tyler. You and Jackie and all the members of the club."

They locked up the house and walked back to Tyler's car in silence. It was almost evening now, and it had finally occurred to Tyler that he had been supposed to meet with his folks about his decision on the garage tonight. He sensed Katherine knew what was going through his head and just wasn't saying anything. With what had happened to Mack, she was letting it lay for now, but he wasn't so sure his father would, or could for much longer.

WISDOM AND WISHES

Tyler and Katherine hadn't been in the car more than a minute and had just gotten back on the road when his cell rang. It was the hospital.

"Yes, this is Tyler," he said as he pulled over to the side of the road while listening to the voice on the other end. "Okay, thank you. Thank you so much for calling."

"He's stirring," he said, looking hopefully at Katherine. "That was the nurse. He opened his eyes a few times. He seems disoriented, she says, but that's normal. She thinks it would be good for someone he knows to be there because his vitals have stabilized a bit and they'll be taking him off the ventilator as soon as he regains full consciousness. They may even move him from ICU into a regular room tonight."

Tyler turned the car around and headed back towards the freeway, and then turned to her thoughtfully, "Would you mind going and being there with me?"

"I wouldn't want to be anywhere else," she said, putting her hand on his.

They drove back to the hospital while Tyler called his mother on the way to update her on what was happening and the fact that they'd learned relatively little about Mack's family that was of any use. When they got to the hospital, they asked for the nurse that had called at the front desk of the emergency room and about five minutes later they were summoned back into the room they had sat in before to talk with the charge nurse.

"The cardiologist on duty this afternoon says that the immediate danger of Mr. McLean's situation has passed," the nurse who came in began as she sat down in front of them. "However, he has suffered a very serious incident and damage to his heart. His vital signs have progressed enough that he feels we will be able to transfer him to a room in the cardiology department within the hour, at which time you would be able to go in and see him. He hasn't attempted to speak yet, but he's nodded and acknowledged that he understands what happened to him."

"When you say he suffered damage to his heart," Tyler asked, "what does that mean? Will he be able to make a full recovery?"

"That's something best to ask the cardiologist about," she said. "Right now we're just concerned about getting him stable. I can tell you I don't think he'll be leaving the hospital anytime soon, and at times patients in his condition can have a follow-up incident so we will be monitoring him closely. But once he's settled in the room and fully alert, we think it'd be good for him to see a familiar face or two. Like I said, it should be inside the hour and we'll come get you as soon as that happens."

"Thank you," Tyler said. "I really appreciate it."

"Were you able to locate and contact any of his family?" she asked as she got up to let them out.

"No," Tyler replied. "Unfortunately we didn't have much luck as yet. I think we're his family, at least for the moment."

They walked back and took a seat in the waiting room.

"I don't like the sound of damage to his heart," Tyler said, running his hands through his hair and looking down at the floor worriedly. He looked up at Katherine and spied a small room with vending machines in it just over her shoulder at the far end of the waiting room.

"Can I interest you in dinner, Ms. Anderson," he said suddenly, forcing a small smile as he nodded in the direction of the room.

"Sure," she said smiling back at him, "as long as you're buying. I don't even have my purse."

They chose a handful of things to share, a soda and cup of coffee for Katherine, and went back to the waiting room and began eating like they hadn't in a week.

"Well, I guess that's at least a little better," Tyler said as they finished the last of a bag of chips.

"Assuming he's communicative and understands what's going on," Katherine said suddenly. "Do you think we should ask him about family?... And do you think we should tell him we read those letters? Those things might upset him, but if Mack's as private as you say, maybe he does keep in touch with someone back in Scotland and you just don't know it. It could be just over the phone, or via email. I didn't see a computer in his home, but I assume he's got one in his office. What if his parents are still alive, or he has a sibling, a cousin, anyone?"

"Yes, Mack has a laptop that he often takes back and forth from the office to his house," Tyler said. "For someone who seems pretty old school, he's surprisingly computer savvy, but I don't know if he uses it to keep in touch with anyone. Let's wait and assess his condition before we ask him anything, but I think we should keep the fact that we read those letters to ourselves for now. I'm not sure how he'd feel about that. I'm just relieved that he's awake."

They sat there for another twenty minutes while Tyler related a handful of stories about Mack that he remembered from over the years and the little things he seemed to just now realize that Mack had either done or said that had ultimately shaped how Tyler viewed a lot of things in life.

"You know, I'm not sure I ever really appreciated what a big influence he's been on me," Tyler said at one point. "I mean, in my mind I guess I always just thought of him as my golf coach, and my boss this past year. But only now do I really realize how much of what I learned from him had almost nothing to do with golf."

"Well, I've always been aware of it even if you haven't," Katherine said smiling and looking at him in mock exasperation. "For years all I heard was Mack said this, Mack said that, or Mack thinks this. I remember thinking at one point when we were back in high school that all your dad really had to do was change his name from Jack to Mack if he really wanted to talk you into taking over that garage."

Tyler laughed genuinely for the first time in a while. The fact that Mack was at least awake had lightened their moods a bit and they were just enjoying each other's company.

Their moment was interrupted by a voice from the door leading back to the ER. "Mr. Foster?" came the call.

Tyler and Katherine got up quickly and headed in her direction.

"He's been moved," the nurse told them as they approached and she held the door for them to step back inside and motioned for them to sit down. "This is Dr. Stephens, he's the cardiologist on duty. He can tell you a bit more before you head up."

A tall, thin, salt and pepper-haired man in his mid-fifties stepped forward and shook both Tyler and Katherine's hand.

"Mr. McLean has suffered a serious cardiac incident," he began. "He was unconscious for quite a while, and while we were able to revive him and he's stabilized, he's by no means out of the woods. His heart is significantly weakened and he's at risk for another incident in the short term. We've moved him to a room in the Cardiology Ward for now. At the minimum we are likely going to have to schedule him for surgery, once we assess how soon he can handle it, to introduce multiple stents to insure normal blood-flow in some areas. I will be consulting with other members of our staff, however, there is also a strong possibility that he may need open-heart surgery as well."

"Really?" Tyler responded. It suddenly sounded much more serious than he had hoped. "He can recover from all this, though, right?"

"Well, that depends upon your definition of recovery," the doctor said. "It's a little too early to say exactly what percentage of recovery he can expect to experience if things go well, but I will say that something approaching even an 80-90% recovery is unlikely. This was a life-changing incident and if he makes it through, he will be forced to make significant changes in his life and his lifestyle. We can hope for the best, and a lot of it will be on him."

"Can we go in and see him now," Tyler asked. "Is he awake, alert, does he know what happened to him?"

"Yes, you can. He's been responding to the nurses, albeit slowly. He's spoken a handful of words since he's been off the ventilator and even cracked a small joke. We've told him why he's here and what happened and he seems to not quite remember the incident yet. The important thing at the moment is to understand that he's in a delicate state right now, and while I believe it will be comforting to him to see familiar faces, it's not a good idea to get him too excited so I would try to be as reserved as possible and refrain from talking to him about subjects in which you know he may have a strong reaction."

"Okay, I understand," said Tyler. "Where do we go?"

"It's on the second floor," the doctor said. "Nurse Jenna will show you. You'll have to check in with security right before the elevator."

"Thank you, doctor," Tyler said, and they both got up and followed the nurse down the hall towards the elevator and awaiting security guard at the desk. He gave them adhesive name tags with the patient's name and room number on them and they headed up. When they got to the next floor, nurse Jenna handed them off to another nurse and gave her instructions as to who they were there to see. They followed her down the hall past a nurse's station where a half-dozen others were working, and then made a quick left into the first open door past the station.

Tyler wasn't quite prepared for what he saw. Mack was in the room, apparently sleeping, with his head rolled to the side opposite the door. He was hooked up to all sorts of monitors that were beeping indiscriminately and an IV. Sitting there hooked up to all that equipment and in a hospital gown, he seemed a shell of his former self, even though Tyler reasoned that he couldn't have really lost any significant weight since the day before.

"Mr. McLean," the nurse said softly, "there's some folks here to see you. Are you still awake?"

Mack turned his head very slowly in their direction and opened his eyes. At first he looked a bit confused, as if it took a moment for his eyes to come into focus, but as recognition crept over his face, a warmth came along with it.

"Appears I'm not in as good of shape as I thought, Tyler," he said and then smiling ever so slightly he continued, "Ya' may need to find someone else to caddy for ya' in a few weeks after all."

And then, as if he had just realized Tyler wasn't alone, he turned his head a little more.

"Oh, hello, Katherine. It's good to see ya'," he said smiling weakly. "I trust you're taking good care of this wayward boy for me?"

"Doing my best," she said smiling back at him. "You know how stubborn he is though."

Mack smiled and almost laughed a little in response, but it appeared that just speaking was a bit of an effort, so he saved his strength.

"It's just good to see you awake," said Tyler. "How do you feel?"

"Oh," Mack started, then paused as if he was looking for the right words. "I guess I feel about like ya' do when ya' come into eighteen one under and double the last to shoot over par... a bit deflated ya' might say."

Tyler chuckled knowingly and Katherine rolled her eyes in mock exasperation.

"You two never stop thinking about golf, do you?" she said.

Mack did laugh this time, but it was a weak laugh that he seemed to realize wasn't the best idea so he cut it short.

"Mack," Tyler decided to risk, "I'm not sure how exactly to ask this so I just will. Is there anyone you'd like us to contact to let know you're here and what happened?"

Mack stared up at the ceiling with the question and his eyes got a bit far away. He didn't look back for a long moment, and when he finally did, it looked as if his eyes had gotten a bit watery.

"No," he finally said, and then when Tyler had just about decided he was going to leave it at that, he continued, "Outside of y'all, Jackie, and everyone at the club, whom I imagine have heard about this by now, I can't really say that I do. I mean, there's a few golf buddies I have who might like to know, but no family anymore if that's what you're asking... My parents passed on years ago, and I had no brothers and sisters, and only one cousin I know of, but I haven't heard anythin' from him in more than twenty years. My life is here, and I can't imagine anyone else I once knew back home would really even remember me at this point, or much care even if they did."

"Okay," Tyler said, seeing it wasn't exactly easy for him and deciding to let it go. "I just wanted to make sure you knew I will take care of whatever you need for now and if that means contacting anyone you just let me know who, where, and how."

"Ya' could go feed Bogey for me," Mack said, looking suddenly concerned. "How long's it been since..."

"It's okay," Tyler said. "They gave me your keys. We went and got your car and I already stopped by the house and made sure Bogey was taken care of. It's been less than a day. He's fine, but if you think he'll be lonely I can bring him home until you're out of here. Mom's always there and she'd be happy to keep him for a while."

"Thank you, Tyler," he said. "And work? Have ya' got things handled there, too?"

"Yes," Tyler said. "I've already spoken to Tom, and he and I will cover it for now and we've got Kevin outside who can man the counter in the afternoons if we need him. You don't need to worry about work, we've got it taken care of. You just worry about getting better."

Mack lay there a moment longer looking up at the ceiling, and Tyler wasn't sure if he'd gotten tired and needed to rest, or if he was just off somewhere thinking. He turned back to them after about a minute and looked at them, his face heavy with emotion.

"I suppose it's a little sad that a man my age has only work and one small dog to worry about... But then, I suppose those are the choices I've made," he said looking at them both, his gaze passing back and forth from one to the other... "Now that I look back upon them, I suppose I do regret some of those choices. When you're young it's easy to let pride cloud your judgment... The pillars of your principles alone can support you for a long time, but if ya' blindly cling to them for too long this is what happens... Ya' end up alone."

"I'm sorry," said Tyler. "I really didn't mean to bring up a sore subject. I just..."

"It's okay," Mack replied. "I'd be reflecting on these things whether ya' brought them up or not... I've avoided thinking about some things for far too long. I guess I was afraid of the conclusions I'd come to... Sometimes fear has a clever way of showing up disguised as pride... I suppose the most important thing is to recognize that before it causes ya' to make decisions that can't be undone."

Tyler and Katherine looked at each other knowingly, but said nothing. Having read the letters, each had a pretty good idea exactly who and what Mack was talking about when he spoke of choices he regretted.

"I think you need to rest, Mack," Tyler said. "I'll take care of the shop and Bogey, and you just take care of getting well for now."

"Thank you, Tyler," Mack said. "You've turned out to be quite a golf professional, even though I know ya' wish those two words were in the opposite order. You're an even better man, though, and I've been blessed to have ya' as a friend… But now that ya' mention it, I think you're right. I feel like I need a bit of a nap."

Mack closed his eyes and Tyler and Katherine quietly let themselves out. As they walked out of the hospital and back to the car, they seemed both lost in thought. It wasn't until they were most of the way back to Katherine's that Tyler finally broke the silence.

"I really want to thank you for today," Tyler began as he suddenly pulled into the small parking lot of Bacon Memorial Park. "You don't know how important it was to me to have you there despite everything."

"Of course," Katherine replied, looking at him and smiling warmly. "I know. I'm glad I could be there. And despite the fact that I know you think sometimes I blame him for, well, you know… I don't."

"There's something I need you to tell you," Tyler said, turning off the car and reaching out to take her hands in his in almost one motion.

"Despite what I know you already think I had decided about the garage," Tyler began, "I spoke with Mack for a long time yesterday after work about what was in front of me. I stayed well into the evening after that, wrestling with the choice that I had to make and all the potential ramifications of that decision. I know how much sense choosing to take over the garage makes on the surface, and how much my parents just want what's best for me, for us. I think I still instinctively resisted, though, at least partially because I resented the fact that both of you seemed to be forcing me to choose between a life here with you, and who I am."

"I don't think that's quite fair, Tyler," she interrupted, suddenly defensive and stiffening.

"Please, let me finish," he cut her off, raising a hand to her lips tenderly. "Mack told me yesterday that I'd have regrets no matter what I decided, and that I just needed to figure out what regrets I could live with... Well I did, even though I really struggled with how unfair it all seemed. I understood why my parents needed to put that choice to me right now, but I also knew that no matter what I ultimately decided, they'd still love me, even if they were disappointed in me. What I couldn't come to terms with, though, was whether or not you would... I will always regret it if I never even try again to make the Tour, Katherine. I know I'm good enough, and I want to prove that, not to anyone else, but to myself... I know also, though, that I will regret it the rest of my life if I give up a life with you just to try... I don't want to make that choice, but I'll make it for you, Katherine. I'd give that up to be with you... Not being with you is the thing I would most regret..."

Katherine started to cry and threw her arms around him, burying her face in his neck and sobbing.

"Oh, Tyler," she said through her sobs, but as she did, he pulled back slightly, almost awkwardly and looked into her eyes.

"Katherine," he continued, and she suddenly realized he hadn't been finished. "I just told you I would give up everything that's important to me, give up who I am to be with you."

"Who you are is a lot more to me than how well you hit a little white ball, Tyler," she replied, suddenly confused and wanting him to understand how much she respected who he was.

"Obviously, I get that, Katherine," he continued, "but that statement alone tells me that you still really don't get how much more golf is to me than hitting a little white ball. And how much that statement diminishes who I am. I'm just not sure someone who doesn't play will ever really get that, and maybe it sounds like I'm trying to attach more significance to it than is appropriate, but golf is more than just a game to me, Katherine. It's something I feel like I was put on this planet to do. And so when I say I'm willing to give that up, I guess I just need you to understand how much I'm really giving up, and how much you're really asking."

Katherine sat there quietly for a moment. She seemed to be weighing her thoughts and trying to choose carefully what she'd say next.

"I'm really sorry if you feel I've underestimated how difficult this has been for you," she began slowly. "In my mind, I believe I've always recognized what this meant to you, but maybe I've been selfish, too concerned with my own needs. And I suppose there's a difference between recognizing and really understanding."

"Well, there is," Tyler replied, "and please don't think I'm diminishing you now when I say this, but first of all, I'm not sure anyone can ever *really* understand if they've never felt like they were truly born to do something. And secondly, after everything that has happened today, it suddenly occurred to me that I don't know the answer to one very important question. And it wasn't until after we read those letters that I began to realize what that question was... Would you do the same for me?"

Mike Dowd

ON KNOWING GREAT MEN

Two weeks passed and Mack was still in the hospital with no date for his impending surgery set. Tyler spent his days opening the shop, and his afternoons and evenings at Mack's bedside, getting instructions for what needed to be done at the club, in the short term, as well as from a longer perspective. As much as Tyler had learned about being a golf professional in the past year from watching Mack, there was so much more to running the club than he had realized, and Mack was giving him a crash course so he could take care of everything in his absence.

Mack was still weak and slept a lot. He wasn't getting any worse, but he didn't seem to be getting stronger either as Tyler had suspected he would once the immediate emergency had passed. The doctors had visited frequently, and Tyler had pulled the one he had originally spoken to aside on one of those occasions to ask him about it. "As I mentioned previously, his heart has been weakened, and this may be as good as he gets until we can get those stents in. We were hoping to see him get just a bit stronger first, but I think we may be getting to the point where we are going to have to schedule that surgery anyway because it may be what's keeping him from getting stronger."

Mack had plenty of visitors from the club, including old Garrett Williams who came by to keep him company and play cards with him nearly every morning when Tyler wasn't there. Mack had been the face of the club for more than thirty years, and the Board of Directors had declared that he could take as long as he needed to get healthy and his job would be there when he returned. They were impressed with how Tyler was handling things with Mack's guidance, and with the busiest part of the season behind them he knew he could handle most of what came up as long as he had a little input from Mack.

And that is where things stood when the deadline came to pay the entry fee and sign up for the first stage of Q-School, which was now little over a week away. Tyler was sitting with Mack that evening and learning all about the budgeting process as the time was fast approaching when they would need to be prepared for the following year. He had brought Mack's laptop to him from the club and they were going over the spreadsheet when a reminder popped up on the screen. 'Q-School Entry Deadline tomorrow.'

Tyler looked up at Mack a little surprised. "You keep track of those types of things?" he asked.

"Well, I had a bit of a vested interest ya' might say," Mack said looking up at him with a hint of a smile. "When I first set that little reminder, I assumed ya' would be playing. And just in case ya' hadn't been able to save up the money, I was going to offer to pay the entry if that made things easier. Ya' haven't even brought it up since I've been in here, so I don't know what you've decided, but just in case you're letting money stand in your way I want ya' to know the offer still stands."

Tyler looked at him speechless and after an almost uncomfortable amount of time had passed he finally asked, "You would do that? I don't know what to say… I so appreciate it, but I've got the money, Mack. I saved all year for that, and besides, you're my coach and my caddy. And I just can't take off for a week or maybe more now, not with you in here. Tom can't run the whole place by himself every day."

"Well, considering everything you're doing for me," Mack said gesturing and looking around the room, "it's the least I can do to thank ya', but selfishly, it's a bit more than that. I told ya' the story before, about how I wasn't quite cut out to play this game for a living. Despite that, I believe I'm a pretty fair teacher of it. And thanks to growing up around *my* old man, and a number of his old cronies, I've witnessed first-hand plenty of those who have played at the highest level and I've got a pretty fair eye for those who have the ability."

"I… I hope you aren't mad about this," Tyler said suddenly, "but when I told you we went by and fed Bogey initially and took your car back, well, Katherine and I took a look around the place because the folks at the hospital here thought I should see if I could find anything that would help locate family we should contact like an address book or something, in case…"

"In case I didn't wake up?" Mack finished for him. "Why would I be mad about that, Tyler?"

"Well, I felt a little uncomfortable poking around through your place without your permission is all," Tyler replied, "and even though I understood it was necessary, I was sort of worried that *when* you woke up you might not have liked it. Anyway, we were looking through your old desk in the garage and found your teaching bible… We thumbed through it, honestly I could have set there and studied it for days, but that's not why we were there. We didn't come across much that would have led us to being able to locate anyone you knew, but there was a picture in there of a big strapping guy standing alongside Tony Jacklin watching a kid swinging. Was that your father? And was that you swinging the club?"

Mack looked off out the window and seemed to be really far away all-of-a-sudden. When his attention finally returned, he began slowly.

"Yes, that was my father. The big guy, not Tony Jacklin," he said smiling. "And that was me. My father grew up competing against them and many of them were friends. Tony, Christy O'Connor, Bernard Gallacher, Peter Alliss, and many others. He loved toting me around when I was a lad to all the big tournaments and showing me off at the driving range to the other players, bragging about how I was going to grow up to help us knock the tar out of the damned Yankees someday and get The Ryder Cup back… Sort of ironic, I suppose, that I ended up being one… You know, he just missed being selected for that famed '69 Ryder Cup Team, and really would have been if it hadn't been for the fact that he didn't get along with Captain Eric Brown, a fellow Scot who he'd had a bit of history with."

"You've got so many stories, Mack, and you never tell them," Tyler said wide-eyed. "You grew up around all those great players?"

"I met a lot of the famous American pros at that time, too," Mack said, "at The Open Championship when my father played. Nicklaus, Palmer, Trevino, Watson, Weiskopf, and even that blow-hard Johnny Miller. The Tour was more like a fraternity in those days, and even though my father didn't play on it, he played in enough big events over there that he came to know a lot of the players over the years and they were all much more approachable back then. Many years at The Open, when my father missed the cut, we'd stay for the final two rounds and just follow the players I wanted to follow. I loved to watch Arnie and Trevino. They played with style, and Arnie was a true gentleman. He came and played a practice round at my father's invitation at our home club one year when he was preparing for The Open at Carnoustie. Just Arnie, his regular Open caddy, my father, and myself."

"Your father knew Arnie? You played with him?" Tyler exclaimed. "This is unbelievable."

"Well, my father had met Arnie a handful of times at The Open in the late 60's and early 70's, and was even paired with him in the first round one year. But it really happened because my father knew his regular Open caddy, Tip Anderson, pretty well. In those days, when the money on Tour wasn't what it is now, it was traditional for the Americans to use a Scottish caddy. They couldn't afford to bring over their regular caddy, and so they would just pick one up over there and Arnie used the same man every year and became good friends with him. He talked Arnie into coming up and playing a tune-up at our club. I was about 17 at the time, and a pretty good player already, but I was nervous as hell and sure didn't show much skill that day."

"Amazing," Tyler said, suddenly not only finding he had an all new respect for his coach, but wishing he'd spent a lot more time in the past decade talking to him like this. "You've never told any of these stories, at least not to me anyway. No wonder old Garret Williams wanted to bring you over to be our pro long ago. He must have been impressed as hell and thought it was quite a coup to land a pro with such a pedigree."

"Well, I told those stories a lot more early on," Mack said, "back when I was young and worried about impressing everyone here with who and what I knew. But those days are long gone, and the more removed I got from them the more it felt kind of sad... There's a pretty big space between just knowing great men, Tyler, and being one... At some point I guess I figured it was time to start working on the latter. I think I was tired of riding those coattails, and to be honest, a lot of those old stories reminded me of things I kind of wanted to forget."

Mack stopped speaking and Tyler let it lie to see if he was going to expand upon his last comment, but he didn't. Tyler thought about the letters, and he guessed what some of those things might be, but he wasn't going to embarrass his coach by telling him they'd found them, let alone read some of them. He felt a little shame at the moment for it, but at the same time knew it was kind of important. After it was apparent Mack wasn't going to elaborate, he decided to try a little different angle.

"Was your home club The Peterhead Golf Club?" Tyler asked.

Mack looked up with a bit of a raised eyebrow. "How'd ya'come up with that?"

"Kind of a guess," Tyler said, "but when Katherine and I were taking a look around I saw that big map with all the golf courses in Scotland on them. The Craigewan Course in Peterhead was the only one that had a red dot on it. Kind of looked like you'd taken the point of sharpie and just pressed it down there a few seconds or something. I remembered you said it was a seacoast town, so it sort of made sense."

"You're quite an amateur detective, Tyler," Mack said with a genuinely warm smile. "...And you're correct. Peterhead..."

Mack looked up at the ceiling first, then out the window as if he could see out across the green walking space and the woods beyond all the way to Scotland.

"S'been many years since I've been back," he finally said. "Oh, I went back about a dozen year's ago when my folks passed. One right after the other, almost. It was just before we started working together, actually. Cancer caught up with my father, that and the whiskey maybe. He was just seventy. It was quite an occasion in the Old Blue Toon. He hadn't retired as the professional there until a couple of years just before that and was kind of a local celebrity. Mum went just a year later, a much quieter affair. I had to arrange the burial myself and there were just a few friends and the polite and appropriate attendees from the club. I was their only real family. I didn't really want to think about Peterhead much after that, and I guess I sort of stopped telling most of those old stories around that time, too."

Tyler privately wondered whether he'd encountered Mairi upon his return, his old friend Thomas, or anyone else from his past, but he didn't want to divulge they'd uncovered anything more than that, and it seemed this last part was more than a little painful for Mack to recollect, so he didn't press him for anything else.

"So, I think it's my turn to ask the questions again, Tyler," Mack said. "What did ya' tell your father about the garage?" Mack asked. "Ya' were supposed to have done that by now, weren't you?"

"Well, yes…" Tyler responded a bit hesitantly. "I had just about resigned myself to taking them up on their offer, but with everything that happened after you went in here, I realized some things that made me question that decision."

"Oh," Mack replied, looking somewhere between disappointed and curious. "What was that?"

"Well, first of all, I decided I needed to ask him to disclose how much the offer was to sell it. He was a bit reluctant, at first, but he finally did and that's when I realized just how much they were really giving up for me. It was just too much to pass up. And as much as I appreciated what they were trying to do, I couldn't in good conscience allow them to do that just for me. I mean, with what they'll be getting he could always just re-open it somewhere else if he really ended up regretting the decision, but I don't think he will. They deserve to take a step back. My mother deserves to travel a little and they should enjoy life some. Besides, as good as my father's business has been, there's signs that times are changing. The name All-American Auto was more than just a nod to his football days, it was his calling card. He only worked on and restored American classic cars. You know the type, mostly muscle cars from the 60's and 70's that were built back at a time when you could actually work on them. There just aren't as many of those around as there used to be and it's getting harder and harder to get parts for 'em, and almost impossible to work on anything built much after that."

"Ya' say this all very matter-of-factly, Tyler," Mack said. "I know that wasn't an easy decision. How did Katherine take it?"

"Well, in truth, it was the hardest thing I've ever done," Tyler said, staring out the window with a pained look, "and the biggest part of that was because I know how much she wanted me to take it. I mean, she was conflicted too. She understood that it was a great thing for my folks and, truthfully, she loves them as much as I do and is happy for them. But that doesn't change the fact that she's disappointed."

"Will she get over it?" Mack asked.

"I'm not sure, but I'm just not my father. This is who I am, Mack," Tyler continued, grabbing the Butler Bluff logo on his polo and pulling it from his chest for emphasis. "I'm a golfer, not a mechanic, no matter how much money is in it, and you're a big part of that. It's not just about trying for the Tour. I want to be involved with the game on some level, regardless of how that ultimately works itself out… And despite all that, I had decided to give it all up if that's what it took to be with her. At least until it occurred to me that if she was really going to force me to choose then she obviously wasn't willing to do the same. As much as Katherine says money doesn't matter, I'm not so sure her perspective hasn't changed now that she not only knows exactly what I'm giving up, but because she's got some pretty good opportunities of her own. She wants to settle down and start a family in the future, the near future, and my decision makes it harder for us to do that in the short term."

"I get that, I mean it's something I want too, at some point, but I need to establish myself in some way before we can. Sure, taking over my father's garage would have gotten us there sooner, and I was ready to do it, but I realize now that in the end that would have just sucked the life out of me. I can't explain it, but I just need to make it on my own."

"Ya' don't need to explain that to me, Tyler," Mack said. "Look where I ended up."

"…Well, I guess maybe you do understand," Tyler replied after thinking a moment. "I just really think to do that you ultimately have to like doing what you're doing. I know Katherine doesn't want me to be miserable, but I think she's having a hard time not seeing my decision as choosing to chase a dream over settling down and building one with her. I believe we can do both, but she's not so sure. Sometimes it makes me wonder if she's really in love with me, or with the idea of someone she wishes I was, but I'm not. We're spending some time apart to think about things."

"I figured something must have happened," Mack said. "I didn't ask, but I sort of knew since the only time she's come by to visit me is during the day when you're at work. I wouldn't give up on her, lad. We all struggle with what we think we need and who we think we're supposed to be when we're young, and much of that is the baggage we carry around from our youth. Taking some time is a good idea. I've learned a thing or two about making hasty decisions in my life and you don't want to be looking back years later and wishing you'd thought things through a bit more."

"Well, I feel like it's more about whether or not she'll give up on me at this point, Mack," Tyler half laughed, but with no real amusement on his face. "She knows how I feel and where I stand, and she just needs to decide if she can accept me for who I am."

"So, I suppose that brings us back to my earlier question about Q-School," Mack said. "Are ya' ready?"

"I didn't sign up, Mack, not after what happened to you," Tyler said, "How could I have?"

"You've worked hard and another whole year has gone by," Mack said. "If it's what ya' want to do, Tyler, ya' need to see it through. I've already spoken to Tom and a few members at the club and they'll cover things for ya'. We aren't going to be all that busy, and everyone knows how important this is to ya' so we can't let my little situation here keep ya' from that opportunity. Besides, I'm buyin'."

"I don't even have a caddy," Tyler said. "I told Gabe I wasn't playing and so he's off to Europe somewhere and Tom obviously can't do it."

"Why don't ya' take Jackie?" Mack said. "It'd be a great experience for him. Ya' know how to play the game. You don't need anyone's help, other than toting your bag, and Jackie's plenty big enough to handle that. You've just got to get your aunt to let him skip a few days of school."

Tyler sat and thought about what he was saying. Ever since Mack's heart attack, he had given up on the idea of going to Q-School. As much as it had disappointed him after all the work he had put in, he brushed aside those feelings as selfish in the face of obviously much bigger life issues. Mack needed him more than ever, he thought, and after all he had done for and been to Tyler, he felt the least he could do was to take care of things until hopefully he could return to doing some things himself.

"Do you really want me to?" Tyler asked. "I don't know; I haven't hit a ball since you got sick. I don't know if I can be ready now."

"Ya' know, if I'm honest, Tyler, I do," Mack said with a weak smile. "I'd have never talked ya' out of taking over for your father, but since you've already passed on that, I don't see why ya' shouldn't. I've always wanted to be able to say I coached a player that made it to the Tour. I'm not sure I quite realized why that was so important until now, but I suppose it's the only way I'd ever be able to say I finally one-upped my own old man. And you're ready, Tyler. You're more ready than you've ever been. I think the important question is whether or not ya' really want to?"

"Well…" Tyler said after a moment, "I mean, ya' know I want to. I want to prove to myself that last time was a fluke. I know

I can do it. And I can't explain it, but just proving that to myself feels more important than anything.'"

"Then I think ya' need to get that entry in, lad," Mack said. "And start practicing a little. Ya' don't want to go out there completely cold."

LESSONS FROM Q-SCHOOL

When Tyler asked Jackie about caddying for him at Q-School, it was if he'd offered his birthday present, Christmas, and a trip to Disneyland all rolled into one.

"I can't believe it!" Jackie said. "You really want me to go with you? I won't let you down, Tyler. You just tell me what you want me to do and I'm there!"

"Well first I need to talk to your mother," Tyler told him laughing. "You'll be missing school, obviously, and I don't want her to start thinking I'm a bad influence on you."

Tyler's aunt Candace hadn't put up much of a fight once she'd seen Jackie's excitement. He'd have to get all his homework in advance from his teacher and Tyler had to promise to make him study each and every night after dinner. But considering everything that had happened with Mack she understood it was a unique situation, and she believed that Tyler was probably right. If Jackie wanted to find out if he was cut out to head down this same road someday, the experience inside the ropes of an event like Q-School would probably be invaluable.

The issue of the garage behind them once and for all, his folks were supportive, even encouraging, and the day before they headed off to St. Louis his father even made a point to tell him so over a little send-off dinner they had held for him and Jackie and his parents.

"I want to make a toast to my son," Jack began by raising his glass just before they dug into the near feast his mother had spent most of the day preparing. "I know I may have sounded at times as if I haven't been in favor of this path you've chosen, but I just want you to know that isn't the case. Your mother and I have always wanted what's best for you, and I just wanted to make sure you always thought everything through when it came to your future. I know from experience how hard it is to have a life-long dream pulled out from under you, and I guess at times I believed I was trying to spare you that same pain. I realize now though, that having your dream taken from you and not realizing it, and just giving up on it are different things completely. It's a tough road you've chosen, son, and I admire you for not taking the easy way out and seeing it through whatever happens. And I wish you luck."

"Thanks, Dad, I really appreciate that," Tyler said.

When Tyler called Katherine to tell her what he was doing, the conversation didn't go quite as well. She'd agreed to stay on with the ACS through one more Gala that fall if they would agree to move up the date. She'd declined one of the job offers she'd had, but couldn't put off the other beyond October. She'd become the face of The American Cancer Society in Poplar Bluff, after her performance and handling of the event the previous year, and most everyone in town knew of it and understood why she needed one more year to train her replacement to help insure a smooth transition. She was busy, for sure, but her somewhat dismissive tone with Tyler said as much as she did about where things stood, and what he was about to do. He knew she was having trouble reconciling her feelings about his decision in regards to the garage, and there was likely some guilt involved in those feelings since she knew he'd unquestionably done the right thing by his folks once it was clear how much money was involved. She seemed almost to resent how easy the size of the offer had made that decision for him, and how it had clouded the path to that idyllic future she had felt they had been oh so close to.

There was more to it than that, though. She hadn't been at all happy when Tyler had suggested that maybe she wasn't willing to sacrifice for him as much as he was ready to give up for her. But she hadn't exactly had an answer either, even though she knew that refusing to support him would be hypocritical.

"No, no, I get it," she said to Tyler a bit exasperatedly after his initial explanation of Mack's offer and his desire to see Tyler give it another shot. "That's a very generous offer, and you can't let Mack down. But you can't tell me he had to twist your arm too hard either, Tyler."

"I really don't think that's fair, Katherine," Tyler said a bit wounded, and then continuing after a long pause, "Sure, this is still important to me, but we've had a lot of long conversations in the past couple of weeks, and I never realized just how important it is to him. And all things considered…"

"Okay Tyler," she said, "I'm just really busy here. I understand. We can talk when you get back. It's just that I'm assuming this means I need to scramble to find your replacement now since I guess you'll be missing the Gala?"

"Well," Tyler said, "that was something I was getting to. The final round is on Saturday. I have no idea what time I will draw, it depends on how well I'm playing, but if it's a late time there's a possibility I couldn't drive all the way back here in time. Do you think you could have a back-up plan just in case?"

"Oh, sure, Tyler," she said a bit sarcastically. "I've got plenty of applicants to choose from."

"I'm sorry, Katherine, I really am," Tyler said, "but this only comes around once a year and I totally understand what an inconvenience it is for you. After what happened to Mack I hadn't even planned on signing up, and if you hadn't moved the Gala up this year it wouldn't have been a problem."

"Don't worry about it, Tyler," she said, "just go play your game and I'll figure it out."

"There's something else I wanted to ask," Tyler said, knowing he was on thin ice with her already. "I was hoping you could find a few minutes to stop by each day while we're gone and check in on Mack? He's still really weak and I'm worried about him. He just sleeps most of the time and they want to do that surgery in two weeks now, whether he gets stronger or not. It doesn't make any sense."

"Fine, Tyler," she said pointedly, "I'll take care of that for you too. Anything else?"

"Look," Tyler said, "I know how busy you are, and I'm sorry to ask this of you. I wouldn't if I didn't think it was important. I know I owe you big time, Katherine."

"I'm just busy, Tyler," she said. "I'm happy to check on Mack. Just go, because I've got to get back to what I was doing. I'm running out of time."

"Thank you, Katherine," Tyler said. "That means a lot to me."

***

Q-School that fall was right back at the scene of the crime, The Aberdeen Golf Club, where he had missed qualifying the previous year after his disastrous final round. Aberdeen, true to its name, was a Scottish links-style course, and one that, in retrospect, would have been great to have Mack on the bag for. It was a beast at more than 7200 yards from the Championship Tees and notorious for being windy, with challenging gusts whipping up out of the river valley beyond almost every afternoon.

Tyler and Jackie arrived a day early to get in a practice round and check out the condition of the course. Tyler had taken Jackie out with him for a few nines after school the previous week and had him carry his bag so he could show him what was expected of him as a caddy, not only from him, but what he would need to do to make sure he stayed out of the other players' ways and could handle the responsibility.

"In the end," Tyler told him smiling, "just take my lead. It's not that hard. Gabe hadn't ever caddied before either last year and he did just fine. And besides, I think you read greens better than Gabe does anyway so I figure I'm a few shots ahead already."

The practice round proved to be invaluable for both of them. Tyler re-familiarized himself with the course, and Jackie got over the nerves he was obviously experiencing all the way up to St. Louis. When they got to the hotel and checked in early that evening before heading off to dinner that night, he seemed to finally exhale.

"Whew!" Jackie said, sitting down on the bed exhausted. "I guess that wasn't so bad. I expected the other guys to be all stuffy and cranky, but most of 'em seemed alright. I am the youngest caddy by a long ways, though."

"Well," Tyler said, "that was a practice round. Everyone's pretty loose on a practice round. They'll get a lot more tight-lipped tomorrow, and just make sure you don't go clanking those irons around in the bag looking for a club during any of their pre-shots. Especially after one of 'em makes a bogey. A lot of these guys would bite their own mother's head off for breathing too loud after they make a bogey."

They went to dinner that night and returned pretty early so Jackie could study and they'd get a good night's rest. Tyler's tee time the next day was 8:15, and they'd have to arrive about 6:45 am for him to get in his usual 90-minute warm-up routine in. Tyler wasn't as nervous as he thought he'd be when the morning came, but as they got to the course he began to get emotional about the fact that Mack was sitting back in a hospital bed in Poplar Bluff instead of being here with him. He was glad he had Jackie with him, and was enjoying seeing the enormity of the experience through his eyes. At the same time, he missed his coach. And now that he knew even more stories about Mack's life, his experiences growing up in the game, and all the great players he'd been around, he regretted even more not having taken him as a caddy last time. What things he could still teach Tyler and what other amazing stories did he still have lurking up his sleeves that he'd yet to tell?

The emotion he felt arriving at the course that morning carried over into the first handful of holes, and he inexplicably found himself three over par after 7 holes and unable to stay focused on the task at hand. He kept flashing back to his rounds the previous years and what he might be asking Mack if he were there, instead of Jackie, and it was Jackie, in truth, that brought him back a bit after his third bogey.

"Am I doing something wrong, Ty?" he asked on their way to the next tee.

"What?" Tyler said turning to him as if he'd been awoken from a nap.

"You seem like you're somewhere else," Jackie said. "I don't know, but you asked me what I thought about the break on that last putt and then you just went and putted it while I was looking at the line without even waiting for me to answer. Am I doing something wrong?"

"Oh, sorry, Jackie," Tyler said, "I guess I was just thinking about Mack."

"I wish he was here," Jackie said. "I'm obviously not a very good caddy."

"Nonsense, Jackie," Tyler said, rubbing his hands in his hair in a rough playful motion. "I'm the one swinging the club, Jackie.

I've just got to get out of my own head. Thanks for reminding me of that. I'll get it together now."

And he did. Tyler ran off two birdies in the next five holes and then held on with pars through number 16. On the seventeenth, a mid-length par 5 without a lot of trouble coming into the green, Tyler found the green on his second shot with a beautifully played approach and after rolling in a twenty-footer for eagle, he was back to one under par for the day coming into the difficult eighteenth.

A year earlier, the eighteenth had been where his Q-School dreams unraveled. After coming up short on the second shot, and landing in the water after he'd ignored Gabe's advice about taking an extra club, he'd spent most of the next eight hours drowning his frustrations in beer and barbecue, and his final round disappointment was the predictable penalty.

This time, Tyler remembered Gabe's advice, and when the wind was quartering into them from the right, he asked Jackie for two extra clubs.

"Are you sure?" Jackie asked after Tyler had asked him for a 5-iron at 165 yards, a distance that was usually no more than a 7-iron for him, and sometimes even an 8.

"I'm sure," Tyler said. "That wind's coming in from the right and you can't feel it as much from here because we're shielded from it by those big mounds up there behind the green and to the right. If I get the ball up in that wind too much it'll knock it right down in the water."

"Okay," Jackie said, handing him the club. "You're the boss."

"I learned that last year," Tyler said, winking at him as he addressed the ball. "The hard way. Watch."

Tyler took what looked to be about a three quarter backswing and knocked the ball down low under the wind with a long and low follow-through. The ball started out about ten yards right of the green and when it rose to just about the level of the mounds behind the green, the wind hit it and moved it ever so gently to the left towards the awaiting green. It hit the ground on the middle right of the green, took one brief hop, and rolled down the slope towards the pin that had been tucked up behind the lake in attempt to lure players over that direction.

"Wow," Jackie said in true admiration and giving Tyler a fist bump. "Now that was a pro shot!"

Tyler laughed and after proceeding to the green a few minutes later, he two-putted for a routine par and a first round 71. A respectable one-under par. He'd hoped for a little better start, but considering his first few holes, he was satisfied and told himself he was bound to have a little rust to knock off, all things considered.

They had lunch in the clubhouse after the round and a few guys Tyler knew from junior golf, college, and various other events he'd played in over the years came by and said hello, and Tyler introduced Jackie to them all as his little brother. Jackie was having a blast, and Tyler was glad he'd taken Mack's advice and brought him with him. In truth, he'd helped with more than just shaking him out of his early round funk, as he'd seen a few breaks on the greens that Tyler hadn't initially been convinced of. And helped him stand over more than a couple of putts with a little more conviction than if he'd been just reading them himself.

When they were done with lunch, Tyler said he wanted to putt some and hit a few shots out of the practice bunker before they headed back to the hotel. He'd felt good about his ball-striking and just wanted to get a little better feel for the greens and the bunkers which were both quite different than they were at home.

Tyler's tee time the next morning was an hour later, and with the extra sleep, he arrived at the course a bit fresher and feeling confident after the way he'd finished his round the previous day. After starting the round with a couple of routine pars when he got a little overly aggressive with his birdie tries, Tyler settled down and ran off a stretch of five birdies in seven holes and turned in a scorching 31 on the front. Jackie was fired up, trying to retain himself with each successive birdie, but it was showing through in his expression even though he was doing his best contain it in his body language.

"Lot of golf left to play," Tyler said to Jackie when they stopped in the locker room briefly at the turn. "Can't get ahead of yourself, Jackie. I could just as easily turn around and make five bogeys on the backside if I'm not careful. Can't sign your scorecard until you've played all eighteen," he said, repeating one of Mack's favorite phrases and smiling.

Tyler didn't, though, and when he came to the seventeenth, he'd added three more birdies along with a handful more fist-bumps with Jackie until he found himself looking at a twenty-foot eagle putt for the second day in a row.

Jackie handed Tyler his putter as they began to line it up, and then, a bit of a sheepish smile added, "I don't know if this is a good time to ask or not, but you don't happen to know what the course record is do you, Ty?"

"Nope," Tyler said flatly and completely focused. "And if I want to make this putt, I don't want to."

Jackie stepped back and got out of his way without saying another word and Tyler calmly drained the putt to go ten under par for the day. Twenty minutes later they'd walked off the difficult eighteenth with another routine par and Tyler had carded a new course record of 62. The guys in Tyler's group congratulated him and as the word began to spread in the next twenty minutes or so, Tyler had more than a few people coming up and interrupting their lunch to congratulate him on the round, and even a couple of local newspaper reporters who wanted a comment on the round and his thoughts about the prospect of qualifying. Tyler thanked them all, graciously, and said very politely that he'd be happy to make a comment if and when he did qualify for the next stage.

After hitting some more putts and greenside bunker shots, Tyler and Jackie went by the scoreboard to see where things stood after round two. He'd been in the middle of the pack after the first round, but his stellar second round put him in second, behind only some guy named Garrison Diehl who'd shot a pair of 65's in the first two rounds.

"Well, Jackie," Tyler said with a bit of gleam in his eye and a pat on his back, "I suppose we'll have to go get that guy Diehl tomorrow."

"That was the best round of golf I've ever seen, Ty," Jackie said. "You didn't make even one bogey. Have you ever even shot a 62 before?"

"Sure," he said, "but never in competition. I did it once in high school, and a couple of times in college during a practice round, but it's nice to do it when it actually means something."

"You were so focused out there," Jackie said. "You were just in a zone. After a while I just wanted to get out of the way. I was afraid I'd mess it up."

"Golf gets that way sometimes," Tyler said. "When you get on a roll you feel like you can birdie every hole, and you're surprised almost when you don't. Just about the time you start thinking about what kind of number you're going to put up, though, you usually find it all comes back down to earth. Even though they haven't always been in competition, I've had enough rounds in the mid to low sixties at this point to know that when you get it going you just have to roll with it and keep playing your game. Don't change anything, don't start playing more conservative to protect it, or worse yet, more aggressive because you get cocky or greedy. Either of those is the kiss of death and then the bogeys inevitably start coming. You asked me on seventeen if I knew what the course record was. I had a pretty good idea I was close, but I do my best to not even think score when I'm out there. You've got to just keep hitting that one shot that's in front of you. Every single time I start thinking score it's like the karmic hand of the universe reaches down and knocks my ball in the woods, or worse. Remember that, Jackie. It may sound cliché, but you can only play one shot at a time."

"Still, that was amazing," Jackie said. "We should call Mack and tell him."

"Let's not get ahead of ourselves, Jackie," Tyler said. "It's only the second round and there's a lot of golf left. We'll tell him in person when it's all said and done, and we've qualified. He'll be more impressed with that than one hot round."

The morning of the third round dawned, and being in the lead group, Tyler had a lot more time to warm-up and think about what he wanted to do that day. With a tee time of almost noon, he figured he was going to have to play most of the round in the wind that tended to roll in every afternoon at Aberdeen. The course had been ripe for picking the day before, an uncharacteristically windless day, and Tyler had taken advantage of it. But today was going to be different. They had only just got out of the car when the cool autumn breeze that hit Tyler's face told him it was a whole new ball-game.

"Par's gonna' be a good score today, Jackie," Tyler said as he pulled on a wind-shirt he had taken out of his bag and took his putter and a handful of balls and rolled them out on the green. "Won't be any 62's out here today."

"It's cold," Jackie said, pulling on his own jacket.

"Yep," Tyler said, "and you feel that breeze? We didn't get that until after lunch yesterday. If it's like this at 9:30, it'll be twice as much by the time we tee off and by the time we get to the back nine it's gonna' be at least 15 to 20 miles per hour, with gusts of maybe more. It'll be an equalizer for sure. The guys going out early this morning are going to have a big advantage. We're just going to have do the best we can today and take what it gives us. Pars will be good."

Being a low ball hitter, Tyler was a good wind player, and he actually enjoyed the additional challenge of figuring it out and hitting the types of shots that you needed to play in those situations. Playing in the wind in a practice round or a casual event was one thing, though, and having to deal with it when you were playing for your livelihood was another thing altogether. When their tee time rolled around almost two hours later, Jackie realized Tyler had been right.

"Wow, it's really starting to pick up," Jackie said. "You might be right. It's gonna' play a lot tougher today."

"A couple of things to remember, Jackie," Tyler told him as they waited for the group in front of them to tee off. He was really enjoying walking Jackie through all his thought processes and teaching him the things he knew he would need to know as he got started on this journey. "First of all, when the conditions are tough and the weather is bad, half the guys will just give up mentally and use that as an excuse for why they play poorly. If you just stay focused, keep grinding, and do your best, often a score you wouldn't normally be too happy with ends up being half-way decent."

"That makes sense," Jackie said. "Remember the second tournament I played in this year? It rained like the devil for half the round, and some kids even quit. I didn't play real well, and I was soaked when we got done. I shot a 90, and I wasn't too happy about it, but when it was all over I actually took third place. I just kept playing because all I kept hearing in my head was Mack telling me to never give up. *Quitters don't finish in the money, Jackie*, he always tells me."

"Where do you think I learned it?" Tyler said laughing as he slapped Jackie on the back. "Now the second thing to remember in the wind is you have to take at least an extra club or two and swing easy. The harder you swing, the more spin you put on the ball and it climbs up in the wind and flies even shorter. You don't want that. Spin looks cool on TV, but it's no friend in the wind."

The third round turned out to be every bit as difficult as Tyler had told Jackie it would be. Fortunately, Tyler was pretty energized coming of a good night's sleep and with a course record 62 under his belt, he could afford to be patient. He managed a birdie on the outward nine, off-set by a couple of bogeys that were the result of unexpected gusts of wind that knocked a pair of well struck irons down and into greenside bunkers. When they turned at one over, Jackie looked serious, Tyler thought, and for the first time he worried if this was beginning to be a lot physically for him.

"You okay?" Tyler asked him as they stopped at the clubhouse for some water and a granola bar. "You almost look like you're worn out."

"No, I'm fine," Jackie said as if Tyler had woken him up from something. "It's just tough out there today and I don't know if I'm much help. Don't get me wrong, Ty, I love being here. I mean this is the coolest thing I've ever done, but I don't feel like I'm really helping. I wish Mack was here. I feel like you're the one coaching me out there, and you're supposed to be thinking about your game."

"Is that all it is?" Tyler said smiling, but not wanting to laugh at his young cousins' concern. "To tell you the truth, Jackie, I think Mack actually is here. I think he knew exactly what he was doing when he told me to bring you with me. I've enjoyed the hell out of this, and sharing with you everything I do out here in hopes that it will help you at some point. And if you must know, I think it's kept me from thinking too much. I can't quite explain it but just talking to you about what I'm thinking on each shot, explaining what I intend to do, and then executing it just seems to keep me right here in the present. And that's what you need to do in competitive golf."

Jackie smiled at the thought that he actually was helping Tyler.

"Good," Jackie said. "I was starting to worry you regretted bringing me."

"Don't be ridiculous," Tyler said. "Whether or not we qualify, and I do mean we, Jackie, I wouldn't change this for anything, and I can guarantee we're both gonna' learn something from it."

They started the back nine with a birdie on ten, and after seven straight pars they found themselves in the middle of the fairway on the difficult eighteenth, albeit 50 yards shorter than usual due to the almost 25 mile an hour wind they had in their faces.

"Well," Jackie said, "I guess we don't have to wonder if there's any wind up there we can't feel because of those mounds today. It's blowing."

"You've got that right, Jackie," Tyler said. "How far we got to clear the water?"

"About 210," Jackie said, looking at the yardage book with all their notes from the practice round.

"Might as well be 310 into this wind," Tyler replied only a bit sarcastically. "Give me the 4-iron. We're just gonna' have to lay it out to the right about 30 yards short of the green and try to get up and down for par."

"You sure, Ty?" Jackie asked. "You hit your three wood like 250 usually. You don't think it'll make it?"

"I just hit my driver to a spot 50 yards shorter than I usually do, Jackie," Tyler replied. "That's a driver. It not only goes farther than my three wood, but it's got about four degrees less loft. If I put a three wood up in that wind it'll be lucky to land within 5 yards of the far bank."

"Oh," Jackie said, "I guess I've still got a lot to learn. I didn't make the connection there, but now that you mention it, that makes total sense."

"You've got to use all the information available to you when you make decisions out here," Tyler said. "The worst shots happen before you even swing the club."

"I think I know where I've heard that one," Jackie said smiling.

"Yeah," Tyler said smiling back at him. "I suppose I might have borrowed a few things from Mack along the way. More than *I* even realized."

Tyler laid up safely to just about where he planned, pitched to within about eight feet, and ten minutes later they walked off the green with a par for an even par 72.

"You know, I said yesterday that 62 was the best round of golf I'd ever seen. I'm not so sure that 72 wasn't maybe even better considering the conditions," Jackie said as they walked off the green after Tyler had shaken the hands of his playing partners. Garrison

Diehl had struggled in the wind, giving four shots back to par, along with his second-round lead and the other guy had done even worse.

"I think you're right, Jackie," Tyler said. "Yesterday I felt like I could play another eighteen coming off that green. Today I just feel like laying down for a nap. Let's go take a look at the leaderboard and see where we stand."

Most of the players in the afternoon had gone backwards in the wind, but quite a few of the players who'd gone out early before the wind kicked up had played well. The overall effect was that the field had tightened, with the leaders coming back to the pack and those at the back making their move. Still, with the aid of his stellar second round, Tyler found himself tied for the lead with one other guy going into the final round, followed by Diehl and another guy at a shot back, and another pair two shots back. Three more sat three back, and then a whole host of guys at four and five respectively. It was still anyone's tournament, but with fifteen guys advancing to the next stage, Tyler was in great position.

"You ready to go get something to eat?" he asked Jackie.

"Absolutely," Jackie said. "I'm starving. Where we going?"

"Your pick," Tyler answered, "as long as it's not barbecue."

THE HOLES WE FILL

When Katherine got the call from Tyler saying he likely couldn't make it in time to help her with the Gala because he was going to Q-School again after all, she was at first irritated, then disappointed, then relieved. She didn't want anyone else by her side, it wouldn't feel right, and now she'd not only have to train someone else to do what he'd done, but explain to everyone where he was and why. They'd all say how great it was he was taking another crack at Q-School and how they wished him luck. She'd agree, and then feel guilty because she knew a part of her not only wished that he hadn't gone, but, if she was honest with herself, that he didn't make it. And she knew that didn't really make sense now.

With the prospect of Tyler taking over the garage finally put to bed, the vision of the life they might have had seemed to have gone along with it, and she was honestly conflicted about what she expected from him now. He'd wanted to make his own way, and now he had to. And, if it wasn't through golf somehow, what else was he supposed to do? She suddenly realized the few weeks they'd spent apart while she readied everything for the Gala hadn't exactly done anything to help other than take her mind off things for a while. She knew now that sense of relief she felt about him not being there had a lot to do with the fact that she wasn't ready to answer some tough questions. Questions about where they went next. And more than anything she was afraid of what her answer to the question he'd put to her might be.

Tyler just didn't understand. He had questioned her love for him, saying it was obviously conditional, and he'd accused her of being more in love with her fairy tale idea of the life she wanted with him rather than who he actually was. He had been ready to give up his dream for her, ready to take his parents' offer for her, he said, until it had suddenly struck him that, like the Mairi in Mack's letters, she didn't seem willing to do the same for him. She had supported him all the way up until the prospect of doing so didn't exactly fit into her vision of how she wanted life to be, and then she'd withdrawn that support. And that had stung. Was he right?

A part of her understood, and even admired him for what he was doing. Taking over the garage would have been so easy, would have made their lives easy, but Tyler didn't want to be handed anything. He wanted to stand on his own two feet, and needed to do something that was important to him, even if that meant it was more challenging. He was so determined. He was like a bulldog when he wanted to accomplish something, and she felt that determination was a big part of why he'd ultimately be successful in whatever he put his mind to. And she didn't want him to go through life unhappy just for her. She told him she'd have ultimately supported him no matter what he decided, and she believed that at the time. It's just that she had a hard time standing idly by when she felt he was making a mistake.

But to question her love was an unfair turning of the tables. After all she'd been through for him, after he had left her the first time to run off and chase his dreams, and then she'd taken him back, it was the pot calling the kettle black. They wouldn't even be in this position if she hadn't forgiven and forgotten and been willing to accept what he had done as the folly of youth. But they were older now. She was being sensible, pragmatic, and like his parents, not just looking out for her best interests, but for his. He was the one who'd fallen in love with a fairy tale and who couldn't let go of that dream even when given the opportunity to have everything he said that was really important to him. Was she testing him? Yes, and she had a right to after what he'd done before. As much as he said he wanted her by his side, it was obvious that meant on his terms, and if she didn't like those terms he'd ultimately be gone again if he had the opportunity. Yes, she was testing him, and he was failing.

And then there was Mack. Katherine had come to develop an inexplicable connection to the stoic old Scot, and part of that was because she knew how much he meant to Tyler. He was like a combination of the big brother Tyler never had, and the way he'd hoped his own father had been towards him for so much of his youth. Katherine knew Tyler wouldn't let Mack down once he knew how important it was to him to see Tyler succeed. Seeing the two of them together at the hospital, and being there in Mack's house with Tyler, it had become all the more apparent to her what an influence Mack had been on him. And she couldn't deny the fact that his simple wisdom had played a big part in shaping Tyler's beliefs.

Since the day he'd woken up in the hospital, she'd made a point to go by and visit him every couple of days. She knew he not only didn't' have any family to speak of, but something about knowing a little of the sad story of the lost love of his youth had touched Katherine and made it almost intolerable for her to think of him sitting there in that hospital bed alone. At first she'd gone by on her lunch hour, but if he had any visitors from the club, they seemed to come by in the mornings or early afternoon, so she decided she'd pick up Tyler's slack by going to visit Mack every evening since he wouldn't be there.

"Hello, Katherine," Mack said, opening his eyes and turning towards her shortly after she sat down as if he'd just woken from a nap.

"Hello, Mack," she said. "How are you this evening?"

"A bit tired," he said. "Can't really explain it. I didn't even have any visitors today, until now. Any word from our boy?"

"No," Katherine said. "He never calls me in the middle of a tournament. He always says he needs to stay focused, and he'll tell me all about it when it's over if there's anything to tell."

"Ya' didn't cheat and check the scores on the web?" he asked.

"No," she laughed. "When he wants me to know he'll tell me. I respect that. And besides, I've been a bit too busy to worry about golf. I've got the Gala tomorrow night."

"Oh, that's right," Mack said, suddenly reaching over to his table for something. He pulled out a little zip pouch and produced a check and handed it to her. "I've been meaning to give ya' this."

It was a check for $500. Katherine's eyes got a bit wide as she saw the amount, and then she looked back at Mack with sudden concern.

"This is an awfully big donation," Katherine said since most people gave $50, not $500. "Are you sure?"

"Yes, my dear," Mack said. "I think I'm a bit overdue to give back a bit to this community for all they've given me and I can't think of a better place to start than with you."

"Well thank you," Katherine said with a bit of lump in her throat. "You're very generous, and from what I can tell I think you've already given this community at least as much as you've been given in return."

"You're too kind," he said and then looking up at the ceiling he got a bit emotional, "and it isn't true. When I came here many years ago I don't think I really intended to stay here. It was a stepping stone, I thought, a way to establish myself and make my way on my own. Thirty years later I'm still here, and life just happened. I thought I'd be starting a family of my own, or maybe even return home to Scotland someday to be near family, once I'd made my way, but somewhere along the way it just hit me that this was home. Ya' ever heard that old saying, *life is what happens while you're making other plans?*"

"Yes," Katherine replied, "I think I have."

"Well it's true, Katherine," he said with visible tears threatening to escape his eyelids. "I guess I just kept thinking there would always be more time to do this, or time to do that, and then I woke up one day and my folks were gone. And any real reason to return sort of died with them. Still, I thought there was time to do things. I felt like I was still young and there was still plenty of time to do the things I'd hoped to do or to atone for the mistakes I'd made... And then one day ya' wake up and realize ya' may have played your last round of golf... And the saddest part is, ya' didn't even know ya' were playing it when you did. I guess I just wasn't quite ready to give up the game yet."

"I'm sure you haven't played your last round of golf," Katherine said, putting her hand over his and hoping it didn't betray the shaking she was starting to feel inside. "You'll be back out there again before you know it."

"I don't know, Katherine," Mack said. "I know they want to do surgery, but they're concerned because I'm not getting any stronger and they don't know if I'll make it through it. I feel tired, very tired. I can't seem to shake it. Maybe surgery will help, but I'm hoping I can ask ya' a favor just in case it doesn't."

"Sure, anything," Katherine said. "What can I do?"

"Would ya' take my key here," he said, handing her the same keys Tyler had given back to him after they'd been to the house. "Could ya' go to the house and get me a couple of things?"

"Absolutely," she said. "What do you need?"

"Just two things," Mack replied. "In my desk in the garage, you'll find my big leather teaching journal. Tyler said ya' looked at it so I don't think you'll have trouble finding it. The other thing is in the hall closet, on the top shelf."

"The box of letters?" Katherine said, inhaling sharply as she caught herself.

Mack weakly raised an eyebrow at her, then smiled as her face reddened.

"I came across them when we were looking for something that would help us try to contact your family," she said by way of explanation. "I only glanced at the open ones to see if they were from family, or had any mention of family members you may have had. Tyler knew your father's name, but we figured he might have passed on."

"It's okay," Mack said as he glanced away with a somewhat pained expression. She didn't know if he was embarrassed by what she knew, or just reliving the circumstances of what they'd contained. "Just bring me those, too. It probably doesn't really matter anymore, but I've been avoiding that box for thirty years. As much as it might kill me to know what they say, I don't think I can live any longer without knowing."

***

Twenty minutes later, Katherine was on her way back to the hospital with Mack's journal and the box of letters. She was running through her head whether or not she should just excuse him to read them in peace. They were a private matter, and something he obviously carried some deep regrets about. She truly was concerned about the effect they might have on him in his current state, but at the same time understood his need to see them now. He'd let those letters sit in that box for thirty years, and that avoidance had come to almost define how he'd spent those years, framing them in a sort of sad loneliness. The fear of what might have been in them had obviously been greater than the fear of not knowing. Whatever was inside, there were bound to be more regrets or disappointment, maybe things he really couldn't live with. But with all that had happened his need to know had finally become greater than his pride, his fear of the unknown, or both.

When Katherine walked back in the room, Mack was playfully teasing one of the nurses in his thickest Scottish burr, trying to coax her into bringing him some ice cream.

"I guess I should have asked ya' to bring me one more thing, Katherine," he said as she walked in to the nurse shaking her head at him.

"Mr. McLean," the nurse said, "I'm under strict orders about your diet, and ice cream definitely isn't on the list."

"I'm dying here," he said playfully, "and she won't even bring me a scoop of ice cream. What kind of a place have I ended up in?"

"Oh, Mack," Katherine said as the nurse turned to walk out, "She's just looking out for you. A little less ice cream and you might not have ended up in here in the first place."

"I suppose," Mack said with exaggerated ruefulness. "I didn't realize I'd eaten my last bowl of ice cream, too."

He reached for the large teaching journal first, and she placed it on the mobile table that leaned over his bed for his meals.

"Tyler tell ya' what this was?" he inquired.

"He said it was given to you by your father and that he started it years ago, and it was yours to finish."

"Yes," Mack said, opening the large leather-bound volume and carefully looking at the familiar pages as if he were admiring works of fine art. "It had always been my intention to organize them, get a professional illustrator, and publish the entire work. My father's thoughts on teaching the game were ahead of their time. He was preaching bio-mechanics before people were calling them bio-mechanics, and he had advanced principles of physics incorporated into what he taught long before Homer Kelley came along."

"Who's Homer Kelley?" Katherine asked.

"Oh, it's not important," Mack said. "Just an old engineer who wrote a book many years ago about the mechanics of the golf swing that developed quite a cult following amongst golf instructors."

"From what Tyler has told me," Katherine said, "it sounds like your father was quite an influence."

"I suppose he was," Mack replied, "but we were very different people. He was a big, strapping, typically loud and jovial Scotsman, but at the same time quite a deep thinker when he wanted to be, especially about anything golf related. He had quite a few advanced theories. I took more after my mother, I think. More soft-spoken, contemplative, and almost devoid of the outgoing Hollywood personality of my father. Our thoughts on teaching were very different, too. I was more of a feel player and I was drawn to the secrets of the mental side of golf and the battle against yourself. Too much in the way of swing mechanics made my head spin. In the way of a book, though, I think it would have made for a nice balance. You would have both sides of the coin, so-to-speak."

Katherine nodded, not one hundred percent grasping everything he was saying, but letting him say it without interrupting.

"I'm sorry," Mack said, suddenly realizing what she was likely thinking. "This is probably like speaking Latin to you."

"No," Katherine said, "I get it. Your theories, like yourselves, were very different. I think that only makes sense. It's very seldom that a father and son see completely eye to eye on something, so it only stands to reason."

"You're a very wise woman," Mack said. "I think it took my father passing away for me to finally appreciate all he had developed and his thoughts on teaching. In the end, I believe incorporating elements of what we both believed is important, and that is what I did my best to impart upon Tyler, and now Jackie."

"Well it obviously worked," Katherine said. "I'm no expert, but from what I understand Tyler is the best player to come out of this area since the club was founded. And if you listen to Tyler, Jackie might end up being even better. I don't think it's too late to publish that book Mack, and with the testimony of those two it can't help but be a best-seller."

"Maybe," Mack said, "but there are a lot of pages left to fill in here. As much as I've contributed, I think there is much more to be covered yet, and I think I'm going to pass it on to Tyler to add his part once he's more fully developed his own theories."

Katherine felt tears well up in her own eyes now as she heard this. She saw plainly how much this book meant to him. It was not only his father's life's work but his own, and he wanted to pass it on to Tyler.

"I obviously never had kids of my own," he said, turning his head slowly to look at Katherine and smiling, "but Tyler's been as close as I could have hoped for and I've been lucky to know him. I know it takes a special woman to understand and love a man who lives this life. It's demanding. But I know you're a special woman."

With that he took an envelope that had been sitting on his table and tucked it inside the journal, closed it, and tied a nice bow in the ribbon holding each side shut.

"Now," he said, "I suppose we ought to have a look at those letters."

"I can go," Katherine said, a bit embarrassed suddenly and wanting to respect his privacy.

"Nonsense," Mack said. "You're the only other person who's ever read them. Don't you want to know how the story ends?"

"Well," Katherine said, "I read them to Tyler, and we both felt kind of bad about that. But at the time we honestly just wanted to try and find out something that would have helped us get in touch with family or friends we weren't trying to be nosy. They're kind of private though. Are you sure you want *me* to know what they say?"

"Yes…" Mack said, pausing as if he was looking for the right words. "I guess I want at least someone to understand the choices

I've made and why. I know they may have been wrong, proud, cowardly, stubborn, just plain stupid, and probably a lot of those things all rolled into one, but I had my reasons."

"But you stopped reading them once she broke it off and sent the ring back," Katherine said. "Didn't you even wonder why she kept sending them?"

"Well, I read those first few letters so many times I could probably quote them word for word," Mack replied. "The final one, though, hit me in a way that I just couldn't handle reading any more. I'd lost my fiancé and my best mate. Lost them to each other. And I was alone in a new country, thousands of miles from home and powerless to do anything about it. The combination of anger, resentment, disappointment, bitterness, and betrayal I felt was so strong I nearly burnt the whole lot of them a hundred times. I couldn't bear to open the rest of them to read about how Thomas had finally relented, and I knew he would. How they'd gotten engaged themselves. How they hoped I could be happy for them and, despite everything, how they actually wanted me to be in their wedding. Ya' see, Thomas and I were like brothers. We'd sworn to be each other's best man someday. But there was just no way... I know it probably sounds foolish now, but I thought all those things and more when I was younger."

"Were you that sure they'd ended up together?" Katherine asked. "In her last letter Mairi made it sound as if Thomas would never betray you in that way."

"Mairi was an attractive, alluring, and determined young woman," Mack said matter-of-factly. "If she really wanted to be with Thomas, he couldn't have ultimately resisted her. And Thomas, well, he really was a great mate, a true friend, and I actually understood why she'd fell for him once I hadn't been around. I think in the end I was afraid that he truly was the better man, and that it was my own foolish pride that had caused me to lose her to him. If I'd never left, it'd never happened... but I did. I'd paid the price for my selfish decision. I knew she didn't want me to go. I knew she didn't relish the idea of leaving everything she knew and everyone she loved. Yet I still stubbornly talked her into it because I knew I could. But once I was gone, and she didn't have me there every day steeling her resolve, telling her how it was going to be fine, how she would adjust, how we'd make new friends and everything else, she'd eventually succumbed to what she really wanted. And I gave all that up just because I thought in order to be a man I had to make my own way."

"I get your feelings, but I don't know..." Katherine said, pausing a moment as she contemplated all he said. "It doesn't add up to me. She wrote more than one letter after breaking it off. Maybe it was an impulsive decision, a weak moment, and she regretted it. I'm a woman, Mack, and I know this... If I'd moved on, gotten engaged, or even married, I wouldn't keep writing my ex fiancé."

"I guess we won't know until I open one," he said gesturing to the box. "But even as expensive as it was back then, I'd convinced myself that if she really regretted her decision, truly, she'd have called and begged me to take her back. She didn't. And writing is a lot easier when you've got something to say that ya' know isn't going to be easy for the other person to hear. That's how she ended it. After that, at least in my mind, each letter just felt like more things I wouldn't want to hear. Maybe I was wrong, but I was hurt and proud and determined to just move on."

Mack looked through the box, thumbing through the unopened letters until he'd settled on the first one following the last opened letter and pulled it out. He looked at the envelope, read the front of it silently and felt the yellowing paper in his hands. All-at-once, he slipped a finger under a part of the flap that the seal had separated and tore it open. He pulled the single folded page out and hesitated just slightly before unfolding it. He looked at it and began to read. He paused after a few moments and looked away briefly, almost as if he needed to compose himself, and then he continued.

More than once Katherine averted her eyes, feeling almost voyeuristic and wanting to give him some sort of privacy to have whatever reaction he needed to have. She started to rise, thinking she would just walk over to the window, leaving her back to him so he wouldn't have to feel her eyes on him, but he put a hand on her arm to stop her.

"It's okay," Mack said softly while a solitary tear finally made its way slowly down his cheek. "I was definitely a fool… it seems… But I guess there's not much I can do about that now."

He laid the letter across his chest and exhaled what Katherine could only imagine was thirty years of suppressed emotion. After a few seconds he handed her the letter, saying, "Go ahead."

Katherine took it from him, but still reticent, she waited until Mack nodded and said, "I'm sure."

Angus,

After my last letter, I'm hesitant to write because, if I know you like I think I do, you'll be just as likely to burn this as read it. As painful as it may be, I need you to hear this because something terrible has happened. First of all, I need you to know that every bit of the anger, disappointment, and whatever else you feel needs to be placed squarely upon me. Ever since I sent that letter I've been terrified that, despite my assurances, you might believe your faithful Thomas' intentions had something to do with what I did, but I promise you they didn't. I did quietly come to love him, but I had never expressed that because after knowing him, I believed his honor and devotion to you would prevent him from ever returning that love. In my weakness, though, I've made a horrible mistake, and made a bad situation worse. Before I wrote you, I thought I'd considered everything. And when I finally did I thought I'd said enough, and thought enough about all of it before I wrote it, to last a lifetime. I'd rehearsed in my head so many times what I needed to tell you, but for some reason I'd never thought about what I'd tell everyone else, and so at first, I didn't.

It was hard enough to tell you in a letter, and it took so much out of me that I didn't want to tell anyone else. I was so embarrassed and ashamed for not remaining faithful to you after showing off my ring and telling everyone about our great plans that I just wanted to avoid it and foolishly believed that somehow it could just go away quietly or would get easier with time. A couple of weeks went by, and when nobody asked, and you didn't write, call, or come rushing back to try and change my mind, I became even more convinced that what I had done was right, and that I really hadn't meant as much to you as I'd silently hoped because you'd obviously given up on me so easily. Someone had noticed, though, and one night after we'd closed and just he and I were mopping up, Thomas finally got up the nerve and asked me why I hadn't been wearing my ring. I swear, I hadn't a clue what to tell him, and I just broke down right there in front of him. I'd kept it all inside and it all just came flooding out of me. I sobbed and sobbed, and told him how I'd ended it because I just couldn't bear the thought of leaving home, my family, friends, everything I'd known, and how embarrassed I'd been to tell everyone.

He was so kind and just sat there next to me letting me cry it out, and that's when I got weak. I looked up into those gentle eyes of his and realized he really had no idea how I felt. I said, "You really don't know, do you?" He just looked at me puzzled, and so I told him. "I couldn't bear the thought of leaving you, Thomas. Can't you see that, you blind fool?" Well, if you didn't believe me before when I told you how honorable he was, what he did next ought to erase all doubts. He got up, took a step back, and looked at me with a combination of what I can only describe as shock and pity.

"I'm truly sorry for you, Mairi," he said after a moment. "You're a good woman, a better woman than I've the right to hope for, but Angus is my best friend, my brother. I'd never be able to live with myself." And he turned, put his keys on the bar, and walked out without saying another word. I was

horrified. Not only by what I'd revealed to him, but his reaction. I don't know what I thought he'd do, but I didn't think he'd just walk out. I thought maybe the shock of what I'd revealed was more than he could handle at the moment, and he'd need time to think, but I think now that even I may have underestimated how truly devoted to you Thomas was.

You see, Angus, he's never come back. Not just to the pub, but anywhere. He's left Peterhead altogether. He phoned the owners the next morning, apologizing, and saying he needed to resign to go be with some ill family, but as far as I know he doesn't have any family. His mother died when you were lads, he said, and he never knew his father. I know he stayed with you and your folks after his mother passed until he was out of school and old enough to take care of himself, but I've checked with them and everyone else, even his landlord, and nobody knows where he's gone. I'm such a mess now, Angus. I know this may be hard to understand after everything I said, but I miss you, and I'm so worried about Thomas. Where would he go? I needed to tell you all of this because even if you hate me, I couldn't stand the thought that maybe because of me you now hated Thomas, too.

He's been a brother to you, and I don't even think you've talked to him since you left. I think that's hurt him. And now I think I've hurt him too. It's such a horrible mess I've made and I still can't tell anyone. The two men I love are now gone, and with each passing day I become more convinced that I won't hear from either of them ever again. I'm sorry for the mess I've made of all our lives, Angus. And I hope someday you'll be able to find a way to forgive me.

M.

As Katherine looked up from the letter to Mack, she had a lump in her chest and realized her own eyes had become full. She didn't know what to say and waited for Mack to respond as she handed him back the letter.

"It would appear my pride may have cost me not only a good woman, but a great friend," he said finally. "I never spoke to either one of them again because I couldn't handle the betrayal I felt. And the thought of them together. Now that appears to have been misguided. What a foolish young man I was, Katherine."

After a few moments, once she realized Mack had slipped back into his thoughts, she asked, "Did you not see or hear of either of them when you went back for your father's or your mother's services years ago?"

"No," Mack said. "Don't get me wrong, I didn't exactly seek them out. I was still bitter and couldn't stand the thought of the family they might have had and the life they'd built when I obviously had none of my own. Peterhead is a small town, though, and Mairi said she wouldn't leave it. They couldn't have missed that my father had passed. He'd been like a father to Thomas, and when they didn't show up, I took it as a slight towards him, and a sign that neither of them could face me after what they'd ultimately done. I guess I was wrong, and as painful as it is to have been wrong, it is somehow a relief to know all the terrible things I've thought about Thomas over the years appear to have been wrong."

"There's still a couple more letters, though," Katherine said. "Are you going to read the rest?"

Mack just sat there and didn't answer immediately as he stared back into the box, but didn't make a move towards them. He looked so tired and weak, and Katherine had the thought that the emotion of this might be taking what little strength he had out of him.

"Maybe you should just rest," she said after a moment. "You can always read the others tomorrow after you've slept a little. I know this isn't easy."

"I've avoided this for thirty years, Katherine," he said turning back to her. "The biggest regrets I have in life are in this box... I was so proud, so headstrong, and so foolish. I guess I somehow believed I could keep all those feelings just locked away like that and I was so determined not to be hurt again that I wasn't brave enough to risk letting anyone else in. I guess it's sort of a sad irony that my heart is what ultimately failed me. Maybe it's appropriate..."

"You're going to get through this," Katherine said, trying to be encouraging. "Once you've had that surgery you'll get your strength back and you've got so..."

Mack raised his hand shakily to cut her off. "Please, Katherine, I appreciate what you're trying to do. They'd have done it already if they weren't afraid it'd kill me... another cruel irony I suppose. The very thing that could save me just might kill me. I'd have liked to seen Tyler fulfill his dream. He's a generational talent,

Katherine. More importantly, though, he's a good man. But then I think ya' already know that. When you do what I do you're lucky if ya' see talent like his come around once in your lifetime, so don't be too hard on him for having a hard time walking away from what God has given him.

"It's hard to explain, Katherine, but a real man needs to make it on his own. He needs to know that he can take care of and provide for his family and the people he loves on his own merits. Without that, you're left with a bit of a hollow feeling, a kind of hole inside you that you can't ever fill with any amount of someone else's money. I understood that as a young man. What I didn't understand was no matter how much you fill up that hole, your life is still empty unless you've got someone that you can truly share it with. I know that now, and despite the friends I've made here and the good life I made for myself, I realize that it's been just exactly that… for myself. And there's nothing left in these letters that won't serve to do anything but confirm that one way or another."

Katherine just sat there, not knowing what to say or do next. She wished Tyler was here. He should be here, not her. Then, maybe it was easier for Mack to talk about all this with her than it would have been with Tyler, or any other man for that matter. He was weak and vulnerable after so many years of doing his best to put up such a stoic façade, and she was not only sympathetic to that, but understanding.

"I think you're at least partly right, you've had enough for one day. And whatever's in there can wait till at least you're back on your feet and a little stronger," she said with a note of encouragement.

"Maybe you're right…" Mack said, looking back at her from the place in the ceiling where he'd almost burned a hole in it with his gaze. "I'm not sure this old man can handle much more. At least not today. I'm tired, my dear, but I want to thank you for coming to sit with me, and for listening to me. I'm sorry for unloading all of this on ya'. It wasn't right of me to do that, but I'm grateful for it. I've dealt with so much in this life on my own and it's nice to have a sympathetic ear. Tyler's a lucky man. Now please, go. I've taken up too much of your time already and I know how much you have to do yet for tomorrow."

"It's been my pleasure," Katherine said standing and leaning over to kiss him on the forehead. "And thank you for sharing it all with me. It's been an honor. Tomorrow's the Gala and I'll be really busy, but I'll check back in on you Sunday, and Tyler ought to be back by then."

Mack smiled, nodded slightly, and closed his eyes as Katherine turned and walked away to the sound of his soft breathing mixed with the incessant beeping of the monitors he was hooked up to. As she walked out the door, a nurse was entering and Katherine stopped her.

"Can you keep a close eye on him tonight?" she asked, almost choking on the request. "He's awfully weak, and I'm afraid for him right now."

"We definitely have both eyes on him, miss," she replied. "As often as we can."

Katherine decided to run down to the cafeteria on her way out and get a cup of coffee to go before she left. She had a number of last-minute things to tie up for the Gala and would need to go back to the office for a few hours tonight. This visit with Mack had left her drained, emotionally and physically, and she needed to recharge her batteries in order to finish everything she needed to. Ten minutes later, with the first drink of hot coffee, she felt the warmth of it creep into her limbs and wake her from the emotional haze she'd been in, and then, in stark contrast a sudden clarity and a cold feeling washed over her completely... And she knew he was gone.

Mike Dowd

THE LONGEST WALK

When Tyler and Jackie got back from dinner that night, they decided to play a game of cards. The anticipation of the final round had both of them a bit restless, and since they had a late tee time Tyler decided an hour or so of some mindless entertainment would help them both relax and get a good night's sleep. Cards was something he and Jackie had always turned to on those rainy day family occasions when they couldn't go outside, and Jackie had of late been imploring Tyler to teach him how to play poker. He'd seen a lot of it on TV and wanted to know how to play all the games. 7-card Stud, 5-card Draw, and especially Texas Hold 'em. Having already given him a basic grasp of those core forms, Tyler had decided it was time to teach him some of the more exotic games. Poker was something Tyler and the guys on his team had played a lot in the dorm at Vanderbilt. For four years Tyler had whiled away many an afternoon eating chips and salsa, drinking Milwaukee's Best, and becoming one of the best poker players in Nashville. At least in his own mind.

"Okay, Jackie," Tyler said, "this one's called 727. What you're trying to do is get as close to 7 or 27 as you can. You start with two cards. Numbered cards are worth their face value and face cards are worth a half."

Tyler taught Jackie 727, Criss-Cross, Omaha, and a couple of other games in the next hour until he could sense Jackie was starting to nod.

"Why don't you get some sleep, Jackie," Tyler said. "We've got a big day tomorrow and I don't want you pooping out on me on the back nine. I'm going to go out in the hall and make a quick phone call."

"Alright," Jackie said. "I am getting tired."

Jackie got ready for bed and Tyler went outside in the hall and closed the door behind him. He suddenly wanted to talk to Mack. He was a little wired still and knew he'd have a tough time sleeping, so he thought a few words of advice from his coach would be helpful. He'd really wanted Mack here this time around, and while he was thoroughly enjoying this time with Jackie, he felt a couple of words from his long-time mentor might be invaluable going into the final round.

He called the hospital's main number and hit the extension for Mack's room. The line rang and rang, but no one answered.

"Probably asleep," Tyler said softly to no one in particular, but he was suddenly concerned. He'd had a couple of texts from Katherine saying she'd been checking in on him in the evenings, and all was status quo, but something nagged at him so he decided to text her to see if she'd been in to see him today.

"Hi, you see Mack today?"

He saw that it was received, but no immediate reply came. About ten seconds later came the one-word response from her.

"Yes."

Tyler waited for her to expand on it as he suspected she would, but when another ten seconds went by, he typed.

"I phoned the room and there was no answer. Figured he was sleeping…"

Instead of a response, Katherine's name and smiling face came up on the screen. She was calling.

"Hey," Tyler said, feeling suddenly uneasy as he picked up the phone and began pacing down the hall. "What's going on?"

"Tyler," Katherine said on the other end. "I'm sorry, I'd decided not to call you. I know you've got a big day tomorrow, but once you texted I didn't know what else to do."

"It's okay," Tyler said. "You went to see Mack today? What's up?"

Tyler heard Katherine swallow hard on the other end, and then inhale sharply before continuing in a faltering voice.

"Mack is gone, Tyler."

Tyler stopped where he was walking and fell back against the wall as his knees buckled. He slowly slid down against the wall until he was sitting on the floor.

"W-what do you mean?" Tyler said, already knowing the answer to his own question.

"He's passed, Tyler, peacefully," Katherine continued through audible sobs. "I'm so sorry, and sorry I'm having to tell you over the phone like this. I wanted to wait until you got home and tell you in person. When you asked, though, I-I just couldn't lie. I didn't want to tell you until after your final round tomorrow in case you were doing well."

"What happened?" Tyler asked, still not believing what he was hearing. "He's supposed to have surgery to fix everything."

"I was here," Katherine continued. "I came to visit him tonight. He was very weak and tired. He was concerned he wouldn't make it to surgery, or at least make it out of it, and so he asked me to go to the house and get him a couple of things."

"What?" Tyler exclaimed more than asked, still in stunned disbelief and not processing what he was hearing. "What could he possibly have wanted?"

"He asked for his teaching journal…" Katherine replied, and then stopped, sniffling and trying to collect herself, "…and the letters."

"The letters?" Tyler asked, still incredulous. "I don't understand. Why now? I can't believe this. Why did he need those? Why does this have to happen?"

"I'm so so sorry, I don't know, Tyler," she replied through her sobs. "But he seemed to sense what was going to happen. He said he'd avoided those letters and what they might say for thirty years, and it was time he finally knew."

"Is that what did it?" Tyler asked, almost accusatory. "What did they say? Why'd you even go get him those things? He obviously wasn't strong enough to handle whatever it was."

"Don't you think I haven't thought that, Tyler," Katherine said defensively. "It felt like a dying wish, and how was I supposed to deny him such a small thing. I feel terrible enough as it is. What was I supposed to do?"

"I'm sorry," Tyler said quickly, "I didn't mean it like that, I-I just can't believe this. Was it that bad?"

"I don't know, Tyler. He was very emotional. He only read one while I was with him, and he learned that his friend Thomas hadn't betrayed him like he thought he had. He was very emotional and had a ton of regret about how he'd thought of him for all these years, but he was somewhat comforted by the news at the same time. After that he said he didn't know if he wanted to read any more. He said it wouldn't change anything and after reading the one he wasn't so sure he could handle whatever else he might learn."

"Well, what happened then?" Tyler asked.

"I agreed, after seeing how emotional he was and what it was taking out of him. I said the others could wait until he was stronger and more rested. I told him goodnight and asked the nurse to keep an eye on him and I left for the cafeteria to get a cup of coffee. I've got the Gala tomorrow, as you know, and I still had to go back to the office to take care of some last minute things. Ten minutes later, I'd gotten the coffee and was about to head back to the office when I somehow just knew. I hurried back upstairs and found him appearing to have gone to sleep. At first I was relieved, glad that I'd been wrong. It looked like he'd opened and read another one of the letters after all, though, which lay in his hand across his chest. I was about to take the letter from his hand and put it away in the box when I suddenly realized the monitors had stopped beeping, and the nurse came in behind me not a second later, excitedly summoning others and asking me to please step outside. I waited just outside as they attempted to revive him, but about fifteen minutes later the same nurse came out and found me in the hall."

"Mr. McLean has passed," she said. "Peacefully. He apparently just went to sleep and they were unable to revive him."

"…I should have been there," Tyler said after a few moments. "I'm so sorry you were there by yourself to handle that, Katherine. I should have been there…"

"You're where he wanted you to be, Tyler," she said, "and you couldn't have done anything."

"I could have been there. I should be there," Tyler said. "I'm coming home."

"There's nothing you can do, Tyler," Katherine said. "And I really don't think Mack would want you to do that on his account. He wanted to see you succeed, Tyler, and unless you're already out of it, coming home now isn't going to accomplish anything. I asked and they say they won't do anything for a couple of days and I can help you organize a service if you want when you get back."

"What am I gonna' do?" Tyler asked, more to the heavens than Katherine. "What do I tell Jackie?"

"Well, I think you just need to tell him the truth," Katherine said. "I'm sorry, Tyler. I know that won't be easy. This hasn't been easy."

"I know. I understand…" Tyler replied. "Thank you, Katherine. Thank you for being there. I'm so sorry I wasn't there with you. You don't know how much I appreciate you always being there and what that means to me."

"You're welcome," she replied. "I wish you were too, but honestly I'm glad that I was able to be. I can't exactly explain it, but I think he was strangely comforted by my visits. We had kind of become close in the past few weeks. He really was a special man, Tyler. Are you going to be okay?"

"I… I don't know, Katherine. I really don't know," Tyler said as he exhaled heavily. "I've got a lot to think about, and I know how much you still have to do yourself to get ready for tomorrow. Please just go ahead and do that and I'll talk to you when I get home," Tyler said. "I know all you do is hard enough as it is without having this hanging over your head… you really are amazing."

"Okay, and thank you," she said after hesitating a moment, seemingly at a loss for words now. "Tyler, I… I've just got to go."

"I understand," he said. "I'll talk to you tomorrow." And then they both hung up.

Tyler just sat there for a few minutes with his head in his hands trying to figure out what he was going to tell Jackie. I should have been there, he kept thinking. In the end, he decided Katherine was right and he went back inside the room, but found Jackie fast asleep.

Tyler turned off the light and laid down on the bed. He rolled this way and that, but try as he might there was no way he could sleep after what he'd just learned. After about twenty minutes he decided he needed to take a walk so he could think. He slipped out of bed quietly, pulled on his jeans, his tennis shoes, and a jacket. He wrote Jackie a quick note and left it on the bed where he would see it in case he woke and slipped quietly into the hall. Once he was outside, Tyler just started walking without thought as to where he was going. He walked through the small lobby of the hotel and out the front door into the night.

What had just happened? What was going to happen? He'd not only just lost his boss, but his coach and long-time mentor. Most importantly, though, he'd lost a friend. More than a friend. Mack had said that Tyler was as close to a son as he had, and in truth, he knew he looked to Mack for help and advice more than he did his own father. It dawned on him suddenly that, aside from the time he was away at school, Tyler had actually spent more time in the last ten years with Mack than he had his own father, too. And he seemed to be just now scratching the surface.

Mack had taught him so much, and not just about golf, but about life. His simple, understated, but profound wisdom was something Tyler now realized he not only admired, but had subconsciously imitated. Mack had a way of slipping little things into a lesson, a discussion, or even just an observation that made you think. He wasn't outspoken, listening far more than he spoke, but when he did you listened. Because you always knew it would be something worth hearing.

A soft rain began to fall and Tyler realized suddenly that he had no idea where he was going. He had been just walking down the frontage road the hotel was on towards the bright lights of the commercial district down the street from his hotel, and not knowing what actually lay in front of him. He passed a big box store and some fast food restaurants and he suddenly realized he was standing in front of the big red barn that was the BBQ joint he and Gabe had spent far too many hours at last year. He frowned at the memory that in some ways seemed a lifetime ago. He felt like he'd done more growing up in the past year than in four years away at college and had a hard time reconciling with the memory and how foolish he'd been. Things were different now.

His thoughts turned back to Mack and how disappointed he was because in some ways he only just now seemed to really be opening up to Tyler. He had a whole treasure trove of life experiences and stories he'd never even shared with Tyler when he was growing up. Was Mack right when he said that at least part of that was because he'd never asked? Had he been so self-absorbed when he was younger that he hadn't really even been interested in the life behind the man he'd been learning so much about life from? The regret he now felt was for not asking more questions, not being more interested, not asking Mack to tell more stories was something that tore at him. He'd never be able to hear any of them now, and he knew there was so much more to learn.

And what about the club? Mack had been the face of Butler Bluff for thirty years. The foundation around which everything there seemed to be built. He'd shepherded the club and all its members through the past three decades and touched more lives there than anyone could count. He was a friend and mentor to a lot more people than just Tyler. When anyone thought of Butler Bluff they thought of the stoic old Scot. And while Tyler had always known he was originally from somewhere else, in his mind, Mack had always been there as far back as he could remember. That other life before

Poplar Bluff almost seemed like just another story, one that belonged to someone else. Where would the club turn? What would they all do without Mack? Tyler had worked there less than a year and learned a lot from Mack, but it wasn't really until the past few weeks since Mack had fallen ill that the full scope of everything that Mack was responsible for had become clear to him.

The rain began to fall harder and turned Tyler's thoughts back to golf and what tomorrow meant. He wasn't prepared to get soaked, so he turned back in the direction of the hotel and looked for the shelter of a storefront awning to wait out the squall. The course was going to be soft tomorrow if this kept up, and that meant guys were going to be able to shoot a number. Players who might have been too far back to make a move on a typical firm and fast blustery day at Aberdeen would get their chance. That all seemed so insignificant now, though. Tyler was confused by how detached he felt from that reality and tomorrow's outcome in general. He wasn't nervous like he thought he'd be, not at all. Something about what had happened with Mack seemed to bring into focus what was most important, and being nervous over a game of golf, even one as important as the final round of Q-School, seemed almost laughable at the moment. So much in life was so fragile, and so much more important. And after all the years he spent dreaming of this moment, he found it almost hard to believe he felt that way suddenly.

He thought of Katherine. So much of what they'd been through seemed to be starting and stopping. So much of what they'd seemed to be struggling with was figuring out how each of them, and their individual places in the world, fit with each other. Tyler knew they each wanted to be together, but each of their visions of what together looked like had been what they so struggled to rectify of late. While Tyler had spent half his life dreaming of life beyond Poplar Bluff, and the wide world of opportunity that lay out there, it seemed, at times, that Katherine had spent as much time dreaming about a life whose borders weren't much beyond Butler County. Despite her own opportunities, she didn't seem to need anything more than she already had to be complete, except maybe someone to share it with. She appreciated all the simpler things in life, appreciated them in a way that made them seem profound. Everything she wanted, and wanted Tyler to want, seemed so obviously to be the things that Tyler's head told him were the things that were most important in life. But the awareness of that didn't make it any easier for his heart to walk away from everything he was and had been. Katherine was home. But Tyler, like Mack had, felt the need to forge his own path. And no matter where they were in the world, as long as she was with him, it would be home. And golf had always been the key to opening up that door.

God had given him a gift and to waste that would be criminal. He'd heard someone say once, maybe even Mack, that the saddest thing in life was wasted talent. He had a rare talent for the game, and he knew that. He saw the game in a way others didn't. It was a chess match against the course wrapped inside a battle against yourself. But at the same time, for him, it was an expression of himself. He could hit shots other guys couldn't, or wouldn't, and part of that was not just that he knew how to hit them, but he saw them before they were struck. Like an image in his mind, or the replay of a shot he'd hit before, and once his mind had drawn it up his body knew how to execute it. He didn't have to tell it to, it just did. He could feel the shot before he hit it, somewhere inside. Maybe it had something to do with how many times he'd hit similar shots before, and maybe it was something else altogether, but he had that and he knew it was unique. Tyler didn't go so far as to believe that golf was so important that the almighty had actually intervened on his behalf, but there were days when it almost felt that way. And while he knew the game was impossible to master, for him at least, some days it became almost comically simple. And so while he was not given to arrogance or self-aggrandizement, the thought of being asked to give that up felt like something akin to asking Mozart not to compose, Michelangelo not to sculpt, or Picasso not to paint.

The rain slackened just a bit, and Tyler decided he ought to start walking back before it came down hard again. He couldn't believe Mack was gone. And he couldn't believe he hadn't been there for him. Despite the fact that Katherine said there was nothing he could do, and common sense told him that even had he been there things likely wouldn't have been different, something nagged at him about the fact that he wasn't. He might not have been able to do anything about Mack, but he had left Katherine alone to deal with something so traumatic, and he knew he should have been there. It must have been terrible. He couldn't even imagine, and on top of it all she had to go and run the Gala tomorrow night and act like nothing had happened. She'd known Mack for years, and he'd always liked her, but their relationship had never moved much beyond polite acknowledgment and a handful of casual dinners with Tyler over the years after events. That had changed in the past few weeks, and because she'd grown closer to him, he knew how hard that call had to have been for her to make. These past few weeks had only served to reinforce for her how truly special Tyler's relationship with Mack had been, and how special he had been. Tyler should have been there. And not having been was going to be something Tyler knew he would regret for the rest of his life. In the end, he was only here because of Mack. He owed so much to him, and it suddenly became so clear to him how much getting through Q-School, and qualifying for the Tour, had been something he had been doing not just for himself, and not just to prove he could do it to himself, but how much it had been for Mack. Because he knew how much it meant to him, and now he was gone.

As Tyler walked up in front of his hotel, the rain suddenly stopped. And as the door slid open, revealing the brightly lit lobby beyond, it was as if the clouds had parted, and with it a complete sense of peace began to well up in him, and he knew what he could do.

IT JUST WASN'T MEANT TO BE

Katherine felt numb all day Saturday. She'd worked nearly as hard this year to bring the Gala together, and she knew after what she'd done last year the expectations were even higher. She'd felt so excited last year as the event neared, but with Mack's heart attack, her looming career decision, and the unsettled nature of what her and Tyler were going through, things just didn't feel the same. She knew she was organized, and after having gone through it once already she was confident that everything was coming together. But she had mixed emotions about the whole night. She'd indicated to everyone that this was very likely her last Gala, as she would be moving on to take another position, and so she had hoped to leave on a high note. But she felt like the energy had been sucked out everything. She'd been hoping to find someone she could train, someone to take over the event when she was gone, but no one really suitable had stepped up. Karen Gibson was still involved, but she had a new grandbaby and didn't have the requisite time or inclination to be that person. And most of the other interns and volunteers they had didn't have the level of commitment needed. The event had become her baby, and she'd begun to despair that it was going to die. And she had a hard time reconciling with that because of how hard her mother had worked to make it a reality.

And as much as she had to do, she just couldn't get poor Mack out of her mind. He'd essentially died in front of her. She, of all people, was the last person he'd spoken to, and she couldn't help feeling like she could have and should have done more, or something different. Maybe she shouldn't have left him when she did. Maybe she should have asked to have the doctor come in and look at him since he seemed so weak. And maybe she shouldn't have brought him those letters. Reading the one had obviously taken a lot out of him, not just physically, but emotionally, and once she'd left, he'd obviously decided to read one more. And that's how she'd found him. With that last letter across his chest. When she found him as she did, it hadn't occurred to her to look at it, but she now wondered if it held some shock, disappointment, or final revelation; opening the door to a fresh wave of regret which had resulted in Mack just finally going to sleep for good.

And calling Tyler to tell him about it had been one of the hardest things she'd ever done. Something like that should be done in person, and she'd been so afraid of how the news would affect him, especially if he'd been playing well. Qualifying was so important to Tyler, and he'd worked so hard for so long to get where he was. She couldn't stand the idea that this would cause him to falter, and she knew Mack would turn over in his grave if he knew he'd been the cause of Tyler not qualifying.

The afternoon had progressed as planned, and despite the fact that Katherine felt she was only there in body most of the day, her preparations had everything humming along as they should have. It was nearly 6:00, and as the time for guests to arrive approached, she ran down her last-minute instructions to Jenny, Karen's youngest daughter, who'd agreed to stand in for Tyler when he'd abdicated that responsibility to return to Q-School. She was a pretty girl, and pretty sharp too. She seemed genuinely interested in the Society and the event, and would have been a great trainee. But she was a senior in high school with plenty of opportunities and would be preparing to head off to college next year before this event came around the next time.

As she was pointing towards the door and explaining how they would greet people as they arrived, the door opened and Tyler walked in wearing a tuxedo and looking about as handsome as she'd ever seen him. He walked up, took her hand, kissed her gently, and acknowledged Jenny.

"Sorry I'm late," he said matter-of-factly. "What can I do?"

"W-what's going on?" Katherine asked in disbelief, yet happy to see him. "I didn't think you'd be back until later tonight."

"You don't think I'd miss something as important as the Gala, do you?" Tyler asked smiling slyly. "You only work all year for this night, and after how much you've been there for me I wasn't about to let you down."

Katherine looked at Jenny, who was smiling now, and asked, "Did you know about this?"

"I think I'll go help my mother with the silent auction, Katherine," she answered as way of a response. "It appears you've got things covered here."

"What happened?" Katherine said turning to Tyler, still shocked to see him.

"We can talk later," Tyler said, pointing to the door where the first couple had just made their entrance. "It appears you have guests. Do I need to know anything different than last year?"

"Uh, no" she said, collecting herself. "The table diagram on the easel is the same." And then, just before the couple was close enough to hear her, she turned to look at him and smiled, "Thank you for being here."

****

The evening went as smoothly as Katherine had hoped, in truth, better than she'd hoped. Somehow Tyler being there had made her feel right about everything again, and she'd regained her energy and focus on the evening and every one of her guests. Her speech, while less personal than last year, came off every bit as well as she'd focused on how cancer had touched the lives of so many of the families in their community. And when she lifted the veil on some of the more well known cases by telling the very human side to their stories, there wasn't a dry eye in the house by the time she was done.

Tyler had handled his duties as effectively as last year, and all the while smiled and was gracious in a way that she knew had to belie the way he was truly feeling only twenty-four hours after finding out about Mack's passing. And what about Q-School, she thought. They weren't in a position to exchange more than a small handful of words throughout the evening, and she couldn't help but think that only the fact that he must have played well could have been buoying his spirits enough to make it possible for him to get through this evening as well as he was.

As things finally wound down, and she'd thanked the last of the guests for coming, she finally turned to Tyler who was standing at her side once again and smiled as she grabbed a bottle of unopened champagne from an ice bucket near the server's station.

"Shall we go to my office?" she asked with a smile while nodding in the direction of the same place they'd spent that time talking after last year's event.

"Show me the way, madam," Tyler said formally, offering his arm to her.

They walked out the back doors of the Community Center and to the little business office where they'd sat in private to talk before. At first they didn't speak. Katherine was still in the afterglow of the evening, and it wasn't until they got inside and Katherine slipped off her heels and settled into the over-stuffed couch that she finally relaxed, and the reality of what had transpired in the past twenty-four hours came flooding back.

"I'm so so sorry about, Mack," she said turning to Tyler suddenly. "With everything this evening, it got pushed to the back of my mind. But that's no excuse. He was an incredible man. I just wish I'd gotten to know him better earlier. I can really see why you were so close to him."

"I feel the same way, to an extent," Tyler said. "I mean, I've known him forever, but it only seems in the past year did he really start opening up. Talking about his past and all his experiences. You know he really lived quite a life before he came over here."

"Oh," Katherine said, getting up suddenly and heading over to a box of things she'd locked up in the office prior to the event. "I think he meant you to have this," she continued as she pulled out the large leather-bound teaching journal and the envelope with Tyler's name on it.

"Thank you," Tyler said, putting it on the small coffee table. "I'll look at it later."

"My God," she exclaimed suddenly. "Being here, and everything this evening and with Mack has thrown me I guess, but what happened? With Q-School, I mean. Why are you even here? I didn't think you could make it back in time."

"Well, I didn't know in advance how many players there would be, and I figured if things had gone as I'd hoped I might be cutting it close," Tyler replied. "I mean, I reserved the tux in advance just in case, but I didn't want you counting on me and then end up letting you down…"

"Oh," she said, giving him the time to say what she figured wasn't easy.

"You know, it feels almost surreal to be saying this now… but in the end, I really believe it just wasn't meant to be," Tyler said finally, not meeting her eyes, but looking at the floor and running both hands through his hair in apparent disbelief as he leaned forward in the couch.

"I'm so sorry," Katherine said genuinely, instinctively reaching to put an arm around his shoulders, but then withdrawing somewhat awkwardly before he looked up. "I know how hard you worked for it… What are you going to do now?"

"Well, the way I see it," Tyler said as he looked up at her with a surprisingly contented smile, "Jackie's gonna' need a new coach. He and just about everyone else at the club."

"I see," Katherine said, taking a sip off the bottle of champagne and handing it to him. She suddenly didn't know what to say. Before tonight, before all that had happened in the past twenty-four hours, she had worked herself up to the point where she was prepared to tell him what she'd decided. But now she couldn't hide the indecision in her heart.

"What's the matter?" Tyler asked confused. "This isn't exactly the reaction I expected. I thought you'd be happy to hear I wasn't going anywhere. I know it's taken a lot for me to get here, but isn't this what you really wanted?"

"It was," Katherine replied hesitantly, unsure of her words, "it's just that I'd finally come to the conclusion that it wasn't what you wanted, Tyler… and I guess I just don't know if I believe that it really is… I know you have a gift, Tyler, and I understand that kind of gift isn't something you just walk away from. What happens when next year rolls around, and the year after that. Are you telling me you will really be content not trying again? Are you really going to be satisfied with the idea of taking over for Mack, if the club will even have you, or isn't that just the interim plan?"

"Wow… with all that's happened, Katherine, I think that's pretty harsh, and unfair I might add," Tyler said. "And besides, you don't understand."

"I'm sorry, I didn't mean it to sound that way, but let me finish," Katherine stopped him as she shook her head. "God, I wish you'd qualified. It would have made this so much easier… You see, the start-up I've got that final interview with this week has changed their plans, Tyler. They're not coming to Poplar Bluff. If I get the job, they want me to move to Kansas City now. It's a really good opportunity, Tyler, and I was honestly considering taking it."

"What?!" Tyler almost shouted. "After all your talk about not wanting to leave home and everyone we know and love you want to up and move to Kansas City? Where does that leave me? I can't believe I'm hearing this."

"Tyler," she said softly. "You were the reason I wanted to be here, and I know you really still don't. You want to play the Tour. I get that, and this town, this life, I don't think any of it will ever be big enough, or good enough for you, Tyler... and that includes me. Without you, everything in this town will just remind me of what might have been. What we could have had..."

"We can have it!" Tyler protested. "I can't believe I'm hearing this. I love you Katherine, and I'm not..."

Katherine cut him off again, throwing her hands up in front of her face to shut him down and glancing away as if in pain.

"Stop, Tyler," she said, crying now but indignant at the same time. "You know as well as I do you were prepared to leave me behind if you didn't succeed in talking me into traipsing around the country with you when you'd qualified. And you and Mack both had me convinced that you were good enough to do just that. I'm beyond sorry it didn't work out, but you knew I was less than excited about that lifestyle and that didn't even make you think twice about pursuing it. Did you really expect me to just hang around here once you'd made it? Didn't you take me serious, or did you think I'd ultimately just come around to the idea?"

"Of course not, but..." he tried to interject, but she again stopped him mid-sentence, shaking her head and almost shouting over him now.

"You left me once, Tyler, and, despite all your assurances, you were prepared to do it again if I wouldn't buy in. And even though I'd finally come to terms with the fact that I would, despite all my reservations about that life, I was ready to support you so you could realize your dream until it hit me that you were going through with it with or without me. How am I supposed to feel about that? How can I trust you anymore when you were prepared to leave again at the first opportunity? And what am I supposed to do now that I have a great opportunity and a chance to fulfill goals and dreams of my own? Just give them up? I might have been willing to do that five years ago, but I told you before, Tyler, I'm not the same girl."

"But this is what you wanted," Tyler protested, upset now and gesturing wildly to everything around him. He still obviously couldn't believe what he was hearing.

"But I needed you to want it too, Tyler," she said, lowering her voice slightly as she tried to stay calm herself through her tears while folding her hands to her chest. "You still don't appreciate what you have right here, and that includes me. Did you ever stop to think that maybe this was your real gift, that I was? No, because you've never really wanted any of this as much as your dream. You ended up here, Tyler, you didn't choose to be here, and I can't live the rest of my life knowing in the end you settled for it, settled for me, once you'd run out of better options."

Tyler got up, he was shaking now, and seemed as if he was going to start to say something, but then he just shook his head and stared back at her with a look of angry disbelief she'd never seen in him. Katherine indicated for him to sit back down and was about to tell him to just calm down, but now it was his turn to interrupt her and he waved her off before she even got the words out.

"You've been right about chasing a dream, Katherine, you're just wrong about which one of us was doing it," he said coolly. "Life isn't some Hollywood movie, Katherine, and I'm so sorry the reality of ours hasn't measured up to the nice little fairy tale you've built up in your head. And you know what else? You don't know a damn thing about the choices I've made!"

And with that he turned for the door, only pausing long enough to pick up the teaching journal Mack had left to him on the coffee table, and to call back with a tone of finality as he walked out, "Congratulations on your event."

Mike Dowd

A FINAL GOODBYE

Five days later, Tyler found himself at Mack's memorial service. The preparations had come together mostly thanks to a small group of ladies at the club who'd insisted on Memorial Gardens and then a reception afterwards back at the club. Tyler would be a pall-bearer and speak at the reception, along with old Garret Williams and a small handful of other members that Mack had grown close to over the years.

The day of the service, Tyler was in as unhappy a mood as he'd ever remembered being in. He'd practiced what he wanted to say about Mack, but it didn't feel good enough or that he could say enough about the remarkable man who'd left such an impression on him. Try as he might, though, speaking in public wasn't Tyler's strong suit, and despite his fury with her, Tyler secretly found himself wishing he'd had Katherine's help. This was her department, not his, but he'd just have to make the best of it.

The morning had dawned just as drearily as Tyler's mood, with a steady drizzle ensuring a sea of umbrellas and a shorter graveside service than Tyler felt was warranted for his friend. Mack was gone, and despite the fact that Tyler knew there would still be tales told of a handful of his exploits around the club on and off for years, it just didn't seem a fitting end for the man who had been such an influence on his life. He deserved more than just a simple day and a simple service to remind the world of the person he'd been. It was so unfair, Tyler thought, yet in some ways perfectly fitting for the man who lived so simply, and ultimately probably was what Mack would have wanted.

As the grave-side service concluded, Tyler scanned the armada of mostly over-sized golf umbrellas that had materialized and was pleased at least that the crowd had been quite large. The majority of the attendees were members of the club, some employees, and a handful of fellow golf professionals from the area. But his folks, his aunt, uncle, and Jackie were there too. Katherine had come, as he knew she would, but they hadn't spoken since the night of the Gala, and she'd stood opposite of him, along with her father, and he couldn't even bring himself to meet her gaze.

As people began filing back to their cars, the rain suddenly halted and a small break in the clouds allowed a few hopeful rays of sun to escape. As the majority of the umbrellas went down in response, Tyler noticed two individuals he didn't recognize still standing silently at the gravesite, looking down at where the casket lay in wait of burial. The first was an exceedingly tall and broad gentleman who looked to be roughly 60 years of age and most out of place in an ill-fitting suit that obviously hadn't been tailored correctly for someone of his build. The second was a pretty, strawberry blond woman of roughly half his age. She held a single rose in her hand, and as she tossed it down upon the open grave, she looked up crying at the much larger older man and he pulled her into a familiar embrace.

The scene was uncommonly intimate, more appropriate of family who'd just lost a loved one, but so out of place and unlike anything else that had taken place that morning that it caught Tyler off guard. Who were these people that seemed so distraught at Mack's passing, and why hadn't he met them before? Tyler suddenly felt it appropriate to introduce himself, and maybe invite them to the reception at the club in case they hadn't been. As he slowly walked over to the two, not quite wanting to intrude on their moment, they looked up at him, since most everyone else had by now begun moving in the opposite direction.

"Hello there," Tyler said by way of introduction and extending his hand. "I don't believe we've met. Tyler Foster. Mack was my boss, and my coach, but mostly my very good friend. I'm going to be speaking at the reception."

The older gentleman, who Tyler could now see had close shaven reddish gray hair, shook Tyler's hand and replied in a thick Scottish burr.

"Guid mornin'," he said solemnly, extending a meaty hand to Tyler. "Angus was like my brother…, name's Thomas, Thomas Lawrie. And this is Agnes," he said as he turned to allow the younger woman who'd somewhat collected herself now to extend her hand and address Tyler.

"Guid ta' mait ya', Mr. Foster." Agnes said. "Ye knew Angus well then?"

"I suppose as well as anyone," Tyler replied as modestly as he could. "He sometimes said I was as close to a son as he had, but I think that was mostly because of our age difference. I suppose I thought of him more as a big brother."

Agnes looked at him with a sad expression he couldn't exactly place.

"He was me…" she stopped suddenly, as if she was fishing for the right word, or wasn't exactly sure of what she was about to say. "…Apparently he *was* me father," she said finally.

Tyler just about fell over, and as he leaned on the tree next to him to steady himself Thomas put a concerned hand on his shoulder.

"Ye okay, Mr. Foster?" he asked.

"Yes, yes, I'll be fine," Tyler said, inhaling sharply. A moment later he collected himself and stood up straight. "It's just that I recently learned some very personal things about Mack's, or Angus' past. There were some things that came up about you, Thomas, but he never mentioned anything at all about having a daughter... I hope I'm not speaking terribly insensitively here, but knowing what I know, and knowing him as I did, I honestly have a hard time believing he had a daughter, or at least one that he actually knew about. Is that possible?"

"A believe you're right," Thomas said, "and that's wha A've been tryin' to tell Agnes here for the past couple of weeks since she learnt of him, but she needed to find out for sure. A knew Angus as well as anyone, despite our lack of a relationship for the past thirty years, and so A agreed to try and contact him for her, ta find out wha he really knew, and that's how A found out he'd passed. In truth, it never really set right with me tha he turned his back on his own flesh and blood."

Agnes was wiping tears from her face with a handkerchief now and Thomas put his arm around her.

"A'm sorry, Mr. Foster," she said sobbing. "It's just tha me mum finally passed about ten days ago, too."

"I'm so sorry for your loss..." Tyler replied.

"She had cancer," she continued, trying to collect herself, "...but in her last days she said she needed to finally tell me where me name came from, and that's when she told me all about Angus. They'd been engaged, she said, with plans to relocate, but she said she broke it off a couple of months after Angus left for Missouri because she realized she just could'na leave home. She said she wrote him repeatedly and tried to call him ta tell him once she found out she was pregnant, but it all went unanswered. Once A was born, though, and he still had'na responded to any of her attempts to contact him, she said she stopped trying and decided that he was dead to her, and vowed that was all she would ever tell me in order to spare me the pain of his abandonment."

"This is just so unbelievable," Tyler exclaimed shaking his head, "…but there's something I think you really need to know, Agnes. Angus never even opened most of your mother's letters. I really only learned about his engagement to her recently. He's always been a bachelor. I guess it was something I never really questioned, but when he had the heart attack my girlfriend Katherine and I went to his house to try and find something that would help us get in touch with any family he might have had because he was unconscious. We found almost nothing personal at all, but a box of letters from your mother was in his coat closet. We felt bad about reading a few of them, but we were trying desperately to find clues that would lead to family we could contact. There were at least seven or eight letters, but he only opened the first three, the last of which being the one that she sent back his ring in when she broke it off and it mentioned nothing at all about the prospect of a child."

"So ye don't think he ever even knew about me?" Agnes asked with a strangely hopeful note in her voice.

"No, I honestly don't," Tyler said.

"A guess that's part of why we came all this way…" she continued. "A just needed to ken, A'm not sure how A expected to find tha out, but A just had to ken more, and learn a wee bit about who he was, and A suppose who A am."

"He said he was so devastated when she broke it off that he never opened the rest of the letters, and if he didn't open the letters he probably wouldn't have taken her calls either, and in those days most people didn't have answering machines. Once he awoke in the hospital, though, he ultimately asked for those letters, and Katherine went and got them for him because I was out of town. She asked him why he never opened the rest and he said he was just too hurt to hear all about her life without him. In that last letter he'd opened, she confessed that she'd fallen in love with Thomas, and Mack, Angus I mean, felt so betrayed that he said he couldn't bear to hear any more about what he imagined was their life together, their wedding plans, or their pleas for his forgiveness."

Agnes turned to Thomas now with a confused look. "Ye told me mum tracked you down in Aberdeen right before A was born?"

"She did," Thomas replied a bit defensively all of a sudden. "She bribed me landlord for the envelope from a check A'd sent him tha was postmarked in Aberdeen. We had a patron at the pub who'd been talking to me about a job there with his company, and A'd decided to take him up on the offer. How she found me there, A still dinna ken, but ye ken how persistent your mum was, and she was desperate and almost 6 months pregnant by then. She could'na hardly work anymore and could no longer hide it from anyone. She said she just could'na go to her folks and tha A was the only one who would understand. So A took her in."

"She could'na go to Granda an Granny?" Agnes asked in disbelief.

"I ken tha sounds a bit strange, Agnes," Thomas explained, "but yer dear old Granda wasn't always the kind-hearted jovial old soul ye knew. He was stern and extremely hard on your mum when she was growing up, and had been furious with her for agreeing to marry Angus and move here in the first place. She could'na bear the idea of his reaction and disappointment in her once he'd learned of the pregnancy."

"So ye married Mum instead, givin' her an honorable way out?" Agnes said, connecting the dots.

"Well, it just did'na happen like that," Thomas replied. "At first, A told meself A was looking after her for Angus, as A was a bit skeptical about the fact tha he would just abandon your mum like tha, and figured he'd eventually come round, but as time went on A became angry with him for not livin up to his responsibilities. Before A would'na, allow me feelings for her to go anywhere. That's why A left Peterhead. A knew A could'na trust meself round her once A understood she had feelings for me too. A could'na do tha to Angus. It wasn't honorable, but the more time went by and he did'na respond, did'na contact her, it changed things, and A convinced meself it was he tha was being dishonorable."

"...Did ye ever really try to contact him?" Agnes asked tentatively after a moment.

"Yes, like A told you on the way over, more than once," Thomas replied, "the last time was right after you were born, A threatened ta come here meself and track him down, but your mum would'na allow it. She just wanted ta move on. She understood him not wantin' anythin' ta do with her, but she was bitter and did'na feel he deserved a relationship with you since he would'na even acknowledge you."

"Well, he could'na acknowledge somethin' he did'na know about," she replied, still obviously struggling with the fact that her father hadn't ever been made aware of her existence.

"A'm sorry, Agnes... In truth, A did'na push her too hard. By tha time, A was so in love with your mum, and A was truly afraid of wha might happen if Angus actually did come back, afraid of where that'd leave me... Sure they were at odds, but they were young and had ye in common, and if he said he'd return, would they get back together so they could raise you... Nae, A could'na bear tha thought, and so A told your mum, and meself, A would shoulder Angus' responsibilities and raise you as me own. A convinced meself it was the right thing to do, but in all honesty, A can see now that maybe it was just as cowardly as it was honorable... A'm very sorry, dear."

The three of them just sat there in silence a moment, digesting all that had just been revealed. Tyler felt a little uncomfortable being included in such an intimate discussion about their lives with two people he only just met, but then he realized too that he was integral in helping Agnes to put certain pieces together.

"It all makes sense now," Tyler finally said turning to Thomas. "Angus was so hurt and so convinced that you and Mairi had started a life together after she broke it off and revealed her feelings for you that he just buried himself in work here to try and forget her. And while the how and why that happened wasn't anything like he'd imagined, it's what ultimately took place. Who knows what exactly might have happened if he'd actually opened the rest of those letters thirty years ago, but I know Mack, and I believe your instincts were correct Thomas. He had absolutely no idea Agnes even existed. And had he ever learned that she did, everything would have changed, and I don't think any of us would be standing here right now."

They all returned their attention to the still open grave, the flower-covered casket, and the man who was the reason they found themselves unexpectedly meeting there on a soggy Missouri morning.

This was all too surreal, Tyler thought. He'd only just learned of Thomas and about Mack's past recently, and now a daughter? It's as if the characters from Mack's life had come to life right out of a book after all these years. That somehow made it more than just a story. It was real. These were the consequences of choices Mack had made long ago. And they were standing right in front of him trying to make sense of it all, too. And how much had all those choices, some made by people he didn't even know half way around the world, affected his own life? If Mairi or Thomas had ever tracked Mack down, or if he'd ever read even one of the letters, or gotten the phone calls that would have made him aware of his daughter, wouldn't he likely have gone home as Thomas feared, possibly never to return. And how different would Tyler's life be if he'd never even known Mack? Would he have fallen in love with the game in the same way if he'd been introduced to it by some other coach? Would he have turned out to be the same player he was, or even the same man he was? Would he have ever even been exposed to the ideas and the opportunities it gave him for a life outside of Poplar Bluff? A vision of the life that might have been suddenly flashed before Tyler's eyes, and he was just Jack's Boy again, working at the garage, taking it over during the day while Katherine sat in the kitchen at home, teaching their own little girl how to bake cookies as they waited for him to come home from work. He swallowed hard as he suddenly realized how much he yearned for that simple, uncomplicated vision of how life might have been and now would never be. How many lives could change as a result of just a small handful of choices made by a small handful of people? It was both poignant and mind-boggling even to consider.

"Oh… for what it's worth," Tyler said suddenly amidst his reflection. "It might be a small thing, but I just remembered something that may be at least somewhat comforting to you, Thomas."

"What's tha?" Thomas said looking up at him from Mack's resting place.

"Mack did finally read at least one of those unopened letters Katherine brought to him in the hospital. In it, she said Mairi confirmed how loyal to him you'd been when she'd finally broke down and confessed her feelings for you in that weak moment. She told him about how you just up and left and what you had said. She said it was really hard on him and he felt awful for all the feelings of betrayal he'd carried around with him towards you over the years. Unfortunately, I'm quite certain he died with tremendous guilt about the loss of such a true friend."

Thomas smiled weakly, but Tyler sensed more regret than relief in him with what he said.

"Anyway, I wanted to invite you both to the reception," Tyler said after a moment. "I know they announced it at the end, but I doubt you know your way around town. You're welcome to follow me. I'd really like you to come. Mack didn't have any real family here, so it'd be really good to have you both there."

"Thank you," Agnes said, putting her arm in Thomas' and leaning into his big shoulder in a gesture of reconciliation. "We'd really like tha. And A'm so grateful you introduced yourself, Tyler.

A'm not sure what all A expected to gain by coming here, and A know Daddy here thought A was a wee bit crazy for insisting we come all the way Missouri to find tha out. In the end, A guess it was some sort of closure, and somehow A think A'm much more at peace with all tha happened now. A think maybe we both are. A'm sure there are more things A'll think to ask ye once we're there, but if ye don't mind, for now, A can be content if ye'll just tell me this… Was Angus truly a guid man?"

"The best," Tyler said with emphasis and a newfound clarity. "I wouldn't be where I am, or the man I am today if it weren't for him. And if there's anything I can do for you to help in any way while you're here please just ask because it won't even begin to scratch the surface of my indebtedness to him."

"Thank ye, Tyler," Agnes said, smiling warmly at him.

They headed off in the direction of the cars, but as they did, it dawned on Tyler what was likely in that final letter Katherine had mentioned Mack had read, and the one he was still holding on to the night he passed. It had to be the one in which Mairi had told him about Agnes. And the fact that he had learned he had a child somewhere in the world, a child whom he'd never known existed, whom he'd missed seeing grow up, and missed knowing, had been too much for him. Even a heart as big as Mack's, one that had born thirty years of heartache and regret in solitude, couldn't bear the weight of that. Agnes had learned a lot that day, but this was something she didn't need to know, Tyler thought. How could you tell a woman, one who'd only just learned of the existence of her real father, that his learning of hers was likely what killed him? No, there are some things in life it's better not knowing, and so this was a secret Tyler would take to his own grave.

HE'S ALL YOURS

When Tyler wouldn't even look at Katherine during Mack's service, it helped a bit with the misgivings she was having about her decision. Despite the fact that she had already convinced herself that her reasoning was sound, her heart was having trouble feeling good about it.

For starters, she was experiencing a tremendous amount of guilt for the timing of it all. When she'd originally considered leaving, Mack was just in the hospital, and she'd envisioned Tyler coming back home to tell her, and everyone else, that he'd qualified and was moving on to the next stage. In that context, her decision made so much more sense. Tyler would be off chasing his dreams again and so it was time for her to move on with hers. Now Mack was gone, and Tyler was back in Poplar Bluff, making her decision to leave and the reasoning behind it more than just a bit harder to justify.

And now Tyler had accused her of actually being the one who was chasing a dream. She wanted to pass that off as hypocrisy at its finest, but for some reason she was having more than a bit of trouble doing that. Something Mack had said in the hospital about pride, standing on the pillars of his principles, and ending up alone kept ringing in her ears, eating at her, and feeding all the doubts she was struggling to pass off. Was there something to what Tyler had said?

A couple of days before Mack's service she'd interviewed for the position and they'd offered it to her. She had such mixed emotions. She loved Tyler, and in a weak moment had almost cancelled the interview and called him to apologize. For some reason she didn't, though, and only a nagging thought that he was essentially doing the same thing could explain why she kept moving forward. When they presented her the offer, they said they needed an answer that day, and some part of her knew that if she'd had more time to think she'd have likely changed her mind.

She'd turned the tables on Tyler, and now she not only didn't feel any of the self-satisfaction she'd told herself she'd feel for years after their initial break-up, she was actually feeling bad for having done so. She'd wanted him home, wanted him to settle down, and now he was, and he appeared to be resigned to that fact. She'd so wanted that to be his choice, though. And now she was the one leaving Poplar Bluff, leaving to make her own way, and leaving him behind. Because, she reasoned, if circumstances had been different he'd be the one abandoning her, all over again. His *only* opportunity was right here now, and that fact alone kept her moving forward. Had he chosen to take over his father's garage, to finish his degree, or even chosen to stay right where he was and work for Mack as an assistant, she not only could have accepted it, she would have supported it. But he didn't.

And so her small car was packed to the hilt and she was off to Kansas City. The job wouldn't start for another ten days, but with her father's help and some furious internet searching, she'd found a small apartment in the area she wanted to live in and she needed to get some things settled in advance. With Tyler out of the picture, her father had insisted on coming with her to help, and so they'd rented a U-Haul for the bigger stuff and spent the previous day packing it up.

It was a crisp clear fall morning, and with more than a five-hour drive ahead of them, Katherine told her father she was going into town to get them a couple of coffees and fill up before they got on the road. As she pulled the cap off and slid her credit card in the pump, her thoughts were interrupted by a vaguely familiar voice from just behind her at the next pump over.

"Good morning, Katherine," it came politely, if a bit flat.

Katherine turned to find Whitney Robertson, and despite the fact that she knew Whitney still worked at the club, she realized she hadn't seen her, much less thought of her, since that forgettable morning almost a year ago when Tyler was giving her a golf lesson.

"Whitney," Katherine replied, nodding her head, but barely looking at her in a somewhat less than cordial gesture. God, why did she somehow still find herself jealous of this woman?

"Where you off to?" Whitney asked, noticing Katherine's loaded car and apparently willing to ignore the brush off.

"Kansas City if you must know," Katherine replied coolly. "I've accepted a position there with a company that's really growing at the moment."

"Really?" Whitney said, genuinely surprised and seemingly confused as she walked up to her now, "But, what about you and Ty? I really thought you two was all gettin' married, having two kids, the white picket fence, and the whole living happily ever after thing. I miss something?"

"He's all yours, Whitney," Katherine said, trying to act disinterested, but almost choking on the words and the thought that went with it as she said it. "I've got to warn you, though. I don't think you, me, or anything else in this town will ever be good enough for him."

"Wow…" Whitney replied, taking a step back and putting her hands on her hips as she stared at Katherine in amazement, "I guess I always gave you more credit than you deserve, Katherine, but you really are a pretty stupid girl."

"What?" Katherine said, finally really looking at Whitney with a challenging stare that might have started something when they were younger.

Whitney laughed pityingly as she shook her head in disbelief.

"Prideful boy. He didn't even tell you what happened at that qualifying tournament did he? God, it's all over the club, all over town for that matter, and you obviously don't have a clue."

"Oh," Katherine replied, still trying to act disinterested as she pulled the nozzle out and put the gas cap back on as she prepared to get back in the car, "he told me alright… It wasn't meant to be. Just like the last time, and probably the next time, too. Well, I'm not waiting around for the next time."

"I don't think you get it," Whitney said sharply, stopping her before she got inside. "I really don't think he intended there to be a next time."

"Is that what he told you? Believe what you want, Whitney," Katherine said bitterly. "I'm tired of believing in him. I need to believe in myself now."

"Katherine," Whitney said shaking her head and ignoring her, "Lord, I don't even know why I'm telling you this, but… You say he told you it wasn't meant to be? Well it sure could have been. He withdrew from that tournament before even playing the final day. He was tied for first place, Katherine, and pretty much guaranteed of moving on, and he up and quit. Tied for first place, Katherine, and he just quit and came home… And if you really think he did that for me, his old man, or even his little cousin, then you really are a whole lot dumber than I always thought."

With that, Whitney turned on her heel and walked back to her car, leaving Katherine just standing there speechless… What had she done?

COMING HOME

The day after Mack's service, Tyler was back at work, opening up the shop bright and early. There was some discussion amongst the membership as to where they would turn next now that their pro of thirty years was gone, but when word of Tyler's decision to withdraw from Q-School had spread, along with his desire to step in for his long-time mentor, a groundswell of support had grown to give him the opportunity. He had gone to the Board of Director's only a couple of nights earlier, humbly expressing his intent and admitting there would be some learning curve, but he promised to ask for help when he needed it, to be a great student, and to work tirelessly to learn the things he yet didn't know. Tyler's grandfather had done a little behind the scenes politicking with the board to give him a shot, but in the end Tyler had impressed more than a handful of the board members in his own right with his commitment to the club and what he'd already done in Mack's short absence for them to be willing to at least give him the chance to prove himself.

As he sat down in Mack's old chair and looked around the familiar office, it felt a bit surreal. He still couldn't believe Mack was gone and the thought that this would be his office now seemed almost blasphemous. All of Mack's personal things were still around, his pictures on the wall, his golf clubs in the corner, and a scattering of training aids. There was an antique sign on the door that read "Experienced Golf Pro – Hooks fixed, slices straightened. Low hourly rate". He'd always loved that sign and knew it was something he'd be keeping. As he continued to look around the room, his glance fell on the big leather-bound teaching journal that Mack had left for him. He'd brought it here the day after Katherine had given it to him, and in the whirlwind of emotion and preparations for the service, he'd forgotten there was a letter Mack had left for him stuffed inside the front cover that he'd yet to read. He untied the thick ribbon that kept it closed and drew out the envelope with his name on it and slowly opened it up.

Tyler,

If you're reading this letter, then I will assume that I am no longer with you. I can't say how much I have appreciated working with you over the years and how much your friendship has meant to me. I had always hoped to compile these thoughts on the game of my father's and mine into a book of some sort one day, but it never seemed quite finished. Maybe our study of the swing, the game, and all the many lessons we learn from it never will be, so I leave it to you now, in the hopes that you not only will be able to learn from it, but in time add to it and maybe see the day and time when it feels ready to share with others. I truly hope that you reach your goals in the game, and qualify for the Tour, if it's what you really want. I know that you're good enough, but if you don't, please don't let that be something that detracts from your relationship with it. We each have our own unique journey with it and give back to it in our own way, and I can tell you that for my part, it has made my life rich, even if hasn't made me wealthy.

To that end, I want to leave you one more thing, just in case you ultimately choose to follow in my humble footsteps. I know you gave up much if you chose this route, and I know you and Katherine have hopes of settling down someday. And while this game has provided well for me, I know raising a family today can be an expensive proposition, despite my lack of experience with it. Having no family, nor any children of my own, I want you to have the house and I've made all the arrangements. It's not big, but it's close to the club, and it's paid for, and hopefully enough to get you both started on your own journeys in life. Please take care of my good little Bogey, too. He's been a faithful companion and even now the idea of him being alone makes me sad. I know you'll pick up where I've left off with Jackie, so I've no concerns whatsoever for his bright future, but please do your best to tell him goodbye for me, and let him know I wanted him to have my latest set of clubs, and his choice of any putter from the garage once you think he's ready.

Being typically a man of few words, Tyler, I think this letter is already longer than I'm usually inclined, but I hope it makes up for all the things I likely should have said along the way. I'm proud of the man you've become and hope that at least in some small way some of the things I've done or said have helped and will continue to help you in the many long years ahead. And so I leave you with this... Life, like golf, is a journey, and one that is best played boldly. Never lay-up, play it safe, or leave an eagle putt short. Don't judge each day by the number you put on the scorecard, but by how you shared that time and your experiences with others. Each round eventually must end, so make sure you've loved the playing of it and those with whom you've played to the fullest. For it's not that the end comes too soon, it's that too often we wait too long before we really start to play. Because when it's all said and done, you'll never know the feeling of pulling off that remarkable recovery if you only ever try for safe pars.

Live and love life my friend. And don't look back,

Angus McLean

As Tyler put down the letter on the desk, the full impact of his loss hit him in a way it hadn't quite yet. When Katherine had first called him to tell him, it had been disbelief. A numbing surreal feeling, and almost denial of the reality of what he was hearing. With each passing day in between that moment and the service yesterday, a creeping acceptance had come, culminating in the deep sadness he felt for the loss of his friend that was only capped by the revelation that Mack actually had a family, a daughter he had never known, and one who'd unfortunately been just as blind to his existence. It was so tragic he thought, and his only comfort had been to think that somewhere Mack had to be looking down at the beautiful young woman he'd never known and smiling upon her and the grandchildren who'd never know him that had remained back in Scotland with their father so they wouldn't miss school. That and the fact his best friend Thomas, his brother, the one who'd kept a watchful eye over them for so many years, was still just as faithful as he'd ever been.

Tyler tucked the letter safely back in the envelope and placed it back inside the teaching journal's front cover. As he got up from the desk, he heard the front door of the golf shop open and figured it must be one of his dew-sweepers, the small handful of guys who showed up just as the sun rose most every morning to beat the crowds.

"Good morning," Tyler said as he walked out of the office and looked up to see Katherine.

"Good morning, Tyler," she said with a bewildered, almost wild disheveled look on her face. She was dressed in jeans and a loose-fitting sweatshirt with her hair pulled back and seemed almost out of breath. She didn't appear to have intended to be at the club just at the moment for sure.

"Is it true?" she asked as if she'd asked a question of him already.

"Is what true?" Tyler asked a little confused, not only by her question, but her presence here at this early hour dressed as she was.

"Did you really just come home, Tyler? Did you really just give up on your dream when you were that close..."

Tyler looked at her, then scanned the floor as if he might find the answer to her question there, but then back to her after a long moment. He still felt like he should be upset with her for how she'd treated him after the Gala, but he found suddenly that he was all out of fight.

"Yeah," he replied slowly. "...But that's not how I see it anymore. I tried to tell you that night, but you wouldn't even let me finish, and the more you kept talking, the angrier I got."

"I don't believe this. I'm such an idiot!" Katherine exclaimed. "And I'm so sorry, I was so wrong all along. I see that now, but you can't have done this!"

"It's what I want, Katherine," Tyler replied, still calm and seemingly measuring his words. "I know it's taken me a while to figure this out, but as much as I was chasing a dream, I was at least as much running from somewhere I'd spent half my life convincing myself that I didn't want to be. I left you once, Katherine, and if I learned anything from it, it was this... Kentucky Blue Grass isn't any bluer in Kentucky than it is in Missouri. I walked around aimlessly outside the hotel in the rain for hours that night after you called, and it wasn't until I got back that it finally hit me... The last place I want to be when something important happens in this life is in some hotel room somewhere while you or someone else calls to tell me about it over the phone. I never wanted to leave you again, Katherine. But you were right, because if I'd gone on and qualified that's exactly what would have happened."

"But it's what you've worked your whole life for," Katherine said in tears now as she moved closer to him. "You can't really just give it all up like that. I can't allow you to do that. What am I saying, you've done it, can you undo it? I can't live with myself knowing I've caused you to give it all up. I know everything I asked of you, and so I know what I'm saying now doesn't even make sense, but I can't let you do that, not for me."

"It's not just for you anymore, Katherine, it's for me," Tyler continued, putting his hands on her shoulders now and looking at her with a peace in his eyes she almost didn't recognize. "If I'd done it just for you I probably would have always resented that, but I didn't. I know I'm good enough now, and that's good enough for me. Everything I *really* want, and everyone who's most important to me is right here. I'm so sorry I left you, and that I hurt you. And I understand you being afraid that I might just do it all over again. It isn't easy to trust your heart with someone twice. When I left after high school, at the time, it was what I thought I needed to do to get where I thought I really wanted to be. A thousand times I was going to call you, and I didn't because I listened to my head instead of my heart. I knew if I did I would end up right back here, where I was meant to be, but the last place I thought I was supposed to be. I was scared of what I thought I'd be sacrificing to be with you. And you were right, I just wasn't ready yet.

"If I hadn't left after high school I would have always wondered what might have been, would have thought I'd settled for less than what I could have been, and that wouldn't have been fair to you. I won't wonder anymore. My dad told me once that you only get so many chances in life to figure out what's most important. Hell, it might be the only thing he's ever said I've actually listened to, but I know what that is now. I know that the real sacrifice would have been to give up the most important person in my life just to chase a dream. When I withdrew, Katherine, I chose us, and I chose you."

Katherine started to say something, and then, seemingly at a loss for words, just leaned into him and threw her arms around Tyler, burying her head in his chest almost sobbing. And when she looked up to face him again, she finally let go, kissing him in a way that told him she never ever would again.

"Oh my God you don't know how long I've waited to hear that, to really believe that. That's all I ever really needed to know. I'm so sorry I ever doubted it," Katherine said as she finally broke their kiss.

The golf shop door opened and Katherine broke off their embrace, red-faced, as she suddenly remembered where they were.

"Oh, I'm so sorry," she said, turning to the man who'd walked in the door who now looked more embarrassed than she did.

"I can come back," he said to the both of them. "I'll be on the practice range if Pete's looking for me, Tyler."

"Okay, Mr. Williams," Tyler said a bit embarrassed. "I'll let him know…"

"Maybe not the most auspicious way to start off my first day as the boss," Tyler said, turning back to Katherine, a little flush now in his own right and smiling a bit sheepishly. "Well, I just hope you're alright with settling for a little old small town golf pro…"

"Oh, I'm quite alright with that, Mr. Foster," Katherine said, smiling back at him. "Everything's going to be more than alright from now on. Remember when I said I wasn't like your mother, Tyler, that I wouldn't always just be here?"

"Yeah," he replied, "why?"

"Well," she said, "you know how much I love her, how much I respect her. I immediately regretted that. And despite how upset as I was, I somehow knew I was lying the moment I said it."

And with that she leaned forward and kissed him once more, beaming with a kind of joyful glow Tyler had never remembered seeing on her.

"I'll see you tonight?" she asked as she broke it off slowly. "I've got to go unpack."

"Why don't you wait to do that until after I get off," Tyler said smiling back at her mischievously.

"Why's that?" she asked arching an eyebrow.

"I'd like to take the future Mrs. Foster to see her new home first," he replied. "It really needs a woman's touch, and then maybe together we can figure out where everything will go."

ABOUT THE AUTHOR

Mike Dowd is the author of the ***Lessons from the Golf Guru*** Series, and is a featured writer for ***GolfWRX.com.*** He has been Head PGA Professional at Oakdale Golf & CC in Oakdale, California since 2001. He has served three terms on the NCPGA Board of Directors, Chairing both the Growth of the Game and Communications Committees. He was the PGA's 2013 Bill Strausbaugh Award Winner, and a 2016 Teacher of the Year Nominee. He has introduced thousands of people to the game and has coached players that have played golf collegiately at the University of Hawaii, San Francisco, U.C. Berkeley, U.C. Davis, University of the Pacific, Missouri Valley State, C.S.U. Sacramento, C.S.U. Stanislaus, C.S.U. Chico, Whittier, William Jessup, and Dordt Colleges, as well as on both men's and ladies' professional tours.

Mike currently lives in Turlock, California with his wife and their two aspiring LPGA stars where he serves on the Turlock Community Theatre Board, is the past Chairman of the Parks & Recreation Commission, and is a member of the Kiwanis Club of Greater Turlock. In his spare time (what's that?) he enjoys playing golf with his girls, writing, music, fishing and following the foibles of the Sacramento Kings, the San Francisco 49ers, the San Francisco Giants, the New York Mets, and, of course, the PGA Tour. You can find Mike at mikedowdauthor.com and mikedowdgolf.com.

Mike Dowd

Made in the USA
Middletown, DE
06 May 2019